Barker's Rules

"You don't want to break them"

By Alec Pangia

Editing: Brielle Bogdzio, Marisa Marie Langel

Cover & Jacket: Nikki Rae Colligan, Alec Pangia
Interior Design: Alec Pangia

Manufactured in the United States of America

This one is for Jenn, who took my dream and brought it to life.

Table of Contents

About Me

I was born in Philadelphia, and raised in South New Jersey. I represent One True Promotion, a social media brand dedicated to the promotion of fellow artists. I wrote my first novel straight out of Stockton University, where I studied Literature and Creative Writing with the goal of publishing my stories. Today, I double as a fiction author and a student of special education, hoping to use both my writing and my work to provide a helping hand to my fellow citizens.

Instagram: @alecpangiaauthor
Twitter: @APangiaAuthor
Facebook: Alec Pangia – Author

Instagram: @onetruepromotion

Prologue

The Grier Family

Se}ptember 27ᵗʰ, 2028, was cold and damp. All morning it had rained and by noon Martin Grier couldn't see anything but gross, depressing, gray. The policeman sat in his squad car, warming up with coffee. He was sitting on a speed trap on a back road that had its busy days and its, well not busy days, like this one. So he sat there, drank some coffee. Watched the road.

Christ, I'm bored as hell, he thought. Martin went to take another sip, and spilt it as something flew by on the road. It must have been at 120 miles an hour, give or take. Well, that was all it took. He charged into pursuit, lights flashing, alarm sounding. He had to match speeds with the idiot to catch him, and he felt like if he turned the wheel slightly left or right he'd go spiraling off the road. When he caught up, the offender began to slow, eventually pulling off the road and onto the muddy gravel. Martin did the same, his heart now starting to simmer down. Having to chase them left him livid, and as he emerged into the cold autumn day, he slammed the car door shut behind him.

This one's a teenager, drug addict, or both, he decided. Arrogant teens got under his skin about as deep as a metal hook, and drug addicts were even worse. Either way, he was going to hate this. But twenty years of experience on the force allowed him to keep himself composed. He casually approached the vehicle. The window was still up.

Asshole. He tapped hard, and the window came down.

The man looked grungy. His hair was jet black and thick, a beard of the same color covering the face, mostly scruff. He looked uncombed and Martin could smell his sweaty, unclean skin even from outside. His eyes were hidden behind thick sunglasses and he sat still with a half grin on his face. His clothing was all black.

Great, Martin thought at the sight of this Gothic speeder. His face had a primarily young appearance, with no wrinkles or excess fat of any kind, but still his head was large as well as his Adam's Apple. Not a boy, definitely a man. Maybe mid thirties.

Curious, he glanced in the backseat, and saw duffle bags. That could either be traveling supplies, or something worse.

Though he was approaching fifty, and gaining a bit of a stomach, Martin delved into the zero tolerance, badass reputation he'd built up for years, and used it for confidence.

"License and registration," said Martin, hand near his gun.

The man grinned. "Yes sir." He shifted in his seat and dug in his jacket. All the while he smiled, and Martin got a good look at his shiny white teeth. When Martin read the license, the name was "Ryan Downs."

"You know why I pulled you over Mr. Downs?" he asked.

"Speeding?" the man asked with a raised eyebrow.

"Correct. You been drinking?" asked Martin.

He shook his head. "Not a drop." When he gestured, he took his time. Slow shakes of the head, slow movements of the hands.

"Are you high?" Martin asked, taking a half step back.

The man turned his head to Martin with a condescending, arrogant twist of his mouth. "Are you?"

Martin's chest tightened. "Can you read?"

Ryan Downs looked away and shrugged. "I made it through high school."

"Oh good. Then you must have noticed the sign that said 45 miles per hour? Or did you just, you know, whip right past it?" said Martin.

"Ah, that must have been it," he said with a snap of his fingers.

Martin glanced at the duffle bags again. "What you got in the back?"

"Sandwiches, napkins, bottles, zip locks, condoms, lubricants…" He folded in his lips. "Umm, tin foil, ketchup packets, some books."

"Shut up," Martin said. "I get it. Step out of the car."

The man grimaced. "Excuse me?"

Martin dropped his hand near his weapon, ready. "Step out, of the car. We'll see how sober you are." He took a few steps back. "Now."

The man groaned, and the door opened. A pair of long legs hit the concrete, and the man rose to tower over Martin. He wore a dark trench coat with long murky pants and black boots. Gothic as hell. Tall, broad shouldered. He removed the black glasses, revealing a pair of yellow eyes.

"Go on," said Ryan Downs. "Do your thing."

Martin took out his flashlight and sprayed light over the man's eyes. Downs recoiled and let out a gasp.

"What the hell's your problem?" Martin asked.

The man rubbed his eyes and groaned. "Sensitive." He frowned at Martin, and something gave the police officer a chill. The man didn't glare, but his eyes were cold, emotionless.

Like a murderer.

Martin had met them. He arrested a mass shooter at the mall years ago. If they weren't strung out, they just had this look. The same look Downs was giving him. Except he was inches away, and unrestrained. They were on a back road, miles away from town.

"Are you done?" Downs asked.

"Yeah, I'm done. Get back in your car." Martin heard his own voice quivering.

The man smiled and bowed, then got back into his car. Without another word Martin returned to the squad car and began printing the ticket. Despite the weird and over the top body movements, from what Martin could tell he wasn't under any kind of influence. He glanced back at the car repeatedly, once noticing that the man's hand was now hanging out the window as if he were smoking. Only instead of a cigarette his middle finger was hanging, tapping the side of the car. It stroked his nerves but he knew the man would claim ignorance to the gesture. Why bother? He walked back. The man had put his glasses back on.

"Have a present for you," Martin said, handing him the paper.

The man snatched it up and read the print like he'd just been handed a manuscript, lips moving slightly.

"You're not from around here, are you, Mr. Downs?" said Martin.

"None of your business, officer." He was still reading the ticket as if it were a book.

"But it's true, no?" Martin looked back at the duffel bags. "You're a drifter."

Now the man looked up at him. Martin could see the outlines of the yellow eyes through the black shades. "What's it to you, sir?" Then he stopped and stared at, of all things, Martin's chest. "You think yourself above me?" He curled his lips and shook his head. "Cops."

Martin leaned in close, hand on his gun. "I stand for law and order, son. The same law you broke. And you're really pissing me off."

Through the shades he stared everywhere but into Martin's eyes. Then he nodded with a bent lip. "I used to get along with cops." He smiled. "Sometimes."

"Sometimes?" Martin said. "Son, I suggest you start remembering those times. Now beat it. And don't let me catch you out here again. Clear?"

Without hesitation, the man smiled wide at him, and Martin's chest flipped.

"Yeah, officer. Crystal." The black sunglasses turned away and the mustang's engine came to life.

Martin returned to his squad car. He took a sip of his coffee and watched as the offender slowly rolled away, no more than 35 miles per hour. The man hung his hand out the window as if he were relaxing at home, this time with all of his fingers together. He drove at a sluggish pace all the way down the road until Martin couldn't see him anymore.

And once he was alone, Martin let out a rather deep breath.

Asshole, he grimly thought.

***

Debra Grier habitually checked her calendar every morning. Today was October 4th, 2028. She had an important conference at 10:00 am, and was given the morning to prepare for said conference. So while her husband and daughter were busy scurrying about, she was casually enjoying the first slow morning she'd been gifted in weeks. Coming out of the shower, she neatly combed her wet hair and wrapped herself in Martin's least favorite bathrobe: bright pink with a yellow duck at the stomach. Her daughter wasn't much more fond of it than her husband, and Debra only wore it due to a large gaping hole at the rear of her usual robe. But as much as Martin would have loved for her to wear that every morning, she had her own dignity and her daughter's mental stability to consider. So yellow duck it was.

When Debra walked down their stairway, carpeted with a cream color, Martin was at the door in full uniform. He was husky and well built, and she noticed a few more gray hairs she'd rather not mention to him. His gun was already strapped to the belt, and she stole a quick eye at his small stomach that had prompted a renewed gym membership. He saw her coming and smiled under his very thick beard, then he saw the robe and grimaced.

"Gotta go," he said and walked halfway out the door.

"Get back here," she ordered.

He rolled his eyes and smiled. She came to the bottom of the steps and he met her there. She softly touched her lips to his. Nineteen years of marriage and every kiss gave her the same butterflies as years ago.

He pulled away, a scowl on his face. "Happy now?"

She chuckled and patted him on the shoulder. "Nobody's looking."

Martin looked over his shoulder, out the open door. "Who knows who's looking?"

She laughed again. "Oh, go to work. Have a nice day."

"Yeah I'll try," he said with a dark expression. He picked up his car keys.

Debra suddenly felt bad. "Hey. Don't let them get to you, okay?"

His eyebrows went up high and his mouth curled up. "This coming from you."

"Mine are children, I'm supposed to let them get to me. As for the beasts I face today well, in one ear and out the other. I always say."

Martin was nodding his head. "Supposed, to let them, get to you. In one ear and out the other." He grunted. "How precious."

She nodded. "Mhm. And then I whip 'em into shape before they end up in your backseat."

"Maybe you can start with our daughter."

She lightly struck him. "Don't be a jerk. She's just fine for her age."

He scratched an itch in his beard. "Make sure she stays that way and I'll admit your qualifications."

"As if I owe any of them to you, boss." And she hit him again.

"Mom!" Their daughter, Melanie, appeared at the top of the steps, a grimace on her face that told them she'd rather be in bed than going to school. Her blonde hair looked damp. "Mind if I borrow a few cue tips?"

"Sure honey," Debra said.

"Thank you," said Melanie, turning away, then stopping. "I can just walk in and grab them?"

"Yes dear," said Debra, having thought that was obvious.

"Your mom's are the little ones," Martin called. "Make sure you don't grab mine. Sometimes I toss them back in."

"Ew!" Melanie shouted.

"That is such bull," said Debra.

"She likes my humor," Martin said with a smile.

"I don't think she likes it anymore than I do."

Melanie reappeared quickly. "Thanks Mom!" Then she looked at her father and let out a sigh. "Dad, you're gross."

Debra pointed up the stairs, "I like her humor."

"She's sixteen. She doesn't know humor."

"I don't know. I think she's a natural."

Martin scratched his head. "Bit better at that than driving."

"Didn't go too well? I forgot to ask."

"That is why you need to whip her into shape," Martin said. "She almost killed me."

"Really?" Debra said, crossing her arms just above the yellow duck. "Sorry I missed that."

Martin shook his head. "She thinks its funny. My loving wife." He put on his hat and walked out to the car, muttering all the way. "Out to get me, all of them. My daughter jerks the car around like a damn mule. My wife thinks its funny."

"Oh, come on, it was her first time," Debra said. She was halfway out the door, watching him go.

Martin clicked the keys and lights flashed. He stole one last glance at Debra. "Christ woman, go back inside."

She played with the pocket of her robe. "You really hate it that much? I think I could go shopping in it."

Martin rolled his eyes, blew her a kiss and got in the car.

As the car pulled away she shut the door behind her.

Even with a few hours to kill, it never hurt to get into work clothes. She dressed in a blue suit with a white shirt underneath, liking the effect the blue outfit had on her hair. It made it look more red than brown.

Debra walked down the long white hallway and toward her daughter's green bedroom. Melanie would be leaving soon.

***

Melanie was tying her shoes. She was still drowsy and lost in the thoughts she woke up with: clips from "The Godfather" and "A Very Long Engagement," two of her favorites. She fully awoke when she gazed upon her reflection. Florescent lights were her least favorite thing in the world, highlighting every little thing she hated about her face.

By the time Melanie was done obsessively washing and applying makeup the marks were all faded. Then she threw on a white tank top, denim jacket, blue jeans, and started to tie her shoes. She wished she'd gone downstairs to tie them, instead of sitting on her bed. All she wanted was to fall backwards and sleep. In moments her mother arrived to dash those hopes. She gave a cute little knock on her open bedroom door.

"All packed up?" she asked.

Melanie yawned. "Yep." She stood up and hoisted her book bag over her shoulders. No going back now.

"Everything okay?" Debra asked.

"Tired," she said.

"Join the club," Debra laughed. Melanie hated that phrase. It always felt condescending. Then her mom followed up with, "Don't go out with wet hair. It's cold."

"I'll go if the bus comes," she spat back. "I mean I could just go back to bed."

"Yeah, no," Debra said. "Getting your test grades back today?"

Melanie sighed. The last test had just been the worst, and she'd forgotten until now that today she was getting the grade. "Yeah."

"Not looking forward to it?" Debra asked.

"No, not really."

Debra crossed her arms and adopted a frank tone. "Did you study?"

Yes. For hours. Days. The thought pounded Melanie's head, but that wouldn't earn her mother's sympathy. Not without results.

"I studied. I'm just bad at it, okay?" she pleaded.

"I told you, you should consider getting a tutor," her mother said, closing her eyes, raising her chin.

Melanie pressed her fingers to her forehead, getting even more tired. "I don't want to spend extra hours studying math. I don't get it. I never will get it. I want to put it in a ditch and bury it." She let out a sigh.

Her mother smirked. "Well, I'll get you a shovel and you can bury yourself in there with it. You're smart, you're artistic, all of those things. You'll get through the uglier stuff with some initiative."

"I have initiative!" she snapped. Debra fell back for a moment, and Melanie felt terrible. She knew her mom was just trying to help her. That's what parents did. "Sorry. Sorry, I'm just tired."

"Yes, well, so am I, but I'm not snapping or yelling, am I?" said Debra.

"No," Melanie said, defeated.

Her mother inched into the room and tapped Melanie's shoulder. "Nope. I deal with stress in funnier ways," she whispered, like there was someone around she didn't want to hear. "I just forced your father to kiss me in my bathrobe. In front of the neighbors."

She saw the mental image of the duck robe, and almost burst out laughing. "Oh, my God, did they see?" She cupped her hands to her mouth.

"I'm not too sure but I think so," said Debra, smirking.

Melanie started to crack up, and she felt more awake. "Oh, my God, mom."

Debra chuckled. "Go on, you'll miss your bus."

It was almost time to go, so she might as well stop dreaming about going back to sleep. She scurried back to the bathroom to check her face one more time, then she ran down to the kitchen to grab a few granola bars. Melanie was perfecting the art of sneaking snacks in class. Her mom was waiting for her at the door. She gave her a kiss on the cheek and walked out into the chilly morning.

The bus arrived just as she made it to the stop.

A few seconds later the bus was carrying her to school, and she got out her IPod. The day went on with all the same momentum. Unless she was sitting in class she never stopped moving.

Melanie didn't pay attention much in Geometry. She'd given up. Right now Mr. Donalds, a short, plump, bald man, was giving the whole class a very detailed lecture on College Preparation and responsibility, but Melanie was thinking about pictures. She couldn't help letting her mind wander, here at the mercy of the man in power. Instead of math equations and plans for her future, her mind was filled with visions of buttons on the camera, setting aperture, getting the shutter speed just right. Once or twice, Melanie daydreamed of success, of being like just like Timothy Hogan, one of her icons. She returned to reality when a small sheet of paper hit her desk. She flipped it over and read the numbers. 35/100.

If there was one thing Melanie hated, it was math. This was probably the lowest test score she'd ever received. The test had been awful, just a long hour of blanking out again and again. When her mother asked, she said it went "fine." Now she'd have to face the music and this was grounds for a retest, which her mother would insist she take. Melanie let out a groan.

She wondered just how angry her mother would be, what kind of day she'd had. If it was going to be bad, maybe she could bail tonight and stay at Emily's. Her stomach turned at the thought of the yelling and the upcoming lecture. That and the numbers themselves took a few blows to her self-esteem. Thirty-five. A number like that just made you feel stupid. But, she reminded herself that some people just weren't good at certain things. Her friend Emily was good at everything. Oh, she couldn't wait for the gloating.

There was a nice big F on the paper, and it made her mother's voice pop into her head. You're not a failure. You're a smart, kind, mature young lady, with as much left to learn as anyone else your age. You're very good at photography. You get all A's in English and your Language classes. You'll do fine.

Her mother was very good at telling her when she was wrong but also that she thought she was wonderful, and had faith in her to do better. And yet, the fact that her mother worked at this very school, made Melanie feel like she was somehow always being watched. In short, she just couldn't wait for school to be done. To live out on her own. To explore the world. To be her own person. She couldn't talk to her parents about this, especially her dad. She didn't know how to word it without offending them.

Donalds trudged around the room, between desks. "And remember," he said in a thick Italian voice. "The one's who mean it, will excel. The ones who don't, are going to stay in school for…" he laughed. "A long time!" He thought he was funny.

I'm just done, she thought.

The bell rang, and like an explosion, she was in a crashing wave of students, over powering Donalds's "Have a safe weekend."

In the hallway, Emily walked up beside her. Her friend had red hair, silver earrings and bright green eyes. Clothing wise, Emily had a purple fetish, to the point where Melanie removed purple from her own wardrobe.

"What ya get?" Emily asked.

"A thirty-five," Melanie made herself say.

Emily hugged her schoolbooks to her chest like a newborn. "Ouch! You bombed it."

"Thanks, Einstein," Melanie muttered.

In response, Emily look ahead of them and said, "Well, I got a 98."

"Why would I want to know that?" Melanie irately asked.

"Cause you're my best friend." Emily poked her on the shoulder.

"Yay, me," Melanie said.

"Oh come on. You're such a goth sometimes." Waving her hands, she added "Smile!"

"I think you mean Debbie-Downer," Melanie remarked.

Emily snorted. "Hell no. Have you ever actually sat down with a goth? They're scary! Never happy."

"Sounds like me." Melanie didn't smile. "God, I'm gonna get such an earful when I get home."

"And then you'll get a nice gourmet dinner and some words of encouragement after your mom calms down. Better than my mom." Emily shrugged her head. "My mom's a, well…"

"A bitch?" said Melanie.

"Fuck you, bitch," Emily giggled back.

Both girls laughed. Outside, the air was cold but the sun was hot, its light bouncing off the yellow armada of school busses.

"Thursday night?" Melanie asked, adjusting her heavy backpack.

"Thursday night!" Emily said, hugging her. "Can't believe I'm seventeen."

"You should have a hot guy sneaking you into bars by now," Melanie joked, secretly hating the thought.

"Ew," Emily said. "I'd rather take you…anyways, it's gonna be fun. Hope you'll be able to come."

"They won't ground me. They're not that mean." Was it bad that she was still thinking about camera tricks and short cuts, not her failing math scores?

"Yep!" Emily said. "Well, gotta go. Try to make it out of junior year, will ya?"

"Bye," Melanie muttered as Emily was already trekking away with her books hugged to her chest. Melanie gave her a gentle wave and got on her bus.

Now that Emily was gone, Melanie retreated to her role as the silent girl in the back of the bus. She took out her headphones and started listening to her favorite music as the bus swung around the curb.

Fifteen minutes to her house. Fifteen to lean her head against the window and listen to Josh Groban, Opera, and Disney. She didn't listen to any of the popular stuff, and thankfully, she'd stopped caring about that last year. Melanie didn't need other people's approval; her mother taught her just to embrace what she loved. So she did. Bu it left her few friends at school. It was hard to talk to people you had nothing in common with. The sound of kids on the bus talking was background noise to the sounds of "Under the Sea," "A Whole New World," and "Friends on the Other Side." Josh Groban's "Oceano" came on shuffle, and his beautiful, loud voice drowned out everything.

As the bus drifted Melanie thought about her mother. She was in for a disappointed look and a lecture, she knew. But maybe later, after they were done talking about mathematics, Melanie could ask her mother something. There was something on her mind, something she wondered if she was capable of doing. And she wanted her mother's opinion. She always did. Melanie loved talking to her mother, asking her advice. Why did today have to be a bad test day?

By the time she approached her house, still humming tunes, the sun had gotten a little bit warmer, heat massaging her cold skin. Her suburban park was always quiet, not many kids living there at all. The bus door closed behind her and with a loud grumble it drifted away. Melanie approached the front door, and saw a series of odd sights. A brown Mustang she didn't recognize was parked right in front of her house. Was it a friend of her mom? Dad? And then the second odd sight: a police car in the driveway. Dad shouldn't be home yet. What was up with that?

Melanie put one hand on her backpack as she approached the front door, reaching out with her free hand. And when she got there, it was creaked open. A sudden but deep chill crept down her neck, and she didn't know if she should go inside. No, that was ridiculous. This was her house. Melanie eased the door open.

All of the blinds were drawn, leaving the house dark as night. Melanie set her things down on the sofa. There were no voices. The TV wasn't on. No footsteps upstairs. Nothing. In all the silence it was easy to hear anything, including the dripping faucet in the sink. Next she heard the frantic buzzing of a fly caught in a web. She glanced at the bug, then at the spider, and looked away.

"Mom?" she called. No answer. "Dad?" Nothing. "What the hell are they doing?" she muttered.

If the house was this quiet then they couldn't be inside. Were they next door? That didn't seem likely. They weren't very fond of the neighbors, and the neighbors were hardly ever home anyway. She'd almost forgotten the Mustang. Maybe they had a visitor? Then it clicked. They might be in the backyard, showing a guest around. It was still odd that Dad would come home just for that. Maybe Uncle Russell was visiting. She couldn't remember what kind of car he drove, and it could have been new.

In any case, she crossed the dark house to the back door, sandwiched between a closet to her right and the washer and dryer to her left, some dirty clothes piled in front of it. Melanie slipped her hands through the blinds on the backdoor's window. Outside, everything was golden; a nice haze over the neighborhood. She looked over her shoulder. Everything in here was dark. She opened the door leading outside and looked out into the small square backyard.

Empty.

She shut the door and walked back into the dark.

"Okay, so they're not in here or out there…What the fuck?" She spoke quietly, as if she didn't want the silent house to hear.

In the middle of the foyer, right next to the stairs, she stood in place, moving her fingers aimlessly, nervously. She put her hand on the railing. "Mom!" she yelled.

She heard something.

A bump. Like something hitting the floor. She felt numb for a moment, reassured that her mother was up there, yet concerned for why she didn't call back to her. She took out her phone and dialed her mother. They had to be next door. She turned to walk away from the steps when she heard the master bedroom door open.

Melanie switched the phone off and turned back. "Hello?"

A tall man dressed in black walked to the top of the stairs. "Hello!" he said.

Melanie screamed and ran for the front door, but before she could touch the doorknob, a sweaty hand grabbed her wrist. He'd reached her in seconds, and his grip was so painful she thought he'd break her wrist. She dropped her phone. He was pulling her up the stairs. She dug her heels into the ground but he forced her up the steps, smacking her against the walls. She went to strike him and then both of her wrists were in his grasp. He kept pulling and pulling and she slid upward as if the stairs were ice.

They were at the top, hallway dark as a cave, in front of the master bedroom. He held her arms at her sides.

"Won't you join us?" he asked.

She screamed again and was thrown through the door, face planting on the carpet. Someone was crying, and the voice sounded weird. The dresser was to her right and the bed to her left, on the ground in front of the bed, her mother.

Her mother was tied up, hand and foot, crouched on the floor, her hair mussed up and her face red. She was barely dressed, just the clothes she would have woken up in. Something black was stuffed in her mouth and duct tape held it there. Her mother screamed, and the same sweaty hands grabbed Melanie's shoulders, pulling her up. She tried to pull herself free and strike back but he kept her arms secured and forced her to her knees.

"Who are you? What do you want?" Melanie yelled.

"Quiet," he said. Her mother screamed even louder. "I said, quiet, Debra. Do I have to kill your daughter?" Melanie tried to pull her wrists free but they were held tight in what felt like one hand, pain shooting up her arms and making her numb.

Something ripped behind her, and she felt duct tape behind wrapped around her wrists, holding them firm as cement. He held her down by the shoulders as she tried to get free again. She tried to swing out of the tight grasp. She threw her head back and hit him in the stomach. He shifted but his feet stayed planted. He was holding her in a way that kept her from looking back.

"Get off me! Get off! Help!"

A hand clamped tight over her mouth and she smelled hot skin. Melanie forced her jaw open and managed to bite him. It did nothing. Not even when she tasted blood.

"Tasty?" he asked.

Something touched her throat, and she knew at once to stop. It was cold, thin, and sharp. She shifted in place and felt a little bite, just the tiniest cut. But it made her numb and nauseous. Melanie was quiet now, letting the blood from the hand drip down her lips. She could vomit at any minute now.

The knife was held so close to her throat she felt if she moved too much she'd be sliced. And now her arms felt cold. She couldn't feel her hands.

The man leaned down and whispered in her ear. "Shhhhh."

Her mother was the only one making noise, trying to say something that sounded like "No."

But when Melanie felt the knife pressed against her neck, her mother stopped. "Please," Melanie muttered, thoughtless. "God, please. Please don't."

"Now," said the man. "I'll take the knife away, if you stay calm…and stay still, and quiet." His voice was somewhat deep, still retaining a younger, medium pitch. It was raspy and seductive. "You see?" he asked her. "It's your choice. Not mine."

Sick and numb with a hand over her mouth, Melanie had no way of answering him. If she nodded, she was afraid she'd cut herself on the knife.

"Can you do that for me?" he asked. "Just stay calm? I'm not going to hurt you. I'm going to take what I want and go. Okay?"

He pulled the knife away, and she breathed in deep. "Is that okay?" he asked, still holding her mouth.

She nodded, and so did her mother, as if instructing her.

"Good," he said, and released her.

She saw the cut she'd made on his hand. Very small, just a little thumb sized stream of blood. Melanie could look over her shoulder now. She saw him in full view. He was very tall, and all in black.

He wiped his hand against his pants and then he took a pillow off the bed. He slipped off the pillowcase and brought it to her mouth, wiping the blood from the bite off her mouth. He grabbed her again and forced her to lie on her stomach, spending all of ten seconds wrapping tape around her ankles. She felt the small bones in her ankles bash together like magnets, and now they were stuck.

She looked up at the stranger at her mother, who was hyperventilating.

"Mom?" she said, fighting tears. "Are you okay?"

Her mother nodded. Melanie looked over her shoulder again, best she could.

He was standing over them, completely relaxed. He took a deep breath and put his hands on his hips. His coat was black and his face was white. Scruffy black beard, hair under a dark beanie, and yellow eyes. He also had gray boots. He stared down at Melanie, a skyscraper about to fall down on her. But for the moment she was safe and he was only looking. She hoped.

Melanie felt light headed, sick. Not long ago she was chatting with Emily. She thought she was coming home to a lecture. To an argument. She thought she was going to be angry with her parents, sitting in her room, still secretly putting all her attention on photography. She didn't expect this. No one would expect this. She didn't expect to be tied up. And she didn't know or want to expect what was coming next.

Closing her eyes and opening them again, she allowed some of the anxiety to come out, and couldn't stop a few pathetic whimpering tears. It fed more grief to her mother, who broke down, face red.

"Mom, I'm sorry," she whispered. "Sorry...I'm okay."

The intruder dug into his back pocket and pulled out a wallet. He fished through it and took out a driver's license. He laughed.

"Ryan Downs...Good one." He showed the ID to Melanie and chuckled. She felt like she'd missed a joke. He stared at her like he was waiting for her to laugh.

"What do you want?" she asked.

"Shhhh," he said. "None of that."

"Please. Don't hurt us. If you want money you can have it."

"None of that!" Though insistent, he still hadn't raised his voice. "Let me go get Martin." He turned and opened the bedroom door.

Martin. "Dad? Oh my God. What did you do to him?" She tried to roll onto her back. "Where's my dad?"

He was back kneeling over her now, and he rolled her onto her back so she could look up at him. "What did I say?"

She kept her voice down. "Where is h—"

He put a finger to her lip, hurting her front teeth.

"Enough," he said softly, as if to a small child. He tapped his finger against her mouth a couple of times and she remained stiff. He stood up. "You'll see in just a few moments...spend some time with mom." He looked over at her mother and smiled. "Yeah...spend some time..."

He turned and walked away quickly as Debra growled at him, like she'd rip him to pieces if she could.

"What did you do to him?!" Melanie shouted.

But he was gone. She turned her head to her mother, still lying on her side.

"Is Dad okay?"

Her mother leaked a few more tears and shook her head.

Melanie squeezed her eyelids. She wanted to be lying across her mother's lap, with a hand stroking her hair. On the sofa. Watching movies. Eating popcorn.

A sound of a body being dragged toward the room signaled the man's return. He threw Martin into the room and Melanie shrieked again.

"Oh my God!"

Debra remained silent. She'd already seen it.

Her father was covered in blood, held up by the collar of his work clothes, which were ripped in several places and stained red. His sleeves were rolled up so Melanie could see several small puncture holes: black, messy, and dried blood crusted on top. And what made Melanie want to vomit again was her father's face. It didn't look like a face. It looked like a rotten, smashed plum.

While the intruder held him up with his left hand, his right hung loose at his side. He smiled again at Melanie, almost possessively. Then he looked down at her father.

"Look, Martin. She's home," he said, and the back of her neck numbed.

Her father was looking straight at her, and Melanie realized that through the swollen eyes he was awake. His jaw moved. His mouth opening halfway. It hung there for a moment while he (to the best of his ability) took in the sight of his daughter.

Melanie struggled to get into a sitting position. She managed to curl her legs and press herself upward with her elbows. Now she and her father were face to face.

"Daddy...Are you..." She wanted to comfort him. But the face. It made her sick. "Oh my God."

"Melanie," he slurred in a voice that had no tone or pitch. Just scratches and gargles trying to form words.

The man tightened his grip on the collar, as if Martin was a grocery bag. "Think you can move on your own, sir?"

"You," Martin's deformed face twisted into a ruthless glare. His fingers slid on the carpet, and he started to dig them in.

The man let him go and Martin fell sideways, stopping himself on his hands.

"Good job," muttered the intruder.

Martin was horizontal, his knees holding him up, his face pointed at the carpet, his hands flat and his arms bent. "You..."

"What's that?" the man said, leaning over Martin.

"You son...of a..."

The man straightened himself up like a cartoon character, wearing a fake dumbfounded expression. "Oh, more of that?" He looked at Melanie with the same mock surprise. "You have a passionate man living in your house. Did you know that?"

"Leave him alone," she pleaded. "Please, stop. What do you want? What do you want? We'll give you anything."

"That's encouraging," he said. "You want me to leave dad alone? I guess I could...could I Martin? Can I trust you?"

"Fuck you." Martin's head was lower to the ground now, like he was about to do a push up. But Melanie knew he was just struggling to stay awake.

The man curled his lips and looked back at Melanie. "I'm gonna need your help," he said.

"Dad, just lie down, please." Melanie kept her eyes on her father, ignoring the intruder. "Dad, you're hurt. It's okay. I'm here."

Martin forced himself up with a savage growl.

"Dad, no!" Melanie squirmed and tried to stop him but it was too late. Her father rounded on the man with his elbow, and the man caught it. Then he flattened his hand and pushed the back of Martin's elbow and Martin was on his knees again, screaming. Her mother was crawling towards him and Melanie was backing away, hitting her head against the dresser, screams drilling into her ears. The man brought his fist down on the top of her father's head and he felt flat, only moaning quietly.

Her mother was right next to her father now. He lifted his head up and she saw their eyes lock. Then he looked at Melanie, and her mother did too. It was the most bizarre portrait of her parents she could have imagined. One face covered, the other destroyed. Martin's glare returned. He wheezed like an old man, and cocked his head in the direction of the intruder.

"You keep your hands off them…you hear me?"

The man had a mellow scowl on his face. "I hear you."

"What do you want?" her father drooled out. "Take it. Take it and get out."

"I'm taking it now." He cracked his own neck and gasped. "Well part of it."

"Leave—!"

The man grabbed him by the throat and mouth, one hand on each, and Debra was trying to say something to him.

"Shut. The Fuck. Up." With each slow word he pressed harder on her father's neck.

"Leave him alone," Melanie begged, starting to lose her voice.

Melanie heard a few small sobs from Martin before he spoke again, still wheezing and hissing. "Leave them alone…take me."

He took his hand off Martin's throat and stood up. "I'm going downstairs. Keep the noise down Martin. Okay? If I hear anymore, your daughter will be first. It's the duty of a parent to protect his children, isn't it?"

Martin dipped his head down. "Fuck you."

The man dropped the knife in front of him. "Pick that up, and cut your wife's legs free. I'm going to take her downstairs. Then I'll be back."

Martin picked up the knife and brought it near Debra's ankles. All the while Debra fixed her pitying gaze on him. Melanie felt pity as well. Martin could barely make a small cut in the tape. He had to grab it with two hands, and spend time sliding it back and forth to start the cut. His hand quivered too, as if his muscles weren't working.

"Oh, for God sake," said the man. And he shoved Martin aside. Martin hit the ground and gasped. The intruder sliced her mother's legs free with a few quick strokes. Then he pulled her to her feet, pointing a finger in her face. "I wouldn't do anything too aggressive, now. We all just came to an understanding. Just walk nice for me. Go ahead." They were vanishing out the door. "That's it. Good, Debra."

His voice grew distant.

Melanie's eyes burned, her tears making wide stains on the carpet.

"Dad," she said. "Daddy, are you alright?"

His face was pressed against the carpet. And Melanie got a look at his back. There was huge red stain on the back of his uniform, much larger than any of the others.

"Dad!" she said insistently, not too loud. "Are you okay?"

He pushed himself up. The plum looked sad and a few tears leaked out. "Oh Melanie." He crawled toward her. "Oh, Melanie…are you okay?" he asked her.

Her eyes and nose were hot with moisture. She nodded, starting to break down.

"Listen," the odd voice said. "Stay calm…It'll be alright. I promise."

"But you're hurt…"

And the plum grinned. "You know your old dad…Melanie." He slowly pulled himself closer and closer. "It's okay. Just relax."

"I am relaxed," she said. "You look terrible. You need help."

"Don't worry…listen…when he comes back." He was very close to her now. And he put his fingers on the tape on her ankles. "When he comes back… I'm gonna let him kill me."

"No!"

"And you are gonna let him. And do whatever he likes…this isn't about you, it's about me…He's crazy…he'll leave you alone if he gets…me." He didn't sound afraid or sad or angry. Just out of breath. Like he was going to pass out. His body bloody and mangled. He'd transformed into a slug.

Every second she spent looking at this disfigured version of her the man she loved more than any other clawed at her heart. He hooked his fingers around the tape.

"No, dad. Don't! Just leave it. Please…I don't want him to hurt you anymore." She barely choked the words out.

He shook his head. "Melanie…you have no idea…you don't…you don't."

"What?"

He put his head down at her feet.

"Dad!"

The intruder reappeared with his cell phone pressed to his ear. "Yes, I need an ambulance fast. A police officer and his wife, gravely injured. In the house. 22nd Edgewood Drive." He hit a button and slipped the phone into his pocket. "A little too noisy up here. Don't you think?"

At her feet, Martin was mumbling. "I've got you baby. I've got you."

"Please. Let my dad go." Her words were choked between sobs and her face was probably bright red. "Please. He's so hurt."

"I just called an ambulance."

Her father was motionless. "Please!" Melanie said. "Please…look at him."

The man kicked him and Martin came back to life, moaning and coughing.

"See? He's fine." He knelt down next to her and cut the tape on her feet with one strike. Then he pulled her up. On her feet he was still very tall, at least six feet. "Come on, you. We're doing downstairs."

"Why?" she demanded.

"So I can take what I want and go before the medics and cops get here."

Her father was rolling onto his back when Melanie was pulled out of the room and down the stairs.

When they got down to the living room, Melanie saw her mother sitting on the couch. She was still tied, but he'd taken off the gag. Still she didn't say anything. Her mouth was firmly shut and her eyes closed, face red.

The man forced Melanie to her knees right in front of her and Debra opened her eyes.

"Melanie," she said.

"Mom," she said before fully breaking down, neck hurting as tears welled up.

She could hear the man walking toward the back door. "The medics are coming, the medics are coming. Yay, everybody goes home happy."

"Fuck you," Debra growled. "Melanie," she said quietly. "Melanie, look at me."

Melanie obeyed. Her mother looked very aged, eyes tired and skin wet. But her look was serious and firm. "Don't say anything to him. You understand? Don't say a word."

Melanie nodded. All she wanted was her mother's arms around her. She wanted to disappear somewhere safe. Far away from this man.

"It'll be okay. It'll be okay, I promise. I promise, Melanie, when this is done you'll be sitting right here on this couch. Perfectly safe. You understand?"

Her mother sounded so sure of herself that Melanie believed her for a minute. But when the man came back into the room, gliding like he was on ice, her doubts got the better of her.

Not the knife. Not the knife. Not my neck. Please.

But she didn't beg. She didn't say a word, as her mother commanded.

"Medics are coming," he muttered, standing next to Melanie and her mother.

"You mentioned," her mother said dismissively.

"Great news...time for me to go."

"Good," Debra said. "And never come back." It didn't sound like a plea, but Melanie knew it was.

The man walked away from them and pulled the blinds open an inch. A small bit of golden light trickled into the room.

"Anything you'd like to say to your mother, Melanie?" he asked without looking at them.

Melanie turned around. "Say?"

He turned to face them and she looked away, eyes on her mother. He said, "Yes, before I end this."

"End?" And then it hit her. "No! Don't hurt my mother. Please, don't. Please. Please."

"Melanie, I said don't talk!" her mother yelled.

"What do you want?" She turned around to face him. "Money? Do you want money? We don't have any. But I have a rich friend. I-I could take you there." He gave her an intrigued look as he approached. Melanie went on, "Lots of money. I could call her on the phone right now. They're just around the corner. You'll be set up for life. I could call right now." He reached down on the glass coffee table and picked up his roll of duct tape.

"Money, huh?" he said.

Melanie nodded frantically. "Jewelry. Silver." What else? "Diamonds."

He ripped off a long strip of tape.

"Sound good?" Melanie asked. "I can get you whatever you want."

"I hope you will," he said, bearing his teeth.

"I will, I prom—" He pulled the tape around her jaw and pressed it against her lips. She tasted glue and couldn't say a word. When he was done pressing and smoothing it against her skin he walked past her and stood before her mother. All Melanie could do was watch now.

"Did you hear all that, Debra? How sweet was that?"

"Leave her alone," her mother said.

"Instead of saying something to you, she tried to save you. Wasn't that just wonderful...very big person, your daughter."

Melanie was flabbergasted. Why would he call her a big person? Why did he care what she did?

"You want to kill me?" her mother said. "Kill me. But let her go. Leave her be."

"I won't hurt her...I promise you that."

"Get on with it then. Take what you want and get the fuck away from my daughter."

"Okay, Debra. As you wish." He chuckled.

The living room was silent now. No buzzing. No faucet dripping. No cars outside. Nothing, but the dark.

He walked behind Melanie and started fidgeting inside his bag. Melanie could turn all the way around if she really tried. She tried to talk through the tape, tried to convince him to take her up on her stupid fake offer. Anything to get him out. But as she turned, he rounded on her, and some kind of black bag came down over her head. She smelled fabric and saw nothing but dark. Then her mother drowned out her ears.

"No!" her mother wailed. "Not my daughter! Not my daughter! You son of a bitch, get off of her!" Melanie felt the man's arm around her and then she was flipped horizontal and raised into the air. She was over his shoulder. "You put her down!" Debra yelled. "Put her down, now! Stop! Melanie! Melanie! Melanie!"

Her mother's voice grew distant, and she kicked and fought as best she could. On the way out she slammed into the sides of the door. It slammed shut behind her.

He moved quickly. She felt the hot sun only for a moment before she was stuffed into the backseat of a car. She screamed and writhed, then his fingers pressed against her neck, and she lost a lot of energy. She couldn't breathe. She was passing out.

Her last thought was of her mother. She'd wanted to ask her about a picture. What her mother thought she was capable of. Instead her mind drifted into the dark.

Chapter 1

The Power Plant

Justin Barker always got what he wanted. Today he wanted Melanie Grier, and here she was, lying trussed and hooded across the backseat. It occurred to him that if she threw up, she could choke, so he drove at a modest speed of fifty miles per hour. It lengthened the trip, but who was complaining? He loved to travel.

Barker repeatedly glanced in the backseat to look at his prize, once or twice noticing the truly arousing pose she was in. Not this one. This one gave him a kind of excitement he really wasn't used to. What a catch, that day on the back roads of Fargo. Following Martin Grier home to teach him a lesson had turned out to be a life changing decision. He had intended for his trip around the country to last longer, but this little development forced him to return home. He needed a place to settle her in, to sit in one place and get her adjusted. So after a full year of hopping from place to place, Justin Barker was headed back home to New Heim.

The drive went on for hours, and he played his favorite music all the way. Gothic artists such as Tarja Trunen, singing of lust and desire. It made any car ride all the more enjoyable. As always, he kept the music low, just loud enough to process the melodies. Over the course of the long drive, Melanie nodded in and out of sleep. He heard her stir multiple times, saw the hooded head look around in the dark, unsure of where she was. He heard her cry and moan and try to plead with him through her gag. Once she screamed.

"Quiet," he said. "Or I'll cut your throat."

She obeyed, and he smiled.

***

When Melanie turned twelve, her entire family visited. She remembered seeing them come through the door and randomly thinking, Emily's family is so much bigger. In the Grier family, you couldn't have a lively party without inviting some friends as well. Her father had one brother, Uncle Russell, who was something of a loner. Once Melanie heard her mother say to her father that his brother would rather play with guns than women. Her mom's parents, Margaret and John, came to every party, and they were Melanie's favorite people in the world. Her grandpa was never short a funny joke or kind words, and her grandmother gave the warmest hugs and never seemed to stop talking about how wonderful Melanie was. Then there was her dad's mother, Grandma Beth, who had some health problems over the years and didn't talk very much. But Melanie loved her dearly, and when she came to her 12th birthday she brought her a very expensive present. She talked all day with her grandparents and thanked everyone for her gifts. It was the perfect day.

The next day Melanie had gone to school, and Emily wasn't there. She must have been sick. So Melanie looked around at her classmates and didn't know what to say. She didn't know who to approach. Or how to do it. Most of the kids didn't think much of her. They gathered into their own groups, and some of the others Melanie didn't like, thinking they were mean. Her teachers had no interest in talking to any students. Melanie learned a long time ago, that she could be perfectly social and nice with her own family. But outside, in the real world, Melanie was afraid. Afraid to speak. Afraid to move.

Now, even if she willed it, Melanie Grier could not speak or move.   She woke up with her head against a car seat, feeling a pair of arms around her. She tried to kick with her bound feet, but it did nothing. He dragged her out into the cold air and set her down painfully, her knees scraping against gravel.

Finally, the hood slipped off her head.

Her hair was caked to the sides of her face from sweat and her scalp was itchy, but at least she could see. Twenty feet in front of her were pine trees. To the left, about thirty feet over, was a curving road that led somewhere she couldn't see. But in the distance, past the curving road, she saw the outlines of houses. Did people live there? They would help her, if she could get the tape off her mouth. A long time ago, back in middle school, she remembered goofing around with Emily and having her mouth taped. It had been very easy to push a strip off with her tongue. Now it was cocooned over her jaw, packing down her hair and making any attempts at wrenching free painful.

She could do it though. Tape could come loose. Melanie looked to her right, trying to keep her eyes on him. There were bright lights. About another thirty feet to her right was a huge tower buzzing like the cicadas in the trees. It was a large power station with lots of silver towers. They were large, about twenty stories high, and at the ground there was a long square gate wrapping around the area. Right in front of that, a small square building, for whoever worked at the station. Her kidnapper was walking up to the door of the small building.

He must have been nuts. Delusional. Whoever was inside that building would save her, would identify him to the police. She didn't have to get the gag off or scream or try to run. She would be saved.

Her kidnapper turned and looked back at her, smiling again. Melanie felt like he was about to lunge at her, and started tugging at the restraints on her arms. He turned away from her, chuckling eyes on the door.

He knocked on the door. After a moment, he knocked again, and again.

The door flew open and a small plump man appeared. He had a gun in his hand and a glare on his face but when he saw her, his eyes went wide. He'd come out ready to chase someone off, but when her kidnapper turned to face him, he went stiff.

"B-Barker," he said with wide eyes and twitching fingers. He tucked the gun through his belt, putting his hands up. "You...you, you're back." He smiled, but even from this distance, Melanie could see how petrified he was.

The man had called him Barker. That was his name.

Barker kept his hands in his pockets and twisted his shoulders like he'd just worked out. "Hi there, Charlie," he said to the plump man. He pointed at Charlie's stomach. "You look good."

The plump man put up his hands. "Well, wel—welcome back!" He laughed. "How was your trip? Hm?"

"Good." He glanced back at Melanie, and she looked away, trying to free her wrists. When she looked back at Barker he was eyeing all the electrical towers. "You're still manning the station, I see," he said.

The plump man's terror practically had an odor. "Yes! Of course!" He made a point of tracing his finger past every single tower. "Have been ever since you left!"

"This whole past year?" Barker asked.

"Yes. Of course. You know, in case you came back," said Charlie with a half-graceful nod of his head.

Barker stepped closer to the plump worker. "Good man!" He slapped Charlie on the shoulder, and the plump man winced. Barker put his hands on his hips. "So is it still powering the houses over on Copper Ave?" He jerked his head to the left, toward the road Melanie had been inspecting. The road leading into darkness. That was where she would be taken. She tried to work the gag off.

Charlie looked in that direction. "Yeah, it should be. I don't really ever go over there but I mean...I could go check it out." He shrugged. "If you want."

Barker kept his eyes on the dark road. "No, no. No worries. I'll go check it out. Just figured I'd ask," said Barker. He turned back to Charlie, so Melanie couldn't see his face anymore.

"Okay, well, you just let me know if you need anything. Sound good?" Charlie said.

"Sounds great," said Barker. "You're one of the good ones, Charlie. One of these days I'm gonna give you a nice plump reward." Then he put his finger over Charlie's heart, like a pistol. "On that note, don't go talking around town about me being back. Okay?"

"Of course not. Your business is your business," Charlie said. This man was no rescuer.

Barker laughed.

Melanie pressed her tongue against the duct tape. It tasted like glue, but she felt it starting to part from her face. She had to get away now. If she could scream loud enough someone over in those houses would hear.

"Where were you thinking of going?" she heard Charlie ask.

"125, Copper Avenue." Barker sounded eager.

"Matt Sect's old place?" Charlie said.

"That's the one," Barker said.

Melanie pushed with her tongue and strained her lips. Glue ripped from her skin and cold air crawled up her jaw. "Help! Someone, help me!"

After four words, Barker's arm was around her throat, squeezing so tight her tongue tasted glue and cold air. She faded in seconds.

Chapter 2

The House

A long time ago, the press had labeled Justin Barker a serial killer. Technically, they were right. He had a long enough list of victims to make the cut, but unlike most serial murderers, he didn't have a specific pattern. He killed whenever he wanted and whoever he wanted. They didn't have much in common, and maybe one day he'd kill them all. Although he was forced over the years to embrace the art of planning, Barker was a creature of impulse. He took whatever he wanted. Tonight he wanted a new home.

And here it was, the house of old Matt Sect. It made Barker's stomach tingle, to sleep in Matt Sect's bed while the young mobster slept in the ground. He could hardly wait until–

"Mmmmmm." The body over his shoulder stirred. He had a hard time telling if Melanie was waking up or dreaming. For now, the safest thing would be to get her nice and secure in her room.

It was dark out, but he knew the siding was brown. The windows were cracked. The front door was open, and Barker could see the outlines of graffiti in the dark. He knew what they said.

Faggot

                                       Murderer

              Rapist

Pig

How unimaginative. Barker would have preferred "monster." A ridiculous exaggeration, but closer to the truth. He walked to the front porch, carrying Melanie over his shoulder. Having her so close excited him, and he grew more and more impatient. When would he get to know his new friend?

Barker walked in and flipped the light switch. The dark shrank away and light spread in seconds, like blood from the jugular vein.

"Power's on," he said to his sleeping friend, giddy with excitement.

Inside was as he remembered when last he'd visited the mobster: the kitchen area to the left of the door: consisting of a long counter with multiple cabinets, a table that could seat four people off to the right, near the pantry and the refrigerator, and a small island in the middle of all that. To the left of the front door, a living room: A long sofa facing the door, an arm chair on the other side facing the sofa. All the way to the right was a small nightstand with a television on it. The TV would have to go. Straight ahead from the front door, dividing the living room and kitchen area, the hallway leading to more rooms and the stairs going up.

Upstairs he expected to find three bedrooms and a bathroom. One bedroom turned into an office by Matthew, another full of boxes and dust, and one that would be Melanie's. The carpet in the living room was blue, and the walls were brown. The kitchen was built on white tile.

His last house had been destroyed in, of all things, an air strike. There were people in this California city that would go to great lengths to take his life, but he would never let them have it. He loved it too much. Again and again they tried to take it by force, and to his amusement, fourteen years later they were still trying.

He walked upstairs. At the top, there was a bedroom to his immediate right, a bathroom straight ahead of him, and another room wedged between them in the corner. To the left, the hallway was short and narrow, leading to the master bedroom. He didn't want that. He wanted the extra room, downstairs. He turned to his right, to the closed door. This was for Melanie. He grabbed the doorknob and felt a buzz of excitement dancing in his stomach. The door was thinner and lighter than he remembered, but he would make do. He turned the knob and the door opened. Inside was black as a cave, and he entered to greet the dark.

Perfect.

***

Whenever Melanie woke up, the first thing she noticed was whether or not she was comfortable. It was dark and hot but this mattress was soft, the pillow even softer. She wanted to just stretch and go back to sleep, eyes heavy in that half awake state. She felt the urge to stretch her arms. But she couldn't. Her arm was stuck, held above her head. She tugged at her left arm, and found it held the same way. She tugged both arms multiple times but couldn't move them. There was something hot and stringy around them. She realized after a moment that it was rope, that she was still in her clothes from school, and at this point she was fully awake. She lifted her head and clenched her jaw. That was when her teeth bit down on something. It was soft, like silk, but kept her mouth open, wrenching her jaw. She tried to cry out and found her voice strangled and incoherent. A spasm made her jerk her legs upward, but they were held down no different than her arms.

Then it all came back to her in a huge wave. Her mother. Her father's horrible plum face. Being stuffed into a car. Hours of darkness and bumps on the road. The power station. Screaming for help.

And now she was here. Where was that?

Although she couldn't move very much, she was able to lift her head enough to look around the room. It was small. You could maybe cram in as much as six people. The door was to her left, and this bed was shoved all the way to the right. Next to her on the right was the wall. At the foot of the bed, there was a tall dresser. At the left corner, near the door, was a futon, stuffed into a space that looked like a closet without doors. Melanie whipped her head around looking back and forth at both walls. She stopped and looked straight ahead. Between the dresser and the futon, there was a window, the blinds drawn. If there were anyone nearby, anyone at all…

Melanie tried to push out the gag with her tongue but it was tied so tight, she could barely close her mouth at all. After a few failed attempts, she bellowed in terror.

Oh, my God. Mom. Oh, my God. Help.

Melanie screamed again, as loud as she could. She managed a good look at the ropes on her wrists. Upside down her hands looked like two stones dangling in the air. She wrenched against the rope so fierce she felt her skin burn. No matter how many times she tried, nothing changed. She rocked the bed, writhed and twisted in place, but the cords barely moved. Her shoulders were cramping now, and she could do nothing either than lie still. That was when real panic set in. Her stomach turned and her chest tightened. She had no use of her arms and legs. If he came back, if he brought the knife, she wouldn't be able to do a thing. Her throat was suddenly cold and numb.

She tried the gag again. That couldn't be as difficult as the ropes. It would come loose if she tried hard enough. There had to be someone nearby. She remembered the station. She'd seen houses. There had to be someone.

If she could just call for help, if someone would cut the ropes…

She was exposed. If he came, she wouldn't be able to fight. He could have his way and she would be stuck lying right here.

No. No. Please. No. No.

She tried everything to work the gag out of her mouth, but it only strained her jaw. Fighting the pain, she started trying to bite through it.

When that didn't work she took another fierce rip against the ropes.

Nothing. She rested for a moment.

Then she tried again.

Nothing. Her right wrist was bleeding now. Melanie had lost the energy to scream.

That was when the door creaked open. He peaked in like a curious little sibling, but he reminded her more of a reptile. He slithered in with his eyes fixed on her and nothing but cold blood. He smiled. It was the same smile: wide, almost exaggerated, but mostly relaxed.

"Welcome home," he said. She felt tears coming and looked away.

"Aw," he said. "You're crying…yeah. I get that. I actually enjoy that. Quite a bit."

The last thing she wanted was to give him what he wanted, but she couldn't help it. Her eyes were heavy and they pulled her face down onto her shoulder. It was getting hard to breathe without coughing.

Melanie moved her wrist around, senselessly, just to do something.

"Careful," he said. "You're bleeding."

His footsteps drew closer, and her heart thumped faster. In preparation she looked at him again. He'd ditched the coat and his hair was even more disheveled than before.

"I don't want to make you cry." He rocked in place. "Okay? I want to get to know you…Melanie Grier."

Hearing her own name in his mouth made her scream again. She thought he'd choke her or hit her, but he stayed still. Smiling.

"Oh, I like the passion. I like it a lot." He reached down and rubbed his hand through her hair. Then he turned and walked out of the room. The door slammed shut behind him, and she heard a loud click. The lock.

Melanie was alone again, and might have just narrowly dodged rape and death at the same time. She let her head fall back on the pillow, biting down on the gag.

Help. Someone. Mom. Dad. Come and find me, please. Please.

***

Barker rested his head against the wall, the images of Melanie's fruitless struggles seared into his brain. He was tempted to go back up, back in, and watch her some more. Or he could just play with the camera. Yes. He could do that. Speaking of which, what was he going to do with the stunning photo he'd taken before she woke up? It was the best he'd taken in years; it needed to be framed, but not where Melanie could see it. That might be awkward. It would go in his room. His room. He silently thanked Matt Sect for the house, and the mob families in general for clearing out this part of the city for his limitless use. And he thanked Martin and Debra for the gift.

He was enjoying her so much already.

Chapter 3

Eat Up

Melanie didn't want to sleep. She didn't want to be even more defenseless, but eventually fatigue just took her. For a moment, she didn't think much about the cords on her limbs or the thing in her mouth and just dug her head into the pillow, stretching her neck.

And then she was free. Outside, unbound. She walked side by side with a man in black. They held hands. On and off.

It was a cold day in summer. Although there were no marks on her wrists, she felt wet sticky blood against them. The man was telling her all about McDonalds, of all things. And then a metal door behind them came crashing down, crumbling into bricks, and the black dressed man ran away. Melanie turned to face her father.

Where were you? he demanded. Where were you, Melanie? Where did you go? Where did you go, Melanie? Where were you?

She felt herself pop back into reality, which was now a stuffy dark room. Feeling a deep spasm in her right arm, she tried to adjust herself, but failed against the tight ropes. Instead she just cried. She hated crying. She'd always do it privately, never let anyone see. Well, there was no one here and her life was on the line. She could cry all she wanted.

Melanie scanned the room for anything that might help her escape, but there was nothing, not even coat hangers in the closet. There was nothing sharp, to cut rope with, or anything heavy aside from the small T.V. Just a bed, a futon, and a dresser. And even if there were something sharp, she couldn't get off the bed. Why was she even bothering? To keep herself occupied she studied the door to her left. From the side, she couldn't see how sturdy it was, or how easy it would be to break through it. The window was covered. The blinds looked old, like the kind people used in their houses ten years ago. Just thin strips all sown together. She wondered if there was anything under the couch. Weapons? Belts? Maybe she could choke him. All she needed was to be untied and left alone for a little bit. If there were anything to use, it still wouldn't be easy. She'd never touched a weapon in her life. Her father had never even let her touch his guns, although he had taught her some basic self-defense. If she could take a good jab to Barker's head, he'd be unconscious. Then she could kill him.

Melanie couldn't believe what she was thinking. How would she kill him? Put a pillow over his head? Stomp on his skull until it broke? No, she'd need a gun or a knife. And then she could run and never look back. That last thought sounded wonderful, aside from the fact she'd probably throw up three times before she got out the door.

There had to be some way. She had to get free.

A bird squawked outside the window. A second later it squawked again from what sounded like a whole block away.

Inside, there were no sounds except the footsteps coming up the stairs.

No. No, please. Not now. Not yet. Please.

The door opened, creaking loud. It was old and wooden, probably not that hard to break through. That's why he tied her up.

He strolled sluggishly into the room, dressed the same as before, in a black shirt. He stood and looked at her with his hands on his hips, but he didn't say anything. She made eye contact for a moment, trying to win some pity. When she received no answer, she looked away, staring at the dark wall. There was a click, and light flooded her eyes. She squeezed them shut as the weight on the bed shifted. Barker was sitting over her, hand pressed into the mattress.

"It is four o'clock in the morning," he said. He rubbed his hands together. "I couldn't sleep. How bout you?"

What did he want her to do? Answer? She just looked at him. Waiting.

Now that the moment of shock had passed, and her eyes adjusted, she realized the light in this room was actually very dim. If she wanted to read in this room, she'd either change the bulb or go to a brighter room. But she could see him clearly. At this distance, she analyzed every detail of his face. It was a large head, with all jet-black hair. The hair on top of his head was very thick, multiple layers. His eye brows were thick and pointy looking, giving him a menacing glance. And yet when he smiled, underneath tons of black scruff, he seemed totally relaxed, not angry or aggressive. He looked like he just wanted to talk, and yet he looked like a freak. His eyes were yellow, with a hint of brown. She also noticed that his pupils were a little bit narrow. He looked very strange.

The odd eyes drifted down and he patted her knee. "So how you doing up here?"

Melanie tried to kick his hand away and he drew his knife, the screeching metal bouncing off the wall.

She screamed and went still, pleading with her eyes.

Barker winced but stayed calm and collective, like one of her teachers. "Do I need to use this?" he asked.

Melanie shook her head and tried to talk. Her jaw pinched and strained against the tight cloth, and all that came out was gibberish.

"If you don't scream, I'll take it out. Okay? Give me some hint that you understand," he said.

Melanie looked directly into the yellow eyes and made him a promise by nodding her head.

He nodded back and grinned, showing off his perfect teeth. "Good," he said. "Yeah...that's it." He sounded turned on, voice scratching and then dipping, and she wanted to inch backwards.

Relief seized her when he put the knife away, and turned to revulsion when his hand fell on her forehead. She whipped her head away but the hand found her again. There was nowhere to go.

"I want to see your face," he said. He gripped her head and forced her to look at him. "That gag looks cute, but I want to see your real face. May I see it?"

His skin was so hot. It was starting to hurt. Christ, after awhile it might have actually burnt her.

"May I see it?" he said, more serious, insistent.

Melanie nodded. The warm hand left her and then ten hot fingers were at the back of her head.

Melanie felt another wave of relief as the knot came undone and the scarf fell limp from her mouth. She spit it out and breathed normally for the first time, hearing her real voice again as she gasped.

"Please," she whispered. "Just tell me what you want. I'll give you anything just please don't hurt me."

His hand clamped over her mouth. "Shhh. Relax," he said. After a moment he released her jaw and said, "None of that."

Melanie couldn't stop herself. "Don't hurt me, please."

"My, my. Do I have to put it back on?" His voice was still calm. "Just be quiet for a moment, silly."

She obeyed, and kept her eyes locked with his. Barker squinted at her, like he was contemplating what she was. He traced one finger down the side of her face.

"It's nice to meet you. My name is Justin Kyle Barker."

Melanie sniffed. "Justin?"

His left eye squinted. "Barker. Don't call me Justin. Understand?"

She nodded. "Okay."

"Good." He cocked his head to the side. "Do you have a middle name?" Melanie nodded, and after a moment he half chuckled, like a little pop. "Well, what is it?"

"Jean," she said.

"Melanie Jean Grier," he whispered. "Beautiful. Lovely. And what do you go by? First name? Second?"

She felt a cramp and tried to adjust herself, sneaking in another attempt at the rope on her wrists. "Just Melanie," she said.

He nodded. "Melanie." Up and down his chin went, like he was mulling over some great wonder of the world. "It's such a lovely name." When he whispered there was a little musical tone to his voice, like he was about to get some kind of present. She fought off nausea at his obsession with her.

Next he said, "So, is there something you'd like to say to me?"

Melanie was afraid of angering him, but there was only one thing she could bring herself to say. "I'll give you anything. Anything."

At that he leaned down and she thought he was going to hit her or choke her. But instead, he put his right hand up as if to surrender. "I won't hurt you, dear. I promise." His eye twitched again. "If you don't make me."

She tugged on the rope. "I won't. I promise. I promise. I just want to go home."

"Home?" he said.

"Please. Just tell me what you want. I want to go home."

Barker's face folded into a frown and to her dismay, he looked confused. "You sweet thing…you don't know what this is." He ran his hand through his own hair, and spoke cautiously, like he didn't want to come on too strong. "I won't hurt you. I certainly won't rape you, if that's what you're afraid of. But, understand this. I am not letting you leave. You can never go home."

A weight fell on her chest. She had no response and she felt her jaw quivering. Never. The word bounced around in her head. She gathered up a little bit of courage.

"Why? What do you want from me?" she asked.

He waved his hand. "Enough of that. I know this is a little upsetting but it will all be alright. For now, let's just get to know each other, starting with you. I want you to tell me about yourself, not just ask me the same thing again and again. So there it is. That's what I want and I'll settle for nothing less." He cocked his head. "Good enough?"

"No," she spat. "I don't understand. Why are you doing this? Why did you hurt my parents? Why?"

He shushed her again. "Your parents are just fine. I made sure of that. Your father is a strong guy. I didn't do anything to him the doctor can't fix. You heard me call the ambulance on the way out, didn't you? I was just having a bit of fun."

She sprang against her bonds.

"He looked dead, you bastard!" The hand smacked against her mouth and squeezed her jaw. Her bravery faded.

"You will not speak to me that way."

She was panicking inside, wanting nothing but to scream and cry, and she felt light headed. Tears dripped down her cheeks. Somehow, she managed to nod, and his grip loosened. She'd met many different people with firm handshakes and high temperatures, but Barker dwarfed them all. In fact it was generally hotter and stuffier in this room with him sitting so close. Melanie forced herself to speak, even if it only came out in whispers. "If they're really okay…can I talk to them? Please?"

Barker smiled. He was still relaxed, even when he threatened her. Nonchalant, was the word she'd recently learned. "Maybe. If you behave," he said.

Another important question came to mind. "Where am I?"

"You're in New Heim," he said with a wave of his dancing fingers. "A rather run down city in Washington State."

Washington. Dear God. She was so far from home.

He shrugged. "Best get comfortable, Melanie." He glanced at her wrists. "I can treat those cuts. I don't have the materials yet but I'll go get them. You'll be alright."

He stood up.

"Don't…" She blanked out, thinking instead of her parents, and some of the things she'd never get to say to them.

He stopped. "Don't what?" he said.

Melanie was still thinking of her parents: her mother's terrified, tear stricken face. That wasn't the last time she wanted to see her mother.

"Don't ignore me, Melanie. Finish what you were saying," Barker said.

Melanie was crying hard now. "Don't…leave me here, please."

He paused for a minute, and then asked, "Are you hungry?"

Staring through tears, Melanie could only gawk at his absent-mindedness.

When she didn't answer, he leaned closer. "Are. You. Hungry?"

"No, I'm sick." She was too tense, nauseous, and light headed to even consider eating, but her words made him giggle.

"You're not sick," he said, straightening up. "Don't worry, you'll be fine. But you'll need to eat soon."

She tried to sit up. "I am sick. Please, don't leave me like this. I'll die if you do."

Her words seemed to affect him, as he stared at the wall. After a moment he looked back down at her, frowning.

"Well, then…you should come downstairs with me and eat."

"Okay," she said.

"Promise me, Melanie," he warned. "If you come downstairs, you eat."

She leaned up best she could. "Anything. I'll do anything."

Barker smirked. "I like the sound of that."

When he bent over her a horrific stench came from his armpits. It was like he didn't ever use soap or body wash. He tinkered with the rope behind the mantle, and she felt it start to loosen. For a moment all of her fears and worries dissolved as she started to regain control of her arms. At long last, it was undone, and she pulled her arms down in front of her, shoulders cramping horribly. There were spikes come out her back and she stretched numerous muscles as he started untying her feet. When she was fully untied, she scrunched up her legs, rolled up like an armadillo.

"Up," he said lightly.

Melanie hesitated for a moment, but when she remembered the knife, she was quick to obey. Melanie stood up next to Barker now, measuring their difference in height. He was three feet higher than her, a giant.

He took her arm before she could do anything and led her out the door. The first thing she saw was a very small upstairs hallway: One door seven feet ahead, closed, a bathroom to the right, and a door to her immediate right, a companion to her room. The stairs were to her immediate left.

As they descended, she found that the carpet was tan and the stairs had one landing between the top and the bottom. At the bottom he pulled her into a dimly lit hallway with flickering bulbs. There was a closed bedroom door straight ahead, and a hallway to her right that must have led to the backyard, and probably a laundry room and such. To her left was the front of the house, which she immediately realized was the kitchen and living room. A much smaller house than she was used to.

In the kitchen there was a small table, like one she'd seen in a college dorm once. He sat her down in one of the chairs and examined her wrists for a moment. "Oooh," he grimaced. "These are bad. I'll make sure I get those treatments soon."

Ironically, next he pulled out handcuffs. She tried to move but they were already around her hands, loose. Not tight enough to hurt the red marks. Then he took out another pair and put them on her ankles. Melanie let him do it, afraid to cross him again. He walked away to the counter and opened the refrigerator.

"I hope you like turkey," he said. "Cause, well, that's what we have."

"That's fine," she muttered, still looking around the room.

The kitchen had white tile floor, and a small island next to the table. There was nothing on the counter, and possibly nothing in the drawers. The house seemed like it had been abandoned. Now she wondered if he had just found the turkey meat in the refrigerator of an abandoned house. She hoped she was being fed something halfway decent. On the floor of the kitchen, there was a lot of dust. And that was it. Dusty but no mess anywhere.

She looked over her shoulder.

From the table, there was a sofa straight ahead in the living room. And over by the door, an armchair. There was a nightstand in between them all the way at the wall that must have had a TV on it at some point. A white cable wire stuck up into the air, with nothing to plug into. Maybe she could plug it into Barker's eye.

Barker had a plate out, and was fitting the turkey cuts on the bread. With a kitchen knife he took one slice. Just one. Slow and perfectly straight, like a cook.

The sight of the knife made her panic again, and she jerked against the cuffs. Her hands and feet were all useless, and this was something she'd just never experienced. Any time in her life she'd ever been scared, for any reason, she could run or fight. She could do something. Now Melanie had no use of her arms or legs. It was her job now to just sit and wait at this monster's mercy.

Barker walked over, plate in one hand, with a little skip to his step. He set the plate down in front of her and sat down across from her.

Melanie sniffed the meat. She placed her cuffed hands near the plate and pulled up the bread, peeking. There was nothing to suggest the meat wasn't fresh, and she was suddenly very hungry. But how could she eat in front of him. He sat there and stared at her, like a face on an army poster. She looked at him and then at the meet, the nerve to look directly at him coming and going. He was waiting for her to eat, and probably to tell him it was delicious. He was so bright eyed, his smile so stretched; his face so pale he could have been a zombie. Any minute not she might see bugs crawl out of his mouth.

The yellow eyes went wide. "You need water, don't you?" Before she could answer he was up again, back at the counter. He opened a cabinet door and out came a glass.

As he was filling it he asked, "Are you in any pain?"

"What?" she responded, placing her cuffed hands on her lap, fingers locked.

He shut off the faucet. "Pain. Discomfort. Are you feeling any?"

"Yes," she said, afraid of what his response might be.

He turned to her with a guilty look, lips curled in a frown. "Sorry." With the glass in his right hand, he went stiff. Motionless. A statue.

"I guess…I guess I could be nicer…yeah, I could be nicer," the statue said. He came back to life by shaking his head and shrugging. He came back to the table and set the glass down next to the plate. He sat back down and said, "At some point, restraints won't be necessary. And you'll be going in and out of this refrigerator at your own free will. All that stuff."

"Oh," she said. "Okay."

"Go on," he said. "Eat up."

Melanie picked it up slowly, inspecting it a second time. It was just, normal, fresh turkey, and like magic, she was now hungry. She tore into the sandwich, biting into bread, leaf, and meat, feeling a mixture of flavors roll to the back of her throat and down. When it hit her stomach, she felt much more relaxed.

Barker leaned on his elbows, hands under his chin. As she took her last few bites she kept her eyes on him.

"How is it?" he asked.

"Good," she muttered with a sniff.

"I should hope so," he said. "It only took a couple seconds."

She drank the water, feeling cold liquid go down her throat and through her body. It was the most incredible thing she'd ever felt, like all of the pain and stress in her body was momentarily washed away and cleaned out.

"Good," he said. He folded his hands like she used to do in school. Then he reached over and dragged the empty plate to his side of the table. "Melanie Grier," he whispered.

Although she wanted to ask again what he wanted, for more detail, she just said, "Thank you," she said. "For the food."

"You're welcome," he said. "Would you like anything else?"

She wanted to go home. That would be nice. Melanie raised her hands. "Can you let me out of these?"

"Maybe," he said. "If you promise to keep behaving."

"I promise," she said.

He hesitated, but then reached into his pocket and pulled out a small key. "It's nice to be talking to you," he said.

"I don't want to talk," she mumbled.

His face changed, a frown quickly flashing, then replaced by another smile. Shit. He was going to hit her. He was going to hurt her. But he didn't. He stretched and yawned, showing all of his teeth.

"It's getting late isn't it? Why don't we go to bed?"

"Okay," she said, heart slowing down to a normal pace. "Am I going to be tied up?"

His fingers tapped the table rhythmically as he spoke. "I'd like to let you sleep like a normal person, instead of a…well..." His eyes rolled around. "Something to that effect. But first you need to make me trust you, of course. That'll take time." He came over to her and knelt down, starting with the feet.

There was a fierce gust of wind outside, and then a noise. Barker ignored it for some reason, but the front door was just pushed open. "I'll be good," she said, eyes on the door. "You can trust me."

"I would like that," he said. The cuffs fell off her feet, clanging loud as they hit the floor. He stood up fully now and took hold of the cuffs on her wrists.

He nicked her cut and she flinched. "It hurts," she said.

He made a "ch" sound with his mouth, and turned the key. "I'll bet it does." The cuffs hit the table.

Melanie instinctively went to rub her wrists but he caught her wrist first. With his large hand, he gently massaged hers.

"Think you can sleep peacefully tonight?" he asked. "We can talk more tomorrow."

"Okay," she said.

"Good," he smiled, hissing the word.

He gave her a tug and she stood up. He let her wrist go and started to talk to her. She faced him with her head down.

"I was thinking that I might not have to keep you tied up much at all…We can discuss some rules tomorrow. I've been contemplating them. What do you-"

She slammed into him, throwing all her weight forward. He didn't fall back, but she managed to shove him aside. Then she charged out the door and into the dark.

Chapter 4

The City

A t first it was difficult to see. All she knew was that straight ahead of the house there was a huge fence. She could go left or right, and chose left. Melanie refused to stop running. Any temptation to stop, any pain in the chest, stomach, legs, head, were nothing compared to what would happen if he caught her. Unless the road winded or hit a dead end, she kept running straight, building distance from him. Then she would try to find people.

It was difficult for her to take in her surroundings while running so fast, but from what she could tell, he'd brought her to a house on one incredibly long road. No neighbors, unless maybe if she'd gone right instead of left. Eventually, after ten full minutes of running, she found more houses. There was a street sign that told her she was on Copper Avenue, and another sign above it that told her she could turn onto Crate Drive. She remembered the hand on her wrist, a man who had been down her steps in moments, strong as a giant, and kept running straight.

The wind pounded her face and pressure built in her lungs. Houses soared by her as she ran, gliding out of her view like the images in a montage. She felt cold air and smelled dirt and grass. The streetlights were on and the moon was out. A dim mixture of blue and orange lit the path. Eventually, she had to stop and catch her breath. She heaved and placed her hands on her knees. When she felt air flowing through her chest she straightened up and pushed her hair out of her eyes.

She was standing at another right turn, off Copper and onto Cotton Drive. Melanie looked back and tried to measure the distance she'd just run. It had to have been eight about eight blocks. Barker was far behind her.

Melanie took the right turn onto Cotton Drive, and saw it was a long, winding road. She could only see six or so houses before the rest were obscured behind the behemoth she was looking at now. It was very wide with two garage doors and a porch that winded around the side. All of the lights were off, and there were no cars in the driveway, but they could have been in the garage.

Melanie walked up to the house and started pounding on the door, the sounds of her fist echoing across the street. The thought of Barker hearing her knocks, wherever he was, made her start to knock softer. But no matter how many times she did no one came to the door.

She walked off the porch and tried to see if she could peak inside, but the blinds were drawn. Next she back up into the middle of the yard, to look up into the second story windows. There were no signs of movement.

She turned and looked at one of the other houses. All of them had this look to them like there was no life inside of them. The entire block was silent. There weren't even trees on this block, no bugs singing. Just silence.

Melanie walked into the middle of the street. Looking more closely, the last house before the road wrapped around the bend, had an open garage and an open front door. There were no cars in that driveway either, and although it was dark, the garage looked messy. And the door, when she walked closer, looked broken. Like the place had been looted.

Was anyone living on this block? Chills seized her and she turned around, walking back to Copper. There was still a long way to go on Copper. It was one of those roads.

If I keep going this direction there must be people. Someone, somewhere. There has to be one person. One family. There has to be someone.

Melanie couldn't understand why not one person would be living in this part of town, if that was in fact what was going on here. But on some level, she understood why Barker had brought her here. He'd brought her somewhere far away from people, from anyone who might interfere. And she had to find her way back to wherever those people were.

Melanie was looking straight ahead on her long path. There had to be a neighboring town. Unless this was part of a city. In her curiosity she turned to survey the area, eventually looking back the way she came.

Far in the distance, a couple blocks back, Barker was walking toward her. Melanie almost stopped breathing. He looked small so far away, like a little child all dressed in black, strolling in the pale moonlight. Her heart jumped and she screamed before she ran.

"Help! Help! Help! Somebody help!" She bellowed and howled as she ran. "Please! Someone help me!"

Every block she passed was as silent and still as the last, and when she looked back, she couldn't see him anymore. She was far ahead of him, and freedom felt more in reach.

Copper Avenue finally ended. She could go left or right. Like a wave, her body drifted right. And now she could see something more concrete. A landmark, a sign of civilization. In the distance there was a huge skyscraper, mostly obscured by all of the dark buildings to her left, but it was lit up with purple lights, and stars speckled above. It looked alive. Occupied. Safe.

She ran again, towards the lights.

Her path eventually brought her to a left turn into an alley. At the end of the alley was a right turn into another alley with an option to go left or right. She was in between some sort of large chain of apartments. The smell was unbearable, but she only noticed it once or twice. It was worth the trouble. She zigzagged through the alleys, eventually arriving on a small thin road between two buildings. Two her left, about fifty feet away, was a marvelous sight. In the shaft between the two large buildings, on the sidewalk, there were people walking by. Melanie ran to them, and stepped into a den of bright lights.

The road was large and wide, and the sidewalk thin. She could hear car horns honking, see people walking ahead of her. At the end of the road there was something you would only see in a city: five different little green signs nailed to a large post. Just past it, the road turned into a triangle, veering off into three different roads separating three sets of buildings. The intersection was busy with crowds walking on the little white bridges painted into the concrete. And every building had lights on and people in it. Most were either shops or restaurants. Some had people standing outside smoking, or texting, or just standing. Everywhere she looked, something was going on.

She didn't know what to do, which building to pick, which person to approach.

Calm down. Don't be stupid. You need the police. Ask where you can find the police.

She scurried down the sidewalk to the right of the alley, afraid that Barker might emerge and drag her back into that dark slit. As she walked near the diamond shaped intersection some people started to stare. She probably looked like a monster, with her hair mangled as it was, and bloody cuts on her wrists. Her clothes were probably awful too. The intersection was the worst part. Hordes of people blocked her path and there was no right, left, north, south. Everything seemed like it was spinning.

The crowd closed in on her and made a lot of noise. She couldn't breathe. She couldn't sit down. She couldn't relax. And she didn't know where to go. Melanie asked them for the police, but no sound came out. Instead she gasped for air.

Several of these people bumped into her, oblivious to the fact that her wrists were covered in red. Cars zipped by on the roads. Some people across the street were yelling, either partying hard or getting into a fight. She didn't know.

"Excuse me. Ex...excuse me. Excuse me, I—"

A trio of people her age had walked up close to her. Two boys and a girl, boys dressed in blue shirts and the girl in white dress. She had flowing dark hair and the boys were both blonde. Brothers?

"Excuse me. Please. I need the police station," she said.

They looked at her incredulously. "What the fuck? Are you high?"

"No! Please, please, help me."

The girl started digging into her purse, and Melanie hoped she would call the police. Then the girl pulled out change, and something in her snapped.

She grabbed the girl by the shoulders. "I'm not begging! Please, I was attacked!"

"Oh hell no," one of them said and roughly shoved her aside. Melanie almost fell as they scurried off. She thought about chasing after them but she was suddenly on her knees. Crying.

She pressed her hands against the concrete, buried in this forest of chaos. Surrounded. Helpless.

You need a phone. Get someone's phone. Call the police. And your parents. They'll come.

It was hard to think right now, but she got back to her feet. The sidewalk was more clear now, and she looked to her right. A large man was standing beside her, smoking as cigarette. He wore a sleeveless leather vest and he was bald and brawny. He was standing in front of a restaurant that read: ShipDeck, Bar and Grill. She couldn't help noticing the inside of through the window: there seemed to be several booths with red cushion and mahogany wood, and pirate statues on the walls.

She addressed the smoking man, rubbing her cut wrist. "Excuse me," she said. There was a pinch in her arm. Rubbing stung just as much, but made her feel she'd accomplished something.

The man cocked his eyes at her and blew smoke out his mouth. "Whatever you're selling I'm not—"

"I need help! Please, I need the police!" she shouted.

"What for?" he said, flicking the butt of the cigarette and dropping some ashes to the ground.

"I was kidnapped. I escaped. Please, do you have a phone?" She realized she was crying again, and for a moment she grasped her own head.

A man walked out of the restaurant, wearing khakis and a red shirt: a waiter.

"If this is some kind of scam, kid…" the bald man was saying.

"Please, can I just use your phone?" she asked. "I need help."

He groaned. "Sure," he said, reaching into the pocket of his jacket.

"Hey," said the waiter. He was a slender man with a buzz cut, deeply tanned and sporting a tiny chin beard. "What's your name?" he asked her.

"Melanie," she answered.

"Melanie," said the waiter, nodding. He walked to her, standing beside the bald man. "You say you were kidnapped?"

"Yes," she said, insistently.

"By who, exactly?" said the bald man, crossing his arms.

The waiter shot him a grimace, then looked back at her. "Melanie, why don't you start at the beginning?"

"I…I…" She remembered the first time she saw Barker, and her mother tied on the floor. And she was expected to recount it. On the sidewalk. In front of people. Coherently. She started to heave, and pressed her hand to her mouth. A wave of dizziness made her stumble and suddenly the waiter was touching her. "Hey, why don't we sit down?" he said.

She let gravity take her as the gentle hands pressed into her back.

"Geez, kid," she heard the older, bald man say.

Melanie was on her butt now, back against the stony building.

"There we go," said the waiter, rubbing her shoulder with a very soothing touch. "Now we're sitting," he laughed.

She smiled back at him, but she couldn't stop the tears.

"It's okay," he was saying. "I'm going to call the police. Okay?" His eyes were focused on her and he was frowning.

She felt deep gratitude toward him, and noticed he was very handsome, the tight shirt showing off his muscles.

"I'll do that now," he said, taking out his phone. He pressed it to his ear and kept his eyes on her.

A realization struck Melanie. "Can I use your phone? Can I call my parents? Please?"

"First let me call the police. Okay?" His eyes darted left, in the direction of the phone. "Yes, hello. I'm reporting a crime."

He got up and took a few steps away.

"Hey, kid," said the older man, throwing his cigarette to the ground and coughing. He pulled out an IPhone and extended his hand. His face was twisted like he was in pain, or not getting enough air. But he held his hand out patiently, waiting for her to grab it. She gently pulled it from the embrace of his fingers, clutching the device tightly.

"Thank you," she said.

"Make it quick would ya?" he said, coughing again, a fist to his mouth.

Melanie dialed.

The excitement brought her back to her feet. The phone rang. She held it with her right hand, her left hand to her other ear to drown out the noises of the street.

It rang. Again. Again.

Melanie faced the street, anxiety burning in her. In fact she did feel very hot. He wouldn't pick up. No matter how many times it rang. No answering machine. Nothing.

He had to be in the hospital. Maybe he didn't have his phone. What about her mother?

She dialed.

The phone rang.

To her right, Melanie heard the waiter talking. "She says she was kidnapped. Could you send out an officer? I-what?" He waited for a moment, and then said with careful annunciation, "Carl. Banning." He had his hand in his pocket as he spoke, and walked back and forth a couple steps as he spoke. He seemed unable to figure out where he wanted to place himself. His eyes widened, "Thank you. Thank you very much."

He took the phone away from his ear and walked back toward her.

Her mother's phone was still ringing. Again. Again. Again. Again. Why weren't they picking up?

"Melanie," said Carl, now very close to her. "Why don't we go inside until the police show up? You can go the bathroom and, maybe wash those cuts."

She looked down at her wrists, dark rings in place of what might have been bracelets. She pulled her sleeves down over them.

"Can we just stay here?"

"Sure. Sure. That sounds good."

So Melanie stood on the concrete, waiting for help to come, Carl Banning's hand on her shoulder.

"What's your full name?" he asked.

"Melanie Grier."

"Melanie Grier. That's pretty. Are you hungry? At all?" Barker's words.

"No. I'm fine."

Carl nodded his head and rubbed her shoulder. "Okay. Do you feel sick at all?"

Actually, for the first time in awhile her stomach was fine, her organs seemed to be in the proper positions. "I'm okay. Really."

"Okay, that's cool." He looked away from her and watched the traffic, folding and unfolding his hands. She stared ahead, taking everything in. She decided this city was more massive than Fargo.

The door opened behind them and a girl walked out wearing the same clothes as Carl, except she had short shorts. Her short dark hair sat on her head like a hat. "Hey. Jack is looking for you."

"Um," Carl said, looking at Melanie then back at the waitress. He scratched his head. "Yeah, um." He walked over to the waitress and Melanie barely heard their whispering. She turned away and continued to watch all of the people and cars. The cars zoomed by unless the traffic lights were red. At a crossroad people were huddled together like a cult. They reminded her of some geese she saw crossing the street when she was little. She didn't remember where that was. Some family trip. She remembered the geese lingered in the road, and she thought *Isn't that dangerous?*

Horns went off every few seconds. In fact it was a wonder Melanie heard any of the whispering behind her.

"Kidnapped? Oh my God."

"Yeah. Just tell Jack I'll be back in when the cops show up."

"Is she okay?"

"She will be. I didn't ask who took her. I mean, do I really want to know?"

"No. Let the police ask her."

Melanie kept her hands at her sides, only moving to scratch an itch every few seconds. She had a lot of those now. On her cuts.

The bald man with the IPhone had wandered away.

And replacing him was a cop car, pulling out of the line of traffic and up to the curb right in front of her. She heard the wheels against the gravel and dirt, and took a step back.

Carl walked up beside her and pulled her back an inch. He was taking the role of protector, and Melanie was the person being introduced.

Two Martin Grier's walked out of the car. One was a large burly man with a deep tan and a long mustache, like an upside down "U." He also had a small "X" shaped scar on his cheek, and gages in his ears. The other was a young man, maybe twenty. Or Twenty-five. Melanie wasn't very good at that. But he was thin and had a lot of hair: combed on his head and a connected mustache and beard, all brown. The burly man walked up to them and put his hands on his hips, seeming eager to get down to business. The thin man stood beside him, hand sitting open on his gun holster: relaxed but vigilant.

The burly man pointed his finger, "Are you Carl Banning?"

"Yeah, that's me," said Carl, voice quivering for a moment. He was still braver than Melanie, who said nothing.

The burly, X scarred officer flashed his badge and said, "I'm Officer Gene Brolin." He held his hand out right and stuck out his thumb sharply. "And this is Officer Macklin. He's British."

"Now that's professional," said the thinner cop, in a voice that did in fact sound faintly European.

Brolin ignored Macklin and said, "We're here about a kidnapping." His eyes went straight to Melanie's wrists. "Must be you."

Melanie nodded, fists clenched in apprehension. Brolin turned to Carl.

"Mr. Banning, will you step over here with me?" He pointed at Melanie. "Tom, handle this."

Brolin took Carl by the shoulder and led him away from Melanie, and the young cop stepped forward.

"Where's he taking him?" Melanie asked, eyes following the burly cop and the kind, caring, waiter.

The young man said, "He's just having him state his report again, for the records."

"Oh," she said. She didn't like Brolin. He seemed uninterested. Mean, even. Her father wouldn't ever talk to a victim that way. He may have been gruff and stern but she knew he would have cared. In a missing person's case, her father was the type who led the search party.

"Can I have your full name?" the officer asked.

"Melanie Grier."

"Melanie Grier. The first thing I want you to know is that you'll be alright. Do you understand?" His face and tone were both very serious, and Melanie believed him. He seemed like a kind, caring man.

"Yes." She nodded speedily. "Yes."

"Okay. Good. Now tell me what happened." His pen and pad were ready.

"I...I."

Macklin's eyes met hers. "I know you've been through a lot but we can't help you if we don't know everything. Don't leave anything out."

"I...I was at home. In Fargo. And I-

"Fargo?" Macklin's eyes were wide, mouth open. She noticed that his thin brown beard was very neatly trimmed. "You were taken from Fargo?"

"Yes," she barely said, voice caught in her breath. "I live in Fargo."

"Who took you?" he asked, pen pressed against the pad. "Did you hear a name? Can you describe his face?"

"He said his name was Ryan Downs but...that was a lie. I heard a man call him Barker. I don't know if that's true either. He was tall-

"Barker," said Macklin, eyes wide. "Justin Barker?"

"I, I don't know. You know him?"

Macklin's eyes drifted down, mouth open. Then it closed and he folded his arms. "Go on. Sorry to interrupt."

"He...he broke into my house. He took me. He..." He'd nearly killed her father, he'd done God knew what to her poor mother. Melanie's fingers were vibrating in place. Her whole body was vibrating. She caught herself and tried to find more words. "Then I was in the car. I couldn't see anything. Then he took me out of the car and we were in a power station. And there was a man there. Named Charlie. I called for help but he knocked me out again. Then I was in a house..." She remembered the rope cutting into her wrists. Maybe it would be easier to talk faster. "He took me downstairs and I ran out the door."

Macklin's arms were still folded. "Where did you run from? Tell me everything."

"I don't know! I've never been here before. It was dark. Everything was dark. Empty houses. No street lights. Please! You have to help me?"

Tom put his hands on her shoulder, and his touch was soft and warm. "It's okay. It's okay...I'm sorry. I just needed to know. You okay?"

She put her head down and tears forced their way up again.

Macklin's voice was gentle, like a mother's. "One last thing. Just one last thing. Do you remember a house number?"

She tried to remember. Barker had said it. 125 something. It was something sharp, or jagged. Did it start with a C? "Copper! 125 Copper, something."

Macklin nodded his head. "Okay, Melanie. Um." He looked down again. "Wow, okay, um." He closed his eyes and rubbed them. "Could you excuse me a moment? I'll be right back." He smiled at her.

Then he walked over to Brolin. In the next few minutes she saw the two cops talking back and forth. Brolin cast her a few angry glances. Why was he doing that? She wasn't the one who committed the crime.

Apparently he was done with Carl, because the waiter walked back over to her, looking very concerned.

"Hey," he said.

"Hi," she said.

"You doing okay?"

"I don't know."

"It's okay. They'll take care of you."

"I don't trust the one," she said, looking at Brolin.

Carl looked back at him and grimaced. He spoke quietly. "Yeah he's an asshole. But they're still cops. They'll keep you safe. The other guy seems alright."

"Yes, he is." Although Macklin seemed more interested in the information she had and less in helping her. She didn't expect that from police. She expected them to be heroes, like her dad. But she could give them the benefit of the doubt. Macklin had said, he needed information to help her. He did want to help her. And maybe the other one did too, even if he had the personality of an ox.

In moments, the two cops walked back over, and it was the ox who spoke. "Alright Melanie. We're gonna take you back to the station. You'll be safe there until we figure this out. Sound good?"

"O-okay."

Tom opened the door. "Don't be afraid. It looks scary but it's supposed to."

Before she got in the car, she looked back at the waiter once more.

His face was regretful, like he wasn't ready. "I guess this is goodbye, huh?"

"I guess...thank you," she said to him. He'd been so kind. He might have just saved her life.

"You're welcome," he said. "Good luck."

Chapter 5

The Station

There was a moment in the car ride when Melanie thought it was all starting again. In the car with strangers. Cops, yes, but strangers, just like Barker. Why should she trust them? They could kill her just as easily. She needed to be home again, with her parents. People she knew she could trust without a moment of doubt. These men were dressed as cops. How did she know they were who they said they were? Badges. They'd shown their badges. Still, Melanie wished for the power to read minds. Without it, she was powerless. A rag doll.

To comfort herself, Melanie thought of her father. She thought of the car, the badges, the way they handled the situation. These were real cops, and she needed to relax. A better idea came to her then. She closely studied where they were going, in case she needed to jump out of the car. A warped newspaper headline flashed through her mind before she remembered, the doors locked from the inside.

Macklin was talking to her. "You said he hurt your father and mother. What was their condition?"

"Horrible," she said.

"Do you think anyone called an ambulance?" Macklin asked. "A neighbor, or any kind of witness?"

"Actually," she said. "He did. Before he took me."

The cops looked at one another, and she saw Brolin's eyebrows go up.

"Why do you think he would do that?" Macklin asked. The way he spoke to her sounded genuine with curiosity, like a detective. That was her anchor. That was what made her trust the situation that she was in, and brought her heart to a normal pace.

"I don't know," she said. "He's crazy."

"Damn right," said Brolin. "Quit making her relive it, Tom. It doesn't matter anyway."

Though Macklin's face was mostly shadowed, Melanie saw the way it twisted. "Doesn't matter?" he said.

"They're thousands of miles away. All that matters is what happened since she got here."

"I'm sorry, Gene. Am I being too human?" Macklin asked.

"You're being stupid. The Chief's gonna want to see her. So it's really none of our business."

"Oh! None of our business?" Macklin said. "You know, Gene, protect and serve means actually giving a damn. I'm awaiting the day you actually do your job." He smiled on his last words, an aggressive obnoxious tone in his voice.

"Keep it up and I'll request your transfer, kid," Brolin said.

"Humor me," said Macklin.

Her father told her once about the good cop bad cop routine, and how it involved using a good cop and a bad cop to test the reactions of a witness. Melanie felt like she was participating in an unspoken interrogation, watching the good and bad cops spit back and forth at one another. And none of it made her feel safe.

In the next few moments they arrived at the station. A large sign read "N. H. P. D." and the walls were brown brick, chipped in several places toward the bottom. Bushes and flowers stood in mulch beside the front doors, and tiny trees were lined up behind the mulch.

Inside, the station was small and dark. But small only in the sense that the ceiling felt close to her head. The actual inside seemed very complex, with many different hallways leading who knew where and a bushel of computer desks in front of her. The checkerboard floor was polished shiny and there was an army of officers in their way. Many of them nodded their heads to Macklin and Brolin as they walked past the reception desk in the front, through the crowd of desks, and toward the back hallway. They stopped onto a dull blue carpet and made one right turn. Now a thin hall, lit by white florescent lights, brought her to two large wooden doors.

When they lead her through she saw a large black box with a massive desk in the middle. The desk had picture frames on the right and folders on the left, in the middle there were a few sheets of paper lit up by a desk lamp. A small metal bar read "Captain Ryan, Chief of Police." Behind it sat a tall and buff man, uniformed in black with four buttons down his chest and golden stripes on each sleeve at the wrists. A black cap sat upon his head. He had a rectangular gray chin beard, and she couldn't see how much hair was under the hat.

"Sir," said Macklin.

"Sir," said Brolin.

"Macklin. Brolin," said the Chief, sounding very unfriendly. In fact, if Brolin was an ox, then the Chief was a rhinoceros. He lounged back in his chair with his leg folded, right elbow on the desk. He looked at Melanie with bright green eyes. "This is the girl?"

"Yes, sir," said Brolin.

"Sit," said the Chief.

Tom pulled a chair out for Melanie to sit and she did so. She wasn't sure what to do or say next.

The Chief propelled the discussion himself. "You claim to have been abducted, Miss..." He looked at her inquisitively.

"Grier," she said, clearing her throat of some bile after.

"Miss Grier. Tell me everything." He brushed his lips with his knuckles.

"I...I came home from school one day and he was there. He..."

"Sir," said Macklin. "If I may."

The Chief stayed lounged back as his eyes moved to Macklin. "Go ahead."

"She's been through a lot and she's already told me about what happened. I could sum it up for you."

The Chief raised his eyebrows, not specifying that he was waiting for Macklin to continue. When Macklin caught on he said, "A man came into her house in Fargo. He attacked her father and her mother. And then he took her. He brought her to Ghost Town, and as soon as he untied her, she escaped. And here we are."

The Chief grimaced. He rubbed his thumb and index finger together, still lounged. "Melanie, describe him to me in detail."

This was easy. It was like painting a picture. "Someone called him Barker. He's really tall. Pale. Black hair. Messy. Scruffy beard. Wears a long coat. And he's always smiling."

The Chief's elbow left the table and he held his head in his hands. Melanie turned to face Macklin and the hungry look wasn't there. He nodded at her with a kind smile, wordlessly reassuring her. She half glanced at Brolin, who's face never seemed to change. Then she turned back to the Chief, who looked angry and stunned. He slapped his hands down on the table and Melanie jumped.

He mumbled, "Shit…why couldn't it just be the mob?"

"The mob?" she asked.

Brolin said, "Well, to be fair, sir, the mob sends body parts into the streets too. Ever see the Godfather?"

"Shut up, Gene," said the Chief. "If Barker is back then this is all going to get messy."

Melanie didn't know what to say. The Chief faced her with stern aggression. "Where did Barker take you? How did you escape?" He made it sound like she'd committed the crime, just like Brolin did. Except he was much more frightening. In better shape and with a meaner glare.

"I ran," she said.

"Ran?" asked Brolin, sounding confused.

"Yes! Look you have to help me please! Can I call my parents please? My father's a cop. Fargo Police. I called but he wouldn't answer. Can I call the Fargo police station? Or my Uncle Russell. Please I want to go home."

The Chief raised his hand halfway. "First tell me where he took you. Where did you run from? In case say, he followed you?"

Barker. Coming here. She went stiff. "Please don't let him take me again. Please."

"Answer my question," the Chief curtly said.

She quickly glanced at Macklin, who frowned at the Chief. "125 Copper," she said.

Macklin cut her off. "That's not too deep into Ghost Town."

"What's Ghost Town?" Melanie asked, looking up at him again.

Macklin turned to face her instead of the Chief. "That's what we call it. That whole desolate area. You said you didn't see any people. That's because the place is cleared out. Abandoned."

An entire area of the city abandoned. "Why?" she thought aloud.

"They hit it with an airstr—"

"Macklin!" the Chief snapped.

Melanie whipped her head around to the Chief. He looked furious, eyes on Macklin. "That's enough." He said, his face like a gorilla. Then he softened his voice. "Did you take statements at the restaurant?"

"Yes, sir," said Brolin. "From Banning. The guy who found her."

"Tom, go back and take statements from the managers and owner if he's there."

"Why?" Tom asked.

The Chief raised his eyebrows. "I just gave you an order. Now go follow it." He waved his fingers as if shooing a mouse.

Tom seemed angry, but he left the room. She wanted to call out to him not to go but she didn't want to argue with the police. She was alone now with both of the frightening men.

"Young lady," said the Chief. "His full name, in case you're interested, is Justin Kyle Barker. He's a serial murderer and rapist."

The words hit Melanie like knives, and she felt cold in her stomach and between the legs. How close had she come?

She pleaded one last time. "Can I call my family please?"

"Hold on," said the Chief.

"Hold on?"

"Yes," he said.

And for a moment the trio sat in silence. Melanie couldn't fathom why they were just sitting there like that, or why the Chief was tapping his hands on the table like he was bored, or why Brolin had stepped directly behind her, stiff like a bodyguard.

Finally she mustered the courage to speak. "You said I could."

"Pardon?" said the Chief.

"I asked if I could call the Fargo police or my uncle. You said I could but first I had to answer your question. I answered it."

The Chief opened is mouth in an "Ah" gesture. Then he folded his arms on the table and frowned like a child. "Yes, I suppose I alluded to that." He gritted his teeth, tapping them together like he was nervous, or unhappy. Somehow he seemed uncomfortable, like he wanted to get up, but Melanie was keeping him behind that desk.

"Alright, child. I'll send you back where you came."

"You will?" She'd be escorted all the way home?

"Brolin," he said. "You know what to do."

Melanie heard a loud snap behind her and turned. Brolin's face was that of a savage beast. She saw the baton right before it slammed into her head.

When Melanie awoke she was cold and uncomfortable, biting down on some kind of fabric. Her head was in so much pain, and she felt like the skin just above her right eye was stretched thin. She knew there was a cut there. And she was very cold. There were cold things wrapped around her. Chains. They chilled her skin. All over her body. She was naked.

She was on her side. Freezing cold, looking at red walls.

Behind her someone clapped very loud. "Well, wasn't that exciting?"

Melanie sniffed and tried to turn over, but the chains held her lying on her right arm, facing the wall. But she knew it was Barker when he pressed his hands into the bed and leaned over her. Even though she couldn't see him in full view, she actually recognized the smell of him. She was nude. He was going to do it. She was done. She wished for clothing. She wished for clothing more than anything. Even freedom. Someone was screaming in the house. It was muffled, like her mother's.

"Don't worry, honey. You were just dreaming." He giggled loudly.

When Melanie tried to sit up, she realized the chains were also fastened loosely around her neck.

She tried to say, "Please. I'll do anything." But her voice was strangled again.

The chains were around her legs too. It wasn't like last time, where she could move her arms and legs. This time she was wrapped up in cold shackles. And naked. Utterly helpless. She cried, and started to think it might be easier to die.

He rubbed the top of her head with his hand. "Never. Do that. Again."

She nodded her head, slowly to avoid strangling herself.

He cupped her head in his hand, fingers almost to the cut. "If you do…I will drive you back to your home in North Dakota. And this time, I will make you watch while I kill your mother."

Chapter 6

Protect and Serve

There were many police officers in New Heim who took the words "protect and serve" quite open to interpretation. And then there was Tom Macklin. He seemed to be one of the few good men who lived in New Heim but he didn't want to believe it. There were people here with kindness, empathy, and above all, common sense. None of them worked for the police, and he was the idiot who came to town assuming that they did.

Tonight, he was just a general idiot. The Chief sent him out the door to take statements he had no use for, from people who did not witness Melanie's arrival at the restaurant. He obeyed, so as to keep his job, but when he turned the engine on, it clicked.

He shut the car off and ran back into the station. Doubtful the Chief truly cared for Melanie Grier. But at the very least he would do his job. He would protect a victim. Someone who hadn't been killed yet. He had to understand how important that was.

He plowed through the station and found the doors to the Chief's office locked tight. He banged on the door but there was no answer, and no voices on the other side.

"Sir?" No answer. "Sir!"

Nothing.

Maybe they were around back. He started to go around but the secretary stood in his way. She was a short woman with dark hair and green eyes, but if looks could kill she'd be more infamous than Barker.

"Don't, Tom," she said in a somber voice.

"Where is he?"

She was a statue. "Didn't he order you to do something?"

"Yes. Does the whole station know?" he asked.

"You should go do it," she said quietly.

"Where is he?" Tom demanded.

She glared, still blocking his way. "Just let it be, Tom." He thought about forcing past her, but she said, "Touch me wrongly and you'll be finding new employment. The Chief doesn't want to be disturbed." The words hung between the two of them for a moment and she finished with, "Get over it."

Tom went out front and back to his car. Before he left he checked around the back of the station, accessed directly by a door in the Chief's office.

It was empty.

Tom was into work early the next day.

He disliked his boss and he despised his partner. Last night both of them vanished into thin air with the victim. Poor girl. Whether he was called upon or not, Tom was headed into the Chief's office for some answers.

He walked by multiple officers that wished him a good morning. Until he reached the two impenetrable doors. Today they were unlocked.

Although it was early morning, there was a glass on the Chief's table of dark liquid. Ed Ryan sat alone and seemed a mess, digging holes in his forehead with three fingers. He picked up the glass with his other hand.

"Macklin," he said. "I didn't send for you."

"I don't care."

The Chief looked up at him. The bags under his eyes informed Tom that his boss hadn't slept all night. "Watch it, Tom," he said quietly.

"What happened last night? Where's the girl?"

The Chief looked at his glass and swirled the liquid. "I gave her back." He took a drink.

Tom immediately assumed he heard the Chief wrong. "You gave her back?" He could believe the Chief didn't particularly care about some kid, but this? With his own two hands.

The Chief had a hand on one of the portraits on his desk. "Yes, I did. And I'd do it again," he said. Tom knew the picture the Chief was holding: a picture of his own ten-year-old son. He looked at the portrait in horror, as if it were in some kind of danger. And then he looked up at Tom. "We don't screw with Barker. Those are the rules. Break them and I'll fire you." He put the portrait down. "Do you understand, Tom? I will fire you. Now get out."

Anger welled in Tom. As long as your son stays safe, the rest of the children in this city can burn. You old bastard.

Out loud, he said, "She's just a kid." And the Chief ignored him.

Tom's thoughts drifted to Melanie Grier, and guilt overtook him. She'd gotten out. She'd been free. And all of this: Picking her up at the restaurant. Telling her she'd be safe. Giving her hope. Only to have her sent back.

He had to do something.

"I understand, sir," he lied. "I won't ask again."

"Good," said Ed Ryan.

"Can you at least tell me where Brolin is? I didn't hear from him or see him coming in."

The Chief looked like Tom had struck him as he shut his eyes and shook his head. "Gone."

"Gone?" Tom said.

He nodded with a twist of his lips, like he could have cried. "I sent him to Ghost Town with the girl. He never came back."

"You think Barker took him?"

The Chief set the glass down. "He went into Ghost Town and he didn't come back."

Try as he might, Tom couldn't stop his next words. "If a missing girl won't motivate you to take action, will a missing officer?"

The Chief slammed the table so loud it could have been a gunshot. "Don't you dare take that tone with me, boy! Bring it up again and you're fired. You hear me?" He jumped to his feet. "Do you hear me?"

Tom had taken one step back. "Yes, sir." He left the office.

If Tom went to one of Ed Ryan's superiors, he could probably get him fired for this, but who would be believed, the veteran with connections or the new kid? And even if he got Ryan fired, how would it help Melanie?

The Government. Different departments. CIA. Special forces. With the right manipulation they could rain hell down on Barker and rescue her. And yet, Stanley Jackson, an old detective, had given Tom warnings. He said that Barker had the Government bought. He didn't know how it was possible, but he heeded Stan's words. Stan told him there was only one way to kill Barker, and the key was absolute discretion.

So Tom couldn't fight with the Chief. But he could fight Barker. He'd intended to for some time now, regardless of Melanie Grier. But an innocent life was all the more reason to take action.

A situation like this made Tom reconsider where he chose to serve. He'd come from San Diego, mainly to escape his father. The cost had been leaving his mother alone in the city, at the institution. But as far as he knew she was just fine, Father as well. Tom saw New Heim as a place he could do good work, but ever since he started, his efforts were hindered, not by criminals, but by senseless complications.

He would not resign. He'd fulfill the oath. Protect the people of this broken city from the worst kind of scum, and settle his score with Justin Barker.

The morning air refreshed Tom. Fall was his favorite season: The gentle breeze and the occasional wash of cold air; The changing of leaves and the vast, empty beach. But his fond thoughts were corrupted by images of the girl. How much time did she have left? Would Barker wait? Sometimes he waited. They'd go missing a week before they turned up dead. If he waited, Tom could save her. He just needed time.

Tom hated the Chief. The thought came back again and again. He was letting innocent people die. Technically, Tom did the same, but only because he didn't know what to do about it. But he would find a way. He would kill Barker. He had to, if not for Melanie Grier, or for the city in general, then for Stan.

Chapter 7

Torture

Before Barker left her that night, he took out a pair of headphones and put them on her head. As they slipped over her ears, her world was consumed by an onslaught of drums. It was some singer she didn't recognize, with a deep, operatic voice.

The drums went, Boom. Beat. Boom. Beat. Boom. Beat. Again. One second between each drum for the next three minutes, while a melody overlapped it and blasted loud lyrics she barely understood.

Boom. Beat. Boom. Beat. Boom. Beat. Boom. Beat.

It didn't take long to feel pain in her ears, and she couldn't see very well. The light was off and the door was shut. She was alone, having just been unbearably close to Barker, nude.

Normally, without clothing, she felt lighter. But with the chains, she felt much heavier. The window was open, cold air crawling up her skin. The chills made her hairs stand up and her nipples harden. She'd never been so mortified. This couldn't actually be happening. Melanie Grier could not be chained to a bed in nothing but her skin. Despite the gag, she took a breath and bellowed for help.

Moving too sharply rung the chains against her skin, so she had to be still. Sweat rolled down her skin, cuts had formed on her limbs, and her head was in so much pain. There was padding and gauze over it that started to itch. More cold air forced its way into the room and made her shiver and her nose run.

It would end any moment. He'd sent her a message and the torment would end soon. She understood. It was like being a child on the playground. If a girl or boy twisted your arm or put you in a headlock, when you cried loud enough they would let go and start to laugh and mock you. But they still let go.

The chains had to let go soon. It would end. But he was gone. He hadn't come back yet. The music bombarded her ears and every time she twitched she felt a little shock of lightning.

She couldn't turn over. When she tried, the chains held her tight. She imagined this was how it felt to wear armor. Something that just holds you. Doesn't let anything in or out.

She felt a tickle between her legs (probably sweat) and that broke something inside of her. She strained so hard against the chains she felt like her neck and shoulders were twisting around while the rest of her was held in place. She thought the bed might snap in half. But the restraints did not give.

She was stuck. That was what it was. Not kidnapped, not held prisoner, just stuck.

Boom. Beat. Boom. Beat. Boom. Beat. Boom Beat.

The guitars continued and then died out as the drums became more prominent. Then the drums were gone, replaced by the woman breathing loudly. Breath. Beat. Breath. Beat. Breath. Beat. Breath. Beat. One loud heave. Then silence.

Melanie heard a loud scream downstairs.

"You like that?" Barker was yelling. "You like that? Right in the head?" He was laughing.

Music started again with a loud boom that made her ears close up, and whatever was going on downstairs remained a mystery.

Occasionally, as the songs rolled on, she tried to wiggled her wrists out of confinement. It was hopeless, but it kept her busy. She wasn't hungry, but if she was, she'd probably have to deal with that as well. Beaten, exposed, chained, starved. How soon until she was killed?

Melanie had to find a way out. If she couldn't get out, she had to find something inside that would keep her alive. She couldn't just roll over to this. She would not roll over to this, but she had nothing. Inside the room there were red walls, a bed, an empty dresser, a sofa with cushions. There was nothing. No. She had chains. If he undid the chains, could she strangle him with them. She'd seen that in movies. And her father had once taught her how to knock a man out. Jab the palm of your hand into his nose, send a spasm up into the brain. If you detached the nose bone you could kill with that technique, but Melanie didn't have that strength. Nor was she capable of wrestling with Barker, apparently. He was so strong.

Her father knew the world and was paranoid to leave his daughter alone outside. He'd made sure she was prepared, should she ever be far from home. But Melanie hated danger. Hated risks. She always stayed close to home on her bike. And as a teenager, she didn't go very many places at all. She hadn't run off and walked into trouble. She'd come home, like any other day.

And Barker was waiting for her there.

Hours passed.

The songs went on and on. And at one point, as the drums raged on mercilessly, she understood the lyrics.

> *I just want to get close to you.*
> *Taste your love, so sweet.*
> *I just want to make love to you.*
> *Feel your body heeeeeat.*

Melanie screamed as loud as she could, and her voice sounded like an injured dog with a muzzle. When she lost her voice, she buried her face and sobbed uncontrollably.

Eventually, sleep took her. She ignored the chains, the blood, the pain, and faded into thoughts of food and ocean water. She must have slept a great portion of the night, because she drifted in and out, again and again, forgetting the torture for however brief a time. She hardly noticed when the chains started to loosen, and slide off her, when someone was tugging at her body. She just wanted to keep sleeping.

By the time she was fully awake, Barker had set her down in the kitchen chair. He was zip tying her feet and her hands, securing her to the chair with one wrap of duct tape.

She was still naked. And the sun was coming up. She felt sicker than ever, sitting in the kitchen naked, waiting for him to start touching and violating her.

Hands zip tied behind her, gag still in her mouth. He wasn't going to feed her. Maybe he'd put food in front of her, just to mock her before he did the deed. And the police wouldn't save her. She'd learned that.

Dirty cops, her dad called them. He only ever said it to her mother, when he thought Melanie couldn't hear. But she did. He used to come home from work fuming. Angry. Talking about coworkers, about wrongdoing. Things he didn't respect or condone. He never admitted it to Melanie. He always told her that the police protected and served. That they were there to watch over her. He wanted her to think the world was a safe place to live. And right now she hated him a little bit for that.

Barker was leaning against the island, wearing a wife beater and holding a thin book in his hand. He let it fall open and studied it closely, a bag dangling from the fingers of his left hand. When he spoke he used a different voice: deeper and sharper, with the consonants annunciated.

"Good news. You are special. But not because you were born with some inherit right to the world. You have no right to the world. The CIA, the police, the guy next door, you name them, all reserve the right to blow your fucking head off if they so choose."

Melanie stared at him the entire time. It was easier when he was looking at something else, when those amber eyes weren't probing her.

"To them and the rest of the world you're no different than an ant in a farm. But you are special." His eyes met hers, and she turned her head. "If you choose to be," he finished.

Melanie bit down on the gag and spent some time admiring the fine wood of the table, anything to escape those eyes. After a moment he was closer to her and talking again. He still used the carefully annunciated voice.

"Choosing to be special is not saying 'Look at me, I'm special!' and doing nothing about it. The guy next door still reserves the right to blow your fucking head off." He paused and chuckled. In his own voice he said, "I love this part." He cleared his throat for the final paragraph. "So blow his head off first. Or just put the tip of the gun to his head and warn him…Warn him what happens, if he tries it again. Saying you're special doesn't make it so. Proving it does. And here with all of us, you damn well better prove it. If you want to stand at the top of the food chain, then start marking your territory. You were born with a gift. What can you do but use it?"

She heard the book snap shut. He grabbed her chin and forced her to meet his gaze, which was alarmingly intense. He held the closed book in front of her and she read the title: Awaken and Feast, by Aethon Armata. "A very close friend of mine wrote this…I haven't seen him in fourteen years…but I'll never forget those words."

He let go of her and she looked back down. In the next few moments the large bag dropped in the chair diagonal from Melanie and Barker was sitting across from her, staring off over her shoulder. "I was a very different person when he first showed me this. If I could talk to him now…"

He went quiet for a moment, and Melanie watched him as his mind sailed backwards. He laid the book on the table and his fingers danced on the cover.

He returned to reality promptly, with a fixed gaze and a smile. "I'm coming up with a book of my own. Even smaller than this one. And instead of writing it…" He pressed his finger against his own head. "I want you to commit it to memory. My little book of rules."

Barker reached for the large plastic bag and switched its place with the book. He emptied the bag, and Melanie groaned to hold back a scream. It was bloody, ripped fragments of a police uniform. Hyperventilating was inevitable. She knew that those clothes belonged to the man who hit her, the man she'd heard screaming downstairs.

There was blood in several different places. She didn't want to think about what happened to him and she hoped beyond hope that Barker wasn't about to walk her through the process.

"As I said, I didn't like him hurting you. I would have preferred that the Chief simply held you until I arrived. But don't worry, I taught Mr. Brolin a lesson." He winked at her.

She could feel tears forming in her eyes and stared at the clothes. A person wore those. And now he was gone. Stuffed in a bag. No casket. No memorial. Just taken apart and stuffed somewhere. Despite what he did she felt pain for the way he died, but even worse, she was afraid that would happen to her.

When a tear leaked down her face, Barker said, "I'll have you know he was quite the apathetic bastard. One time he found one of my dead girls, and spit on her. Guess he didn't like being woken up at three in the morning." He snickered. "I, uh, sometimes attend my own crime scenes. They can't ever manage to spot me."

She hadn't heard anything besides several of the girls I killed.

"What you did last night." He paused, and Melanie locked her eyes with his, waiting for his retribution. "It was…" He smiled with what looked like affection. "…expected. If I were in your shoes…I'd have done the same damn thing." He chuckled. "I forgive you. As long as you won't do it again."

She nodded frantically, and even tried to tell him. Relief lit her up and brought her energy. She was going to live.

His smile vanished. "Now listen very carefully. You understand? Nod your head."

She nodded.

Stone faced and emotionless, he said, "I'll untie you and give you a towel. You will go upstairs, to the bathroom…" His head turned sharply to the side. "Fuck! I forgot to get you toothpaste…Damn it. Knew I forgot something." After frowning for a moment, he looked back at her. "Anyway, you will go upstairs, take a nice hot shower. Then you'll go in your room and shut the door behind you. I'll have clothes for you in there. You'll get dressed and stay in your room for the rest of the day, rest of the night. You won't come out. Not even for food. I'll bring it to you."

She nodded.

He was still intense, but not angry. In fact he spoke like he was reading out of that book. "Do all of these things obediently, and you can sleep tonight unbound. Like a normal person. Keep the window shut, get under the covers. Nice and warm. Would you like that?"

She nodded.

"You don't want a repeat of last night, do you?"

She shook her head, hating the thought.

"Good." The smile returned, gentle and sympathetic. "So go upstairs. Wash up, put on some clothes…Yeah…Lets have a nice, nice day."

She nodded, and pointed her fingers up toward the gag.

He giggled. "One last thing. Tomorrow morning, I will let you out of your room, and we'll eat breakfast down here. Then I'll give you some rules to follow. Understood?"

"Yeth," she said.

He smiled and slithered out of the chair, coming towards her as she tensed up. And everything in her was screaming, begging to be away from his hands. "I like you. And I want to be nice to you." He cupped the back of her head. "I haven't even looked at you. Not once. Not like that. I'm your friend. You understand?"

Friend? No friend would do this to her.

He slid his hand down the back of her head, and tightened his fingers around the knot of the gag. In a few moments it was undone and she was able to spit the fabric out. Then he ripped the tape off her torso, which hurt a lot. Then the zip ties on her hands and arms. Melanie wasted no time covering her breasts.

He handed her a white towel. "Upstairs, now," he said gently.

Melanie took it and ran up the stairs, straight into the bathroom, slammed the door. She leaned her back against the door and slid down for a moment, dropping the towel beside her. She hadn't been killed or raped. For the moment, she was safe.

And now at the very least she had privacy. But what happened the night before, the torment, the humiliation, it stuck in the back of her mind like a leech. She held her own hand over her mouth as she fought tears and inspected the bathroom. It was dusty and dirty, little stains on the coloring of the tiles. She got up and walked to the sink. There was so much dust on the sink she wouldn't dare put a toothbrush on it. Not if it was going into her mouth. She was afraid to even run the water. There was a mirror right in front of her.

And for the first time since the morning before she left for school, Melanie Grier saw her reflection.

She didn't look like herself. Her lips were chipped and red, her skin pale and her eyes sunken in. Right where Brolin struck her there was a large, wide Band-Aid. She peeled it off, not intimidated after all of the duct tape. The cut was red with a circle of blue around it that seemed to spin. It looked moist, like the wound was still open. Her hair was mangled and her eyes bloodshot. She could have screamed at the sight of herself, but all she did was watch her bloodshot eyes leak water.

Eventually she sank to the dirty ground to let it all out, gripping the side of the toilet like a drunk. Why would a cop do that to her? She'd escaped. Why didn't they help her? They'd sent her back, thrown her back in. Melanie called for help and no one listened, except for the bald man and the waiter, Carl. Unless he was a superhero, she needed the police. And they left her to rot.

Melanie wiped her eyes. She had to help herself. I have to get out. She pulled the curtains open, finding dust but no other filth. I won't stay here with him. I won't. I'll escape.

Sniffing, she turned the faucet. Water washed away the dust and she meekly stepped over the wall of the tub. The water was loud, yet softer than that awful music. It was hot on her skin, but even when it grazed her cuts, not nearly as painful as the chains or ropes. After awhile it felt like a massage. She basked in it, leaning against the wall, the streams sliding down her face an amalgam of tears and rain.

There in the water, Melanie plotted.

Chapter 8

Listen

When she left the shower and walked to the room, she found a pile of clothes sitting on the couch. The chains were gone and the bed was made. On the couch there were stacks of clothes. She pulled the door shut behind her and dug into the piles, putting on underclothes, a pair of adidas shorts and a black t-shirt. She straightened out her damp hair and took a moment to stand still, hugging her arms around herself. Melanie still hated the man who did this to her, but he'd given her the one thing she wanted if she couldn't have freedom: clothes.

Melanie decided that she would never be naked in this house again, unless she was washing in the bathroom. The bathroom would be her one sanctuary. The rest was Barker's domain. Her hair was a wet mess and he hadn't given her a comb. There was also a box of large Band-Aids. She took one and smoothed it over the cut on her head, flinching only once.

There was a footstep at the door and then she heard the door lock. So this was it. She was just staying in the room for the rest of the day. Her mind settled for a moment on the overall situation of captivity. She had to have done something wrong. Something to earn a severe punishment. Maybe she never went to church enough. Her father had taught her that she didn't need to go to church to have faith in higher power, and that she never had to justify her beliefs to anyone. He told her once that she should tell anyone who called her a sinner to "fuck off." Her mother said the same, although she spoke more appropriately.

Maybe she was mean to the other kids at school. Her mind flashed to Ronnie Kessler, a younger boy who just used to rub her the wrong way. He was loud and obnoxious and just overwhelming to be near on any stressful day. More than once she snapped an attitude in his direction. She didn't remember being downright cruel, but maybe she wasn't the best judge of that. Maybe that was Barker. She could have neglected Emily, received some sign or call for help from her friend that she obliviously ignored. Or maybe she'd just been an ungrateful bitch to both of her parents.

Ghosts of her tied up mother and bloodily beaten father stared at her. Melanie tried to help them, but she couldn't. She'd been too stupid. She could have called the cops immediately. She could have gone to the neighbor. Melanie could have screamed and alerted the whole neighborhood, sending Barker running. But instead, she gawked at the bottom of the stares long enough to get caught. She was stupid and thoughtless.

That was why. This wasn't punishment. Melanie hadn't done anything to deserve any of this. She was here because she was stupid and careless, and scooped up by a monster much smarter. Well, maybe she could be smart now. And turn the tide. She pulled the blinds open. It was bright and sunny outside. The backyard was very small, the fence a perfect square beneath her room. Beyond that was a long empty field of grass leading to more houses.

Melanie looked out over the rooftops and saw blue skies. She wanted to sprout wings and fly, be in the center of all that vast blue space. Then she noticed something even better than wings. There were two small roofs beneath her window. She didn't get why people built their houses like that, but those two little landings would make it easy to get from here, to the ground.

But she wouldn't. Not with him awake. With that thought, she drew the blinds and did the only thing she wanted to do: crawled into bed. Buried in her covers, she tried to force her way out of this world, and into her dreams. Melanie stretched her legs, feeling the cuts and scrapes flare, but underneath felt a calming numbness in her muscles. For a moment she was reminded of home, a soft cushion beneath her after a long and exhausting day. And then she found her dreams.

Melanie and Emily found a cave, a special place that no one else knew about. They went inside and carved their names on the walls, found stones of different shapes and sizes that they gave names too, put together a long and involved story about the origin of the cave. Once all the details were crafted, the cave belonged to them.

She jumped awake when the door opened. There was a pleasant smell in the room, like cooked meat. A sandwich was on a plate, a glass of water in his other hand.

"Hungry?" he asked.

She nodded and he set it down on the bed, and handed her the cup. She wasn't sure whether or not to drink. He might have drugged it.

He took a fabric out of his pocket and she thought he was going to gag her. But he folded it and gave it to her as a napkin.

"Enjoy," he said.

She thought he'd leave but he sat down on the couch, arms spread. Melanie slowly took the sandwich in her hand, wondering if her hesitation would compel him to give her some privacy. Steam crawled up her nostrils, and the odor was of chicken and ranch dressing. Ravenous, she tore into the sandwich, bread soft, meat moist and hot. Once again, it only took a few bites.

Barker watched her eat, never saying a word. Until his eyes drifted to the window, then to the ground, all in wonder. Moments later he rose and left the room, locking her in. That was all she saw of him that afternoon.

All alone again. Night was coming and she'd slept all day. What to do now? She hummed song lyrics to herself, wishing for a camera. She could probably come up with ten ways to pass the time if she had a camera. Then again, she didn't really have the stomach for entertainment. Not when a killer could walk in the room at any moment. Pulling the covers around herself, like some sort of a cocoon, made her feel guarded enough to get through this night.

So she laid still and pitied herself, knowing that Barker couldn't stop her from doing it. For some reason, that made her feel powerful, safe. Then night arrived and stretched for hours. Melanie hummed varying song lyrics all through the darkness.

At the crack of dawn she'd finally drifted into half sleep. She awoke to a bright light filling the room and the door was unlocking. Barker eased it open and emerged with a bottle of something. Melanie yawned as he opened the bottle. She trembled at his touch, always wondering what was coming next, always wanting him far away from her. From the bottle came cream that he rubbed on her cuts.

"I'll bring some gauze as well," he said. "These will heal up nicely."

He rubbed her wrists, gripping her fingers with his other hand. His massage was unwelcome, but not unpleasant. Through her mangled, messy hair she only looked at him with no concept of what to say. No words came for the man who'd stripped her, tortured her. She only knew she had to stop him doing it again.

"You need a hairbrush," he said with crooked eyebrows.

She nodded, embarrassed.

He placed a hand on her shoulder with fixed, intense eyes. "Talk to me. Please."

"Can I please have a hairbrush?" she said, surprised at the deep, grim rasp in her own voice.

"Certainly. I'll bring you one later today." He folded her fingers into a fist. "But first, my rules."

"Okay," she said.

Barker took a deep breath, and Melanie looked away. She noticed a large clod of dust at the bottom of the wardrobe, plastering itself against the wall beneath the window sill. "Look at me," Barker said calmly. Melanie returned her focus to the hairy, pale face, currently devoid of all but one mild half grin. "Number one. You stay in the house. You don't go outdoors. You don't announce your presence to anyone walking by, although the odds of that are slim. You don't yell out the window, you don't stand in the doorway. Until further notice, you have no relationship with the outside world. Now, are we absolutely clear on rule number one?"

"Yes," she said.

"Excellent. Rule number two. When I'm out, you will be locked in this room. Are we clear on rule number two?"

She nodded.

"Good. Rule number three. At night, while I'm asleep in my room, I'll give you free reign of the house. You can walk downstairs and make yourself something to eat if you're hungry, as long as you obey rule number one. And no banging on the doors, screaming, waking me up…Yeah, none of that. Got it?"

"I got it," she said.

He tilted his head and released her hands. "You realize what these rules mean…right?"

"What do they mean?" she asked, hugging her arms around her torso, sitting Indian style on the bed.

"It means that when I'm home you can roam the house all you like. Go into whatever room, drawer, cabinet you want. Go into the refrigerator whenever you want. If you're ever hungry, and we're low on food, please, do tell me. Okay?"

"Okay," she said.

With a smile showing all of his bright teeth, he flicked a strand of her hair. "Good." His eyebrows danced. "Oh, and rule four, stay out of my room. Got it?"

"Okay."

He brushed her hair, fingers like little bugs on the back of her neck. She closed her eyes and let the insects roam her skin, as long as they didn't bite. Then she heard him say, in a voice that sounded possessed, robotic, "If I were you…I'd break the rules."

She didn't open her eyes. "I won't. Ever. I promise."

"Yes, you will," he said with the shadow of a laugh. "I'll give you three strikes. Understood?"

Eyes still closed, she nodded her head.

"Look at me."

She looked up. His eyes were so big. Dark yellow, and maybe brown along the sides. And for the first time she noticed there was an occasional twitch in his left eye. "Three strikes, and I drive us back to Fargo and kill you and your family. Obey, and I'll be kind to you. Understood?"

She gripped his wrists, gently. "Please. Please, I'll be good. I promise. I'll obey."

He laughed, more than a shadow this time. "You'll be happy I'm not holding you to that. But then, maybe you'll surprise me."

"Thank you," she said on instinct, hands on her knees. "Thank you, that's very kind."

"You're welcome," he said with an enthused smile. "Breakfast?"

Melanie nodded.

The next day, Barker tied her hands and feet and applied bars to her window. That had been a long, loud, and emotionally infuriating process. Seven times over she thought she saw the ladder tilting just a bit too much. Seven times over she wished that he would fall and die. But he never did. After the window was successfully barred, he came in and untied her. He locked the door, and he was gone. Out. Wherever that was.

For three days he came and went, running little errands, locking her up. She had the ability to open the window despite the bars. On the third day, she waited for ten minutes after the brown mustang had pulled away. Then she opened the window and screamed as loud as she could, for as long as she could.

No one came.

The first day Barker brought more toiletries: toothpaste, hairspray, hair conditioner, Q-tips, nail cutters, and nail filers.

The second day she heard him come in and go straight into his own room. She had no idea what he brought back that day. Clearly, something he didn't want her to see. Her immediate assumption was weapons, or something else that was horrible.

The third day he came with books. Stacks of books. "Quality entertainment," he muttered, before extending one of them to her. "And all for you."

When she took the box she almost fell over, but she managed to get it onto the couch. She looked through the top. On the top were books such as The Once and Future King, The Silence of the Lambs, The Giver, and The Godfather.

"Thank you," she immediately said.

His arms were crossed. "You're very welcome." He turned to leave when she had a thought.

"Um, Barker…"

He turned to face her and now she felt a plethora of emotions all at once: embarrassment, resentment, then a sudden chill at putting herself at his mercy in any way.

"Yes?" he said.

"I, um, have um, problems," she said. "You know."

"Know what?" he said, looking blank.

Asshole. Are you really going to make me say it? Ever meet a damn girl before? "I'm sixteen. There's stuff that I need."

He pondered for a moment, and then his mouth fell open. "Oh…yes, you do." He turned his head, still contemplative, and then chuckled. She wanted to throw one of those books at his head, but he was gone and the door was shut. Not locked.

Melanie turned and started tearing through the box of books, finding many different titles, many different things to keep her busy.

It was now October 10th, 2028, just six days since he took her. One more day and it would be a week. He'd already brought her plenty of clothing to wear, throwing away her old denim jacket and buying her three new ones. Evidently, he thought those were her style. Really, the day she was kidnapped she'd just been going for a new look for a change. Regardless, she was happy to see something so outdoors-y, as opposed to indoors-y tank tops, shorts, pajamas.

The past four nights up to now she slept unbound, as promised. The door was locked, the window open, giving her a wonderful view of the bars. The weather had been nicer the past few days. A perfect balance between warm and cool.

When Barker was home, she walked the house freely, ate at the dinner table, sat in the living room after dinner. One day, after dinner, she took all that time to inspect. At the foot of the steps, if she went right, there wasn't much left. Just a washer and dryer, and a back door she wasn't allowed to pass through. Melanie did notice something about the back door, though. The actual door was gone. Like it had been ripped off its hinges. All that was there was a glass swing door. Very light. Very easy. To her right, she looked through the chipped, partly damaged hamper. She found nothing but fabric softener and detergent. There was nothing but dust in the closet in back. If there were things there before, sharp pieces of wood, brooms or mops to break in half or just use as blunt instruments, he'd gotten rid of them.

Melanie turned around and walked past the stairs, into the living room and kitchen area. She scanned the living room. There was dust here and dirt there, but no broken glass, no chipped wood. The living room was in good condition. She could probably chip the wood herself if she wanted a weapon. But how absurd was that? She didn't quite know how to get what she needed, other than finding a way to rip the wooden squares off the wall. And if she did it would take her some time, at which point Barker would ask "What are you doing?" And that would probably be strike one.

She remembered thinking she could choke him or poke out his eye with the loose cable wire, but that was gone along with the dresser where the TV would have sat. There was nothing in the living room but a couch and a chair. The window sill was the dustiest thing in the house. Clearly he didn't care.

Through the window, Melanie saw the unattainable. The outside world, with a red setting sun.

Barker went into his room for a long period of time. He must have been using the bathroom. So she checked all of the drawers. There were forks, spoons, and knives. Knives, right here in her grasp. There was one steak knife.

It chilled her. You could kill anyone with that. Barker could kill her at dinner one night if she said the wrong thing. Or vice versa. If he saw her holding a knife, what would he say? She couldn't draw attention. If she ever wanted to use that, she needed to stop looking at it now.

Melanie shut the drawer.

By the time the sun was down, Barker was still in his room. The door was right there. The outside world was right there. All she needed to do was walk through, but deep down she knew he was waiting for her to do it. The other night he just stood by when she ran out the door and went to the obvious destination. There she'd received no sympathy.

But then, she'd gone left. Toward the lights.

A mad thought forced its way into her mind, and she couldn't fight it off. She knew Barker was waiting, just waiting for her to try something crazy. Maybe the front door had an alarm or something. And even if it didn't, it was large and heavy. He'd probably hear her. Her mind flashed to the back door, so thin and flimsy. If she waited for a windy night, she could slip in and out, and he might never know the difference. And once she was out, if she ran right, into the darkness, she might have better luck. Maybe she could find a way out of the city, into the woods, eventually into the next town over, where the police might actually help her.

And if he caught her, it would only be strike one.

Chapter 9

Ghost Town

On October 16th, Barker and Melanie ate dinner in silence. It had been a quiet six days, with him coming and going and locking her in her room. She'd been doing nothing but reading, but when he moved around the house she listened. Melanie wished she could know what he was doing when he left, but she never heard him talking on the phone or anything. She considered asking him. He was passionate about the two of them talking anyway. So she asked, and he reacted unexpectedly. He looked down at the table with a ponderous expression and said, "Eat."

He'd made spaghetti and meatballs, one of her favorites. So she enjoyed it in silence, never daring to speak unless spoken to. And he never spoke. Now, while Barker was probably sleeping soundly, Melanie was assaulted by nightmares.

She was struggling so much with this test. The teacher hadn't gone over any of the material and the book for the test was issued to the class last week, on a day she'd been absent. But somehow, she knew half the answers, just not enough to pass. So, she looked at the note sheet on her lap, thinking herself perfectly concealed. But the girl next to her elbowed her hard, and reminded her she'd be punished for cheating. After that, she forgot the rest of the answers, and panic built in her chest.

Melanie awoke, damp with sweat. She felt a phantom, wordless terror. It was something primal and basic, like happiness, tiredness, or hunger. It was just plain inexplicable anxiety. In moments she pin pointed the source. Challenging Barker had become the most terrifying thing she could perceive. But she had three strikes.

She was losing her nerve. Maybe it was time.

Over the course of the week, she'd slowly gathered a small assortment of items. She picked them out of the refrigerator, out of the cabinets, as discreetly as she could. One by one she brought them up to her room. She did it when he was either in the bathroom, in his room.

Once she'd pull out a water bottle, and he caught her.

Thinking quickly she'd asked, Can I have this in my room?

Of course! he'd said jubilantly.

So now she had her bag full. Four water bottles. A couple apples just taken out of the refrigerator. Clothes for the trip. He'd set her up.

And then she heard a noise. It wasn't in the house. It was somewhere in the distance. Like a great roar.

A thunderstorm was coming. How could she be so lucky? If it rained, thundered, he'd never be able to find her. Not until morning. She went to the window and stared up at the sky, wondering how long it would be until the clouds masked her escape.

He only locked the door when he left the house. At night she was free to roam. And tonight she was leaving.

He'd gone into his room thirty minutes ago and hadn't come out yet. He'd turned off the lights in the kitchen. It was two in the morning.

It was time.

Melanie put the bag around her shoulders, cloaked in a hoodie for the cold and long silky pants good for jogging. Now it was time to venture downstairs.

Descending the stairs almost made her give up. But he was asleep, he had to be. And she was aloud to go downstairs. She wasn't breaking a rule.

Melanie took one step. Quiet, nimble, like a ballerina, and screaming inside like a ballerina. Then she took another step. Descended further and further, all in the dark.

Melanie reached the bottom. She didn't hear anything behind Barker's door. But she did hear thunder. It didn't sound like it was raining. Something more like heat lightning.

Melanie walked past the dusty washer and closet and stood in the small dark space between the walls. The flimsy door was right in front of her. What if it made noise?

She couldn't do it. She needed someone to rescue her. Someone who could kill Barker. Oh, if someone could just kill him. And she could walk without holding her breath. No one is coming. Suck it up.

Melanie placed her hand on the door, pushed in the little button with her thumb. She stood there in silence for a long time. One hand on the door, the other at her side, a backpack on and cloaked in a dark hoodie. She was probably stiff as a board. Someone could probably paint a great picture. Or take a photograph.

There was a thunderclap, and Melanie pulled the door open. She slipped through and quietly shut it, not letting it bang against the hinges.

Melanie was outside. She dropped to her hand and knees and started to crawl. Not one sound. Not one.

Barker's bedroom was on the first floor, left side of the house. She crawled around the right side, plagued by a nightmarish vision of him waiting by the window, clapping his hands before dragging her bag inside.

She practically tiptoed away, into the front yard.

Melanie turned and looked back at her prison as thunder continued to roar overhead. It was two stories high and had a small light illuminating the front porch. That was it. From a distance, people might not even see her prison. She noticed just above the ray of light there was something on the siding that looked like large thick letters. But she couldn't read them. Nor did she want to stay any longer. It was time to run.

She looked to her left. There it was. Somewhere in the distance, a little bright speck that probably read "Ball Room."

She turned her head from the lights, toward the dark. Melanie crept away from the house, and when she'd gained some distance, broke into a run.

**

Tom Macklin bought a hotdog from a vendor on the streets, wondering how long he had before it started to rain. The man was gray and bearded, with many missing teeth. Every time he leaned over the hotdogs Tom wondered if he was going to feast on hair and sweat. But for tonight it seemed like he was receiving a decent meal. He took the dog, covered in onions and mustard, and paid the man. Then he walked off along the sidewalk, into a deserted alley. He bit into the hotdog, mouth full of steamed meat and sourness. It was a good five minutes before an older man with a baldhead and whiskery face walked into the alley. He wore a trench coat and a fedora. His large nose was as unmistakable as his gruff sounding voice. "Macklin," said the man.

"Ferris," said Tom.

Ferris looked over his shoulder and put his hands in his pockets. "What can I do for you? Make it quick."

"Don't you want a hotdog first?" asked Tom, pointing over at the stand.

"Quick, Tom," said Ferris.

Albert Ferris was an accountant and a smuggler who worked for the Marx Crime Family. The Chief didn't roll over to them the way he did with Barker. The Chief despised Allen Marx and everyone working for him. Tom and everyone else at the station awaited the day they caught the Marx Family, but they were very good at covering their tracks.

"You still in there?" Ferris asked.

Tom wasn't the type to do this, to sneak around and cut deals with mobsters. But tonight was an exception. Tom Macklin had a plan to kill Justin Barker, but it required the aid of the Allen Marx.

"He's back," Tom said plainly.

Ferris raised an eyebrow. "Who?"

"Barker."

Ferris rolled his eyes. "Thanks for nothing, Tom." The mobster turned his back and started to walk away.

Tom called after him, "Does Allen know?"

Ferris paused for a moment, then rounded on Tom. "Listen, Officer. You ought to go home and kick back on your couch. Grab a beer. Watch some Netflix. Don't concern yourself with this shit. And don't bug me."

"I don't like the way you're talking to me, Albert. You might want to make some friends. Just in case you ever stand trial." Although Tom stood firm, he wiggled his toes anxiously.

Ferris raised his eyebrows and smirked. "Really? Cause a boy scout like you is gonna lie to a judge?" He shook his head. "You haven't been doing this long enough, Tom. You're an amateur. You got no business messing with Marx, let alone Barker." His voice dropped from loud and mocking to low and intense. "Now you know how information tends to magically travel back to Barker. Ghost Town ain't far from where we're standing. We shouldn't even be talking about this. Go home."

Before Ferris had the chance to turn away, Tom noticed a hint of concern in Ferris's eyes. He ignored it, and plunged. "Is there going to be another airstrike?"

The mobster's eyes widened and his mouth opened. Then he gritted his teeth. "Careful, Macklin."

Tom put his hands up, and made his next words simple and swift. "If so, I have a better plan. One that won't get innocent people killed, but just might be the end for old Barker. Interested?"

Ferris wiped his nose with the back of his hand. Then he adjusted his own collar. "Tom Macklin, the last honest cop in New Heim, throwing away his title and making a deal with the mob." He scratched his head and spit on the ground. "Forget it Tom. Why don't you go home and mind your business? It'll be good for ya."

Tom thought for a moment before saying, "Allen will hardly have to lift a finger. I'll take care of everything. We both want Barker dead. Turn me away and you'll be making a huge mistake."

Tom hoped to see some intrigue in Ferris's eyes, but instead the mobster looked down the alley, toward the entrance. The vendor was steaming more of the dogs. Tom could see the smoke passing by the entrance to the alley, and hear thunder crackling overhead. Ferris turned to Tom, looking annoyed, and whispered, "What are you offering to do for us, exactly?"

"I won't tell you here. I'd like a meeting with Allen, face-to-face." he said.

Ferris looked perplexed through the annoyance. "That so?" He drew himself up very frank, very business-like. "If you know how to kill Barker, why don't you just do it yourself?"

And now he played his hand. "What I'm planning requires money. Allen Marx has more than enough. And with your help, no one will ever know about this, and I can keep my job."

Ferris finally laughed. "And stay out of prison for conspiracy to commit murder." He shook his head. "Who knew you had it in ya?"

Tom was unmoved. "Follow my plan and you have another cop who owes you a favor, and Barker dead and buried. It doesn't get much better than that."

Ferris snorted. "We'll call you. Good night, Tom."

The crooked accountant turned his back on the honest cop, and smoke continued to rise.

***

The path down Copper Avenue was just as long the second time. Left was miles long, and right was miles long. Barker's house seemed to rest right at the center. Melanie's feet carried her past five streets: Bronze Drive, Selim Drive, Silicon Road, Martha Street, and Silver Drive. As she ran the streetlights only grew dimmer. The clouds continued to produce the echoic noise and the moon was covered. Still Copper Avenue stretched on. The thunder rattled across the landscape, and she started to feel like she was in the growling stomach of a beast.

Keep going straight. Eventually, she would cross the threshold of the city. The outside world had to be just up ahead. This road was her path to freedom, out of this disgusting, dank, horrific place.

But when it stopped, she hadn't reached the end. It simply stopped.

Melanie was standing at the end of the concrete, and if she stepped off, it would be onto gravel. The concrete broke before her, and led to a ravaged, torn up road containing mounds of dirt and several holes. There were puddles too, and the stench was thick and horrendous. She quickly realized that she was smelling sewage.

Her straight path became fields of rubble and waste. She looked to her left. There were piles of wood and cinders where there should have been houses. She looked to her right. There were fields that used to contain houses, now covered in piles of wreckage and charred remains of grass. Somewhere beyond all that was another road, but she couldn't see outside the city. She had to keep going. Melanie walked through the quiet wreckage, careful not to trip and fall in any of these holes. Dancing here and there, walking in diagonal patterns, she made her way across the quiet field. It wasn't a field at all. She didn't know whether to call it a graveyard, a morgue, or a battlefield.

And it didn't end there.

As she made her way through the dark field, she eventually saw another concrete road to her far left. Along the road were houses still half standing, with bits blasted off but not fully destroyed. She stepped onto the concrete and started to walk straight again. The thunder roared louder.

This road winded left like a long hook, and as she progressed, she started to see houses still fully standing. It was also easy to see the sky from the middle of the street. Far in the distance the clouds broke to reveal the stars, but not overhead. It would rain soon.

Melanie started to move faster, running straight down the road. Keep going east. Make sure you're going east.

She came to the end of the road and came to an intersection. She needed to cut across and keep going straight, but from here she gained a perfect frame of what was coming next.

Nearby, up ahead, another bomb had been dropped. She could see the small remains of what used to be houses, little bits of would and metal sticking out of the ground. There was a massive hole in the ground just outside the intersection, where there used to be grass. Cutting across the intersection, she found herself on another straight road. She couldn't find any signs, so she gave it her own name: Desolation Drive.

What made her want to name it was that it was much wider than the previous concrete roads. It seemed to go straight for ten yards before cutting into a fork. The road had been cleared of whatever debris used to lie there, but not everything had been found.

Melanie passed one house with an overturned fence. Underneath, she saw a bony hand. There was something about that that made her sick enough to vomit. When she was done pouring acid and filth from her body, she slowly pressed on, building distance between herself and the body.

Melanie kept going and going, pressing on through all of this wreckage as the storm finally broke. Rain started to fall and an icy cold drop trickled down her face. There was no one here, except for the dead. Desolation and dead people. In that moment, Melanie finally realized where she was.

When the news story broke, all of Fargo was in an uproar. In the Grier household, Melanie came downstairs for a snack of some kind, maybe a snickers bar or Twix to keep her company while she surfed the net. But what she found was her father standing in the middle of the living room, looking tense the way he often did. Her mother was sitting on the couch beside him, one hand over her own mouth, never looking away. Their intensity drew Melanie forth like a magnet, and she saw the whole thing on replay.

A jet had flown over a city on the West Coast and dropped a series of bombs. Hundreds of people were killed and an entire segment of the city was leveled, clearing the survivors all over to the West side. The jet was never found, the pilot never apprehended. The motive was never discovered, all the newscasters kept reminding their viewers was that hundreds of people had lost their lives, and a magnificent society had tanked into depression.

She remembered her father's comments.

Unbelievable, he'd said. *Unbelievable. Disgusting.*

I know, her mother had said. I know, sweetheart. Then she'd noticed Melanie's presence. Oh, sweetie. It's horrible.

Her mother had gripped her hand tight, and Melanie remembered thinking about all of the people who had died. An entire part of a city. And entire series of neighborhoods. So many people. They were all dead. At first she thought to herself that any problem she ever faced, whether it be school, work, or a love life, couldn't compare to the misery happening in that city. Her next thought had been that stepping outside her home wasn't safe, that a bomb could drop on them all at any moment.

Melanie had spent the next four days replaying those thoughts again and again, but as she went through school, weeks upon weeks of a safe journey from home to school, that fear slowly crept out of her thoughts. It was easier for most people not to dwell on news like that, and to enjoy life while you could. Eventually, you believed the world was a safe place again. Melanie, at some point, even forgot the name of that city in the news. But only one year after hearing that horrible story, Barker reminded her.

Here she was, in New Heim, a city that had suffered more than anyone anywhere she knew of. Of course Barker would bring her to a place like this. This kind of place bred monsters. Simultaneous with these thoughts, she realized that at this point she'd built yards, acres of distance between herself and Barker, and she couldn't stop now.

Desolation Drive continued straight and then forked around what used to be some kind of building, maybe an office building or observatory. Continuing brought her to the end of Desolation and into a confusing labyrinth of streets and intersections. But without buildings to block her vision, she could see up ahead, she was only a few blocks away from the edge of the city.

And once there, Melanie realized she'd hit a dead end. Apparently, people reached New Heim by crossing a huge bridge. That bridge was gone, and Melanie overlooked a cliff leading to a river. It didn't matter how dangerous it was to stay in the city with Barker. She couldn't find a way to cross the river in this darkness, and the rain was falling harder.

Flashes of light danced above her and wet pelts assaulted her. As she ran to the left it only grew colder.

Eventually, she found a one-story building. It branched off into four more long one-story strips and ended at a large, three story square wing. It had to be a school, either elementary or middle. The large square was the gymnasium, and for the most part this building was in tact. Somewhere between what might have been B wing and C wing there was a massive hole. Well, she didn't have to worry about a locked door. Melanie ran through a field of dead grass and stepped over multiple puddles and piles of debris before she stepped into the building.

This place was such a mess. It was large and complex, in a large confusing part of town. He wouldn't find her. Although the building was incredibly large. And how many schools were in this area? Maybe he would think to check here. With a surge to her heart, Melanie resolved to find a better hiding place once the storm ended. In the morning, she would head back to the cliff and find a way down. If Ghost Town was a large square, she and Barker were on opposite sides of it now. She was fine. And she would find a way across that river, even if she had to swim across. If her life depended on it, she could do it. But not in this darkness, where she couldn't see through the rain. That was a quick way to drown.

Melanie was staying here for now.

Too restless to stay in one spot, she began to wander the halls. First she walked slow, inspecting small hallway she initially stepped into. The newly formed walls were of jagged broken brick. Small metal poles stuck out into the opening near the top. She felt glass break under her shoe. The hole from which she had stepped in led straight to another, probably then leading to the playground or sports fields. As she ventured deeper inside, the storm worsened. Melanie walked down a long rectangle, as white light flashed and rain pounded the outsides of the walls, echoing and bouncing off the hollow walls. It was like being inside a drinking glass.

Walking, she was slow and cautious, waiting for anything to jump out at her. It was so dark. Not long into her investigation, she came upon a door to her right. It led to a classroom. The lights were out, but with a little help from the lightning, she could see everything for brief moments, and then perceive the outlines of desks in the dark. They were probably covered in dust, and as she drew closer to the chalkboard, she didn't see any lines or shapes, believing it was blank. Habitually, she found a good spot to stand in that gave her a good wide, straight on perspective of the room, wondering if when the lightning flashed she could pull off a photograph.

Children used to study here, before this part of the city cleared out. The children's families might have been dead, or maybe they all survived and decided to go live somewhere safer. Melanie knew she would have. Her mother would have. With her father it was tricky. Being a cop in Fargo, he was sort of married to the city. If they wanted to leave, they'd probably have to leave him. She and her mother used to chuckle about just that, but neither of them ever meant it. Now more than ever, she wished she could see her dad again.

Melanie went back out into the halls, finding no signs of life anywhere and thankfully no bodies. When she came to a corner, she would peak her head around first, in case anything jumped out at her. That's exactly what this was like. Like some zombie apocalypse movie. But everywhere she turned she found only dark corridors, illuminated occasionally by the storm outside. Melanie opened her bag and took a drink of water. A few deep breaths.

With the bottle in her hand, she went forth toward the gymnasium.

The only problem with this large room was that there was a huge hole in the wall toward the top, but it didn't allow much rain to get in. From here she had a clear view of the falling rain and the thunder echoed much louder. The room was wide and tall, of course, vast space on the main floor and bleachers stacking seven rows stretching both of the longest walls. Melanie always thought that gymnasiums in schools were built a little too large. High schools, sure, there were a lot of sports events to consider and the people were bigger. Middle schools? A lot of work went into constructing a monster of a building that kids didn't necessarily need.

Melanie realized that the locker room must be nearby, and she searched the room with her eyes. The locker room might be a decent place to sleep. Something small and compact, with a back door she could use to escape if something terrible happened.

Where was the entrance? She spotted a small opening on the other side of the room, and began to walk toward it.

Something shifted behind her, and she doubled over.

A hand clamped over her mouth and an arm around her torso. Melanie kicked and screamed and the person holding her nearly bent in half. It wasn't Barker.

"Shhh," he said. "Quiet. Quiet. Don't freak out." It was a young voice, around her age. Melanie threw all of her weight backwards and kicked him in the legs. His grip loosened and she pulled away, flailing her arms. He grabbed hold of her backpack, so she let it go and began to run.

More feet hit the ground around her and she stumbled momentarily. It was so difficult to see in this dark, or make out what any of them looked like. She danced in place, moving back and forth, never stopping, never standing still, trying to confuse them. That was when a bright light hit her eyes.

"Get her!" said a girl's voice.

Two more bodies enclosed around her and she was pushed to the ground. Then they were pulling her hands behind her back.

"Be still!" one of them said. "Don't make me shoot!"

Somehow, by their voices, she got the impression they were younger than her.

She wriggled in place, and an older boy's voice said. "Don't move or I'll blow your damn head off!"

There was an explosion louder than thunder, and she lost her hearing for a moment. When it came back, she heard the girl yelling.

"Fire that thing again and I'll fucking put you down!"

Then someone was crouching down next to her. Melanie looked up as best she could. The girl was young and thin, around her age. She had long hair and wore some kind of sleeveless shirt.

"Will you relax now?" she asked.

"Who are you?" Melanie pleaded. "Let me go."

"I'll ask the questions, thanks," said the girl. "What are you doing here? What's your name?"

Melanie could sense there was still a gun floating above her head, and she struggled to find the right words. She couldn't just say she was out for a stroll and decided to trespass. They'd shoot her. "Please, you have to help me. Please," she said. "I was kidnapped."

The girl cocked her head. "Kidnapped?"

Melanie nodded frantically. "Yes. Please, stop. I didn't mean to. I didn't know anyone was here. I'll leave. I'll leave." She tried to get her hands free, but the boy was putting all of his body weight on her.

The girl regarded her coldly, curling her lips. "Kidnapped. By Barker?" She knew.

"Yes! Please. Please help. Don't let him find me."

The girl stood up straight and ignored her.

"Bring her over here," she said.

Melanie felt them tying something around her wrists, and she buried her face in the floor, pointlessly struggling. This all had to be some cruel joke, or just her imagination. She'd fallen asleep in the gym, a realistic nightmare with everything that had happened. There wasn't anyone here in this room with her. There weren't any people in Ghost Town besides Barker. They were all dead.

Chapter 10

Start Over

Melanie hadn't played many video games in her life, but she knew most of them involved doing a task, having obstacles in your path. If the obstacles got the best of you, you had to start the game over. As she sat in a large gymnasium with a gun pointed in her face, she felt like a set of controls operated her life.

She felt like she was on display, sitting on the bottom bleacher with a group of people scuffling around in front of her. Her hands were tied behind her back and her ankles as well. They hadn't gagged her, and she was beyond screaming for help. They just kept that gun on her. The boy holding it was thin and short, with a doo rag on his head. His hands didn't tremble on the gun, and he seemed to know how to use it. Melanie looked around the gym.

The lights weren't working, but the boys were armed with flashlights. Flashlights pointed up, lined up in large supplies. About thirty feet away, there was a fire being built in a pit.

Outside, the rain raged on, lightning crackling.

The boy with the gun circled around her and sat down next to her.

"Don't do anything stupid," he said, with a deep frown.

Melanie didn't answer. She counted them. There were six kids that were either a few years ahead or behind Melanie, and they had two small children with them. Melanie noticed two girls around here age—actually they looked younger—maybe fourteen or thirteen. The two girls were standing with the children, who had to be five and six. They were petting their heads and kissing them lightly, but Melanie saw the girls had guns on their belts, and they seemed capable. There was the largest boy (he had to be eighteen or nineteen) they called Dom. He was the one who'd caught her, put his hand over her mouth, held her down. Then there was another tall boy holding a gun, and the boy sitting next to her, guarding her. Finally, there was the girl who had spoken to her, the leader. She was tall and had long flowing hair and a black vest that showed off her bare shoulders. She wore boots and had jeans on. A cigarette was in her mouth and a handgun was held at her waist. All of the others kept glancing at her before they did anything, waiting for her word. She held a phone to her ear, and Melanie had a good feeling who was on the other end of the line.

Melanie kept her attention on the rest. Dom was still, but jittering in place, while the other boy had torn open her bag and was helping himself to her things.

The boy sitting next to her, pointing the gun, seemed to be a little bit shy. He didn't seem to want to be here. He kept his eyes off Melanie, but never moved that gun.

"You don't have to keep that on me," she said to him, extending her bound ankles to him. "I'm not running."

"Yeah well in case you start freaking out again, I'm gonna keep pointing it," he said. She could tell he was only trying to sound mean.

She snorted, struggling not to break down or lose her breath. "Hard not to freak out when a bunch of guys start grabbing at you."

"You're the one who trespassed," he said. "Not our fault."

"What's your name?" she asked.

"Peter," he said.

"Peter. How long have you been working for Barker?" She had to face that fact. As soon as she mentioned his name, they tied her up. She was being sent back. Again.

It's only strike one. Relax.

"It's a bit more complicated than that," Peter said. Then he pointed at the slender girl on the phone. "I work for Kris."

Melanie studied her. "Is that her name?"

Peter nodded. "Yep. She's our mom."

Kris snapped the phone shut, cursing and redialing. "God damn reception." She put it back to her ear and placed her hand on her hip.

"How old is she?" Melanie asked.

"Eighteen," Peter said. "I'm sixteen."

"So am I," Melanie said.

Peter looked at her then with intense eyes, as if he were sad. "How did you end up here? In New Heim? Were you born here?"

"No, he kidnapped me," she spat.

"You're not from around here, then," he said. She shook her head, a sudden tear trying to jump out. Peter groaned. "This place sucks, don't it?"

Melanie half chuckled, but inside there was weight pressing on her stomach.

Across the gym, Dom began to throw wood onto the fire, and one of the other girls kneeled next to a boy who looked sickly. The two boys had their eyes on Melanie.

Peter was looking at her too. "Your name's Melody right?"

"Melanie," she said.

"Oh, sorry." He turned away from her, clucking his tongue.

Melanie glanced back at the fire. One of the girls was looking at her just like the little ones. And then footsteps were coming near here.

Kris looked nervous as she held the phone to her ear. Melanie looked at the tall, thin girl and saw that her hair was brown and there was a tattoo over her eye. It was like a thin black needle.

Someone was talking on the other line. "Okay," said Kris, swallowing. "Got it." She took the phone away from her ear, extending it toward Melanie. "It's for you."

Melanie leaned forward, so the phone was next to her ear, but she didn't know what to say. She was tongue-tied.

"Melanie?" she heard Barker say.

Like magic, she was ready to cry again. Her stomach numbed and that confusing, inexplicable anxiety seized her all over again.

"Melanie?" he said again, insistent.

"I'm here," she said.

"Ah good…I had a bit of a scare you know. The thunder woke me up, and I went upstairs to make sure you weren't afraid…You were not in your room."

"I'm sorry," she whispered, glancing up at Kris. "I'm sorry."

"Hush. Are they treating you well?"

She wanted to say no, but something within forced her to say, "Yes."

"Good…I'll be over in a little bit. Behave yourself."

"Okay."

"Strike one, Melanie."

The line went dead.

Kris pulled the phone away and then looked at Peter.

"Give us a minute," she said.

"Yeah? You told me to hold my gun on her," said Peter, immediately standing up.

Kris scoffed. "I got it under control. Go."

Without another word the gun was gone and Peter headed toward the fire. Everyone was on that side of the room but Melanie and Kris. She still sat with her hands tied and Kris loomed over her. A few tears leaked down Melanie's eyes, along with some deep breaths releasing the anxiety she'd just built up. Right now she was on guard against this girl as best she could be. The girl looked tough.

"How old are you?" Kris asked, hand near her gun.

"Sixteen."

"Cool," Kris said. She took a few steps back and held her hands on her hips. "Sorry for scaring you earlier. It's not really a safe place we live in. Trespassers are more than likely to kill us. We heard you coming and setup a basic ambush. Nice and dark in here, you see. I understand why you freaked out, but that's not going to help you now. Got it?"

Melanie nodded, shuddering at the strength in Kris's voice.

Kris continued, "If you can stay calm, I'll consider untying you. If you're thinking about running, just know, you won't get past me." She tilted her head toward the fire pit. "And if you did, they'd kill you."

"Just let me go. Please," she said.

Kris shook her head. "Sorry. We don't screw with Barker." Kris knelt down and curled her knee to keep herself close to Melanie's height. "Melanie, huh? Got a last name?"

Melanie looked away, refusing to answer.

Kris leaned over, trying to follow Melanie's face. She said, "When did he take you?"

Melanie considered how much time had gone by since she last pondered the question. They were in the odd hours of the sixth day.

"Tomorrow it'll be one week," she said. Her father was probably still in the hospital. And her mother was probably searching everywhere. Fargo must have been littered with signs.

"And where'd he take you from?" Kris asked. "What part of the city?"

"I'm from Fargo," she said.

Kris flinched. "Fargo? Isn't that, like, somewhere East?"

"North Dakota," Melanie said.

"He took you from North Dakota?" Kris asked, incredulous.

Anger was welling inside her. "Yes, but first he tortured my family!"

Kris was still kneeling, looking down at the ground. She groaned. "Fucking psycho," she muttered. She looked up and their eyes met. "Do you know why he wants you?" Kris asked.

"No," she said. But sex slave came to mind. How could she possibly admit that out loud?

"He's taken a lot of girls you know," Kris said. "And boys. They don't come out alive." Her tone was grim.

That was all Melanie needed to hear for her gut to wrench. "He's going to kill me because of you."

Kris shook her head. "He said the funniest thing to me, Melanie. You know what that was?"

Melanie looked back at her. The girl was smiling, eyebrows slanted the way people do when telling a bizarre story. "What?" asked Melanie.

"He said, 'Keep her safe. She's my friend. And I don't want her harmed.' I asked if he was going to do to you what he did to…others. And he said, 'No. She's like family to me.'" She scoffed and then laughed. "You can't make this shit up."

"Did he say anything else?" she asked.

Kris stood up and started stretching with gritted teeth. "Nope. Just to keep you safe until he gets here."

"Safe, huh?" said Melanie, bitterly.

"I know, dumb word." said Kris. Kris tested her shoulder muscles, tapped her feet and brushed her hand over her gun. She seemed like she didn't know what to do with herself and yet she was ready for anything.

Melanie never thought she'd be sitting in the midst of a gang with weapons all around her. She'd known some thugs, or rather punks who thought they were thugs, at school, but no matter who she bumped into it never affected her. With a father for a cop, some basic self-defense, and an understanding of what not to do or where not to go, Melanie thought she would always be safe.

"Where are your parents?" she asked Kris.

Kris bent her lip, looking bummed out. "Dead."

It struck her, despite everything. "I'm sorry." Melanie wondered for a moment if she actually cared, if she should care about anyone affiliated with Barker.

"Thanks," said Kris, indifferent.

"Did he kill them?" she asked, feeling a spike from the ropes. "Did Barker kill you family?"

Kris scratched her head and scoffed. "Well, the way people talk, it was his fault. Maybe he'll tell you more about that." She cracked her neck, and looked down at Melanie like a child. She reminded Melanie of a teacher. "Did you ever hear about what happened to this place?"

Melanie nodded. "A jet. Someone did this. On purpose." Was it Barker inside that jet? Was he rich? Did he have a yacht or some luxurious, bizarre place he was going to bring her to next?

Kris leaned forward, hands on knees. "It's called an airstrike, kid. I'm sure he'll tell you more." She turned her head. "Hey, Dom! Bring me a cig!"

Melanie turned away from Kris and closed her eyes. Ridiculous stories. Evil cops. Restraints and locked doors. Death threats. Wake up, Melanie. For God's sake, wake up.

Dom was in front of her now, lighting a cigarette for Kris. The girl dipped her face near the flame and a small red dot appeared on the bottom. After a deep inhale smoke streamed through the air. "Thanks."

"Finding out stuff?" Dom asked.

"Mind your business," she told him.

"Fuck you," Melanie muttered. She couldn't stop herself. "Fuck you all." Still she spoke under her breath.

"Ouch," said Kris.

Melanie resolved not to cry. Not in front of these people. She was tougher than that. But eventually, as Kris stood by and blew smoke out her nose, something other than tears came out. Something to the same effect.

"You're just gonna let him take me?" she mumbled.

At this, Kris took the cigarette from her mouth, and inhaled deeply. "I'm sorry, Melanie. Really." Her voice was much softer now, not unlike her mother's. "I do what I have to do." She pointed over at the fire. "For them."

When she pointed, one of the children saw her, and started to come toward them as if she'd called him over.

"Oh, shit," Kris said under breath. "No, no sweetie stay over there," she said. But the child kept coming. "Hey! What did I say?"

The child stopped, and his face bent into a pudgy little grimace. Kris groaned, and motioned the child to come closer.

Closer, Melanie realized he couldn't have been more than five. He was short and stubby, his hair thin and dark and his skin light. His clothing seemed to fit him well, and it didn't look dirty. He didn't have torn sleeves like the older kids.

Right now he looked like he was about to start sobbing and Kris knelt down in front of him. She was rubbing his hands and gently pulling him into an embrace, as the auburn haired girl made her way over. The boy was looking over Kris's arm, right at Melanie, two little sapphires popping out at her.

"Who is that?" he asked.

"She's a friend of Mr. Barker," Kris said, gently, something close to maternal. "Remember when I told you about him?"

"Why is she tied up?" The way he asked was so calm and frank, like there was no real danger. It had actually been a long time since Melanie had been near a small child. And in that moment, Melanie realized something about the girl who was holding her right now. The child made her realize, for just a moment, why Kris would do anything Barker ordered.

Kris shooed the child away with the older girl and turned to Melanie. "Listen to me. He said he won't hurt you. Won't rape you. Won't kill you. Do you understand?"

She hated hearing those words. And they brought her back to that night. On the bed. Exposed. Waiting.

"He is going to kill…" Her voice cracked.

"Did you hear what I told you?" Kris asked. "What he said to me on the phone?"

"So what?"

Kris went on, "I've seen him kill. I've seen him torture. I've seen him rip doors off hinges, run the fuck up buildings. Do you know what I've never seen him do?"

"What?" Melanie said.

"Lie."

Melanie looked up, feeling tear drops fling onto her knees.

"Well you don't know him." She sniffed. "What? What does he have a code?" Just a book of rules.

"I'm sure he's told a white lie here and there. I'm sure your parents run red lights. I'm sure your teachers cheat their taxes every now and then. Everyone tells little fibs. But when Barker is explaining his intentions…" She stopped, and Melanie noticed her eyes were on the ground, and she'd gone stiff. "He doesn't lie."

Melanie twisted her hands to distract herself from the pain. She was getting good at that. Dealing with the pain, finding ways to distract herself. Now she just needed to learn how not to cry or panic.

"He won't hurt you, kid," Kris said. "I promise. If you were dead meat, I'd tell you."

Across the room, the fire started to stretch higher. The two children were kept closest to it. Outside, the storm hadn't stopped. It was only getting worse. Melanie might have noticed the approaching clouds during the day, but she didn't spend much time looking outside, as per the rules. The older boys were feeding the fire and murmuring amongst themselves, and the two girls were sitting together. Kris stayed with Melanie, her eyes fixed on the group by the fire.

Another person entered the room.

He'd come in on the other side of the room, out of the locker room. The boys had seen him and raised their guns, but suddenly there was nothing there. Just an empty doorway, lit by the fire.

"Are you all nuts?" Kris shouted to them. "Put down the weapons."

Melanie thought she sensed odd movement around the gym. For about two seconds, it was like sticks were falling against the ground in various places, even though there were no trees inside. And then someone much larger than all the boys was standing next to her. Tall and broad shouldered. He knelt down so they were at face level, and without a moment's warning she was staring into his eyes again.

And he had the same smile. "Hello, sweetheart," he said.

Melanie tried to answer. Instead she just waited quietly for her judgment.

He scoffed, seeming somewhere between angry and amused. "You don't waste time, do you?"

"I'm sorry," she croaked.

His hot, sweaty hand found her hair, and slid down to fall on her shoulder. "Two more strikes. As promised."

"Barker," said Kris. She faced him boldly, not trembling or batting an eye. Barker took a breath before he turned to her, like he was ready to do business. Kris stood straight and tall, hands near her hips, and waited for him to speak. "Is there anything else we can do for you?" she asked.

"No, not yet. Thank you though, sweetheart." He looked around. "Are they new?" He pointed at the two small ones.

"Yes," she said.

"Two new little ones," he whispered, rubbing his hands together. "And where are the rest?"

"Linden Avenue, at the house," Kris said.

"Why are these two little ones in the work place?" he asked her. Then he hummed to himself. "You're the one who found them, I suppose."

"That's right," Kris said. "Keeping them close so they don't panic."

Barker nodded. "Bring them over here."

"Barker, please," Kris said. All he did was motion with his index finger, and Melanie watched the scene unfold. Kris wore a defeated look on her face, then she whistled over to the others, and the boys brought over the little ones. They went straight to Kris, one hugging her around the waist, the other's hand held firmly in hers.

"What are their names?" Barker asked, eyes jumping between the two of them.

Kris rested a hand on the one hugging her waste. "Jimmy." She squeezed the hand of the child holding her's. "And, Max." Jimmy refused to look at Barker, while Max looked up boldly.

Melanie tapped her foot on the ground. Don't hurt the children. Don't.

Barker knelt and gave the bold boy the same smile he'd give her in Fargo. "I'm Barker. I'll be making sure you're fed." Despite all his monstrous habits, his voice had gotten softer for the children. "Would you like that?"

"Yes," said Max, in a very small voice.

Barker cocked his head toward the other. "How bout you?"

Kris nudged him and the child nodded.

"What's wrong with this one?" Barker asked.

"He's not very trusting," Kris said. "He's a runaway from Nester's," she added.

"Another one," said Barker. "Should I pay them a visit?" he asked.

"I would love that," she said with venom.

He chuckled. "Could be fun. And this brave little fellow. What's his story."

"He doesn't talk much, but he was seriously abused before he got lost. Someone put marks on him."

"Anyone I know?" he asked.

"Maybe one day he'll tell me," she said, squeezing his hand.

"That's nice," he said, and then cleared his throat. "Boys, you do everything Krissy here says, and I'll make sure you eat every day. Sound good?"

The boys nodded.

Barker smiled wide. Melanie recognized it from the first time he saw her face. "Good boys. Run along."

Kris whistled and this time it was Big Dom who came and collected the kids.

"Sorry about that whole mess with Charlie," Barker said. "I promise I'll take better care of you and the rest of them." His voice grew slighty more tense. "As long as you do your job."

"We are. Eyes on the target at all times."

As Barker nodded his head, Melanie squirmed in place, just trying to keep up. "What happened with Charlie?" Both Barker and Kris looked at her, and she continued. "He's the man from the power station, right?"

Barker turned to Kris. "Isn't she adorable?" Before Kris could answer, he said "Kris has been taking care of these kids for more than a year, living in Ghost Town where no one bothers them. They often have to steal to survive and, well, coming to Ghost Town is safest. No one will apprehend them here, because no one comes to Ghost Town when a...certain someone is around." He giggled. "But I was away for a year you see. And I left Charlie to watch over things. But apparently, when Kris last went to him for help, he treated her, well, rather poorly."

Melanie looked at Kris, and the girl elaborated. "Pointed his gun at me and pulled the trigger."

"She's nimble, and Charlie is a terrible shot, so all is well," Barker concluded. "You remember the night we arrived, Melanie? I was showering the man with compliments. I was, um, very disappointed to hear this news. Poor Krissy."

Kris's mouth moved like she was going to retort, but she didn't. She looked at the ground.

Barker said to Melanie, "These young people are loyal to me. They are my eyes and ears around the city, and I am their bank so they can eat. And all is well." His eyes darted between the two of them. "If you ever need anything Melanie, if God forbid something happened to me, Kris here will make sure you are safe."

Kris nodded her head. "It's true." Her eyes and Melanie's were locked. "Anything you need, kid. Ever."

Melanie nodded her head. "Thanks."

Barker laughed and scratched his head. "We'll be going now," he said to Kris. "Be in touch."

"Of course," Kris said. She started to move, but hesitated, looking at Melanie once more. "Goodbye, Melanie." The smile Kris gave her seemed to be genuine, no hint of mocking or teasing. Kris was now bounding off toward the fire, legs carrying her fast, and Barker knife from his pocket, dangling it like a toy. He stepped up to Melanie, and she stepped back from the blade.

"Ready?"

Chapter 11

The Unlocked Door

When they arrived, it was three thirty in the morning and the rain had finally softened. There was still distant thunder and likely more rain coming later. Barker had yawned very loud, ordered her to bed, and then shut himself in his own room. Melanie had lingered for a moment. Thinking about going to the refrigerator for water, but she decided it was better to obey. On her way up the stairs, she remembered something Barker had said in the car, something that was making her heart race.

If you try to run twice in one night, I might get mad.

The room was stuffy. Always stuffy. The gymnasium had been a large square with a hole at the top, so plenty of air could pass through. This room was tiny like a tomb, dark as a coffin. She'd sat on an uncomfortable cold bleacher, surrounded by people who really didn't mean her any harm. Here she was in a warm comfortable bed, with a monster downstairs. Melanie was back. If she tried to get out, the beast would bite her.

However, the rules left some flexibility. She was not aloud to leave the house, but her bedroom door was unlocked. Melanie was aloud to roam the house.

Melanie was sitting on the floor now, rocking back and forth. She was holding her pillow, pressing it against her chest. It felt good to squeeze something. Something soft. She realized sitting there that she was surrounded by gifts. A warm bed. A box of books. A closet full of clothes. But she didn't want any of it. Melanie wanted to be outside. She wanted to get her own books. Her own clothes. She wanted to be with whom she chose. Namely, Martin and Debra Grier.

It had only been a week, but for Melanie it was like she had crossed some threshold. The days were going by. Going by faster. As time went on, her family would forget about her. No, they never would. Never. They would frame pictures of her atop the fireplace. The whole family would remember Melanie. The whole school would remember Melanie. Fargo would remember her, but soon they would stop believing she was alive. And Melanie felt dead. Dead to all of them.

Two more strikes. Was she really going to sleep tonight? In Barker's house?

Two more strikes. The words bounced within her skull. Run, Melanie.

The room was square, a box. The Gymnasium was an even bigger box. And this damn town was cut off from the rest of the world by a broken bridge. Melanie was trapped within a series of boxes. She never escaped, she just jumped into a different one.

"What the hell," she muttered.

Melanie wanted to pace to let out some anxiety. But she couldn't. Barker could not know that she was awake. Quietly, she stood up, and sat down on the bed. She placed the pillow. Let her head fall. She rolled over, burying her face. Everything was blanketed black. She probably looked ridiculous all the times she used to do this at home. Stupid. Whatever she was upset about (a bad test grade, something a mean kid said to her, some horrible thing she heard on the news, or just general sadness) just looked stupider with her face buried in her pillow. Was that really all she could do right now?

The door is unlocked.

It was a different house. Different situation. A dire situation. But she felt stupider than ever before.

Why didn't I just keep running? It was only rain. Why didn't I go back to the city? I didn't have to go to the cops. He would have had to search the crowds. He never would have found me.

"Fuck," she whispered. "Damn it."

She nearly pounded the bed, but then she remembered. Don't let him know you're awake. A thought was rolling around in her head like a spinning wheel. As the thread formed a shape, Melanie saw something ugly. Slowly, it became more and more real. All of her emotions were coming together in a swirling storm, melding into one single mission. In her mind, she saw an open drawer beckoning her downstairs. And yet, a memory of cold chains warned her to use discretion.

I can do it. Such an insane thought. Go down the stairs. Creep into the kitchen, to the drawer, then to the bedroom door. Turn the knob. Then be quick about it. You still have two strikes.

If there was any blessing still privileged to her, it was that she had still had a chance to do wrong, and not be killed for it. In that moment, what she felt was motivation enough.

I won't let him hurt you, Mom. She stood up, silent. Her father's smashed face appeared again in her mind. Barker deserved to die. I won't let him hurt you anymore, Dad.

She would run away. No one would find her. Not until she found her way home.

And now Melanie was at the door of her own room. She slowly turned the knob, careful to avoid any loud clicks.

Slowly, Melanie pulled the door open and saw a hallway of strange shapes. When she was little, shapes in the dark consisted of faces: wolf snouts, tiger fangs, spider legs, any monster that might eat her. Tonight the shapes looked like sticks, guns, squares, boxes. There was a curved rectangle along the floor, a square straight ahead, and two rectangles next to her. All was cloaked in black, nothing but silhouettes surrounding her. But she knew where to step. She knew from last time which spots to avoid. Melanie knew all the quiet places to step.

Then she was at the stairs. To distract herself, to stop herself from panicking, she counted them.

One...Two.

Three...Four.

She arrived at the landing. Thunder roared outside. And she thought she could hear Barker snoring.

Five...Six.

Seven...Eight.

As she descended, Melanie saw darkness moving upwards. She was walking into its belly and wondering if she would ever climb back out. But as the thought came to her, her feet (like a feather) hit the ground of the bottom floor.

The door was right there, but she had no weapon.

There was a thunderclap, but this time it sounded distant, miles and miles away. Melanie practically slid along the ground floor, through the kitchen. If her feet could grow wheels she'd feel much less anxiety.

When she touched the drawer, a chill ran through her. She thought nothing of it, for once, and opened the drawer.

There's nowhere to hide. Just do it and run like hell.

She half expected to turn around and see Barker laughing at her in the living room chair. But there was nothing in that darkness except more stationary shapes: a barrel and a small overturned locker. Melanie had the knife in her hand.

The knife was heavy, so sharp she thought the tip would tear right through her no matter how gently she wielded it. She kept a firm grip on the hilt. Sharp objects, needles, skewers, scissors, had always given her chills. If you tripped, that could be the end.

But now Melanie had another problem. The knife was going to be her best friend now. Her hand was clasped around the knob of Barker's room.

What was she going to do? Stab him? Cut his throat? Maybe she should just go back upstairs. No. He was asleep. And she could do it. In the next five minutes, she could be free.

Prickles of rain hit the house, and moonlight trickled in through the window.

Once she opened the door, she would have to be quick. If he saw her, that was it.

Open the door. Slowly. Make sure he's asleep. Then stab him.

Her hand was still on the knob. Just sitting there. Melanie tightened her grip, and turned the knob.

The lock came undone. Slowly, she pushed the door open. Only a small bit of light made its way into the black cave as she gently eased it open wider.

Barker's room was the darkest in the house. The thick blinds were drawn and right in front of her was an animal. Some massive shape in the dark, making massive snoring sounds. From the brief splotch of light, she saw him lying face up, bare chested, facing the ceiling. She had a clear shot to the heart. Her hand was still on the knob, and in a few seconds it would be time to hold her breath, and let go.

I'll take something from you now.

Gentle on her feet and clenching her weapon, Melanie glided forth. Gaining speed, she let gravity take her and plunged the knife down.

Her wrist slammed into Barker's grasp.

Melanie screamed but still pressed down. He twisted and pain shot up her arm, loosening her grip. Barker pried the knife away from her with his other hand and suddenly she felt it slice her right forearm. As sharp pain gnawed into her flesh she let out the loudest scream she could, everything in her body clenching and going stiff as rock. Barker rose and threw her backwards, smashing her against the wall, gripping her throat. His eyes fluttered like a baby's, not even fully awake.

"Excuse me. I'm trying to sleep," he hissed. In the dark she could see him gritting his teeth.

"Let me go!" Her arm was in so much pain. "Let me go!" she howled, wrenching against his grasp. Blood dripped out, onto the floor.

He squeezed her throat so hard she was sure for a moment she was going to suffocate. At this point she had kicked him several times in the legs, but that did nothing.

She could see his face more clearly, the yellow eyes peering out of the dark just like a wolf. He pressed harder, and she was ready to pass out.

"Strike two. Go. Back. To bed." He pressed against her one last time, and she felt ready to vomit. "Now."

He released her and she fell to the ground. First the knees, then her head smashed against the carpet. She clutched her cut arm and words just poured out of her.

"Please don't! Please don't! No more! No more! I'll be good. I'll be good, I promise. Please! No more! No more!"

"Get up," he said. And then he roared. "Get up!"

Melanie forgot the pain for a moment, chilled. Stumbling, she got to her feet. He was looming over her, straight and tall, sweating like a runner. "Back to bed." He gritted his teeth and his voice dropped multiple octaves. "Right. Now."

Melanie turned and ran up the stairs. She didn't bother counting. She was out of time and out of strikes.

***

Ridiculous, he told himself. Anyone else who tried to kill him would be dead already. Well, as long as he didn't want to play with them first. Anyone he pinned to a wall would be broken right now. But Melanie...he didn't want her dead. He wanted her to live with him. He wanted her company. To talk about photographs and school and all of the things he'd learned when he'd visited the Meridian. He just wanted her. It was bizarre, and it was trouble. This was actually difficult, to stop her without breaking her. He might have almost killed her just now.

Locked door. Barred windows. And bindings...Yes. That was what she needed. It was so simple and he'd underestimated their importance. She needed to be trained. He wasn't the best at that, not the most patient person. But he would do it and do it well. He'd do it for her. Barker reached into his trunk and pulled out a length of rope.

Chapter 12

Marx Manor

om Macklin was not allowed to approach the Marx Family Manor without an escort. So Albert Ferris came by to pick him up, and when they approached the black iron gates, the car rolled between two men with long coats. Both looked strong and ready to shoot at a moment's disturbance. So Tom waited for orders before he did anything.

"We're here," Ferris said, turning the key and looking over at Tom. "Um, get out."

Tom opened the door and stepped out into the cold morning. It was 6:00 A.M., just before dawn. While Tom was supposed to have met with Allen Marx the previous night, no one seemed inclined to pick him up in the heavy rain storm. And that was just the first of many insults he would have to endure throughout this encounter.

The coated hit men escorted Tom out of the car and one of them spoke into a walkie. Ferris stood for a moment, a large ruffled coat hiding all but his large bald head and smug, detached expression. Both of the hit men were a foot shorter than Albert, but appeared ten times as dangerous. Tom looked up at the gates, taking in the playing field. They were about forty-five feet high, keep out anyone who wasn't supposed to be there. To storm Allen's Manor, you would have to bring a tank or a helicopter. He had to chuckle at the thought of performing an airstrike on Marx Manor. Now wouldn't that be karma?

There was a loud screech as the gates began to open. Ferris walked in front of Tom as the two armed men closed in behind. The four of them walked through the gates. As a gesture of respect, Tom wore a white button down and the nicest pair of jeans he could find. The respect wasn't towards Allen Marx personally, just toward the guns that would be pointed at Tom all night.

Tom felt like he was living out a scene from a movie as they glided across a long sidewalk cut through two large green squares. At the edges of the grass, lining the walls, were several different kinds of small trees and plants. The mansion was two stories high with a balcony at the top, stretching all the way around. The outside was brown and the front door was between two cylinder pillars. As they walked up the short stairs to the front porch, Tom noticed that rose bushes lined the front of the house.

Inside was polished. Everything smelled like fresh, clean stone, but Tom felt like he was inside a mausoleum. True, a golden chandelier hung above, but everything else was white marble. Straight ahead Tom saw a passageway leading into the rest of the first floor. On either side of the passage were too long staircases leading to the second story. Up on the second story wall, proudly presented for all who entered, was a large portrait of classic Renaissance art, the Wanderer Above the Sea of Fog. On the first story, standing in the corners of each side, right under the stairs, were two identical sets of statues. Two sets of Three Foolish Virgins, each either hiding their eyes or turning away from something. There were also two identical desks next to each statue, both with a potted plant and two Easton Press bound books stacked on top. What good the books were doing there, Tom did not know. But as he was pushed forth past the desks and through the passageway and into the rest of the house, Tom saw many more examples of classic German artwork.

Tom remembered once hearing a story about how Allen's great grandfather was part of a larger crime family in Germany, before some dispute ended in their defeat and flight from the country. Allen was born in America, but evenly divided between two cultures. The story was more fascinating to Tom than the story of the Maxwell Sect, but Tom didn't spend that much time searching their complicated and bothersome family histories.

The kitchen was something of a small dark tunnel, wide and neatly cluttered with cooking utensils and many different kinds of plates, presented on stands. Multiple islands across the long floor, multiple small tables one could sit down and eat, and to the right a large square area for cooking. The hit men ushered him left, although he merely followed Ferris down the long kitchen and to a right turn.

At this point they arrived at the back room. It was enormous, the ceiling of the second story visible from the bottom. Multiple fans spun above, two large windows stretching from the first to second stories. A third window rested between them toward the top, and was diamond shaped. The carpet was blue and covered in multiple luxury sofas, brown in fabric and wide enough for four people each. On the couches sat four men in suits. They varied in age, but Tom knew each of their faces and each of their last names: Marx. Standing in the corners of the room were tall men, each one of them armed, although their guns weren't visible. Tom could tell by the way they were standing and the way they kept their hands close to their wastes, they were ready to draw.

Tom was forced into an armchair, facing the four Marx's. Each of them regarded him differently.

"So you're the one who's been sniffing around, hm?" said the eldest. William Marx. He was over sixty and had a face with stretched skin and a bright white widow's peak. He was Allen's uncle.

Tom knew that ignoring any of these men would be an insult, while back talking them would be an even greater insult. So he spoke respectfully when spoken too. "I haven't been sniffing. I have merely been discreet. For my own sake."

William nodded while the short, plump man next to him grimaced and snorted. His skin was lightly tanned, like William's, though he had no smug charm, or charm of any kind. This was his brother, Randall Marx.

On the other sofa, to the left, sat a younger man, maybe five years older than Tom. He had deep black hair and a nice clean shaven face. If Tom got close enough, he was sure he'd be able to smell a poignant odor accompanying after shave. This was Stephen Marx, Allen's cousin and William's son. And next to him was his brother, Reeve. Terrific. Tom really was in the lion's den.

Albert sat down on a stool next to Stephen and Reeve, and Tom looking over to his left. At the edge of the room, there was another room. It was raised a level, accessed by two steps, and completely brown, wooden. At the back there was a large bookshelf and next to it, a desk with a man sitting behind it. Tom recognized Allen Marx more vividly than the rest. He'd seen them in pictures and files, but met Allen in person. The man was on the phone, talking about something presumably Barker related.

"Yes," he said. "Yes, that's right." He rubbed his eyes. "Alright, thank you, sir." Unlike the others, he was still in his morning robe. He had a great, thick head of hair, but Tom thought it was so jagged it made him look like a triangle. Allen had a full face with a bit of excess fat, despite having a very thin body. He was a fine American, balancing gluttony with virtue. In Allen's mind, virtue was using the money your parents left you to better the family name. And what more virtuous lifestyle than a nice large middle finger to the corrupt American Government?

Allen set the phone down and yawned. "Mr. Tom Macklin." He didn't look at Tom, only at some paper on the desk. "You were nobody until very recently." Allen's voice was loud and precise, every consonant well annunciated. His accent was noticeably German, but he had perfected his American dialect.

"Now I'm a somebody, I presume?" Tom said. He expected a few laughs but the room was silent.

"No," said Allen, standing up. He smoothed his hands over his cherry colored robe. "No, you're the guy who can help us with our Barker problem." He sounded incredulous.

"Ridiculous," said William. "I told you, Allen, the boy is lying. You should not have let him in."

Allen entered the room. "Allow me to introduce my uncle, William." He pointed passed the stretch faced man and toward the other two older men. The one next to William was short and plump. Allen pointed at him. "This is Uncle Will's brother Randall." Then he pointed at the third man, skinny and black haired, sitting on the other long couch. "And this is my cousin Steve. Stephen Marx. Not a bad ring to it, eh?" Allen stood between the two couches, looking down at Tom. But Tom realized then that Allen Marx was very short, all of the other men in the room towering over him, and Tom himself a foot higher.

Allen's smile was ear to ear, forming a crevasse in his chin. "Stephen Marx," he was saying. "Sounds almost as impressive as 'Allen Marx,' which is very accurate. Got it hand it to all our parents. God bless them." He finished with a proud grin.

There was silence in the room, and Tom wondered if Allen's uncles and cousin actually liked him, or if they just followed him out of fear.

Tom wiped a few wrinkles off his shoulders and ignored all of the eyes on him. Ferris was over Allen's shoulder now, arms folded, looking nothing but uninterested in all of this.

"So," said Allen, with a more serious face. "You can fix our Barker problem."

"I can," Tom said. As the meeting unfolded, Tom remained wary of the many loaded guns in the room, and his own on the other side of the city.

Allen jerked his head and widened the eyes. "I'm listening."

"It's not that easy, Allen." He stiffened as he spoke. "I tell you my plan; you don't need me anymore. If we proceed, I will take the lead. I just need your assistance."

Allen and William both laughed. William said, pointing his finger, "He's funny. I like him. Boy, we don't need a little amateur badge to tell us how to deal with an enemy."

"So why's Barker still alive?" Tom asked politely.

The laughter stopped, and William looked furious.

Tom didn't like this man, and that propelled him further. "You're looking rather gray, my friend. How long have you spent mulling over ways of dealing with Barker?"

"Mind your tongue," Allen said calmly, while William was beyond words. In the back, Ferris chuckled.

"Something funny, Albert?" asked Allen.

"I think your uncle lets people get to him too easy," Albert said.

"Yes, he does," said Allen, hands in pockets, eyes on his uncle. Then they were on Tom. "You bring up a good point, Tom," he said nodding his head. "Barker's been at large for fourteen years. And let me remind everyone in the room, just for some prefacing, that the first time we clashed with Barker it was after he killed one of our own men. So we sent fifty, and he came out without a scratch." There were murmurs in the room, surprisingly, from the hit men. Allen grinned. "You must understand, Tom. These wonderful stiffs guarding us tonight, they have served my family well. But the hit men Barker has killed. That was their families. The fine men who aim the guns for me hate Barker more than I do."

"I'm sure they want him dead as much as I do," Tom said, not insincerely. "But if you don't me speaking plainly, if fifty armed men didn't work, fifty more armed men won't work. You need to think outside the box."

"And you have," said Allen. Tom could tell from his tone that Allen didn't believe a word he was saying.

"I have."

Allen scoffed and rubbed the side of his hip. "Okay, Tom. My patience for obscurity just ran out."

"And I told you, I'm not giving away my secrets. I'm not stupid."

"Careful, Tom," Ferris muttered.

"Shut up, Albert. Why did you come if you're not going to say anything?" Allen asked.

"Because you summoned me," Tom said. He put some extra venom in the word "summoned."

Allen breathed in, his teeth gritted and his breath wet, sounding a bit like his was slurping soup. And then Tom heard heavy footsteps behind him, and couldn't help looking over his shoulder. His stomach sank.

An ogre stepped into the room, broad shouldered, large muscles, and at least seven feet tall. His hair was graying, scalp and face, but both the hair strands on his head and the whiskers on his face looked sharp like pins. He had steely eyes and tonight he was dressed casually.

Allen said, "Ah, Orson, glad you could join us."

"What did I miss?" said the ogre in a deep, gruff voice.

"Not very much at all." Tom turned to find Allen's eyes still drilling into him, a crooked smile on his face. "Mr. Macklin was just sticking his nose where it doesn't belong."

Tom replied. "Your nose never belonged in the Mayor's office. Your nose never belonged in the banks. Your nose never belonged in the station, in our lives, keeping tabs, though I can't say I blame you for that one."

Allen was visibly irritated, his crooked smile faltering before wrenching itself wider. "You wasted your time, Tom. I have a plan to kill Barker, and it's a damn good one."

"What are you gonna do? Send assassins?"

Allen clapped his hands together. "Congratulations! I see a detective shield in your future." Then he concealed them again.

"And I see death in yours."

"Are you threatening my nephew?" said William.

"No," answered Orson Marx. "He's just questioning your nephews intelligence. Like I do."

Allen closed his eyes and his smile was crooked. "Thank you, Orson." And then to Tom, "I won't discuss this with you. Just know, I will always plot against Barker. Until he's a pile of limbs."

Tom absorbed every tiny thing he saw and used it to prove his point. "I guess Orson isn't so sure, since his airstrike didn't work."

"Watch your mouth, you little shit," growled Orson.

Of all the people sitting in this room, Tom found Orson the most deplorable. Maxwell Sect and Allen Marx both devised the airstrike that created Ghost Town, but it was Orson who did the deed. He murdered all of those people. He was a soldier on leave. A fighter for The United States, like a police officer, but on a much higher scale. It seemed to Tom the higher they climbed the more corrupt they became.

Allen raised his finger, his voice overpowering Orson. "The airstrike…did not work. Correct. But we will not give up. One man won't overpower a family like ours. Let alone one thug, rapist." He shook his head. "We'll find a way."

"Said the Sects," Tom remarked.

"A comedian, huh?" said Stephen Marx.

"Indeed," said Orson with folded arms and an overturned lip. "Perhaps we should wrap him up and leave him at Barker's doorstep. Then he'd know what happened to the Sects."

"I know more than you think," said Tom, anger welling within him. He kept his voice calm and polite as he spoke. "No one used to say a word about Allen Marx, or anyone before him." He cast a sideways glance at William. "No, in the old days it was Malcolm Sect, George Sect, Maxwell Sect. All men with real power. Each one a nightmare for every cop in New Heim. All killed by Barker. Now like magic, the Marx family holds all of the power. Well, if you want to lose it all, go right ahead. Go in, guns blazing."

All eyes in the room were locked on him and he noticed William mouth "shoot him" to Allen. But Allen was, shockingly, remaining very calm.

"Are you a religious man, Tom?" asked Allen.

"No."

"I am." Allen folded his arms and paced the room. "God has watched over my family for generations." He brushed his hair. "God takes care of us all and answers our prayers. Except for abominations like Barker. They've been left to rot. But me." He sharply pointed his finger at his own heart. "I was born to a rich couple. Money I would surely inherit. And now I have. I was given everything I own by God. And he won't abandon me now. There are several ways to kill Barker. And at some point God will smile down on me."

Is he serious? Tom thought.

Stan once told Tom, Mobsters are like a foreign culture. They kill people for pissing them off, and then they start talking about God and holiness. They're convinced of their own fucking sophistication while in reality if you backed them into a corner they'd get as petty and animalistic as Barker. Tom needed Stan's strength and confidence now, or he wasn't leaving this house.

Tom kept a straight face when he said, "I can hire a man to kill Barker. A man who possesses all of Barker's skills and more."

At this, Allen raised an eyebrow. "That so?"

The room was still and silent.

Tom felt a sudden surge. "That's all I tell you tonight, Allen. You're not getting a name, address, or anything. Not without some assurances."

"Beat it out of him," William said, and Orson stirred.

Tom jumped to his feet and several guns were drawn. "Lock me up, Allen. Ed Ryan will have one hundred eyes on you and your entire family. I don't think you want that. He's been dying for a piece of you." He raised his finger as guns were drawn, pointing it in Allen's face. "All I'm asking for is your cooperation."

Allen looked angry, like a child backed into a corner. Red in the face, mouth closed. "And what exactly do you need from me?"

"Are you stupid, nephew?" William said. "He said hire. The boy wants money. This is ridiculous. There is no man with Barker's skills. If there were, we would have heard of them by now."

Allen turned sharply. "Shut up, uncle!" William stepped back, aghast. Allen turned to Tom with gritted teeth. "No one seems to know shit about anything. I've heard about the man, or men, you speak of. You don't think I considered that before?"

Tom's chest dropped. "You should consider it again, Allen. Before you get more of your men killed."

Allen scoffed. "Get him out of my house."

Orson walked out of the room and Ferris kept a firm eye on Tom as he was shoved out of the living room and back down the brown hallway. Tom walked with hands behind his back, out the door, across the courtyard, through the gates. He slammed into the concrete as the rusty gates howled.

Chapter 13

The Leash

Melanie had wasted two strikes and now everything was different. Now, her wrists were tied in a knot in front of her, a short rope lassoed to the foot of the bed. She could pull her wrists about five feet from the foot of the bed, and beyond that she was stuck. He'd tied her fingers as well, so her hands stayed in one position. He'd also tied her ankles, making it impossible to get into any kind of comfortable position. Melanie leaned to the side, slouching on the floor next to the bed. As one final punishment, she was biting down on a wooly scarf, knotted painfully tight at the back of her head.

Barker said that she was going to learn how to respect a man like him, and this was the first step. He'd started wagging his finger. If I come up here, and find any of your bindings undone, even the gag, I will cut you again.

Speaking of which, that night he'd covered the wound with material to sop up the blood, not caring that she'd dripped blood on the carpet. Now there were seven spots on the floor that matched the walls.

This time she got to keep her clothes.

The first night of this new arrangement, he left the door wide open, along with the window. There was nothing she could do, only wait for him to untie her, whenever that would be. Her arm was in so much pain. In her easiest moments it was just a sting. But any sharp, quick move of her arm brought a boulder down on it. She wasn't aloud to have any meds.

Pain's just pain. It's true. His eyes were trailing all over the place. I don't want you to feel it, really. I want you to be comfortable, and happy, and feel safe. His eyes settled on her. You'll learn. He'd slammed the door when he left.

The gag was so tight, not only could she say nothing coherent, but nothing loud. Really, all she could do was whimper like a dog.

No light came from outside. Everything was dim. Whatever darkness was outside, it didn't match the darkness inside. Any beast outside—the Chief, the police, the gang— didn't compare to the monster that tied her down. Here there were no boundaries. Here, he decided what she did or didn't do. The darkness, the pain, the misery and grief. It was all arbitrary.

In this darkness, Melanie's tears were invisible, her sobs inaudible. She kneeled up the best she could and looked up at the bed, wishing for the soft mattress. Instead she had the hard floor and the searing bindings. It only proved further that she was out of chances. She had been denied freedom and given small comforts. Now she was denied comfort. Denied any kind of reprieve. Melanie was losing something. A part of herself.

Despair had been explained to her once as the absence of God. There was definitely no God here. Just darkness. All she ever felt was pain, fear, and now loneliness. This was despair. If she could turn back time, just one day, she'd change everything. She wouldn't have tried to kill him. She wouldn't have tried to escape. She would have been good. Waited patiently. Learned more about the city. Questioned him. Found a real opportunity to escape. One without him watching and waiting to take her back. But she couldn't turn back time.

Melanie was despondent. A horrible mutation was occurring within her. Hope was gone.

If you couldn't escape, and you couldn't fight back, what could you do? The first answer that came to her was die. The second was adapt. Her parents had told her that once that to survive is to adapt. Melanie was not a schoolgirl. She didn't have parents, Martin and Debra, or a friend named Emily. She wasn't mean to a boy named Ronnie. She didn't hate math, and love photography. She loved food, water, and to be by herself. What she hated was rope, scarves and knives.

Barker's pet had to respect the hot, bloody hand that fed her, and she loved most to be alone and alive.

He came the next morning, wearing a wife beater and sporting a somber expression. Melanie laid on the floor, groggy, waking up.

"Melanie." Barker took a couple steps and knelt next to her. He didn't quite reach her level, but his legs were bent. "I thought…we had a good thing going," he said, sounding disappointed. "You were wandering free, you were being good. And now look at you."

Melanie avoided eye contact.

He continued, "I give you three strikes. You blow two in an evening." He covered his face with his hand and let out a muffled laugh. "Boy, oh, boy."

As he giggled, Melanie saw that across the room there was an ant on the floor. How did that little guy get in her room? Did he climb the whole house? That must have been quite an adventure to such a little thing.

"Look at me," he commanded.

Melanie grunted behind the gag. More than anything she wanted the option to ignore him, but he was persistent like a spoiled brat. When she looked at his face, her father flashed through her mind. Barker looked stern, in the mood to discipline, but also regretful. It was like he didn't want to be mean but he had no other way of teaching her.

He smiled. "Did you break two rules or three?"

Melanie's chest sank, and her bound hands went up instinctively in defense.

Barker's face twisted multiple ways, mouth, eyebrows, neck. "You ran away. One. You came into my room. Two. And you tried to kill me. That is three, no?"

She shook her head.

"No?" he asked.

You didn't say anything about killing. You never said the words. You said don't run away and don't go in your room. You didn't say don't try to kill you.

He laughed, and it was like he read her mind. "I didn't tell you no trying to kill me…I suppose…well, we'll call it two strikes then." He raised a finger. "One more, dear. One. More."

She closed her eyes and nodded. Melanie used to daydream for hours, but when Barker was in front of her it was like ropes trussed her mind as well. His arm started to slide across her back and she feebly struggled. He pulled her into a warm (too warm) embrace, and she gave up.

As he hugged her tight, she noticed that his body temperature fluctuated. Like a heartbeat, it jumped from lukewarm to fever hot.

"I don't want to hurt your parents, or you. You understand that? I just want you to be good. Please be good." He was literally pleading. He didn't whimper or cry, and his voice never cracked, but it was a sincere plea. "Please don't make me hurt you. Okay?"

She nodded.

She heard him say "Good…good girl."

His lips came down on her scalp, itching her and pressing down with the weight of his head. Then he separated from her and she shivered, arms and legs. A moment later he released her and left the room. Even with his head turned away, she knew he was grinning.

Chapter 14

The Bell

As days started to go by, Melanie quickly became subservient to him. She knew she would have to start doing that to survive him, but currently it was just so he would feed her. When he cut her free and made breakfast, she ate whatever he put in front of her without complaint. Sometimes he would even ask what she wanted. Her answer was always anything, whatever he had to offer.

Being locked up all day, the last thing Melanie wanted was to go all over herself. She was humiliated enough already. Barker had that covered. When he'd given it to her he had dangled it like a toy, same as the knife. It was a small bell, held by a red string. This is for you. Ring it whenever you need the bathroom, or when that special time of the month comes around, and I'll be up in an eye blink. Okay?

He then warned her not to ring it to annoy him, as stated in rule number three. That was all she wanted to do half the time. To ring the bell nonstop, make him regret ever bringing her here. But she never did. She was good. Melanie spoke only when spoken to, and that was only at breakfast, lunch, or dinner. When she wasn't being fed, the gag went right back in. For days, Melanie stayed in that room, lying on the ground, bundled up in storage.

There was nothing she hated more than this. Every day at school, Melanie would plow the halls and walk the fields during gym class. If she survived this experience, this room might cause her life long claustrophobia. She just needed to get out. So as days continued to roll, eventually bringing her to the end of the second week, Melanie was Barker's wonderfully behaved pet.

Every couple of days, Barker loosened the lasso. As the days went on, he granted her more room to move. Finally, on October 21st, he'd stopped tying her fingers, and her feet. If she undid her hands or took out the gag, there would be hell to pay. Melanie dealt with the pain, because it meant she could sleep on the bed, hands tethered to its base.

He also allowed her to wash morning and night. The bathroom was her sanctuary. He never entered. He just waited for her outside the door. So she drew each shower out until the water ran cold, and he waited. If it made any sense to say, he was forgiving. Slowly, he returned her small comforts. Melanie had a wonderful free zone in the bathroom, but when she finally opened the door, he was sitting right there. Then it was back into her prison uniform. No ifs ands or buts.

Melanie had learned something about the world. If you have good parents, they shield you from the fact that the world is a gruesome, bizarre place, where nothing precious to you is safe. Anyone can, and will, take away what you hold dear.

***

October 21st. Barker went over a list of things he had in the house now. The refrigerator was stuffed: Eggs, bread, meat, some pastries, oven pizzas, more ingredients for various meals. He had beer as well, though Melanie didn't like it.

There was no television. He didn't need it, he could find the news and current events on his phone. And Melanie spent her time reading. He'd spent hours across various days picking out a collection of his favorites, and at some point, he would question her about them. Reading was good for the soul and the mind, and hopefully that would help her settle in more comfortably.

It had been over a week since she tried to kill him. The punishment would continue until he was convinced he could trust her. Slowly, systematically, he would ease her back into their prior arrangement. She would be allowed to sleep untied, but with the door locked, then she would be allowed to roam the house again at night. And eventually, if all went well, she would just stay. She would be his, and never want to leave. There would be no more bondage. There would be trust. And finally, Barker would prove his old friends wrong. He would show them all that he was more capable and in more control than they ever predicted. That alone made him smile all the wider.

So what did he have to read? He walked over to the coffee table and picked up a few titles: The Once and Future King. The Silence of the Lambs. The Lord of the Rings. Awaken and Feast.

The last was his favorite by far, a book about him and the man he used to be. He remembered the days of being a Meridian Killer. What an ugly title. Aethon had agreed. Regardless, that was what they were called when they lived in Montana. When every night was a party, and one or two casualties was the minimum.

Of course, while the Meridian technically referred to the state of Montana, mostly the subject of rumor thanks to some very powerful people, the Meridian was a circle. And that circle should have been drawn around any amount of acres containing men and women of this nature. As long as Barker lived in New Heim, this war torn ghost of a city rested within that blood soaked realm.

All in a day's work.

Those were old days, but not his glory days. He was living them now, no longer cursed like the rest.

He wondered what would happen if he shared this with Melanie...she wouldn't understand. Well, maybe he could have her read the book. She'd pick up quickly. She'd know.

She would know about him...no, there was something else. Maybe they could talk about photography.

Yes.

What else was in the house? Toiletries, check. Bath products, check. Then Barker picked through his many wonderful toys and tools with a deep churn of adrenaline. Check.

He wanted a victim...yes he wanted a playmate. Brolin just hadn't been enough. Barker considered the delights he'd taken that night. He'd cut Brolin, stabbed him, drilled him even, made him scream. Felt the blood on his skin. All those wonderful things. But it just wasn't enough.

He wanted a girl. Yes, he wanted to be inside someone.

No. Not yet. Melanie was in a delicate state. And he didn't need to bring chaos into the house just yet. He needed things to calm down between them first.

***

One night, as Melanie tried to sleep, windows barred shut and door locked, the cloth between her teeth started to hurt. She tried to ignore it, but eventually she realized if she left it in she just wouldn't be able to sleep.

If she fell asleep with the gag out, she could awaken to Barker, shaking his head.

Strike three.

If she could just relieve the pain for awhile, that would be enough. Barker was downstairs. She was alone in her box. Maybe for part of an evening, this box could be home to her own rules.

So she reached up and pulled it out and letting it rest comfortably on her chin. The pain went almost immediately, and when she let out a yawn, the cloth slipped down to her neck.

She dug her head into the pillow, rubbing her knuckles against her spit sticky lips, and started humming again.

The Seaweed is always Greener, in somebody else's lake.

Melanie always loved that song, that movie. She enjoyed movies with bright colors. Part of what got her into photography had been an interest in combinations of harsh colors, bringing out all the little details you might not notice at first. She might have been a painter (her mom had initially said that) but Melanie didn't have any skill for drawing, or the patience to learn. Photography had occurred to her during a trip with her parents. They'd taken her to Maine for a few weeks of exploring the woods and taking in the sights. One night as the sun set over water and an assortment of different colored rocks, Melanie saw that all of those colors she used to love could be captured in real time.

When they caught her staring, her father had brushed her hair with his hand, and there was a silent exchange of understanding.

Melanie felt herself fading now, and pulled the cloth back into her mouth. It felt looser than before. Barker would never know. She dug her head into the pillow, and she was back in Maine.

***

On October 25th, Barker sat in the armchair reading The Silence of the Lambs. Melanie was upstairs, either sleeping or sitting around enjoying the punishment.

A text message turned Barker's phone into a bumblebee.

Kris: Marx is coming for you.

Barker sat up straight, holding his phone in two hands.

Barker: Elaborate.

Kris: Two men with guns, staking out Cotton Drive. Two more over at Bronze. Three more in a house around the corner. Might be more even closer to you. They'll try to box you in.

Barker: Hiding? Trashcans? Houses? Holes in the ground?

Kris: Correct.

How many of them would there be this time? If a bombing didn't work, Allen would want to compensate. There would be several. Fifty. Or more. That didn't scare him. If Barker wanted a work out, fifty regular men with guns was the minimum requirement. If he wanted a great challenge, he'd take on one hundred. But there were certain weapons he always needed to be wary of, and there would be many of those.

Barker: Stay out of sight and stay by your phone. You'll be my eyes and ears on the other side of the city.

Kris: I need to get the kids to safety.

There was something in her tone he didn't like.

Barker: You will have the girls watch over the little ones. You, Dom, Adam, Peter, and the all the other boys will patrol the city and watch for the rest. Clear? ☺

It took a moment for her to reply to that one. Maybe the smiley face was a little much.

Kris: Clear.

Barker put the phone away. So, Allen's men were coming. This time, the fight would be intense. Was it finally time to remove the Marx's as he did the Sect's? What an exciting turn of events.

Melanie.

He went stiff. If Melanie got caught up in all of this, she might be killed. The thought weighed over him for a moment and he started brainstorming several different ways to protect her. Even so, for the first time in years, Barker was afraid.

Chapter 15

A Thorn in his Side

Melanie was kneeling on the bed the next morning, reading A Clockwork Orange. Although she was entertaining herself, her hands were still tied in front and her mouth still restrained. There was something fitting about reading such a book in this state. Reading at all while tied up was bizarre, and almost made her laugh. The door opened and Barker stood before her. She closed the book as he walked up to her and reached for the gag. He took his time undoing the knot, but when it fell from her mouth she took a clean breath and wiped the spit from her chin.

"Hello, darling." He shut the door behind him.

"Is everything, alright?" she carefully asked.

He turned from the door and leaned against it, staring around the room. He looked peculiar. Unhappy. Confused.

"Mind if I sit?" he asked, pointing toward the couch.

As if it mattered. "Go ahead," she wheezed.

"Good…we need to talk." Barker sat down on the couch. He stared at Melanie's bed. No. That was just where his eyes were pointed. Melanie adjusted herself more into a sitting position, hands still tied. She didn't know where he was until words came out. "Melanie…I have enemies."

"Enemies?" That was something she never thought about. Who were his enemies? The cops? Someone she didn't know maybe. Was it possible that an enemy could come and kill him? Would they take pity on her, or were they cruel like him?

Barker scratched his own scalp. "When you tried to escape the first time, you learned that the police answer to me. And when you tried to escape a second time, you saw the devastation done to this part of town."

She nodded.

He then asked. "Did you ever hear about that on the news?" And she nodded. "What did you hear?"

"There was…" She stopped. This would be the first time in days engaging in a full conversation with him. She had to remember her place. No more strikes. "They said that there was some kind of bombing. They didn't say much else. They talked a lot about the place, the impact it had on the people who survived, and talked a lot about all the people who lost their lives." She scratched an itch on her right hand with her left, and kept scratching after it had gone. "But they never said anything about how it happened or who was behind it. I always wondered about that. So did my dad." Mentioning him in Barker's presence gave her a start. Their eyes locked, a silence hanging between them. Melanie searched his face for guilt, but his expression, like her own, was barren of emotion.

"It was an airstrike," Barker said.

"Airstrike?"

He nodded, eyes wide. "Oh, yeah. The atrocity was perpetrated by two crime families who lived in this city for decades: The Sect Family and the Marx Family." He leaned forward. "Little bit of history. The Sect Empire was built by Malcolm, and the last person to lead it in New Heim was Maxwell, who, they say, was a severely abused child. He let all kinds of bad people hurt his family, until the last few killed his parents. He grew into a hard man who subjugated everything he could and brought the hammer down on anyone who wronged him. This was the reputation the Sect Family had. The Marx Family, currently led by dear Allen, is a much more boring story. They're so deplorable that Germany didn't even want them. So they got dumped on these shores and started taking advantage of all the right people, including the Sects. I suppose you could debate which family was truly greater. The ones who subjugated an entire populace with fear, or the ones who lied and cheated there way up to the very top." He stopped for a moment, eyes on the ceiling as if he were contemplating it himself. "I digress. Anyway, the Sects and Marxs were mortal enemies. It was rumored that they worked together once or twice against the police, but that was never confirmed. What is confirmed, was the one time they all teamed up, against me." He finished with a proud grin.

"Wow," Melanie said, trying to sound interested. In truth, it was fascinating, but she wanted him to leave.

Barker sniffed before he went on. "Basically, when I became a...powerful human being, I quickly made powerful enemies. Makes sense right?"

Melanie nodded.

"The Sects and Marx's were used to eating dirt from one another, but some lowly, stalking, murderous little peasant like me, gaining turf? Oh no. No, no no. What came after were several attempts to kill me. And after multiple failures and hundreds of men down, they banned together to arrange a bombing. At the time, I was living in this part of town."

"So they blew it up," she said. "And you escaped?"

"I did," he said, grinning with pride.

"How?" she asked, truly curious.

He laughed. "I'm fast."

Melanie knew that all too well, and if people with guns and bombs couldn't stop him, what hope did she have?

He paused, digging into her with his eyes. "After that...I slaughtered the entire Sect Family."

It sounded like a threat, and she felt the urge to gulp. "Oh," she said.

"I would have killed the Marx family too, but..." He was trailing again, and she could tell that whatever he was thinking about was something that took him back vividly, something he couldn't forget. Maybe she was about to find out. But he just said, "There was an incident, that drove me away for a year. That's what brought me to you."

When you kidnapped me and tortured my family. "So now we're back," she said.

"And the Marx Family needs to be dealt with."

"Wait a minute," she said. He looked at her, surprised, and she panicked. "Sorry. I didn't mean to."

"No, no. Go on," he said with a smile.

"I was just going to ask why did the families have to team up to pull it off?"

He snapped his fingers. "Excellent question. You see, although the whole thing was tedious, either family could have pulled it off with the right amount of money. But Allen Marx has a cousin named Orson. Orson is a veteran with military connections."

"Military," she muttered. Then he must have stolen a fighter jet or something. Maybe he owned one. She didn't know much about how that worked.

Barker went on, "Orson flew by overhead and bombed the city, the jet vanished and was never seen again." He waved his hands through the air. "Thus was the birth of Ghost Town."

"Thank you," she said. "For telling me."

He cleared his throat. "What I'm concerned about, is that I have it on good authority Allen Marx is going to try something on me soon. Not that he's coming himself. Oh, no, that'll be the day. But he'll send any number of men with guns." He leaned forward. "I'm concerned about you. Your safety."

And so was she. "What are we going to do?" she asked.

He scratched his nose. "Well, I have an idea. It'll require timing. Exact timing. Something I'm pretty good at. I'll keep you safe."

She wished like hell he would send her away. Somewhere safe. And while he was fighting, she could make her escape. But he wouldn't be so careless. Wherever Melanie went, she would be tied up.

Barker walked over to her and kissed her on the head. His skin was hot. "No reason to fret, dear. I'll take care of it."

He stood up and kept his hand on her head. He looked down at her and their eyes met. On his face now was a look her mother used to give her, when she would cry as a child. "It will be alright," he said. It was like her mother's voice echoed by shredded guitar strings.

***

Barker was thirty-five years old. He was born of a mother, like any other child, but in his own opinion he had been born prematurely. His recreation occurred fourteen years ago. He had waddled in envy, and now inspired greed.

Barker awoke when he found his purpose. His pleasure. His love. Killing. Blood. Blood was the best part. Blood gave him a tingle. There were various ways it could form. Dripping, bursting, spreading like a river, girdling into a black puddle. Over time, various aspects of taking a life provided him with an ecstasy. When they screamed, it took hold. When their eyes leaked tears, turning red, he thought he could see expression all the more clearly. He had so many fond memories of screams. Of crying. Of chains and shackles and muzzles. It all began with a pursuit of blood.

At the age of twenty-three, if it wasn't a weekly routine he'd grow severely frustrated. Today, he could space it out if need be. If he needed to stay out of sight. To watch.

Before Melanie, girls never lasted very long. They were brief incidents in his life. But although the girls themselves meant nothing to him, they were wonderful memories. Barker loved to tie them down and penetrate them more than a boy loved Christmas gifts. He also enjoyed fighting, and that was inevitable with his amount of enemies. He didn't feel for his opponents the way he felt for the girls though. He loved them so much that he'd been tempted to create a photo album, stretching a whole decade, but it was such a cliché. They called him serial killer. Back then he hated it. He was special. He'd discovered something that no one else on the planet ever had. Of course that made him different. Of course that made him individual, unique, difficult to adjust to. They should have classified him as unique. But, no. They needed to put him in an obligatory category. Serial killer. Disgusting. He killed twice as much as normal when he first heard that name assigned to him.

Today, he didn't give stereotypes a second thought. He was more mature now, more understanding of the important things in life. They could call him whatever they wanted, it didn't change his individuality, or how unique he was. His life was his, and his beautiful discovery, he didn't need to share it with any of them. So to Hell with them all and whatever they thought of him. All he needed was Barker, and some playmates to keep the nights exciting.

So photo album? Well, he'd eventually done it. Taken some pictures of what he found especially erotic or artistic. But that was the only reason. It wasn't about the girls. Don't get attached, he told himself. After you kill them, you'll start missing them. Barker had adjusted to the fact that he could have whatever he wanted, and nothing could stop him. But that involved compromising on occasion. If he wanted to kill a girl, but keep her all the same, that just wasn't possible. So Barker rationalized exactly what he wanted.

Barker wanted the blood. And he took it. Oh, he took it.

He'd kept the pictures in a box, not an album, and he only remembered one. A girl on which he'd tied the gag so tight it looked like thin white paper. And her eyes had been so bloodshot. He'd taken a memory of that, and dug it up on occasion out of boredom. What was her name? Names were harder than faces.

Regardless, that picture was scorched in the airstrike. And what a smart decision not to get attached to all of the objects the mobsters had taken away. In truth, they'd taken nothing, and given him Ghost Town. Barker's own personal Meridian, where all who entered never came back. Oh it was so perfect.

Soon would come many more years of memories, after he settled the scores. But Melanie. He also had to protect Melanie. Over the past fourteen years, Justin Barker had gone through many changes. And now he was going through yet another.

He never got attached. He just wanted pretty looking mannequins to cut up. And yet, here was Melanie. The untouchable. Barker stroked the picture of her in his room, asleep with her hands tied and mouth covered up. Like an infant, christened into the dark realm.

It had all started with a photograph. Something small, that triggered him in a catastrophic, vexing fashion.

After the distinguished Officer Martin Grier pulled him over and waved his dick in his face, Barker followed the idiot home.

He'd intended to kill and whatever family he had then, and when he saw Debra he was ecstatic. Good hips. Nice tall, slender figure. Pretty short brown hair. Not only would he get to kill Martin but have some good sex right in front of him. He thought about stringing up their bodies in the likeness of an embrace for when the police came to the scene.

He checked into a hotel, and came back the next night, ready to do the deed. He was theorizing what Debra might look like in her nightclothes when someone else walked out of the house.

He crept in the bushes, leaving his car down the street. And she came outside, holding a camera in her hand. She was wearing a white T-shirt and short shorts, but her long blonde hair was decently combed. There were blue-ish lights flashing inside from the television, and that was either the father or the mother. This was the daughter, he realized.

"Melanie!" Martin had yelled from inside.

"Yeah?" she said.

"Put a jacket on!"

But she ignored him and started pressing buttons on the camera. She put it up to her eyes and started surveying the town. And Barker ducked further into the bushes, afraid for a moment he might be seen. She followed the road beside them and was apparently taking a video. It was pitch black outside. Didn't she know that she needed more light to make this shot work?

That was the moment. Something was triggered. No different than hitting the record button. She must have taken twenty pictures. The cars on the street. The stars. The house. She sat down on the porch and flipped through all of the shots she took, studying them closely, teaching herself things about them. She clearly had a mind for it. Nothing else was important to her. She loved something that Barker used to love, before his interests turned to killing. How much in common did they have?

Then it occurred to him that when he killed her father, he would surely have to kill her too. Right then, something inside him screamed in protest. He wanted not to harm the girl, but not to leave without teaching the cop a lesson. What to do? What to do?

Yes. Barker remembered that momentary confusion. But he resolved it quickly, with giddy excitement. When he left Fargo, Melanie Grier was coming with him, all wrapped up.

Barker had been reckless then, and even as he took her, he'd been unsure of his end game. Would it work? How long would he care for her, before he killed her? When would the game end?

Perhaps it would not. Not ever. In that moment, Barker saw an image forming in front of him. An image of Melanie, clad in black with shortened hair. A knife in her hand, only not quivering this time. A person who understood him. Who walked with him. Ran with him. Who gave him something he had never yet attained. Yes. Melanie was here. She was his. And now it was time to buckle down and groom her. But it would take time. Before he even got that far, these idiots might kill her if he wasn't quick enough.

Fool. Idiot. Fool. Why did you bring her back here? To Allen, and Orson, and all the rest? You'll have to make sure nothing happens to her. No one would take her away from him. It didn't work that way. Not anymore.

***

Melanie was waiting to die. If men with guns were coming here, the odds of surviving were low. So she was waiting to die. There was no point in envisioning what would happen beyond today. Was this it? The last day?

Then again, she was with Barker. The man had caught her in a half second, broken her father, and survived an airstrike. All of that ferocity would be on her side tonight, so maybe she'd survive easily. Either way, Melanie sat in the living room, on the sofa, waiting for the ball to drop.

Barker gave her a knife, just in case. This wasn't from the kitchen drawer. This was one of his. A hunting knife. Heavy and very sharp. It made her feel stronger than the other knife had. Melanie was dressed in jeans, a tank top, and a small hoodie that could conceal her face. Barker had dressed her himself, and handed her the knife with the words, "Careful where you stick that." Then he mussed up her hair and walked away.

He was sitting in the armchair now, right by the window. His feet were reclined and his head was back, eyes shut. His trench coat was folded across his lap. His beanie covered his hair. A black tank top, army pants, and black boots completed the wardrobe for whatever this was. A brawl. A slaughter. Or maybe a catastrophe. She liked that last one.

Melanie had watched him tie one knife to his leg under his pants and sheath the other at his waist. He was so still. Was he asleep? *I could stab him now.* Melanie sheathed the thought and remained still. *No. If I can escape, maybe these men will kill him. The smart thing to do is to do as he says. He said he won't let anything happen to me. He'd said it so genuine, she believed him.*

She concealed the knife under her sleeve, as instructed, and continued reading A Clockwork Orange. Almost done. She hadn't eaten dinner, but her stomach was numb right now. When someone is coming to kill you, you don't need to eat. Melanie Grier, age sixteen, had learned that you typically don't want to eat when you're afraid for your life. And her classmates thought they had issues. *Classmates.* Maybe this was all some Government experiment, and she was really lying in a coma while her classmates watched and took notes.

Melanie Grier. The situation is a man is breaking into your house to kidnap you. You have five minutes to get out. What do you do?

And now:

Melanie Grier. You have been kidnapped, and forced to live out of your environment. You can roam freely throughout the house, make yourself food, use the bathroom, arm yourself with whatever you find in the drawers. All that is certain is that someone is coming to the house tonight and they will kill you. How do you proceed?

And her classmates had pens and paper, and would be expected to write essays on what they saw and what they would do in that situation.

What a fun thought. When she woke up, she'd be angry. She didn't remember volunteering for this test. She shut the book and leaned up. *Come on. Is he really asleep?*

"Barker I—" she started, but he shushed her.

"Quiet."

"But—"

"Quiet." He raised his hand, but kept his head leaned back and his eyes shut. "I need to hear."

"Hear what?"

"Shhhhh."

He looked like he was fading in and out of sleep. Eyes fluttering. Looking closer, she realized the knife he was holding was actually tucked under the arm of the chair, out of anyone's sight but hers.

She tried to read, but she couldn't.

She started humming again. This time it was Belle.

Pop. Glass shattered.

Barker grabbed her and yanked her off the couch. She slammed down in front of the door, and Barker huddled over her.

Right where Melanie had been sitting, directly across from Barker, there was a hole in the wall. She felt dizzy. He'd moved so fast, moved her so fast. The air had turned into little needles and he'd almost squished her lungs. But she was alive. How did he move so fast?

"Mother fucker," he muttered.

"What was that?" she asked.

Barker kept his eyes on the hole in the wall, and turned to the window. "A sniper. I warned him not to send snipers. Brave. Very brave." Still they huddled behind the front door, his arm tight around her.

"You're so fast," she said, catching her own breath.

He smiled. "I am, aren't I? I don't know what rooftop that fucker is perched on but mark my words. I can still catch him."

There were more loud pops, and glass flew throughout the living room. She didn't know how many holes were in the window now. She only knew she didn't want to move. At all.

When the last bullet stopped, she heard a hiss. It sounded like it was coming from the back.

"What is that?" she asked, terrified.

Barker was staring toward the back as well. He looked stunned. "Are they really...Oh, Allen. You're asking for it."

A small can rolled toward them, hissing loud. Smoke began to fill the room. Barker yanked her to her feet, gripped her around the waist, and the front door flew open. Together they hurdled out into the night, reaching the street in only a second. Going at this speed pounded against Melanie's lungs, but when they stopped she was able to breathe. Behind them the house was filling with white smoke.

Then there were three low pops around them, three things hitting the ground.

Barker stopped as white smoke exploded all around them in a huge wave.

As it crept up her nose and down her throat, Melanie's eyes burned and she cried out, going blind. Barker howled next to her, but he didn't let go. His cry was much louder, and he was grunting fast like an animal.

There were voices, and as Barker lifted her again, she heard gunshots.

The wind plowed against her bones, her eyes were burning as if needles were stuck through them, but not one bullet touched her. Though she couldn't see, the inconsistency of Barker's movements told her he was evading attacks from all around them.

At some point, Barker had run so far that the voices were distant. There were no gunshots. Barker dropped her on the ground and she scraped her chin, feeling the icy, rough sting. She could tell when he was standing next to her and when he crouched down. Melanie heard him groan as vomit spattered on the ground next to her. He groaned and gurgled, his breath wet. And then she heard the beginning of a laugh. "Sons a bitches."

A loud bang dulled her eardrums, and Barker seemed to have left her side. There were people screaming, at least two other voices.

"Come on!" she heard Barker yell. More loud bangs flooded in. Melanie stiffened where she was crouched, not moving for fear of getting nicked.

The noise continued. Gunshots were sounding, men were screaming, and Barker was laughing. He seemed to be to her left, then to her right, then about twenty feet away. Only ten seconds had gone by.

There was a spatter, someone gurgling on their own blood, and someone else shrieking. Barker continued to laugh. "Like that? Huh?"

An unfamiliar voice shouted, "Kill him!"

She lifted her head up slightly, perched on her hands and knees. She was completely blind. Her eyes in so much pain she wanted to bang her head against the concrete.

"Run, Melanie!" Barker yelled. "Get up and run! Run straight!"

Melanie tried to obey. She pushed herself to her feet. On two feet she felt wobbly and disoriented, but not for long. It was just the inability to see that made it hard. As instructed, she started to run straight.

"Stop!" Barker yelled. "Stop! Be still!"

She obeyed, and there were more voices in front of her. "What about the kid?" said one.

"She goes too," said the other.

Melanie's throat clenched. She couldn't see. She didn't know where to run. The only thing Melanie knew was that someone somewhere in front of her had a gun, and it was pointed at her.

There was a bang.

Something heavy tackled her, and she lost control of her body, flying sideways. From the speed they were going, she knew she was in Barker's arms. This time, he ran much longer, and she struggled not to suffocate.

When they finally stopped, Barker gently lowered Melanie down. She felt numb, nauseous, and cold. The bullet hadn't hit her, but as she gently hit the ground, Barker continued to lay on top of her. Her stomach pressed against his, she felt something wet, and warm.

He was groaning. "You okay?" he was asking.

Melanie was taking deep breaths. "What…what happened?"

She still couldn't see, but wherever they were was completely silent. They must have been somewhere buried much deeper in Ghost Town, maybe somewhere along the path she had found. Barker was heaving.

"What happened, silly, is I told you to run straight. And then they just, popped right the fuck out of nowhere. There was a gun aimed at your face."

"Did you save me?" she asked in all stupidity. She knew he was bleeding. Badly.

"Yes, you nut," he said. She could feel him lifting himself up. His hands must have been pressed against the ground, lifting him over her like a predator. "Of course I saved you. Ah! I forgot how much bullets suck."

He sounded like he was in so much pain, but he was standing up. She heard his feet tap against the ground. "Okay," he was muttering. "Okay, okay."

"Where are we?" she asked.

"Near the gymnasium," Barker said. "Krissy is around here somewhere, or should be, if she knows how to follow orders. She's going to look after you for awhile. Alright?" His words were so stunted, like it was hard to speak.

"Barker, are you alright?" she asked, haphazardly. And then she something pushing its way up her esophagus. Before she threw up, Barker helped her roll onto her front. Bile poured out of her and splattered everywhere, filling her nose with a sickening odor and spilling against her fingers. With a start, she realized that more footsteps were coming toward her.

"They're here!" she screamed.

"Shhhh," Barker said. She could hear him backing away. "Kris is going to take care of you now."

There was a snap against the wind, and all Melanie could hear was her own unsteady breathing. Someone else was there, kneeling next to her.

"Hey, kid. Recognize my voice?" said someone who sounded like Kris. A warm hand (much smaller than Barker's) touched her shoulder, and Melanie let herself breathe more softly.

Chapter 16

Shelter

I t took thirty minutes for her vision to return. During that time, Melanie clutched her eyes and panicked inside, letting every irrational thought conceivable flood her mind as she lay on the cold concrete. She was helpless without her vision. Anyone could kill her easily. But Kris was with her. The girl was sitting nearby, just sitting, waiting until Melanie could see again. Every minute that went by Melanie kept asking if she was still there, and Kris's voice assured her.

"Where did he go?" Melanie asked.

"To deal with them," Kris said.

"Where are we?" Melanie asked.

"Somewhere safe. Just relax, until you can see again."

As Melanie lay there silently, she wondered how many of the boys and girls were with Kris, but she didn't ask. She didn't want Kris to know she was plotting to escape.

When her vision came back, Melanie saw the stars. It was like a movie, the black disappearing thanks to a small expanding circle. There weren't many clouds. The stars floated above like thousands of tiny lights. Melanie pushed herself into a sitting position. Her chin was hot, her eyes in even more pain, and she still felt fatigued from the gas. But aside from this, she'd gotten away almost completely unscathed.

"Hey," Kris said. Melanie looked to her right and there she was. The girl still had flowing brown hair and her black tattoo, zigzagging like a lightning streak. She was wearing the same sleeveless dark shirt and that was probably the same exact gun in her hand.

Melanie breathed deeply. "I'm good," she said. "I can see."

Kris nodded her head. "Good. You feeling okay?"

"Yeah," Melanie said. She tried to pull herself up, and Kris helped her. Standing up, Melanie looked around, down past Kris's shoulder. They were in fact on Desolation Drive, right by the fork in the road. The cliff and broken bridge would be a five-minute walk. Melanie didn't see anyone else with Kris, but the girl's grip was firm on her wrist.

"Okay. Let's go," Kris said.

Melanie dug her feet into the ground. "Go where?"

Kris rounded on her, looking annoyed. "To base. Now come on."

How hard could it be to get away from her? Barker was gone. Melanie could run now. She yanked against Kris's grip but the girl kept it, albeit not as easily as Barker.

"Don't be stupid, kid!" Kris said as they continued to struggle.

Melanie was nearly free when the gun slammed into the side of her neck. Melanie fumbled, numb, and Kris pulled her hands behind her back, pushing her to her knees. The pistol was against the top of her head.

"Bitch! Try that again and I'll fucking kill you. Got it?"

Melanie didn't want to scream. She didn't want to cry either, so she talked. "Shoot me then. I'm tired. Tired of this."

The gun was still there, but Kris had knelt down next to her, still gripping her wrists. "You're so fucking stupid. How have you survived this long? If you were out here with me you wouldn't last a damn day!" The pistol was practically pressed into her head now as Kris's hand trembled.

All Kris had to do was give it a little squeeze, and this would be it. Melanie would die. That's what she had been expecting the entire time she sat in that living room.

But then, although Kris's grip on her wrists stayed firm, the pistol pointed away from Melanie's head, and Kris's voice was softer. "Listen…if they kill him, you'll be free to go. If you try to run now and he survives, he'll kill us both. It won't matter where we run or hide, no matter how far. He'll obsess over us." There was a moment of silence, where Melanie had a realization. If she cooperated with Kris, she might be able to get away. Peacefully.

"If he dies, you'll let me go?" Melanie asked.

"Yes," Kris said. "If."

All she had to do was wait. Kris would protect her. She promised to release her. It was better than dying here.

"Okay," Melanie said. "I'm sorry. I won't do it again."

Kris's hand twisted on Melanie's skin, making her yelp. "You better not," Kris said.

Kris released her and Melanie tried to soothe the burning on her wrists. Kris said, "Now get up and walk."

The two girls walked through Ghost Town. Melanie had pulled up her hoodie to fight the cold, while Kris let her hair flow freely. Thought they walked side by side, Melanie remained wary of the gun. In the moonlight, Kris looked older than eighteen. Shadows fell across her face that made her right, tattooed eye look like a black streak and her mouth and nose somehow bigger.

If Melanie could get away, get on her own, there were a number of dangers. She might die of starvation, thirst, fatigue, or anything. Or she'd run into someone else who was dangerous. Or even wolves. All of that was more risky than trusting Kris. If Barker died, the entire game would change.

Please die. She kept thinking it over and over. Please. Just die.

Somehow, as the thought came to her, so did guilt. He took a bullet for you Melanie. You can't ignore that.

But her mother. Her father. Her freedom and her dignity. What Barker had done was unforgiveable.

"It's alright, Melanie," Kris was saying. "None of them are in this part of town. You're safe." Kris sounded like she was trying to come back down from the anxiety and fury that has passed between them. Her voice was soft. "You stick with us and none of them will find you."

"Who's we?" Melanie asked.

Kris smirked and pointed over Melanie's left shoulder, across the street. They stopped for a moment. At first Melanie saw nothing but shapes in the dark, but then one of the shapes moved. Momentarily she went back to childhood, watching shapes form in the dark of night. But this shape was a boy moving to lay on his stomach like a soldier.

"Oh," she said, and looked to Kris. "Who is that?"

"That's Adam," she said.

"Are they all here?"

Kris shook her head. "Adam and I were watching this street together before I found you. Some of the others are around too. We're going to regroup now."

"Is Dom here?" Melanie asked, remembering the large boy who had tackled her the first time they met.

"No," Kris said. "He won't be here for awhile. He's in charge of another group. I can explain it all when we get back to base." Kris motioned for Adam to come out of his hiding place and join them. Offhandedly, Kris said "I should be out there leading that group, but I'm stuck baby sitting."

Melanie didn't answer, as Adam came up to them, fully armed.

"What's going on?" he said. He was about Kris's height, difficult to see in the dark but he seemed to have narrow eyes and black hair. He was short and stocky but looked like he could hold his own.

"You know as much as I do," Kris said to him.

Adam had a rifle in his hands, standing to Kris and Melanie's right. "What do we do now?"

"We're headed home." Kris then turned to her left and motioned toward the darkness. The shadow moved, and another of Kris's group emerged, someone Melanie didn't recognize.

It was difficult to see anything beyond moving shadows, but they were all people. These silent spies of Barker ushered her forward, surrounding her with guns, and she felt very much like a fish in a school, all caught in the current.

Melanie was back in the gymnasium. This time, she wasn't tied up. She wasn't sitting on the bleachers. She was by the fire pit, looking across the room at the spot she'd sat on last time. Adam and few of the others, two boys and a girl, were building a fire. As the embers grew she already felt relief from the cold night.

No one was really talking. The situation seemed to have an impact on all of them, but Melanie wanted to know how much they knew. After the fire was built, the girl (who had black hair pulled into a pony tail and very tanned skin) went off and started pacing. Adam was sitting Indian style with his hands folded, rocking back and forth. The other two boys were lighting cigarettes for one another. When she looked closely, she realized that one of those boys was Peter, the one who had guarded her last time.

Kris, of course, was calm and collective, save for a bit of pacing and constantly checking her phone. Melanie sat respectfully, hands on her knees, enjoying the warmth.

Please be dead, she kept thinking. Please die.

Kris drifted over closer to Melanie. When she spoke, she kept her voice low, as she had instructed everyone else to do. "Haven't heard a word from Dom or Barker."

"That's a good thing right?" said Adam. His tone of voice was like one of the children. He seemed calmly curious, unaware of the dire situation he was in. "I mean. The Barker part."

Kris sniffed. "Well. That's worth contemplating. Our friend here would love it if Barker caught a bullet in the throat tonight. So would we, save for the sudden drop in funding."

Adam nodded, looking ponderous. "Right." Just then, Peter walked over to them.

"I don't like this," he said.

"None of us do," Kris said.

"I think we should go back out there. Search for Dom," Peter said.

"No. We stay together," Kris said.

"But—"

"Don't make me tell you twice," Kris said, sparking a tension in the air. "If you're worried about missing any action, all they are doing is some extra surveillance. Then we'll all be together again."

Peter turned and walked away in a fit. "I don't give a fuck about action. I just don't want my friends to die." Peter and the other boy walked to the other side of the gym, while Melanie, Kris and Adam stayed by the fire.

"There's nothing he can do on his own," Adam said. "These are trained killers. We would all be better off staying together in case any of them show up here. More guns, more chances."

Kris nodded her head. "I know. Ignore him. He can be a hothead all he wants as long as he does what I say. That goes for you two as well."

Adam nodded and Melanie started to get impatient. "I'll do whatever you say. But can you answer a couple of questions."

Kris groaned. "Sure. Why not?"

Adam was watching Melanie with casual focus, while Kris's chin and mouth were invisible behind her knees. Melanie tried to organize her thoughts.

"Cans rolled into the house and blinded us. I couldn't see anything. All I've known is that the Marx Crime Family sent men to kill Barker. Some of them were right around the house, but I couldn't see so I don't know how many. Sounded like a small group of people at least." She thought harder. "Oh, and there was a sniper."

"Was there really?" Kris asked, looking nervous. "We didn't see any of them."

"Surely he won't take that out on us," Adam said.

"You don't know him like I do, kiddo. It depends on whatever mood he's in when this finishes. Anyway, you had a question, Melanie?"

"Did you see how many of them there actually are? How many people are attacking us?" Melanie asked.

At this, Kris locked eyes with her. "Not us, kid. Barker. We're all caught up in the crossfire. Same as you. If you must know, we counted up to twenty-five men, throughout Ghost Town. However, since we're all the way at the South East corner, and Barker and you were up North West, closer to the city, things are pretty quiet around here. If I had to guess what's going on right now, Barker is out there luring them somewhere else. Probably into the city."

"Why into the city?" Melanie asked.

"He can confuse them there. There's thousands of people to sift through in order to hit their target. If there's one thing Barker knows, its how to turn the tables." She adjusted herself, stretching her left leg. "Barker's lived here just as long as them. He knows the playing field."

"But he was bleeding," Melanie said. "Losing a lot of blood."

"True," Kris said. "He could just be running. Recuperating."

"But you only saw twenty-five men?" Melanie asked.

"Yep. That's what we found on our round," Adam said. Then he looked over Kris's shoulder and his eyes widened. "Um, Kris."

Melanie looked too. Peter was bounding back over to them. Kris stood up.

"Easy big fella," Kris said. "Don't be stupid."

"I'm going," he said. "We have to find Dom and the others."

"You will sit your ass down and shut the fuck up. That's what you're doing," Kris said, voice hard and words concise.

"You saw what I saw!" he yelled.

Kris raised her hand. "Keep your fucking voice down." She sounded more uneasy than angry.

Peter made dramatic gestures with his hands and fingers. "They slithered right out of the darkness, and slithered right back in. Did you see the size of those guns?"

"There were only five of them," Kris said.

He clapped his hands together. "And they were perfect! Almost invisible. Just like us. They could be anywhere? They could be here right now!"

"So keep your fucking voice down," Kris said again, making a mocking gesture with her hand. "See?" There was silence for a moment. Kris looked around at everyone. "Just relax. We're safe here. We always have been. They don't come down this way. They think its haunted. Remember?"

She finished with a smile and a laugh. Adam laughed, and the girl came back over toward the fire, seeming more relaxed. Kris checked her phone again.

"Nothing from Barker," she said. "Or Dom."

The girl Melanie didn't know said, "I'm sure we'll hear from Dom soon. His round should be up in about ten minutes, given the size of the sector."

"I was thinking that," Kris said. Melanie curled up, paying attention to the fire. But she couldn't be alone, as Adam was paying attention to her.

"Sorry about all this, Melanie. I'm sure it's hard on you." He flashed her a genuine smile, just like the waiter, Carl, had.

"Thanks," Melanie said.

Kris said to Melanie, "Adam's a lot nicer than Dom or Peter. Actually I lied. Peter is very nice."

A couple of them laughed.

"Dom's probably dead," said Peter. He walked away, fuming.

Adam got up to stretch his legs and walked off with the dark skinned girl, leaving Melanie alone with Kris. Every now and then Kris would glance in Peter's direction, making sure he didn't actually leave.

"See what I have to deal with?" she said with a smile.

"Yeah," Melanie said, not having much else prepared.

"I know you don't like me much. I don't like me much." She pointed over her shoulder. "But these idiots and the little ones...they need me."

Melanie's response was instinctive. "You're like a mother."

"I am," she said. "Barker has a lot of fun with that."

"What do you mean?" she asked.

"It means he can get whatever he wants from me. Whenever he wants it. I should have run this past year, while he was traveling. But who would look after the little ones? Most of them—Peter, Elisa, Sarah, even Adam—they wouldn't last a day without a firm hand. And Dom only hangs around here because of me."

"I guess," Melanie said, thinking about those little faces and big eyes. "Do you think he's dead?" Melanie asked.

Kris took a deep breath. "I hope not."

"Not Dom," Melanie said. "Barker."

Kris stared at the fire for a moment before responding, face illuminated red. "We both know what he looked like. Blood was pouring out his side and he actually staggered when he got up." She crossed her hands in front of her mouth. "The thing is, I've thought he was dead a bunch of times. He always comes back. And when he does, it's bad."

"Did he ever get shot before?" Melanie asked.

"Sure," Kris said. "Shot, stabbed, take your pick. Have you seen him with his shirt off?"

"No," she said. "Why would I?"

"'Cause he's a pig? Geez, don't take it personally," Kris said, flushing. "Anyway, I have. Just once. He's got a nasty one under there."

"A scar?" Melanie asked.

Kris nodded. "Big one. He wears thick clothing to hide it. And whoever gave it to him isn't around to talk about it."

"Oh," Melanie said.

Kris smiled, her eyes heavy in that apologetic way. "The scariest thing about Barker, in my opinion, is that he doesn't have many scars. I counted two as a result of stabbing…and I know he's been stabbed more times than that."

"I…I don't get it."

"Me either," Kris said, and Melanie wanted to smack her.

"Didn't you just say?"

"I told you what I've seen. I didn't say I understood it any better than you do."

Kris's phone buzzed, and both girls stared at it with wide eyes. As Kris read the message it looked like her brain was processing a thousand words a second. She glanced up at Melanie, seeing how uneasy she was. "It's from Dom."

Damn it. She still was not getting an answer. Not yet.

Kris stood up and motioned over the others. Adam and the dark skinned girl came first, followed by Peter and the other boy. Kris said, "Dom's group is okay. They are staking out some of the hit men. The bastards haven't left yet, so Dom is keeping everyone out of sight. That's why they haven't come back yet. As long as they aren't seen they'll be alright."

"How many are there?" Adam asked. "The assassins?"

Kris inhaled. "Dom said he counted twenty." There were murmurs in the group, and Melanie felt stiff where she sat.

"Twenty?" Peter said. "But didn't we count twenty-five?"

"How many did they send?" asked an incredulous Adam.

"Everyone just relax," Kris said. "We'll be fine."

The group wasn't convinced. And as Kris tried to quell them, Melanie stared at the fire, letting it dry out her eyes and mesmerize her. Her mind wandered through the questions she wanted answers to, such as when Kris's friends would be back, and what would happen to her then? How many men had Allen Marx really sent?

But most of all, Melanie wanted to know why Barker was so damn resilient, why he was so strong and so fast. No one seemed to have an answer.

Chapter 17

The Crime Scene

Tom called Albert again. The mobster refused to pick up. He had no idea how Operation Kill Barker was going but all he could do for the next five minutes was sit and wait in his apartment. Then it was off to patrol.

Tom's apartment was smaller than he would have preferred, but he'd decorated it to his liking: Picture frames of family memories on the living room dresser, trinkets from his trips across Europe on the coffee table. A couple athletic trophies on the TV, and that completed the decorating. In the home Tom grew up in, when you walked in the door the living room was to the right and the stairs to the left. But in this apartment, to the left was a wall. You'd smash into it if you turned left. There was a living room. A kitchen behind it. A small porch behind that. And a bedroom the size of a cheap motel room off to the left of the kitchen. That was it.

His least favorite thing about it lately was that it left him no room to pace. His watch went off and it was time to go to work. As Tom left his apartment, a sudden chill went through him, mostly due to his many ignored phone calls. He wondered if he would ever return from the night he was venturing into.

Tom's new partner, John Beckett, greeted him at the door of the station. He was Tom's exact age and a lot more husky. Generally apathetic, though not so much as Brolin had been. John was good with a gun and great backup in case things got ugly. He had nothing but contempt for criminals. That made him perfect in a violent pinch. But tonight, he was only the bearer of bad news.

"We think Barker is at it again," he said in his Texan voice.

"What makes you say that?" Tom asked, silently cursing the mobsters. They needed to take his advice.

"Another dead girl," he said. "Age seventeen. Throat cut. Fucker left her on the side of the road." Though Tom grieved for the victim regardless, in his mind he begged not to hear the name Melanie Grier.

As the two got into the squad car to go on patrol, Tom tried to get more information out of Beckett.

"What was her name?" Tom asked.

"Didn't hear that much. Only that she was young. Everyone was chattering about Barker mocking us again, trying to lure us into chasing him to Ghost Town, just so he can catch one of us. I don't know what's up with that guy. And these vacations he goes on. He should just go somewhere else and be done with it. He can't drain much more life out of this God forsaken city." While Beckett went on like a motor mouth, Tom contemplated why Barker would be out here in the city. Since he got back, there hadn't been an incident besides Melanie's arrival at the station. So what was going on now?

"The weird thing," Beckett said. "Is that this one wasn't kidnapped or raped or anything. Just killed. Clothes on and everything. The guys said that it must have happened an hour or two ago. He just ran up and cut the girl's throat."

"Must not have been Barker then," Tom said. "It doesn't fit his M.O." Beckett looked on contemplatively, as Tom turned a corner, green light shining by overhead.

"True. But the victim sure did," Beckett said. "Unless one of the Marx's got dumped recently. Maybe the nephew."

"Makes no difference," Tom said. "Whether it's Barker or the crime family, nothing will get done for awhile."

Beckett said, "Woah. Easy there, sport."

Tom continued to drive. Ridiculous, Allen. Ridiculous. You should have listened to me.

As they reached 6th Avenue, Tom heard gunshots.

"Hear that?" Beckett said.

"Yes," Tom said.

Around the corner, there was a muzzle flash, and the policemen abruptly stopped. Tom quickly counted. One, two, three guns.

Tom pressed his switch. "Dispatch, this is Macklin. We're at 6th avenue. I see three men with guns. Please copy." They drew their own guns, and Tom opened the door. Outside, people were running and screaming. Tom raised his gun. "Freeze! Drop your weapons!"

Bullets bounced off the car as Tom ducked behind the door, Beckett diving to the right. Tom jumped up and fired over the top of the door. He clipped one gunman on the shoulder, while the other ducked and fired. Tom was almost struck himself as he ducked just in time. Beckett fired a number of shots in the direction of the hit men, but they didn't let up. As Tom returned fire, he managed to catch one attacker in the gut, while the other took another shot at Beckett. He clipped Beckett on the shoulder but Tom's new partner didn't stop. The third hit man was a terrific shot, almost killing Tom with a bullet that shattered the squad car's window. Glass flew near Tom's face as he ducked out of danger again. The excellent shot was half around the corner of the alley, ducking in and out to get good shots. But as he pointed to fire at Tom again, he was suddenly pulled into the alley. The hit man who'd been shot in the gut looked up in horror, before returning to his feet. He seemed unharmed.

Kevlar. These are Allen's men. Before the assassin could fire again, Tom fired. The bullet buried itself in the assassin's neck and he crumbled. The final gunman went down at Beckett's hands, shot in the kneecap. Tom and Beckett left the safety of the vehicle. Guns pointed, they crept over to the killers. One was dead, the other still clutching his throat. Tom beheld the choking, writhing man with a sudden surge of fear. This was his own handy work, with his own hands. Tom had killed once before in self defense, and he began exercising coping tactics he had learned. Meanwhile, Beckett put a bullet in the dying man's head.

Honestly, Tom thought to himself. Can't wait for the news reports: Execution or Mercy Killing?

Tom checked around the corner where the excellent shot had vanished.

What he found was a body, slouched and limp against the alley wall, throat slashed wide open. There was no trace of any attacker.

Beckett walked up next to him, and Tom motioned at the corpse. "What do you think?" he asked. "Look familiar?"

"Same as the girl," Beckett said, a ghostly tone in his voice.

Tom looked left, right, backwards, up at the roofs and even the sky, gun pointed in every direction. Where are you? Where are you hiding? In that moment, Tom started to understand Barker's strategy. As he contemplated, his cell phone started to buzz in his pocket. He picked it up and read the caller: AF. Albert. Tom walked away from Beckett and answered.

"What the fuck, Albert? Why are your men shooting at me in the streets?"

"Tom, I'll ask the questions," said the gruff voice.

"No, listen to me, damn it," he exclaimed while keeping his voice low. "Did you kill Barker yet?"

"No, Tom. Barker escaped."

Tom looked back at the body, killed the same way as another tonight. Why two of the same killings? Why did one of them happen to be one of Allen's men, one of Barker's enemies? It might have been a trail. Barker might have been luring the attackers into the city. All he had to do was make a loud ruckus, and people were starting to scream at the sight of the body.

"Tom?" Albert said. "Have you been in communication with Barker?"

"What? No!" Tom said. "How many men did you send?"

"Someone tipped Barker off, Tom. I sincerely hope it wasn't you," Ferris said with venom.

"Of course it wasn't me," Tom said.

"Allen is convinced it was you," Ferris said, sending a chill through Tom's spine.

"Listen. Just let me talk to Allen," Tom demanded.

"Watch your back," Ferris warned. The line went dead.

Chapter 18

"Good" News

T he doors slammed open, sending echoes throughout the gymnasium. Melanie uncurled herself, and Kris pointed her gun at the doors. It wasn't Barker or mobsters. It was two more boys. They searched the room for a minute before bounding towards the fire pit.

Kris lowered her weapon and curled her fist. "God damn it. You idiots! You scared the shit out of me." She slammed her fist down in thin air. "And I told you to move quietly!"

One of the younger boys (both looked thirteen or fourteen) raised his hands. "I'm sorry! I'm sorry. It's just...I have news."

Kris folded her arms. "Talk."

The boy looked like he was about to cry, and Kris unfolded her fist. "What happened?"

Peter, Adam and the other two (Michael and Elisa) were running towards them as well. "Danny!" Peter yelled to the crying boy.

Danny was shaking. "They're everywhere," he finally said.

"What?" Kris asked.

Another boy stepped in front of Danny. "Kris...there might be fifty of them."

"I know, Jack. Dom sent me a message. Where were they the last time you saw them?"

"Gone," Jack said. "They headed toward the city."

"You just said they were everywhere," Kris said. Danny was dropping to his knees now, breaking down. His sobs started to fill the room. Jack spoke for him.

"He's not thinking straight." Melanie looked closely at this boy, Jack. He had reddish hair and freckles all over his face. He wasn't sobbing, but his eyes were misty. "They...they killed Pat."

The whole group gasped. "What?" Kris said, her voice lower than usual, quivering. "We lost Pat?" Danny tried to compose himself as Elise knelt down and wrapped her arms around him.

Jack explained. "We were as far north as we could go, right at the dividing point between Ghost Town and the city. We watched for anyone coming into Ghost Town, just like you said. Well...people came in. They came in on foot in a huge group. Almost saw us too. We got so lucky...we followed. We followed them all the way to Barker's house."

"You were at Barker's house?" Melanie said, over Kris's shoulder.

They all turned and looked at her. Kris stood with a group of boys behind her and two in front. "Give me a minute, Mel," she said, then turned back to Jack. "Go on."

Melanie walked closer and started to study the boys more closely. Danny had been crying, and was trying not to now.

Jack continued, "We followed them all the way to Barker's house. Stayed out of sight. By the time we got there they'd gassed the place. Barker and the girl ran out and got covered up." He pointed at Melanie. "Is that her right there?"

"Yes, it's her." Kris said. "Keep going."

Jack sniffed. "Then Barker was gone. Like wind. They scrambled chasing him and one of them found us. We ran at first, before I shot the guy in the head. But not before…" Jack was breaking up, tears starting to leak.

"They shot Patrick," Kris finished, solemn.

Jack nodded, wiping his eyes. "He was so fucking scared. It's my fault. We weren't supposed to be seen."

"No," Kris said. "You weren't." For a minute she looked grim and stiff. But then she walked forward and pulled Jack into an embrace.

Adam slowly walked back to the fire, right past Melanie. Peter's head was in his hands. Kris released Jack, who knelt down next to the crying Danny. Kris turned to the fire, her fists clenched again.

"And you weren't seen after that?" Kris asked them.

Both boys shook their heads as Jack stood up. Next thing Melanie knew, Peter knocked Jack down to the floor.

"Asshole! You were supposed to protect him!" he roared.

Kris put her gun right in his chin. "Get back. Get the fuck back!"

Peter shouted more at them and Melanie backed away from the crowd, building safe distance. Adam had come forward too, standing near her almost protectively. Peter looked like he was about to fire his gun, before Kris shoved him forward, away from the crowd so that it was just the two of them. Melanie saw a look of horror cross Peter's face as Kris bounded toward him and backhanded him across the face. Peter hit the ground with an echoic thud.

"You challenge me and you're done! You can go out and fend for yourself!" she said. Then she whipped around to the room and pointed her gun. "You will all do what I say. Clear?" Adam's hands were up. The rest looked horrified.

Melanie tried to get a good look at Kris's face. Even though she'd shown her menacing side, Melanie wondered if she could spot any tears.

Kris didn't say anything to Peter. She just stared. She gave him the same look she had given to Melanie, something that said she wished she could do something. Then she turned away. "How many were there?" she asked Jack.

Jack sniffed and said, "Ten," through half closed eyes.

"Ten." Kris repeated. "For a total of fifty-five."

"Ghost Town's crawling with them," Elise said. "The kids must be terrified."

"I thought they went back to the city," Melanie called over. She had been listening intently, even if her presence was unwelcome.

Jack spoke up again, "On our way back, we heard fighting all over the place. Barker was doing his little speed tricks. First he was around the block, then a few more blocks down. Then closer again. Then West. We knew because gunshots kept going off in all directions, like they were waiting for him everywhere. Had all of Ghost Town boxed in." He looked around. "'Cept for here I guess."

"Yeah. They think it's haunted," Kris said. "What happened next?"

"After awhile the gunfire stopped, and as we got closer to home, some of them came from around the block. We hid. They didn't see us. God, at least twenty of them must have passed by. They seemed to be headed towards the lights. Everything was quieter then."

Kris and Jack continued to talk as Melanie heard Adam grunt next to her.

"I'm sorry," Melanie said. "For your loss."

Adam looked at her like he was surprised. "Thank you. That's really sweet." He stared into the fire. "Pat was a lot younger. Middle school…He was one of the babies."

Melanie frowned, her heart dropping. "I'm sorry." She heard Peter talking to Kris.

"They could still be around here," he said. "Just because it's quiet doesn't mean we're safe. These are trained hit men. We need to go." Melanie could hear the terror in Peter's voice, and she felt for him. She knew that terror. She was even feeling some right now.

"Enough of that," Kris told them firmly. "It's horrific, what they did to Pat. But it doesn't matter how you're feeling. Now's not the time for crying. All right?"

It worked. Both of them stopped and started to stand up, looking more composed and ready for action. Peter wandered over to where Melanie was standing and spoke aloud. "They probably killed him. And I'd be happy about that if they weren't gonna kill us too. Allen knows Barker has people working for him. If they see us they'll shoot us on sight."

Somehow, it clicked upon those words. These people spied for Barker. His enemies were their enemies. They were at risk. Being with them put Melanie in more danger, not less. Nowhere was safe in Ghost Town. She remained silent. Peter must have wanted to say something to her, the way he was drifting toward her but she walked away, hiding herself in the dark part of the room, feeling the cold again for the first time in awhile. From there she could see them all in the light.

Kris drifted toward Melanie and they stood together in the dark.

"You okay?" she asked.

"I don't know," Melanie said, with only one question on her mind. "Is it safe here?"

Kris looked over her shoulder. "Probably not. We'll need to move to the house. But first we wait for Dom."

While the gang stayed alert no matter how tired they became, Melanie nodded in and out of sleep. She was lying down by the fire, having rolled over to give her eyes a break from the heat. The room was dark, but grew darker when her vision started to fade, and her senses started to dull. The images in front of her flashed between a group of kids with guns, to Barker lying on the ground. He crawled in a pool of blood, the wound on his side spreading. On his face, no matter how much agony he experienced, a smile was carved in place.

"Hello darling," he would say.

"You're hurt," she would say.

And he would laugh.

Melanie came back. Once she gasped awake, and Kris looked in her direction, but said nothing. Melanie would then fall back asleep, and Barker was there again. Occasionally he showed her the blood on his hand. Occasionally he licked the blood. And once, he mentioned "daddy," and she couldn't sleep anymore.

Melanie sat up, curling herself into a crouching position. It was so cold, and thoughts of her father swirled within her. Oh Melanie. His beaten face, about to cry. Her mother's tears. Her own tears.

Barker was the bringer of pain, and the bullet he had taken for her was penance.

Tonight he bled. So when she entered the dream world again, she thought she might smile back at him this time.

There was a great gust of wind outside, through the hole in the ceiling, when the sentries started to act up.

"Kris! Kris!" They were waving frantically, and Kris had her gun out. Kris bounded toward them, gun cocked.

"What?"

"They're back!" The boys seemed happy. Melanie stood and adjusted her belt, looking for something to do with her hands. A large number of boys walked in, the rest of the gang. There had to be at least eight or nine of them. In the center was the largest boy, the same boy who had captured Melanie during her first visit here.

Kris hugged Dom before asking, "What happened?"

"They're gone," Dom said. "Sorry. It took forever, but they finally all pulled out. They're in the city now."

"Back to the city, huh?" Kris said, her voice loud. The room started to liven.

Dom said, "That was an hour ago. Since then we've been combing all of Ghost Town. We're alone."

Kris stared, looking fierce. "You were supposed to keep me updated. I thought you were dead."

"I meant to," Dom said with a shrug. Kris punched him, but unlike Peter, he just took it and kept standing.

"I could kill you right now," she said. "But before we get to that, are you absolutely sure?"

Dom nodded. "They're gone. You want to head back to the house?"

Kris nodded and breathed. "I think that sounds good." She turned to the group. "Alright, we're headed home."

The room filled with applause, while Melanie remained still and stoic. Home sounded nice, but she would need to be patient.

Chapter 19

Girl's Night Out

The gang brought Melanie about two blocks up from the Gymnasium, on the Far East side of Ghost Town. They approached a humbly built two-story house: one small garage door, one small porch, and not much yard space. Melanie guessed that upstairs had no more than two bedrooms. She didn't get to inspect much else before she was pulled inside. It was much cleaner than Barker's house, and though none of the lights were on, Melanie could tell she was looking at something confined. Up the right wall was the stair case, and to the left was a small living room, just one stuffy square box, and between them both, a passage leading to the rest of the house, probably the kitchen. A small speck of blue light emanated from that back area. The stove was on.

In the living room, the children were huddled together. There seemed to be seven of them, all either five or six years old, based on their size. They were whispering to one another and stopped when they saw Melanie. Fifty eyes followed Melanie as Kris led her upstairs.

What she stepped into was a small room with one little cot in the corner, a small dresser, and a window. Kris stood in the middle of the room while Melanie sat down on the cot.

"He wants you tied up," Kris said.

"I'm not running," Melanie protested.

"Damn right you're not," Kris said, walking over to peek out the window. "If you jumped out this window, you could survive. But two of the girls are standing guard down there. With guns." She made a shooting motion with her finger.

"I'm not running," Melanie repeated.

Kris chuckled. "And there will be a sentry just outside the door. Knock if you need to use the bathroom or anything, and they'll let you out."

"Don't you usually knock to get into a room?" Melanie asked, hands on her knees.

"Don't test me, kid," Kris said with a raised finger.

Melanie grunted and lay down on the bed, stretching out. "I won't bother them. I'll be good right here. All night."

"Not so bad, eh?" Kris said to her.

"No…thank you."

Kris tapped her feet, standing in the middle of the small room. "Remember what we talked about. I don't mean you any harm, Mel. If Barker's out of the picture, I'll help you."

"I know," Melanie said, she kept her eyes closed. "Thank you." Eyes still shut, she heard Kris going toward the door. But when the footsteps stopped, Melanie opened one eye. "What?"

Kris stood in place for a moment, then turned. "Mind if I sit?"

"Sure?" Melanie said. Why did her captors keep asking her that? The farther into this dark adventure she went, the stranger it became. Kris sat down on the bed, cracking her neck.

"I'm just...wondering, if he died, what exactly is your plan?"

"I leave here and find a way home," Melanie said.

Kris scoffed. "Yeah, and get kidnapped by someone else along the way."

Melanie sat up. "I'm not stupid, okay? I'll find somewhere I can make a phone call and I'll let my family know where I am. I'll stay out of sight until then."

"Well, you may not be stupid, but that is stupid," Kris said. "Just stay with us."

Though aggressive, it sounded a lot like an invitation. "Stay here with you guys?" she asked.

Kris nodded. "You can call them right from my cell. They can come pick you up and until then, we'd keep you safe."

"That's...thank you," she said. And it occurred to her that she could reach her parents from Kris's phone, right here in this room. But she didn't want to ask. While Barker lived, she knew what the answer would be. In fact, if Melanie detailed any of this discussion to Barker later, would he feel threatened? Would he hurt Kris? The children flashed through Melanie's mind. They needed their guardian. And besides, Kris had been aggressive and rigid, but kind. Melanie owed her.

"Are the kids okay?" Melanie asked, taking an interest. Her mother taught her to invest in anyone who has invested in you.

Kris rubbed her face, yawning. "I hope. All of this has been a little bit intense. We don't want to tell them too much, but they live in a dangerous place. We can leave out certain gruesome details, but we can't hide the reality of the danger from them." She paused, staring at the ground. "They're okay. They're tough. The girls are entertaining them right now. Keeping their minds off things."

"Good," Melanie said. "I'm glad."

Kris sat back, getting comfortable. "Nice of you to ask," she said, frankly. "If I were you I wouldn't give a flying fuck about anyone else."

Melanie adjusted herself, folding her arms over her knees. "I didn't. Up until now. I just appreciate you looking out for me and...I hope you and the rest of them make out okay." Kris smiled at her, lightly clapping her hands together like she was bored.

"Quite of few of them have asked about you. Since the first time we all met."

"Really?" Melanie asked.

"Yep. Dom has a lot of sympathy for you, even though he looks and acts like a big drone. He said, 'So we're just gonna let that one suffer and die, huh? Go team.' I had to agree with him but, well, Barker is in charge. Peter and few of the others seemed uncomfortable too." She flashed Melanie a grin. "And in case you didn't notice, Adam has a little crush on you."

"He does?" she said, starting to blush.

Kris grinned. "Yeah. He's a cutie pie, most of the time. But he'll never say anything, not while you belong to someone else."

The way Kris phrased it made Melanie's chest drop. She fought back tears, at a loss for words. Kris saw her face and gasped.

"Hey, sorry. I didn't mean to."

"It's okay," Melanie said. "Can we not talk about him?"

"Sure thing," Kris said.

For a moment both girls were silent.

"How did you end up taking care of them?" Melanie asked, breaking the tension.

Kris crossed her fingers together and looked up. "A little over a year go, this wasn't Ghost Town. It was all part of New Heim. This was the shitty part of town, sure, but there were people living in it. I lived here with my mom, dad, and little brother."

"Okay," Melanie said.

Kris nodded. "Things were always tense between my family and I. I wasn't the best student. Rocked it in gym class. Sucked in everything else. They always wanted me to do better. Do better. I just didn't care. And then when I came out, well...things were bad after that."

"Oh," Melanie said. She hadn't guessed that Kris was gay. For some reason she'd thought she'd sensed chemistry between Kris and Dom. But maybe that was just a close relationship, taking on the care of a family together. Siblings.

"I'm sorry to hear that," Melanie said. "Sometimes people just don't understand...things." Way to sound like an idiot, Melanie.

Kris scoffed. "Especially people our age. I got in a lot of fights. And that only made my reputation at home worse. So...one night..." Kris was gone, just like Barker. Her eyes told Melanie she'd gone somewhere else. Melanie didn't know whether to put a hand on her shoulder or to say something comforting. So she stayed still.

Kris went on, "I started sneaking out of the house all the time." Her eyes were wide and dazed now. "Standard dysfunctional family," she said in a half whisper. "And then one night..."

Kris stood up and walked two steps forward. At first Melanie thought it was a lame dramatic gesture. Then she realized Kris was struggling not to cry.

"One night I ran off with some girl. Didn't love her. She didn't love me. But both of us wanted out and away from our families. Oh, God, she was smokin'. Hottest damn girl I'd ever seen. So we were in the business district at this restaurant I really loved...and then a jet flew over the city."

That was all Melanie needed to hear for the weight to fall on her chest. "I'm so sorry."

It was like Kris was speaking at her own funeral. "They killed everyone. Mom. Dad. Most of my teachers. All of the gym teachers. This girl I used to hate. Some guys I was friendly with. Two girls I liked." A tear fell from her eye. "My little brother."

Melanie couldn't find words. She just looked at Kris, almost about to cry herself.

Kris moped like a child, but her voice was grim, detached, and profoundly clear, as if she were documenting the Holocaust. "You know the most frightening part was how many of them I knew. It didn't matter if I liked them or not...You hear about people dying in the news all the time. And they're just stories to you. Far from home. But this. It happened right at home and I knew so many of those names."

Melanie was the opposite. She was the one who heard about the bombing on the news. Melanie had no faces to apply, but standing before her was someone who'd lost a part of herself in this fiasco.

"When I think about my little brother..." Kris was smiling now. "Playing his video games, running around in circles, digging for groundwater in the backyard or whatever weird crap he used to do." The smile faded like water smearing on a window. "And then a bomb falls out of the sky." Her voice broke and she turned away. Melanie knew she was crying and guessed that she wouldn't let it happen for much longer. But she stayed on the bed, hugging her knees.

"I'm sorry about your family. I wish I could change what happened," Melanie said. Kris sniffed modestly, back still facing Melanie. She wiped her face quickly.

Melanie broke the silence. "So after that you guys all came together?"

Kris folded her arms. "Started with Dom." She sniffed. "In the weeks that followed, emergency services ran through the district before they pulled out and labeled it restricted." She turned to face Melanie. "Overtime it became Ghost Town. I snuck in to see what was left of my house, and I found Dom. He had a broken arm and he hid from the paramedics and cops 'cause he was wanted for aggravated assault. So I treated him."

Aggravated assault? Fantastic. "You could treat him? Did you learn that in school?"

Kris had sat back down now. "No I learned on the spot."

"Oh."

"I gave him a scar in the process. I don't think he's ever gotten over it."

Melanie laughed at that, and she was happy to hear Kris laugh too.

"And the others?" Melanie asked.

"They trickled in from different places. Homelessness is a thing in this city, it turns out."

"Well it's really great of you to take care of them. I'm sure they'll never forget you."

Kris gave her a quaint grin. "I'm not dead yet, Mel."

"I didn't mean that," she said.

Kris chuckled and came over, brushing her hair. "Anyway, thanks for listening. Get some rest."

"Okay," Melanie said.

And of course, Kris's knife came out. "This stays between us." Her voice was the same that Melanie was accustomed to. Fierce, guarded, afraid for her life.

Melanie nodded, and Kris left the room.

This was by far the strangest girl Melanie had ever met. And yet there was something attractive about her. Admirable. Likeable. She was holding Melanie prisoner, but Melanie liked her. She really did feel for her. And from the way Kris talked, it sounded like those feelings were returned.

Chapter 20

Gossip

For the next twenty-four hours, Tom did not stop moving.

A series of incidents erupted throughout the city. Phone calls came to the station all day regarding armed men walking the streets. As public panic ensued in normally safe areas, Ed Ryan called all units into action. Now the station was mobbed and Tom was working a special patrol shift. He would get one break in twelve hours, and that was when he would phone Albert Ferris. It was clear to Tom that any and all of these phone calls had to do with Allen Marx's assassins. Ed Ryan probably knew it as well. There was no other man in the city with the connections and finances to hire that kind of force, and since they all knew Barker was back, anyone could speculate the cause.

Tom and Beckett had only seen three. The Chief had already declared Allen Marx as the suspect behind the first incident. However, as they had yet to apprehend any of the gunmen, there was no proof. The lawyers and attorneys were watching like hawks, waiting for the Chief to grab some semblance of proof to put Allen away. Tom and Beckett were sent to patrol the western most district of New Heim along with three other teams. The rest were sent to the North East. Every cop in the city was on duty. No one had caught them yet.

A thought sat in Tom's mind like a rock: the memory of the life he took the previous night. His mind wandered from this to the other thing, but that incident was engraved there. Explaining his perception of the situation to his superiors had been fun. Of course he'd had to withhold what he knew about the Marx Family, withhold any indication that he had been to see Allen. Tom explained that he had shot at center mass, and that the suspect had been unharmed, prompting him to use deadly force.

Their answer? Get on patrol. Well that was good news.

At the moment, Tom and his partner were patrolling the area surrounding New Heim Inner City High School. The building was two stories, different shades of brown and blue spattered across the many wings and halls. Passing the school, they veered East into a long road divided by columns of green clipped grass. Short trees and armies of bushes lined up between the two streets, adding flavor to the bright environment. In fact it was bright (houses ranging from yellow to sky blue) that it was starting to hurt his eyes. A large number of rich inhabitants took refuge here, sticking their heads in the sand, thus making it a decidedly safe neighborhood.

Tom calmly took in the surrounding area, eyes focused along the sidewalks in case any of their suspects emerged. He realized during this trip that he was a rather quiet human being, because his partner simply refused to stop talking.

"An elderly couple uptown saw two men holding guns," Beckett was saying. "Those men vanished. A businessman from the top of his office spotted a man concealing a gun running by. Four bikers saw a couple more. So what's that? About eight men sighted? There's got to be more. After what we saw, we know that bastard Allen Marx is behind it. The problem is, we can't link the men we found to him. As far as the Government knows, they were just three pissed off dickheads with guns."

Tom passed four green pillars, really quite beautiful. But even this safe part of town, especially this part of town, might be concealing whatever operation Marx was running. As Tom contemplated, Beckett was still going.

"But my real question..." he said with a dull but recognizable exaggeration. "...is how did this all start? Particularly, what night did Barker actually arrive back, and what brought him back?"

"Who knows?" Tom said. "If he didn't tear apart handcuffs and knock down prison bars, maybe we would be able to question him."

"Bizarre," Beckett said. "Must be some drug that guy is on."

"I wish," Tom spat out.

"What?" Beckett said.

"Never mind," Tom said. We need to hire a real executioner, Allen. Or Barker will kill us all.

Beckett's cell phone went off. "Yeah?" He waited for a moment, and then his face twisted into a gasp. "No."

"What?" Tom asked. "Who are you talking to?"

Beckett looked over at him. "It's Colton. He's got news."

"What news?" Tom said.

"William Marx is dead."

Tom wanted to stop the car and gawk. "William? Allen's uncle?" The smug, stretched face peered at him from the darkness. "How?"

"How did he die?" Beckett asked into the phone. As he listened Tom saw him grimace and stick out his tongue. "Shit."

Barker's doing, whatever it was, Tom thought.

Beckett hung up the phone. "Station's going to be a riot all night long."

"Or a battlefield," Tom said. After receiving a sideways glance from Beckett, he added, "Let's hope for the best."

For the rest of the day, Tom and Beckett patrolled the garden like district of New Heim, but none of the vermin revealed themselves.

They returned to the station close to evening. At this point, Tom could hardly get a cup of coffee without squeezing through two other people.

"What is this? Disneyland?" he asked aloud.

Around the corner, straight into the Chief's office, at the front desk, in the break room, different people were huddled into groups, chattering and trading theories. Every three seconds in some part of the room, Tom heard the ringing of telephones. More officers were walking in and more were clearing out, going on patrol. Everyone was gossiping. Apparently, William Marx had been found with each of his limbs removed. His face was untouched. There was no symbolic defamation or any message for the police. No, he simply bled out four different holes.

More had happened since then as well. At least ten different gunmen had emerged into the streets, chasing a single man people believed to be Barker. The upped the number of guns spotted in the streets, and no one had been apprehended. Tom knew this situation was one step away from a crisis. No one had been shot yet, or else the squads would already be out.

Tom searched the crowd for Beckett. He found his partner engaged in a thorough discussion with the man who had called them on the phone, Bryan Colton. He had blonde hair and blue eyes, the younger brother of a retired cop who'd once been hailed a hero: John Colton, partner to Stanley Jackson.

Colton was saying, "He'll continue knocking the Marx's off as this goes on."

"Damn," Beckett said. "What do you think Ryan will do?"

"Ryan will do backflips, that's what," Colton said. These men seemed to believe that Ed Ryan would love for Barker to remove the crime family. They seemed to think the man liked being in Barker's service. Tom wagered the Chief was more hopeful that the mob would kill Barker.

Someone tapped Tom's arm and he turned to find the secretary. Her short figure forced Tom to bend his neck and her bright green eyes, hidden behind black-framed glasses, shined in his face.

"Yes?" Tom said.

"The Chief wants a word." Then she scurried off.

Tom groaned as he walked around the corner, into the back hall (cutting through four different people on his way).

Tom stepped into the dark office, the Chief's brilliant, wide desk resting before him. Ed Ryan was tapping his fingers on the table, seeming apprehensive.

"Tom," he said with feigned enthusiasm. "Close the door." Tom obeyed, and the noise from the hallway died out. The two men were alone, and Ryan's eyes drilled into him, same as the secretary's. Ryan said, "I'm about to give a speech to all units. S.W.A.T. is on their way."

"That bad, huh?" Tom said, and Ryan nodded.

"Just in case. That's not why I called you in here."

"Okay," Tom said.

The Chief sat back. "Barker has been sighted. He's roaming the streets. A woman called in and gave a full description matching his. She says that he seems injured, that she saw him limping."

Limping? Justin Barker? Tom felt a burst of energy, though he remained composed. It was exciting to think about. Was Allen smarter than Tom thought? Could he win?

The Chief continued, "An officer will be sent to interview the witness, but that's all. I hope you're not thinking of going out there and doing something stupid."

"Of course not, sir." It was no lie. Tom may have wanted to kill Barker. Tom may have wanted to rescue Melanie Grier. But if the force was mobilizing, Tom wasn't going to abandon his fellow officers, even if half of them were scum.

The Chief was nodding his head. "Good. Let's go." He rose abruptly from the desk, standing two feet higher than Tom, and together they walked out into the lobby. At the sight of Ed Ryan, the gossip instantly started to diminish.

"Listen up, all of you," he said, his voice loud and articulate. "I just got off the phone with Director Ludovich of the SWAT Division. We don't know yet what these people want. Safe to assume Barker, but no proof as of yet. If their target surfaces again, we're expecting a full scale riot. I'll need you all on alert depending on how the situation escalates." He turned in place, addressing some people to his rear. "We will not allow any innocent civilians to die tonight. Is that clear?"

"Sir, yes sir!" they all sang, even Tom.

Ryan nodded. "Good."

The secretary suddenly ran up to Ryan, and he looked down at her, perplexed. She motioned for him to lean down and whispered something in his ear. The Chief's eyes went wide. "Son of a bitch." He then addressed the room. "It appears we have another dead Marx."

The room flew into whispers and canters again, while Tom's gut clenched. He's doing it. He's knocking them off.

As the station caved in on itself once more, Tom realized that it was his turn to go on break.

It took a lot for Tom to get drunk, so one bottle wouldn't do a thing. He'd still be able to perform if he was called. He stood in his apartment, too anxious to sit down. The best thing to do was continue to do his job, let S.W.A.T. take out the gunmen if they emerged. Maybe the Marx's and Barker would all be dead by the end of this. The crime family would be buried, along with any and all knowledge of Tom's wrong doings. The girl would be free. They would all be safe. This would all be over.

Tom downed the beer, feeling its weight on his throat and then chest. He exhaled deeply, wiping his lips, looking around at all of his trophies and photos, giving his eyes and brain something to do.

At 8:00 P. M., his walkie came to life.

He clicked it. "Go ahead."

"All units report. Thirty armed men spotted converging on Main Street. All units report."

It was happening. Barker had drawn them out.

Tom set down the drink and got in uniform. He strapped on his holsters. Stretched his muscles. Armed himself. Went out the front door.

Two guns greeted him, directly in his face. Albert stood behind the hit men.

"What's your hurry, Macklin?" he asked with a gratuitous grin.

Chapter 21

Broken Glass

This time when Tom was brought to Marx Manor, it was with a bag over his head and a gun resting on his shoulder. When the door opened they yanked him out and took off the bag. He stood before the iron gates, and heard something in the distance. His vision was blocked by a long chain of buildings, but he could hear police sirens wailing, gunshots rattling, and faintly he could hear the screams of civilians. Right now, just over on Main Street, a battle was taking place.

"Hear that?" Ferris said.

"Of course I hear it," Tom said. The hit man gripped Tom's shoulder, pointing Tom's own gun at his temple. If Tom moved an inch out of turn, he would be dead. His walkie had been left in his apartment.

Ferris said, "Barker's handiwork. Our men chased him all over the city, but he just kept picking them off. You know what that bastard did? He walked right through Main Street and then stood in the middle of the street. Then he knelt down, like he was in too much pain to move." He rubbed the sweat off his head. "Allen ordered them to go all in when Barker stopped moving, so that's what they did."

He walked over and tapped Tom on the chin, roughly. Tom recoiled but the gunman held him.

Ferris said, "Barker warped away, like he does. And the S.W.A.T. team was there. You know anything about that Tom?"

There was a loud noise and the hit men pulled Tom to his knees. A helicopter flew by overhead, toward Main Street.

"Of course not," Tom said. "I'm on your side in this."

Ferris nodded, lips bent. "Well, Allen thinks you do. Not gonna lie, Tom. This might be the end of your life." He raised his palms. "Out of my hands." They pulled him to his feet.

"Albert, please. If I could just get one word in—"

The other hit man pounded Tom's stomach, sucking all of the air out of him. When the moment passed, Tom exhaled deeply. Still neither of them spoke, the message vividly clear.

"Let's go," Albert said. And the gates roared, sliding left and right.

This time the back room was empty, save for one man. And the man was disheveled, neat hair mussed and tie slightly loosened. He didn't carry himself straight and tall. He was pacing. Then leaning on the desk. Then drinking. Finally, he saw Tom and the others.

"Who's here? Huh?" His small, intense eyes made Tom feel like targets had been painted on his chest. Allen smiled wide, looking like a crazed monkey. "Tom…Tom."

"Allen, what happened?" Tom said.

The monkey's smile widened. "What. Happened?" Tom realized with a chill that Allen had a gun in his hand. "I'll tell you what happened. You fucking pigs fucked with the wrong guy."

Say the right words. Tom put up his hands. "Allen I had nothing to do with this. I offered you a partnership against Barker. Barker is the one killing your men."

The glass left Allen's hand, smashing against the side of Tom's head. He felt the glass tear into his skin as the shards sprinkled on the carpet. His head was searing now and he was on his knees, beneath Allen.

"My men?" the mob boss howled. "He killed my family! My uncles. My brother. God damn it!"

Tom staggered on his knees as he gripped his throbbing head. Behind him, Albert and the hit men guarded the entrance to the room.

"I want Barker dead," Tom pleaded. "Why would I cross you?"

"Because I said no," Allen said. He had everything in the world figured out. Who was Tom to argue? Tom wiped the top of his eye, blood caking his fingers.

"Barker, played us all. I swear." He rose slowly, aware of the guns to his back. Allen motioned for him to stay on the ground, by pointing the gun at his head, so Tom stayed on his knees. "Now, more than ever, you have to consider my offer."

"Last night," Allen cut in. "Three of my men were killed. You know anything about that?"

"Yes," Tom said. "They shot at me first, I was on patrol."

"You shot my men?" Allen said, finger on the trigger.

"My partner killed one of them. Barker killed the other. The third took his own life in the holding cell. Shoved his own hand down his throat."

Allen tried to stifle his laugh. He was halfway to shitfaced. "And how do you know these things? Huh? You seem to know a lot."

"The wound on the third man's neck looked an awful lot like something Barker would do."

Allen folded his lips, still holding the gun up. At that moment, Tom heard police sirens outside. They had to have been on the street, outside the mansion.

"Go take care of it," Allen said. Ferris and the other hit men got up and left the room. Tom and Allen were alone now.

"You stay right there," Allen said.

Tom looked up at Allen from where he was crouched. Tom remembered how short he seemed when they all stood together, but now he looked tall. Allen must have liked that. That's why he had Tom forced to sit down when he first arrived, why he had him on his knees now. It was so true of Allen and his family that despite all of the riches and influence they possessed, here in New Heim they still spent all of their time looking up: at the Government, at the Sect Family, at Barker. That last one had to have been the hardest blow of all. Crouching in fear of a petty, vile man who, in Allen's eyes, had no right to such power.

"Allen," Tom said softly. "He's out there, now. And I can help you. I promise." The gun lined up with the space between Tom's eyes. Allen's teeth were pressed together.

"You can't even help yourself. I don't know why I ever let you in my house."

This pathetic, short man was going to be the end of Tom. The papers wouldn't mention that, because the papers wouldn't say anything. But Allen would remember. And he'd drink to ending Tom's life for the next twenty years.

"You know about them," he said. "You said you already knew what I was planning."

"Yes I know about the Meridian, or whatever it's called," Allen said.

"If you're going to kill me, would you at least tell me what you know," Tom said.

Allen snorted. "Sure! Why not? The Meridian is some place in Montana. People with strange abilities live there, and they are supposedly part of a mercenary organization."

Tom nodded. So far, Allen had gotten just one detail wrong.

Allen went on, lowering the gun and staggering in place. "Rumor has it, they're incredible. They can bust through walls, knock down trees, hurl cars through the air. Crush little punks like you with one hand." He pointed the gun back at him. "Problem is, the director of the organization is, shall we say, particular about whom he selects."

"He'll select me," Tom said. "He has an obligation." Tom watched as the gun lowered. Slowly, Tom rose to his feet again, beholding the mobster as the ant he was. There was a strange look on Allen's face, a mixture of skepticism and greed.

"What obligation?" he said.

"Stan," Tom said. "He denied Stan, and now Stan is dead because of him."

Tom's eyebrows went up and he looked at his own gun like he was about to laugh. "Yeah, that's an obligation. Was your plan always this stupid, or are you just cracking under pressure? Be honest." Allen's habit of pointing that gun in Tom's face was growing intolerable.

Tom said, "I'm told this man, this organization's director, is a man of principal. One has died already from his neglect, and here we are, suffering. Stan also didn't have half the funds that you do. If we work together, we can make this work. I know we can."

Allen frowned. "That's adorable, Macklin."

Tom had his hands up now. "With your help, I can kill Justin Barker. No mess, no fuss, not witnesses. A paid assassin sworn to silence. And I'll put all the money back in your pocket. I swear."

"Well here's what you're going to do first." Allen took a step forward, staggering once. "You're going to go back to your little station and figure out which of my men have been taken into custody. You're going to offer my men some deals." He waved the gun around. "You're going to help me get them out of the system."

Of course. "Fine. Okay."

"And then you're going to kill Ed Ryan."

"What?" This was going wrong.

Over on Allen's desk, his phone started buzzing. Allen ignored it.

"You heard me, Tom. You're going to kill that old bastard, and make it look like an accident. I'll protect you, kid." He was walking towards Tom now. "Sound good, boy?" He shoved the barrel close to Tom's face.

"I can't kill my boss," Tom said.

"Can't you!" Allen yelled.

The phone started buzzing again. Loud, dancing on the desk. And there was another noise. It sounded like it came from somewhere distant inside the house. Upstairs?

"Allen, did you hear that?" Tom said.

"Hear what?" Allen said, in disbelief.

"That sounded like glass breaking," Tom warned.

"Where?" Allen said.

The phone started buzzing again, jumping up and down on the table. Allen's eyes darted from Tom to the phone, to the direction of the noise. In that moment of distraction, Tom took action. He grabbed Allen's arm and pushed his elbow upward. Allen dropped the gun with a loud scream and Tom caught it, quickly emptying its contents.

"You little shit!" Allen yelled, but Tom's focus was upstairs.

"Whoever you are you gave yourself away!" he yelled. "Give it up! Get out while you can!" It was worth a shot, but if the man upstairs was Justin Barker, there was little Tom could do.

Footsteps grumbled up the hallway, and Tom prepared himself for the worst, Allen standing behind him. But it was Ferris and his men.

"Let's go, Allen," Ferris commanded.

"What the hell is going on?" Allen said. But Ferris already had him under the arm, pulling him toward the front. Ferris's sudden boldness surprised Tom so much that he was ill prepared when an alarm started blaring in their ears. It must have been going off throughout the house, and if you were stupid or slow, the raging volume of this sound would alert you that you were in serious danger. Ferris pointed toward the sound of the glass and one of the hit men ran off in that direction, gun pointed. Tom followed Ferris and Allen out toward the front door. He shouted to Ferris, asking to know what he knew, but the alarms drowned him out.

"Shit, shit, shit," Tom heard Allen yelling. "Oh, shit. Oh, Jesus Christ."

In moments they doors flew open and they ran out into the darkness. Ears still buzzing, Tom tried to pop them, and the wound on his head was irritated. Inside, the alarms still went loud, but nothing, no one, had pursued them outside. The gates were opening, the same loud screeches muffling the distant sounds of carnage out in the city. The battle was either dying down, or moving farther North into the city. Fortunately for Tom, none of his colleagues would come wondering about Allen's alarms, with their hands so full elsewhere. His secret was safe but what about his life?

"What the fuck is going on?" Allen demanded of Ferris. "Where are my guards?"

"Calm down, Allen," Ferris said.

Tom looked up. There was a man standing on the roof.

"Ferris!" Tom yelled, pointing up.

As Tom, Ferris, Allen, and five hit men behind them looked up, the figure leapt and cloaked himself in the night sky. The assassins fired and Tom ducked for cover. He saw something small falling out of the sky, and as it hit the ground, Tom's instincts saved his life. He ran as far as he could, before the explosion threw him into the air and deafened him further. Orange light blinded him and he hit the ground rolling. The explosion had been small. His ears were ringing and he had trouble standing. The last time he'd been this dizzy lying down it had been after a night of heavy drinking. He tried to push himself up despite the nausea.

When he turned himself vertical, he saw the hit men were in a craze. Three of them were missing, probably caught in the explosion. The two remaining hit men had abandoned their guns, now that Barker was in close quarters. They drew knives and started swinging.

Elegantly, the hit men slid their blades through the air, but like an acrobat, Barker swayed right and left, avoiding each and every strike. It was like he could read their minds. One of the hit men lunged forward, trying to tackle him. Barker parried the knife and withstood the impact. He squeezed the man's wrist and the man let out a loud cry. Then Barker picked the knife off him and swiped it across his throat, nicking the other hit man in the chin. The first fell, and the second followed, when Barker shoved the knife through his face.

All the while Ferris had been recovering from the explosion, covered in soot, trying to find Allen. He pulled the mobster to his feet, clearly trying to get him to safety. But there were no guards. Barker parted the men, both of whom were apparently unarmed.

Everything had stopped spinning now, and Tom could easily get to his feet. Barker turned his head in Tom's direction, and for the first time their eyes met. Barker looked like a homeless man. His black beard was thick, his black hair mangy, and his face was filthy, covered in dirt. He was also covered in dry blood. But through that mess, Tom saw distinct brownish yellow eyes. They were the kind of eyes you could pick out of a crowd, a slightly different shade than Tom was ever used to seeing.

Barker looked back at Allen and Ferris, but said nothing. Allen was trembling, and Ferris's eyes were wide, his face devoid of any other emotion.

Tires screeched. Doors flew open and voices sounded.

Orson Marx and ten more men charged into the courtyard. They didn't fire for fear of killing Allen. They meant to threaten. Barker threw Ferris to the ground and took Allen hostage, holding his arms behind his back. The mob boss wailed, and Tom couldn't help noticing how pathetic he looked now. Barker was smiling, chuckling, and Tom could see that every story was true. This was a man who killed for pleasure alone.

"Let him go," Orson said in his deep, thick voice.

"You want me to let him go, Orson?" Barker said.

Tom had never heard his voice before. It was not deep, but it wasn't high pitched. It was somewhere in the middle, with a low, almost seductive hymn to its tone. As Tom observed, everything went to shit.

Barker threw Allen down and vanished. The hit men raised their guns and fired, assuming he had taken flight. Tom saw Barker on top of the gates again, and the hit men turned. Barker jumped back to the roof, and they followed. Finally, after the hit men had scattered and shuffled, Barker returned to the ground, and slid around like a roller skater.

Tom had never seen anything like this. Barker ran at an inhuman speed, keeping his body low. As the hit men tried to aim, he ran up to several of them and sliced through their torsos. Blood spewed into the sky and the surviving hit men shuffled and got into a new formation. Orson ran to his cousin, a giant in comparison. He led Allen back into the house, and Ferris followed. They would escape out the back while Barker was preoccupied.

Tom wanted to avoid going into the battle, so he took steps toward the gates. He was slow, making sure not to get to close to the carnage. Barker was just sliding around, avoiding every bullet, and striking when he could.

When Tom was almost to the gate, he got close to one of the corpses. A gun lay next to the body. Tom grabbed it quickly and felt that it was loaded. He aimed at the quarreling group.

A few of the hit men were still up, probably only because Barker was getting dizzy. But still he was able to avoid being struck. There were four men left: one in front of Barker, one behind, one to his right and another to his left. Barker through his knife backwards, burying it in the man to his rear. He then lunged forward and started to disarm the gunman. Two of the hit men fired and so did Tom. He wasn't sure if it was his bullet or one of theirs, but the victim was the hit man, not Barker.

Then there was silence. Tom and the last two men were staring around the courtyard, looking for their prey.

"Shoot that motherfucker," he heard. He turned to find a gun pointed at him. He started, heart jumping. And then blood exploded out of both men's throats, and they crashed to the ground. Tom didn't know if Barker saw him or not, but the killer raced at high speeds into the house, where screaming ensued.

There was nothing Tom could do for Allen Marx. And honestly, the man hardly deserved to live.

The gates behind him were wide open, and Tom Macklin ran.

***

A fun and thrilling game this had been, but as Barker dropped Allen Marx to his knees, he knew the game was ending.

Orson had tried to take his cousin out the back, but Barker got to them in the backyard, flooring both Orson and Ferris. Oh how Allen had squealed. Now the two of them were alone in a dark alley, about four blocks up from Allen's mansion. He could have killed Allen back at the house, but he wanted to leave him in a dark alley, where some bozo might find him. Still, he needed to stop soon. All of that running around had drained him.

He clutched his side, where the pain was still severe. He'd lost blood digging out the bullet, but that was where the blood loss had ended. It was something for which Barker had pride he could not articulate. The only phrase he could think of was that he was simply, perfect, and that sounded asinine. Every now and then the pain spasms threatened to throw him off balance, but he took it, same as everything else.

Allen pulled himself out of the puddle he'd been dropped in, spitting and gasping, covered in filth. Barker needed to savor this moment. Allen was one of his longest standing foes, and this was the end. He looked around the ally. There were no lights. It was pitch black. The brick might have been black, the ground might have been covered in black gravel, and the sky was pitch black. Save for the moon.

Allen was on his feet now, stumbling backwards. He looked like a dog, mouth agape, trembling, breathing heavily and fast.

"You...you stay away...away!" Allen screamed. He presented his fist as if he still had a weapon. Barker took two steps forward, and relished the fact that Allen refused to run. He knew Barker would catch him, and that was the best part. They all knew.

"Almost, Allen. You almost got me."

"Get away!" Allen's eyes scanned the area, and the word "help" was forming on his lips.

"Is that all you have to say?" Barker asked.

"Get back, you sick, demented piece of shit. You're nothing compared to me! You hear me? Nothing! Now get away. Before something terrible happens to you!" He sounded like he was about to cry.

Barker giggled. "Do you know what I'm most proud of, Allen? Some parting words for you."

Allen kept staggering backwards. They were traversing the entire alley. "Stop," Allen said. "Please."

Barker took a deep breath. "I was lying in an alley not so different from this, with a bullet in me and blood dripping out. I dug out the bullet and went in search of fire. I found it." He remembered the little sting, and the orange light, and how quickly it all vanished. "And as the flame closed my skin, I could barely even feel it. It's the weirdest thing. But I like playing with fire, Allen." He laughed out loud.

"Help me!" Allen wailed. "Someone, help!"

Barker jumped forward. He knew the nerve's location by heart, and slid the knife through before Allen could even move. Then he watched, mesmerized, as Allen convulsed, staggered, and swayed. Blocks of blood spurted from his throat, the entire vein shredded. As he gasped for air he clutched his throat, beginning to lose balance. Barker could see the lights already leaving his eyes as he hit the ground. In his last few moments, Allen was still gurgling the blood, trying to talk. Barker smiled. The man had loved to talk, but he never would again.

Chapter 22

New Game

B arker missed Melanie. He wondered if Kris was taking good care of her, and he needed to get back to her. But first he needed to deal with all of these dead Marx's. The battle was over, but he needed a new arrangement going forward. Orson and Ferris were hopefully still back at Allen's mansion. If they were, it would be a simple matter. Barker had done this a million times.

Get in. Disarm. Smile. Make it very clear how unafraid you are. And like magic, they break down.

They were still there. In the backyard of the mansion, concealed by darkness, Barker watched through the large windows as Ferris and Orson argued.

"I want the boy!" Orson was screaming.

"Orson, calm down," Ferris ordered, tapping the air with his hands.

"Fuck you," the deep voiced soldier growled. "I don't take orders from you."

"You ought to," said Ferris. "You're a fucking mess. Listen, we'll find Allen."

Barker almost laughed out loud.

"Fuck you, Ferris. Don't patronize me. We both know my cousin is dead."

"And this ain't helping." Ferris took a few steps back, as Barker drew nearer to the backdoor. "Besides that, I'm pretty sure the kid is innocent."

Orson slammed the wall, creating a tiny crack. Barker admired his strength. He was at the back door now.

Orson said, "Then why did he run?"

Barker cleared his throat, and while Ferris froze, Orson was quick to act.

The first thing Barker did was lunge into the room, knocking Orson to the floor before he could squeeze the trigger. Then he was on top of the giant, holding him down. For a moment they stared into one another's faces. Orson's was tightened with aggression; Barker loved that about him. He quickly disarmed Orson and pointed the gun around the room. He hated using guns, but it was a quick way to gain a captive audience.

He turned and pointed his gun at Ferris's face. The accountant's chin quivered but his brows stayed down, like a bull. Ferris hardly ever dropped his game face. Barker respected that, and responded with his own: a wide twist of the lips.

"Give me your gun, Albert."

"I don't have a gun," Ferris said, without moving.

Orson was on his feet now, looming over Barker. To Barker's amusement, Orson had refrained from charging him.

"You," he growled.

Barker bent his arm up to point the gun at Orson's chin, but kept his eyes on Ferris. "Orson. I haven't seen you since you created Ghost Town for me."

Orson scoffed in reply, but remained still, wary of the gun. Barker looked around the room. The couch was overturned where he and Orson had briefly fought, but Allen's office was untouched, like nothing ever happened. Barker eyed the highly populated bookshelf, and wondered if it was worth browsing.

"Where is Allen?" Orson demanded. Barker ignored him. Albert was still standing stiff, playing dumb.

"Albert, if I have to ask again, I'll start with your youngest."

Ferris lifted his chin and inhaled, eyes twitching, lips curling down. Then he relented, and revealed a gun in his jacket pocket.

"Discharge it," Barker said.

Ferris took the bottom out of the weapon and the bullets fell to the ground like rain. Then he dropped the weapon on the floor, near Barker's feet.

"Testy," Barker said. "Anything else on you?" Ferris shook his head.

"Where is Allen?" Orson repeated.

"Get out, Albert," Barker said. "I want a moment alone with Orson."

Ferris turned and walked out of the room, like a sulking child. Barker spun in place and unbent his arm, taking steps back from Orson. They were now in a Western standoff, only Barker was the only one armed. Orson still looked ready for a fight, his face bold and defiant. How cute.

"Orson," Barker said calmly. "I just want to talk." He put the gun through his belt, pulling his coat over it.

"For the last time. Where is—"

"Dead in some alley. You can go look for him when we're done," Barker said, adjusting his coat.

Orson's face contorted into a grimace that might have broken his teeth, but still he refrained from attacking. Good.

Keep smiling. Game face.

Barker started pacing the room, feeling jittery. "What I want is very simple. I want you to explain to me, in gruesome detail, what happened last night, and all day today. What kind of planning went into it? Who's idea was it? And what was your involvement? After that, you're going to explain to me what happens next." He turned to face Orson and thought he spotted a fast movement. Orson went stiff again, pretending he hadn't tried to attack him. "Careful now, Orson. My patience is a bit thin tonight."

"You want details? Obviously, Barker, we tried to kill you. Again." Orson was bold. Very bold. For a moment Barker considered killing him. Ferris could facilitate Barker's needs. Why keep one giant pain in the ass alive? Still, an adventurous part of him was considering Orson's connections. If Barker ever wanted to have a new experience, he might want access to one of Orson's jets.

"If you don't tell me, in gruesome detail, like I asked, I will cut off your hands."

Then he waited.

After a moment, Orson said, "Last year, Max Sect ordered the airstrike. He made a deal with Allen so he could get me to spearhead the operation, at hardly a penny. I hate you, so I accepted. Awhile later, after the operation failed, you killed Maxwell Sect. After that, Allen sent you a letter. He wrote that the entire Marx Family was threatened into submissions by the Sects, and that he himself forced me into it. He offered you an apology, and cooperation with any of your demands."

"Yes, I remember. Let's skip to the present."

"The letter was Allen's best attempt at a lie. It seemed like you bought it. So after you left for the year, Allen had me start training a special group in prep for your return."

Barker nodded. "Very talented men. I must say. I usually don't have that much trouble."

He felt a spasm, but stayed still. Fuck the pain.

"Well, that's your own damn fault really," Orson said. "You stayed away for an entire year. Didn't keep tabs. We had a perfect window. I kept telling Allen that you were still here, hiding somewhere around the corner, and that we should make nice. After an acceptable amount of time, a year, maybe two, invite you over and..."

"And what? Poison me?" Barker chuckled. "I'd never eat your food, idiot."

Orson nodded. "That's what Allen thought. So we went ahead with the plan, and for an entire year we never heard from you. We plotted the mission for months, figuring you'd stay somewhere in the neighborhood you ultimately picked."

Barker had commanded Kris to keep an eye on the Marx Family. She was oh so good at not being seen. Who was to blame? The target or the operative?

Orson said, "Do I need to say the rest? You were there."

"You trained them?" Barker asked.

"All of them."

"How did you know to use tear gas?" Even as Barker asked, the truth struck him like a nail in his shoulder. "Must have been Stanley."

"Correct," Orson said.

Fucking bastard. I hope he can see all of this, wherever he is.

"Now we get to the big question," Barker said. "How many survived?"

"Nine died against SWAT. Three died against the cops. You killed the ten I brought tonight, along with Allen's guards. You picked off about six throughout this past day, and seven are in custody. Three died against the cops. The rest I haven't heard from."

"I did leave about twenty in the streets of Ghost Town."

"Well, there you go," Orson said.

"That's about fifty-eight total," Barker said. "That all of them?"

Orson grunted. "Yes, that was all of them."

"Really?" Barker asked. "No reserves."

"You killed them all," Orson said, putting up his hands. "You won."

Barker mulled it over. He was sure Orson had some spares, in case of emergency. He'd have to keep his eyes open.

Now to deal with the other little rat. "Ferris!" he called. "Get back in here."

Moments later the accountant walked back into the room, a scowl on his face. "Is it my turn to talk yet, Barker?" he asked as he walked over to stand with Orson.

"I suppose," Barker said. "Not sure if I want to listen. I am truly, severely disappointed in you, Albert."

"Anything but that," Albert said.

Defiance. Really? "Have you lost your mind?" Barker asked him.

"No. I'm just pragmatic. You should be too. There's a lot I can still do for you, and I'll do it. Can we skip the threats?"

Barker swallowed a knot in his throat. "I don't like your tone," he said. That was all. Orson was eyeing Ferris with confusion etched on his face.

"Do you have anything to add to Orson's story?" Barker asked. "Or can we move on?"

"He told you everything," Ferris said.

"What do you mean still?" Orson asked.

The room quieted, and Barker was interested to see where this would go.

"What?" Albert asked.

Orson turned to face Albert directly, shoulder facing Barker. "You said, there's still things you could do for him." He pointed at Barker with his thumb. "What do you mean by 'still'?" Orson's tone was that of a beast about to attack, deep and slow. It occurred to Barker that if he wanted to use Ferris for anything else, he might actually have to step between them.

"Slip of the tongue," Albert said. "Stressful situation."

"Wrong answer," Orson said.

"Go on and tell him, Albert," Barker said.

Ferris was backed into a corner, and he looked down with his face puffing up. "You tell him," he told Barker.

Orson's eyes darted between them.

"No," Barker said. "You will tell him, Albert." Barker loved the idea of hearing the truth crawl from Albert's own mouth, as he fought to keep them back from the giant standing beside him. Albert didn't like it half as much, as he glared at Barker, sucking in some extra oxygen. After a second deep breath, Albert gave in. He put his hands up to Orson.

"I have my own bank account. And a separate account I used to launder Allen's money. Years ago I did the same for Maxwell Sect."

"Yes," Orson growled, fists clenched.

Albert stepped back, keeping his dignity, but the next words were forced. "I have a another account." He pointed at Barker. "For him."

The tank of a man slammed his fist into Ferris's face and the accountant crashed to the floor. When Orson moved toward him and raised his foot, Barker drew his knife. He stabbed through meat and bone, puncturing Orson's knee. When he withdrew the knife blood popped out along with a painful howl. Orson hit the ground, shaking the room. So Barker took out his other knee as well.

"Quiet, Orson. Get up, Albert." He helped Ferris to his feet as Orson's wails turned to stifling grunts. Ferris wiped some blood off his clothing and took small, inaudible breaths, calming himself.

"For the record, Barker. Your funds are fine."

"Are they now?" Barker laughed.

"Yes," Ferris said. "I haven't touched them. And I'm making another deposit tomorrow."

"I guess you have to now that I'm not dead," Barker said with a smile.

The wounded Orson spoke up. "You two faced son of a bitch." His voice was low and restrained. "After all we've done for—"

"Whatever. Get over yourself, Marx," Ferris said, rolling his eyes.

Barker studied Albert's full face and large chin and nose. To Barker, Allen Marx and Albert Ferris were snakes of two different kinds. Allen was a wretched and aggressive bastard, who'd break down into tears as soon as you made him feel defenseless. Albert on the other hand had a bold side to him, grim and gruff in the presence of death. To balance out that one likeable quality, he was a better and more frequent liar than each of the Marx's. Where he daily lied to most people, he very rarely lied to Barker. Rarely was no longer acceptable.

"Yes. Ferris is quite a snake isn't he?" Barker said to Orson. "He handled funds for Sects, currently for the Marx's, and for me all at the same time. Quite a lot of numbers to balance but he's best at what he does, aren't you Albert? But as far as information goes…" Barker took a few steps forward, and cracked his own neck. Albert was stiff as a girl tied to a chair. "With the Sects you told me everything. With Allen Marx, you worked against me. How does that work exactly?" He took out his knife and started playing with it. He let it dance in his fingers and noticed it needed to be cleaned.

"Well," said Ferris. "There was certainly a lot of pressure on my end. With the Sects, I trusted that you were going to kill them in due time. After that, we all thought the airstrike might have scared you away."

"Did you now?"

"You asked me for quite a bit of money after that. I thought you were going away longer than a year. And Allen just took over. What did you expect me to do?"

"You're a feisty little thing, Albert." Much feistier than Melanie, and a lot less pretty.

"The tables have turned, Barker. You've killed Allen and wiped out his cousins, save for this one." He gestured at Orson, cocking his eyebrows. "He's not much without his legs. I'm loyal to the highest bidder. Congratulations, that's you."

"Remember Jack Dawson?" Barker asked, still playing with the knife.

Ferris's mouth fell agape for a moment. He looked chilled. "Yes."

"Who the fuck is Jack Dawson?" Orson growled from the floor.

Ferris turned to him. "The guy who ripped off my account a long time ago. I told you and Allen about it."

"What the fuck's that have to do with any of this?" Orson said, rolling onto his back.

"Poor fool tapped into the funds I had set aside for Barker," Albert said. Then, eyes on Barker, he muttered, "And he found out."

"I did," Barker said, reveling in Ferris's horrified mutters. "I enjoyed Dawson's wife and son, very much."

The room chilled save for Orson's gasps and coughs.

"My legs…"

"You should get that looked at," Barker told him, sheathing his knife. He turned to Ferris. "Are we clear on our roles? I'll make decisions around here." He pointed at Ferris. "You will pay me on a schedule." He pointed at Orson. "You will stay out of my way, and do me favors based on request."

"We're clear," Ferris answered for both of them. But Barker didn't want to hear that.

"Are we clear, Orson?"

"Clear," the giant groaned.

Barker clapped his hands together. "Great!" Then he stared for awhile, letting them ponder what he was going to say next. Ferris's fearful look told him the accountant was reading his mind.

"I'll need a hostage," he said. "Just something to smooth this arrangement over. Albert, you'll bring me your son."

Ferris's eyes went wide, but he didn't say anything.

"Clear?" Barker asked.

A tear fell from Ferris's eye. Barker had seen that before, on Martin Grier's face.

Chapter 23

Settling Down

Melanie waited all day long without a word of news, hoping beyond hope that Barker was dead. During that time she got to see the routine that took place around this house. The gang, mostly the girls, kept the children entertained. Adam's duty was to entertain Melanie, and his choice was magic tricks. She wanted to remind him that she wasn't five years old, but something stopped her. He treated her so nicely, and Kris said he had a crush. If there was one thing Melanie didn't expect to find in this prison it was a boy with a crush. Adam had a deck of playing cards to split up and slip up his sleeves. The first time she'd seen a card trick it was her father, and he botched it. So really, her enthusiasm towards magic was sabotaged early.

Kris never smoked in the house. She would walk out onto the porch. In contrast to the gymnasium, everything seemed more relaxed here. Like vacation. Although Kris walked in and out of the house and in and out of different rooms, Melanie felt the girl's eyes on her. She was always being watched.

Now that sunlight trickled in through the windows, Melanie saw that this house was practically entirely made of wood. There was no carpet on the floor, the walls were mahogany wood, and the space between the stairs and the living room was very small. But through that space, Melanie could see a white stove and oven in the kitchen. They were making dinner, brewing some kind of soup for the little ones, and sandwiches were in the works. Melanie was starving. As she was accustomed to by now, she would eat whatever they put down in front of her.

Melanie was still not aloud to go outside, and the children bombarded her with questions. Where are you from? When did you get here? Do you know about Ghost Town? What's the bump on your head? Did Barker hurt you? What is he like?

Kris had advised Melanie to just say Barker was her protector and theirs. For the most part, the gang kept the kids from "bothering" her, although she didn't mind. She had always liked kids. One of her earliest photo aspirations was to capture children in a playground, under a blue, cloud filled sky. Emily had pointed out to her that she would look like a creep, so she'd better not be seen. Melanie had said many times during her first two years in high school, that although kids could be overwhelming, if you hated them, you were an asshole. They were all children once, and Melanie loved them. In fact, she hated that Barker hadn't set his people up any better than this. Yes, they had a roof, but it was cold in here. The central air didn't work as well as it could, and these were just kids. He was an animal. He didn't actually care. No matter how many bullets he protected her from.

For some reason, at this passing thought, her eyes watered. There were moments, even before her kidnapping, where Melanie felt her eyes growing heavy, but she couldn't pin point what was making her feel that way, just a string of blank but razor edged emotions.

"So photography, huh?" Adam asked her. Melanie came back to reality. Both of them were sitting on the floor, against the wall, arms crossed over knees. Melanie regarded the boy. In the light, he was clearly of Asian descent, with black hair, dark eyes and deeply tanned skin. His voice was incredibly soft, and he was by far the most approachable member of this group. Sitting next to him gave her no start or anxiety, even if he had a gun.

"Yeah," she said. "It's something I've always loved."

Adam nodded his head. "I like movies, myself. Photographers are really important on a film set."

It was Melanie's turn to nod her head. "What movies do you like?"

Adam cracked his neck, a habit that always made her flinch. "I've always loved the Godfather, Citizen Kane, Scarface, James Bond movies," he said. He finished with a laugh. "I know, I'm so interesting."

Melanie laughed. "That's okay. I like a couple of those too."

Adam smiled at her, and Melanie smiled back. She returned her eyes to the floor, finding herself to be a touch more awkward in this situation than she had been in high school.

Are they still looking for me? It's only been a few weeks. Although she missed home, she entertained a vision of Kris and Adam spiriting her away from Barker, forever.

When the sun was down again, Kris approached Melanie.

"He's back."

Her heart dropped. She felt heavier, like she'd seen a glimpse of freedom and it was stripped from her. She should have just knocked Kris out and kept running when she had the chance. Why? Why did she do this to herself?

There was a tension around the group. Most of the children were sitting in the kitchen. The boys sat in the living room, fully armed, and several others were sitting on the stairs. All eyes were on the front door, as there was a polite little knock.

When Kris opened the door, and Barker stepped through, Melanie thought he looked different. Hunched over with his hand on his side. More worn down. He looked around the room with those big yellow eyes and they settled on her.

Melanie shyly put an arm around herself as he approached. As they stood face to face she felt a strange sense of limbo. Melanie was just waiting for whatever would happen next, without coherent thoughts. What happened, was he placed his hand on the back of her head, and gently pulled her into an embrace. He smelled awful, worse than ever, like blood and sewage mixed together. And being this close to him after everything he'd done gave her nothing but dread. And yet, she was thrown by one thing: the gentleness of his touch. For a moment, she actually felt safe in his arms.

"Is it over?" Kris asked.

Barker parted his head and nodded. "Yes." His voice grew louder, projecting. "You've all been terrific…Thank you." When he said it, his voice sounded strained. How easy would it be to escape? Melanie looked at the girls and the children. All of them looked shy, half of them looking away from Barker. Blood spotted his jacket.

"Are they gone?" Melanie asked.

"Hush." He rubbed her shoulder. "It's okay. We're going home."

"Barker," Kris said.

He turned. "What?"

"Are we safe?" she demanded.

"You are safe." He took a breath before continuing. Melanie could tell he didn't want to continue, didn't want any more questions. "There are two remaining, Orson and Ferris." Kris gritted her teeth. "You didn't kill Orson?"

Barker wasn't phased. "No, I did not."

"That son of a bitch killed our Pat! He was thirteen!" The enraged voice had come from the back of the room. It was Danny. The one who'd cried the hardest. All eyes were on him. Barker looked perplexed, and Kris looked stiff.

"Lost one, eh?" Barker said to her.

Kris nodded, and politely asked, "Why didn't you kill him?"

Barker scoffed. "Don't you question me. Everything I do, I do for a reason. You know that." As usual, his scolding was calm and soft voiced. "If it makes you feel any better…" He giggled, phasing out for just a moment. "He's a cripple now."

"Cripple?" Kris said. "Well, I guess that's something."

Barker smirked and turned back to the group. Melanie couldn't stand his long pauses anymore. "They won't be coming back to Ghost Town," he said. "Not unless they're suicidal…which isn't impossible, but don't worry. You're all safe now. Just be smart."

There were some murmurings throughout the room.

"I have some money for you," Barker said to Kris. With an exaggerated, hypocritical grin, he said, "Feed these poor kids." Kris bit her lip and looked at the floor, holding out her hand.

After Barker gave her the money he said again, loud and strained, "If you see any unfamiliar faces in Ghost Town, you tell me immediately. I'll take care of everything. Okay?"

They only continued to stare at him, some nodding their heads. Melanie noticed that Dom had his arms folded, coldly regarding Barker, and Peter looked apprehensive. The girls had all nodded their heads and the little ones stood like small stones. Kris whistled and Adam came over to collect some of the money.

Melanie stood with Barker, unsure of what to say or do until he told her, heaving first, "Let's go."

Melanie was standing between Barker, Kris, and Adam. She wanted to stay. She didn't want to go back. And for certain reasons, she thought they wanted her to stay as well.

"It'll be okay now, Mel," Kris said, and Melanie heard the hint.

Adam looked at her longingly, but only waved at her in Barker's presence. "Bye, Melanie," he said.

"Bye," she muttered. She looked from him to Kris, and then around at the entire group, before Barker gently tugged her and she was swept out the door.

Outside it was a cold fall day, but the sun was shining. "Sorry…about all that," he said awkwardly. "I have enemies."

"You said you'd take care of everything. How?" she asked.

"You'll see. For now why don't we head on back and check the damage. See if all your books are okay."

He opened the door and got in. Melanie hadn't thought much about her books. She'd been in the middle of reading A Clockwork Orange when all of this started. She could get back to it. In fact, if Barker allowed it, that's how she'd spend the rest of the day. She didn't want to talk.

Melanie put her seatbelt on, feeling like a restraint in its own right.

And Barker drove up the partially functioning back roads of Ghost Town.

"Make any friends?" he asked her.

"Think so."

When they pulled up to the house, Melanie immediately spotted the two bullet holes. Inside the gas can was still on the ground, and she assumed there was a broken window somewhere in the back.

"Hungry?" he asked her.

"Yes."

Barker opened the fridge and found a few slices of pizza.

She ate them quickly, not even noticing that they were ice cold. She hadn't had a bite of food throughout all of this. How did they survive? She'd never gone that long without food in her life.

She felt immediately less sick, but her stomach had some pain.

"Thank you," she said, wolfing it down. "Thank you."

He giggled.

Afterward, they walked upstairs. She knew where she was supposed to go, and he seemed to be walking more slowly. She walked into the red room, saw the bed, the couch, the rope dangling out from the foot.

"Sit down somewhere," he said. She sat on the bed and he bent down to pick up the long rope. "Give me your hands," he said.

She obeyed. He put her leash back on her and checked that it was fastened. Then he pulled out a scarf.

"You don't have to—" The scarf forced its way into her mouth. As it coiled around her head she felt the same short breathed, bundled up feeling as always.

"Hush," he whispered, and she wanted to head butt him. But she relented, remembering the rules for survival. Now that she was fastened to the bed, Barker stacked her books next to her. Melanie could reach them easily, though shifting on the bed might make them fall over. "Okay," he heaved. "Have fun." He kissed her on the head.

When the door locked behind him it locked loud, and she was back in her cage.

He'd saved her life. He'd brought her back. And that was it. Melanie was bound and gagged and safe from harm. The books made her want to slap her face. Did he really expect her to read in the dark? Instead, Melanie laid down on the bed, making herself comfortable, arms folded up. She let out a deep sigh, expelling hours upon hours of fear and tension. Though she'd transformed back into an object, she felt relaxed, and almost wanted to laugh.

He had to tie her up. He wasn't strong enough to wrestle with her. He needed to recuperate first. And he would. She would have to be careful. It would take time to find the right moment, but Barker was not invincible.

Chapter 24

Blood

B arker slept. He had seared the wound, but it was drilling into him now. He'd gallivanted around the city, exhausted himself. And now he was lying face up on the bed. Heaving. Straining. Wavering.

Am I dying?

It was never a despaired question. Oh, some anxiety sure. But nothing he couldn't handle. Death might be interesting. Living was a challenge. A challenge to see how long he could go before he caught the fatal bullet.

But what if he died here? Poor Melanie would just be tied down upstairs, all stuffed in the mouth too. No one would find her. Whoops. Well, maybe that would truly christen her into The Meridian. She would either die in her bonds, this house their conjoined tomb. Or she would escape through some ugly, self mutilating manor, either cutting herself to get out of the ropes or breaking her bones against the door to knock it down. Then she would truly belong here. With that in mind, Barker rested his head back, resolving that he would not die. It was an irrational thought. He just needed rest. Something caught his ear. A noise upstairs. Breathing. Stifled. Stifled by a scarf. Melanie was letting out a relaxed sigh. Good. He did the same.

And in his trance, his mind wandered.

Once, when Justin Barker was sixteen years old, he thought he could catch the moonlight over the dark shore of New Heim. He sat on the railing, wearing his long brown coat to shield himself from the chilly night, long boots in case he had to go out on the sand. He had his kit lens attached, a long device designed to capture moments miles away. He didn't want the sand or the waves washing up on shore. He wanted the little pool of light glistening out on the water.

Justin had it just right. He hit the button. What he found was mostly satisfying, the moon wasn't perfect, but the blur was minor at best. The ripples of the water outlined the bottom of the frame. A decoration for a hypothetical new apartment? He'd need to get his mother to sign some documents, and he figured the old addict would come quietly. He was on his way to acquiring his own life doing the things he loved to do. So he jumped down from the railing onto the cement.

A blonde woman stormed by and nearly knocked the thousand-dollar device out of his hand. "Watch it!" he growled.

The woman ignored him. She kept walking, hands under her coat, moving fast, never stopping, like she had only a few minutes to live. And a few minutes later she was dead.

They sprang from the darkness like leaves in the wind. Both of them wore long brown coats and hats, and Justin hid himself behind the steps leading up to the boardwalk, camera firm in hand. They had guns. Justin knew, from his experience in New Heim, that there were two types of men who concealed guns under brown coats: gang members and assassins. The woman thrashed and screamed as the larger of the two men held her arms. The other put his hand over her mouth, while the first spoke to her quietly.

"Calm down. Calm down. Shut up. Calm down," he kept whispering. "Quiet, you fucking whore."

She bit the hand of the man holding her, and it was his turn to scream. The woman was free for a moment as the duo danced around her, but the dance ended swiftly when the whispering man pulled the trigger.

There was a flash of light and thunderous pop, echoing across the sand and then likely drowned by the ocean waves. The whispering man's hat had flown off, exposing his blonde hair and whiskery face. Justin stared at them both as they stood around the body lying in a pool. The whispering man discharged his weapon with a frustrated grimace, and then for a moment they all looked down at the evidence, all backs turned to Justin. So Justin shut off the flash, crept out from his hiding place and snapped a picture. Before he could hide again, one of the mobsters turned.

"Hey! You!" the whispering man shouted. Justin ran, and gunshots rang behind him. But he was fast. He found an alley. He knew they were still chasing him, but he phased into the darkness, gripping his favorite toy, now the only photographic proof.

Later, Justin was banging on a door. He smashed his fist so hard against it he thought he might bloody it.

"Open up!" he howled. "Come on, Stan! Open the damn door!" Finally the lock was undone. Standing there was a man well over twenty-one with frilly dark hair, cut short. He wore a look of pure shock and frustration.

"Barker?" he hissed. "What the fuck?"

"Stan, let me in, please," he heaved.

"It's three o'clock in the morning." His voice was like an older man's, deep and stern, at the moment over layered with something of a whine.

"Please, Stan!" Justin shouted. Stan's murky blue eyes widened and his large Adam's apple danced.

"What's going on?"

"Let me in." Justin looked over his shoulder one last time before Stan ushered him into the dark house with a firm grip. He locked the door behind him and Justin looked on at shapes and outlines of furniture he'd seen many times before. Since late childhood, his closest friend had been a girl, only a couple of years older than him. She was heavily involved with the older cop, and Justin wondered if she were already thinking about settling down.

Stan refused to turn on the lights, but as Justin's eyes adjusted he saw that Stan's hair was disheveled and he was shirtless. Justin had probably interrupted something.

"I'm sorry, Stan, I, I um…" Stan was still rubbing his eyes, trying to wake up.

"Kid, spit it out or get out," Stan said.

"I saw a murder."

Stan went stiff, mouth closed. After a moment of exasperation, he loosened up and his voice grew gentler.

"You alright?"

"Yeah, I'm good. I, um, got it on camera." Justin dug into his bag and pulled out the camera.

The cop's eyebrows jumped around. "Did you now? Well done." His tone sounded more foreboding than congratulatory.

Barker handed him the camera, images set on playback. There were only two. Stan held the camera in two hands with squinty eyes and stretched his jaw for a quiet yawn.

"This is the beach at night."

"Next one!" Justin said. Stan flipped to the next photo.

"There it is, shit. Two men, look like they're wearing suits. Standing around one woman." Stan snapped the camera shut. "Either a bunch of sociopaths having a good time…" He slapped his own forehead. "Or being paid to have a good time. Jesus, Barker. Is this a mob hit?"

"I don't know how clear the picture makes it, sorry."

"Did they see you?" Stan asked.

"I don't think so."

Stan's steely eyes locked onto him. "You don't think so?"

"I mean…yeah I don't think so."

Stan slapped his side. "Damn it. You need to lay low."

"Stan? What's going on?" Andrea, crept into the room, wearing a night gown and a head of giant tangled hair. Justin remembered Andrea telling him once that a lot of people disapproved of her relationship with Stan. Even Justin was apprehensive at first. He was ten years older and cops in New Heim tended to be untrustworthy. But Andrea was eighteen now. She was always smarter than Justin, he was used to being advised, not advising her.

"Nothing, babe," Stan said. "I'll tell you in the morning. Justin, take the couch."

"How do you expect me to sleep when—"

"Do as I say, kid." He sounded like he was sealing a business deal, cool and demanding. "We're not going to stay up at this hour, the only house on the block with lights on, while the mob might still be out looking for you. We'll talk in the morning. Try to sleep, kid, make yourself a drink if it helps. We have plenty." He walked passed Justin. "Come on, babe."

And then they were gone, vanished into the warm cavern they called their bedroom, and Justin did his best to sleep that night, but every quiet moment in the dark inspired echoes of gunfire.

Chapter 25

Hostage

It was difficult to sleep that night. There was so much on her mind. Melanie couldn't decide how she felt about this place tonight. Yes, she hated it, but what else? Outside was crawling with armed men. Here, caged up, there were thick walls between her and them. Was she going about this wrong? Instead of resisting Barker, maybe she should take advantage of him. Be kind to him, get him to trust her. Eventually, she could just slip away. Or try to kill him again.

The thought of trying to play nice with him terrified her, disgusted her. But was it the best way? Melanie couldn't sleep that night. It just wasn't happening. So she played with her fingers, making all kinds of shapes in the dark. She didn't bother taking out the gag. It was just a pinch around her jaw. A small thing.

But although she couldn't speak, different aspects of her mind had full conversations.

It'll be okay, Melanie.

I know. I know.

Be strong. Give him what he wants. And keep your eyes open.

I know. Thanks, Dad.

And keep reading. But make sure you hear him when he calls. Don't anger him.

I know, Mom.

Maybe she could write down these thoughts. She wanted a diary. But that would be a gift from him.

If I prove to him that I can be trusted, eventually I can escape. There has to be a way. I just need to be patient. I need to find the right moment. I'll just have to let him tie me up and lock me up for however much longer. And I'll find an opportunity.

How would he react if she kissed him? She drove that thought out immediately. He hadn't advanced on her sexually. Who knew how he'd take that? That could be the last strike. She needed to start with words. And she knew what her first words would be, the very next morning.

"Thank you for saving my life," she said at breakfast. Barker was probably following the usual routine: untying her for breakfast, lunch, dinner, and bathroom.

He looked at her curiously. Sitting up straight and aside from the occasional caressing of his side, looking much better.

"You're welcome," he said. "That was a riot huh?"

She nodded. "I was just shocked. I've never had a bullet fly at me before, and all the smoke…I'm sorry I didn't say anything until now."

"Well, we don't talk much," he said.

"I feel okay now, better. And…I'd be dead without you."

Barker smiled affectionately. "Thank you, doll," he said. "I'm just glad you're safe." He stood up, and she could see that he wasn't quite better yet. He shouldn't be better for weeks, but Kris hinted that he healed quickly. Right now though, it took him a few seconds longer to stand than it usually would.

"Did you bundle up the wound?" she asked him, feeling brave.

He shook his head, eyes closed, grinning. "I seared it shut with fire."

The thought of that made her grip her own waste. "Doesn't that...hurt?"

He chuckled. "Not too bad." He winked at her, and continued laughing. Melanie felt like she'd missed something. So she went back to eating her eggs. After a few moments he said, "We should be having a guest tonight."

"Who?" she asked. She hoped it was Kris, or Adam.

"One of our friendly neighborhood mobsters. I didn't kill all of them. I left one of Allen's cousins a cripple, and I left the accountant for my own purposes." He flashed her a look. "Our purposes, actually."

"Are they dangerous?" she asked.

"Not anymore," he said. "Don't worry, I'm not letting them inside. I'll keep you safe."

She nodded. Play the game. "I could make dinner," she said.

He looked at her, both surprised and skeptical. "Can you now? And what would you like to make?"

"Whatever you like," she said. "I want to do something for you. To thank you."

He crossed the room. "Planning on slipping anything in my food?" he asked.

She shook her head. "No. I swear. I just..." It wasn't working. She needed to stop talking. She was digging a grave.

He tapped her on the shoulder. "I'm kidding, cutie pie."

"Oh." She let herself laugh a little.

"Do you know how to make a stir fry?"

Of all things. "I could learn," she said. "I know a couple things."

The smile he gave her now was warm, welcoming, nurturing. "I'll do some coaching. How's that?"

She nodded. "Thank you."

"No, my dear." He brushed her hair. "Thank you."

***

Tom looked at himself in the mirror. The spot where the glass had struck him looked like a little thin smiley face, a little red moon peaking out the side of his temple. Allen had hit him just above the eye, and throughout the night his face had been home to a river of blood. Touching it stung like hell, but now that it had been washed, it was just a simple matter of bandaging it. Tom's only gripe was that the mobster had struck him on the head. Everyone would ask where the cut came from, and he needed to get his story straight.

The story: a masked man from the Marx Crime Family attempted to abduct him, leaving a little scratch. Their motive: vengeance for the hit man Tom shot in the throat.

It was October 25th now. Only two days since all of this started. Tom bandaged his head and took it all in. As far as Tom knew, only Orson Marx had survived, simply because Tom had heard nothing to suggest the man was dead. Allen had been found earlier today, a homeless man dragging his body out of an alley. Someone had seen what was transpiring, screamed, and then the police department was on the case. For all Tom knew the Chief was thrilled that the mobster was dead. Tom himself felt more of a detached disappointment, something similar to apathy.

"If you would have just listened to me, you might be alive," he said aloud. "God damn it, Allen." He groaned and carefully placed his hands over his eyes. Even the slightest touch set off a sting in his temple.

Tom was fairly certain he was not concussed. His father had always told him he had a hard head, before continuing to slander Tom's mother with ruthless persistence. The memory of Tom's father brought the scent of alcohol to his nostrils, and he drove out the memories moments later. The priority was Barker.

I can still pull this off. I just need the money. I have the mailing address.

Tom had gotten this information from Stan, and now that he was alone in this fight, he couldn't help remembering a conversation he once had with his old friend.

Stanley had been forty-five when he died. Tom knew him during the last few years. He had been a few inches taller than Tom, with dark frilly hair, cut short, and steely, murky eyes. His features weren't pointy or particularly sharp, but there was hard look to Stanley Jackson. He was a dog, and few dared reach out and touch him.

And yet, when he spoke to Tom, the gruff tone in his voice lifted slightly to reveal a brotherly presence, flaunting his knowledge yet mentoring and nurturing all at once.

"What's the first thing you would do to fix this city, Tom?" Stan had asked him, adjusting his long brown coat.

"I'd get rid of Justin Barker," Tom had said.

Stan's very thin eyebrows had done a little jump, but his expression hadn't changed. "Barker ain't here right now, kid. What would you do if I told you, 'go do it'?"

"I'd snap my fingers and remove the crime families," Tom said. At that time, Tom had made it a point to answer Stan's questions without any bullshit in between. Tom was brand new to the force. Stan was a seasoned detective with a partner of his own. And yet, Stan had reached down to Tom, confided in him.

"Can't snap your fingers to get shit done. What would you do?" Stan said, impatiently.

"I'd catch them in the crime of the century, and see them all behind bars. I'd cuff them myself," Tom said.

Stan chuckled at that. "Yeah. I used to get off on cuffing the bastards myself. Take control of them after they controlled our system and our lives for so long. But you know, Tom. Sometimes it's better to go unseen."

"Never really been my style," Tom said.

Stan had scoffed at that. "You better change that, kid. If you want the mobsters to send assassins to your front door, you can go in guns blazing and take them all down. But if you want to live a long and healthy life, then figure out their weakness and exploit it with discretion."

"Is that what you do?" Tom had asked.

Stan had patted Tom on the shoulder. "Yeah, Tom. That's what I do. Not successfully."

At that moment, a silence had fallen between the men. Stan's eyes told Tom he was elsewhere. If Tom could describe Stan's face, he would say the man was on the brink of crying, never following through.

"One day, Stan," Tom had said. "One day, you'll avenge her. I believe in you."

Stan never smiled when Tom said this, but Tom knew the man was grateful. "So," he would often digress in his sharp tone. "How's that mum of yours?"

Stan loved to tease, but Tom knew the man's heart was true. Stan had become a sounding board for Tom's dark memories of his father. "She's alright," Tom had said. "I actually told her about you. Told her how you're the only one around these parts who ever cared enough to ask."

"Kid, you're breaking my heart," Stan said utterly without emotion. And Tom laughed.

Tom didn't think back much on the smaller moments with Stan. Mostly, he thought about the carcass he found, and the messages left to him. Messages about Barker.

There was a knock at the door, and with Barker on his mind, the timing was far too chilling. Realistically, it could have been Beckett, but Tom loaded his gun just in case. He quietly approached the peep hole and looked through. The large nosed, large chinned face of Albert Ferris stared in, and Tom placed his finger on the trigger.

He creaked the door open and pointed the barrel through.

"Albert," he said.

"Tom," said the mobster, with raised hands. "I surrender."

"What do you want?" Tom asked.

"I want you to be smart for once," Ferris said, twisting Tom's gut. "In this case, pull me into the house, lock the door and keep pointing the gun while we talk, instead of sticking it out here where your neighbors can see."

Though Tom didn't like being declared a fool, he obeyed. He opened the door wider and saw that Ferris was alone, ushered him inside with the gun, and shut the door. He drew the blinds and stood opposite the accountant, gun raised.

"I don't want you in my house a minute longer than necessary so here's what we'll do," Tom said, seeing Ferris break a half grin. "You talk first, then me, then you're gone."

Ferris nodded. "Perfect." He put his hands in the pocket of is coat. "For starters Allen is confirmed dead, along with William, Stephen, Reeve, and William's brother. Orson is alive. Barker stabbed him once in each leg."

Tom raised his eyebrows. "Orson is crippled?"

Ferris nodded. "And essentially the entire task force, save for the apprehended ones, have been slaughtered. So it's just you and me now, kiddo."

"Why did Barker spare you?" Tom asked.

"I thought I was talking," Ferris said. "Barker is keeping me on as his accountant for now, and I expect Orson he'll keep around for, well, whatever. But the reason I came here was primarily to inform you, I'm going into Ghost Town tonight."

"Why the hell would you do a thing like that?" Tom asked.

"Because he invited me." He paused, and Tom could see him gritting his teeth in some kind of emotional duress. "He's taking my son as a hostage."

Oh, God. Not another child. Barker really needed to be buried. "Why are you telling me all of this?" Tom asked.

"Because you're coming with me," Ferris said.

"What?" Tom asked. "I don't think so."

"I've been alive a lot longer than you, Tom, and you're fixing to die at twenty-five. You want to live a long healthy life, maybe you can take a few tips from a professional." He patted himself on the chest, then pointed his index finger at Tom. "You were there the other night, at the Manor. No doubt Barker saw you. Whether you like it or not you're on his radar. So, you're going to come with me and introduce yourself. Say that you were an infiltrator trying to take down Allen, and that you humbly offer him your services in the fashion of Ed Ryan." Ferris paused so Tom could absorb all of this, then said "Clear?"

Tom was still pointing the gun. "I'm not…no, that's ridiculous. I—"

"Need to treaty with Barker. We all do. That's the next play. Unless you want to hang out on your own and get a nasty surprise one night soon."

There was some truth to what Ferris was saying. Was there a way to get Barker to trust him? It would make it easier to work against him. But, by God, Tom simply did not want to venture into Ghost Town, into Barker's nest.

Ferris spoke one last time, "And after we meet with Barker, when we both come back to our homes tonight, after I agree right now to give you a tasty little loan…What are you going to do?"

The weight in Tom's chest lifted, and he started to realize the depth of Ferris's plot. "I'm going to send that letter."

***

It was 6:00 P.M. on October 25th, and Melanie was still living. Spices assaulted her nostrils, and her captor/cooking instructor stood over her. After a long sniff she stirred some more.

"It's all about timing," Barker told her. "Yeah, all about timing. Let the sauce cook into the vegetables." He scoffed as he danced around her, restless but still slow moving since the past few days. "Personally, I prefer rice, but I guess store bought noodles will have to do. Sorry about that."

"I like noodles," Melanie said. Barker giggled.

"Perfect," he said. "So, how often did you cook with your family?"

Melanie continued to stir as her chest tightened. She hadn't cooked very much at all back home, before Barker took her. She wanted to take this steaming pot and throw its contents into his face.

"I asked you a question," he said, pleasantly.

Melanie stirred more aggressively. "I, um, used to help my mom cook. Every now and then for fun."

"What did you make?" he asked, fingers tapping the counter.

"Oh, I can't remember," she said, struggling to remember, knowing he would want more than that. "We made a cake once." She kept her eyes on the food and kept her hands busy. "I begged her to let me help her the next time she made one. We spent hours on it. It was fun." She sensed Barker staring at her, and turned to give him a pleasant smile. He smiled back and silence followed.

Melanie didn't tell him the rest of the story. Her father had come into the room and seen batter all over Melanie's apron. He called her Picasso, and she'd stuck her tongue out at him. He'd stuck his back out, and her mother had made a comment to him along the lines of go be useful. There had been a tense moment, but in the end they all laughed.

Melanie kept this memory to herself. If Barker commented, she probably wouldn't be able to stop herself. And then she would be dead.

When Barker felt like she got the hang of it, he sat down in the living room and started to read Awaken and Feast. There was no sound in the room save for the steaming and crackling of the pot and the sound of paper flipping. Moments later, just as her concoction reached its completion, there was the sound of a loud motor and bright lights passed the living room windows.

"And here they are," Barker said.

Melanie stood at the stove, armed with a kitchen knife. Barker looked at her as he went to the door. "Relax, relax," he said reassuringly.

"It's...almost done," she said.

"Good. This won't take long."

Footsteps approached the door and there was a knock. Barker stood, stiffly poised, then opened the door and vanished outside. Melanie heard his voice and three others a conversation began, and she stood alone in the kitchen. To occupy herself, she turned off the stove and took a smell and taste of the food she'd just made. It burned her tongue but it was delicious. She was proud of herself. As the voices continued outside, Melanie felt like she was tied to the stove. She wouldn't look outside. It was against the rules.

Ultimately, she ended up sinking to her knees, behind the island, where no could see her.

***

Tom followed Albert Ferris up what was apparently Barker's front yard. The grass looked dry and partially torn out in several places. He could tell the house was covered in graffiti, and he braced himself for what was about to emerge from it.

Tom hated Albert Ferris. Walking in front of Tom, waddling next to his father, was Albert's son, Robert. The boy would now be Barker's hostage. He was none the wiser. The boy was disabled. He didn't function very much at all, and if his dad (whom he automatically idolized) said 'get in the car' the boy obeyed. What a disgusting piece of filth. Handing his own son over to this man. There was nothing on Ferris's face that resembled guilt, and part of him wanted to shoot the man.

Now they were standing on Justin Barker's front porch. It was quite cold tonight, but the wind was soft. The boy kept asking his father where they were.

"Where are we, daddy?" Again and again. "Where are we?" The boy was only fourteen.

His father gently shushed him as the door opened. Tom stood awkwardly behind them, looking around, surprised at how unthreatening this house was. Tom expected to find booby traps of some sort if he ventured around the house. He expected nothing but malevolence from the house of Barker.

There were footsteps behind the door, and then it opened. This would be the second time Tom had seen Justin Barker in person, and now he was up close, and facing him. Barker's peculiar yellow eyes darted between the three of them. He stared at Tom the longest, seeming perplexed.

"Evening, Barker," said Ferris.

"Evening, Albert." Barker shut the door tight behind him. "I was just sitting down to dinner, so let's make this quick." He looked at the boy. "And who is this?" He leaned down, touching his own knees.

"This is Robert," Albert said with a restrained growl. "Say hello, son."

"Hello," Robert said, then hugged his father closer.

Barker looked up. "And who's this behind you? I wasn't expecting a third party."

Ferris looked back at Tom, as did Robert. All three pairs of eyes were on him as Ferris said, "This is Tom Macklin. He's a rookie local cop."

"Ah…Why is he here?" Barker asked.

"To pledge some well placed loyalty," Albert said.

"Is that right?" Barker said. His eyes returned to Tom. "Are you then?"

"I am," Tom forced himself to say. "I hope I'm not trespassing. I wanted to tell you in person."

"Did anyone I know send you down here?" Barker asked.

"No sir," Tom said. "If Ed Ryan found out I'm here I would probably be fired."

Barker snorted. There was something about the way he stared at you. No matter how animated his mouth, cheeks, or hands could be, his eyes remained fixed inside his head like too large yellowish rocks. And they zoomed into you in a way, making you feel like Barker was pulling you toward him. "I doubt it," he said at last.

Another set of wheels pulled up behind him, and all of them turned to look. It was a large, intimidating looking truck. The window was rolled down and a girl with long hair sat behind the wheel.

"Shall we, Albert?" Barker asked, and Ferris nodded his head, gripping his son. The trio passed Tom as Barker said, "You wait here."

Tom was left standing at the door of Barker's house. To Tom's left was one thin window. To his right were two very large windows. Likely a living room left and a kitchen right. Tom took a step closer to the door. If Melanie Grier was still alive, she was just beyond this door. If Tom could only ease it open and peak inside.

Instead he turned to watch the hostage exchange. Ferris was kneeling in front of his son as if to explain something to him. The girl was standing behind him. She seemed young, maybe seventeen. She was extremely thin; she must not have gotten much to eat. And Barker towered over the three of them. Robert started to fuss, seeming to get anxious, at which point the girl got close to him and put her hand on his shoulder. The boy was looking at her now, and after a moment of both her and Ferris talking to him, the boy started to look more comforted.

Eventually, Ferris kissed the boy on the head and the girl lead him into the truck. The doors slammed shut, the engine came to life, and the truck rolled away. Now two men that Tom hated were standing in the dark, whispering to one another. Ferris nodded at Barker and turned to start toward the car, and Barker was coming back, toward Tom. The young cop braced himself.

"So, you want to work for me," Barker said, reaching him.

"Correct," Tom said. "I'd like to supply you with police Intel and perform favors for you, similar to what Ferris does."

Barker stood with his hands on his hips and nodded his head. "Might I ask why?"

"I'd like to survive," Tom said. "I'd like to be in your good graces. Not to mention," he stopped there. It was part of the illusion he was casting.

"Go on," Barker said.

"I'd like to help you be more prepared for the next attempt on your life, if and when it comes. That way, we can help you nip it sooner, before the people of New Heim get dragged in."

Barker raised his hands. "But that's the fun part."

Tom smiled at him, wanting nothing more than to see his throat burst red. Barker lowered his hands.

"You know, kid...You look familiar. Have we met?"

Should he say it? Should he confess his identity, his true identity, to Justin Barker? Or should he remain a mystery? Then again, Barker had his ways of finding out the truth, and Ferris warned him he didn't like being lied to. Perhaps a half truth. Or just a simple fact, with no real elaboration. But the truth. The real truth, that Tom had such a burning desire to toss in Barker's face.

"I was Stanley Jackson's partner," he said.

Something changed in Barker. At first, emotion left his face. Then his eyes went wide, and he took a step back. "Stan," he whispered.

Though Barker looked fearsome, muscles proud and shoulders broad, his face now was frozen, like he couldn't let an emotion escape his clutches. And for a moment, from the way he continued to stare and the way he frowned and let his mouth fall open, Tom thought he spotted a trace of envy in the murderer.

After taking a deep breath, he straightened himself back out. Now he looked like a cold hearted, detached cut throat.

"So," Barker said. "Stan's partner." His eyes were fixed on Tom, and the smile was starting to come back. Starting. Just how great a weapon was Stan's name?

"Yes, I was his partner, before you killed him."

Barker shut his eyes at that, and then the smile came in full form. "We don't know each other very well...No...We don't know each other well at all." He rubbed his eyes with his fingers. "Yeah, word of advice." He blinked a few times. "Do not mention Stan to me."

"Understood," Tom said. "I apologize." He even bowed his head slightly. "I want to make things right," he said. Barker took another deep breath.

"I remember you now," he said, nodding his head. "Yeah, you were even skinnier then. Always flanking him. Head darting in every direction, taking everything in all frantic. Every crime scene. Stan was the old dog, and you the pup. I remember looking at you and thinking, 'Look at that little punk.'"

Normally, Tom would be angry. If Ferris, Orson, or Allen insulted him, he'd want to strike them. But looking Barker in the face, he felt more numb than anything. More adrenaline than anger. The challenge was standing firm. "I'm here to offer peace," he made himself say. "I have no conflict with you. It's like Ferris said. You're the biggest player in town."

Barker nodded with a suspicious smile. He glanced at Ferris, out in the street, waiting by the car. The mobster seemed to be watching intently, waiting for something to go down.

The smile Barker gave him then was the same he always used, the way Stan described him. "Run along now, Tom Macklin."

Then Barker strode past him and slammed the door behind him. Tom quickly walked away from the house and when he arrived at the car, Ferris gave him a warning look.

***

Stan's shadow had waltzed onto his property, and Ferris hadn't even warned him. Barker could kill him and the boy right now for that, but he calmed himself. Stanley still mocked him. If it wasn't with his own ridiculous face, it was with ridiculous pawns. He was just like the Sects, mocking him from the grave. The Sects had used the Marx Clan, and Stan had used this young punk. Well, Barker would get to know this little punk a lot better. He would remedy this little situation to his own liking, and he hoped beyond hoped that wherever Stan was now, he was still watching closely.

Barker took a great sniff and realized that the food was still warm.

"Melanie?" he asked. He heard her breathing, shy and reserved. Only a few little breaths escaping. He walked over behind the island and found her sitting on the floor. "What on Earth are you doing down there?" he asked. She looked up at him and he felt his heart soothed. Melanie's look was genuine, innocent.

"I'm staying out of sight," she said.

Barker knelt down next to her, truly moved. This was the first real sign that she was starting to learn. Starting to accept him. He would be able to make this girl into something worth keeping. Something Stan and that raging bitch thought they could deny him of forever. Barker started to see his vision more clearly. A girl who could let the past be past, and embrace a life in the Meridian.

"Good girl," he said. He sniffed again. "Let's eat."

Chapter 26

Transformed

Tom felt like he was stumbling into the lair of another monstrous beast. His nerves warned him to turn back, before the beast noticed he was there. But the deed needed to be done. So Tom finished the letter.

Mr. D. Crawford,

I hope this letter finds you well. My name is Tom Macklin. I am the former partner of Stanley Jackson, a man with whom you once discussed business. Keeping in the agreement you two made, Stan did not reveal any classified information about your organization. What he did mention was that your services may be key in fixing a problem found here in the city of New Heim. Going forward, I want to assure you that you have my full discretion and cooperation. I am writing about Justin Kyle Barker, Age 34, resident of New Heim. Needless to say, our Barker problem has escalated along with this city's death toll. Our children are not safe. I am asking you to dispatch one of your employees to deal with this problem. Stan mentioned the satisfaction that accompanies your services, and for that, I can pay any price you name. If it costs an arm and a leg, I'll pay that. We must stop Barker before he kills again. I know that you found Stan unfit to do business with, but his lone crusade about Barker got him killed. He was a good man. He just wanted justice for his family. We all want justice for our families. Please Mr. Crawford. He's tormenting us. We cannot do this without you.

Thank you for your time.

Sincerely,

Tom Macklin.

***

"What day is it?" Melanie asked. She was sitting on the stool at the island, a copy of The Godfather cracked open in front of her. But she was having a lot of difficulty reading. They had just had a meal together and Barker was allowing her some leisure time. After that, it would be back into the rope's coils.

"October 29th," Barker said. He was rocking back and forth in the armchair, sharpening one of his knives. The loud scraping filled the house, the kind of noise that disrupts your thoughts. Every scrape gave her the impulse to turn and run even though she knew he wasn't coming for her. But as always lately, Melanie resisted every frightened impulse that came to her.

October 29th. Halloween was coming in two days. Did Barker celebrate Halloween? She was afraid to ask. But he kept scraping that damn knife. Melanie decided she didn't care what atrocious Halloween custom he described, as long as it stopped that damn noise.

"Halloween is coming," she said. It worked. He stopped scraping and looked up at the ceiling.

"It is," he said. "Almost forgot."

"Do you celebrate?" she asked.

He narrowed his eyes and widened his lips. "What? Stereotyping me now?"

She shook her head and started playing with the dead skin under her nails. "Just asking."

Barker flipped the knife over and placed it on the arm of the chair, fingers gently cupping the blade like a pet. "I wasn't always like, well this. When I was your age, I didn't give holidays a damn second thought. Especially not Christmas. I didn't have a loving family to spend it with."

That was just what Melanie would have predicted. What else could she learn?

Barker went on, stroking the whiskers on his chin, "When I started discovering my talents, Halloween became my favorite thing. All the scares, gothic décor, ghost stories and all the candy to be had. Oh, how I loved it. It got to a point where I would enjoy a rave every Halloween."

"Rave?" she asked, thinking of a couple different things that could have meant. A wild dance party, a crazy drug high.

"A long list of victims in one night."

She shut her mouth and her eyes, but quickly reopened them to avoid looking too affected. "Oh," was all she said. His victims were probably almost all girls, not different from her. Or parents. People he forced to watch while he made their children suffer. She didn't have any names or faces, but she wanted to start praying for them all, right now. How many people had he made suffer? And how much did all of those ghosts hate Melanie Grier for surviving this long?

"Eventually I stopped that shit," he said. "I suppose I've mellowed out some. Holidays are just gimmicks. I don't do what I do for recognition. And neither should you," he said.

"Sure," she muttered.

"I like Thanksgiving better," he said.

"Oh?"

"Mhm," he said, stroking his stomach. "I find the most expensive restaurant in whatever town I'm in and I gorge myself on their best dishes. Most people go to Country Clubs for buffets, but I prefer a nice quiet dinner."

Maybe that was one thing she could take advantage of. Maybe he would bring something back for her. She could still enjoy her second favorite holiday, after Christmas.

"That sounds fun," she said. She looked over at him and realized his chin was in his hands.

"Perhaps we can find something to do," he said.

"Like what?"

He rubbed his hands against his chin. "There's this wonderful restaurant in the city. I could bring you there."

It was her turn to stare. Did he really just invite her out? In public? What the hell did that even mean? Would he chain her up, parade her around like a toy? Or was he offering to give her something she'd so desperately craved? No. It had to be a trick. He was joking, and she wasn't getting her hopes up. She went back to reading, trying to focus on the words in the book. Then Melanie heard him get to his feet, glancing over once to see him tapping his fingers against the head of the armchair.

"I'm going to tell you something that I don't want you to take the wrong way," he said with a lowered tone. "You don't have to look at me, just listen."

"Okay," she said.

"When we...met. I saw you once or twice before you saw me."

That brought her eyes back to him. "What do you mean?" His feet were moving in place, and she knew that any minute, he would cross the room, put his hands on her.

His face was, for the moment, full of contempt. "Your father and I met about two weeks before I came to collect you. He pulled me over and I hated the way he spoke to me. I followed him home that night, intending to kill him." Finally, he began to move toward her, and the frown began to vanish. "But then, I saw you."

Melanie looked away, catching only a glimpse of his attempt at a friendly smile. She didn't know how to manage this mixture of revulsion and guilty pleasure. He'd butchered her life, taken away so much. And yet to him, she was so damn special. Melanie Grier was more special to Barker than she was to herself.

"You were playing with that camera," he told her, reaching the island. "I knew then, right then, inexplicably, that you and I could be friends."

He leaned against the island, folding his hands. Melanie closed the book, looking at her own hand resting limp against the cover. "How?" she asked him.

He reached over and stroked her hand with his index finger. A thick, hot slug rolled down her scalp, making her itch. "I just need you to trust me. I know things started out a little violent, but I'm not going to hurt you. Not anymore."

Their eyes met, and she had one repetitive thought. To kill him. Melanie was not going to forgive him for what he did. Never. If that's what he wanted he wasn't going to get it. But she had to lie. She had to play the game.

"I'm doing my best," she said, somewhere between pleading and confrontational.

"I know you are," he said. He had a possessed look in his eyes. There was only one thing he wanted to talk about. "You were meticulous with that camera. You knew what you were doing. It meant something to you."

Melanie nodded. "I've always liked it. Photography, drawing."

"You draw?" he asked.

"I'm bad at it," she said, rubbing her forearm. "I've always been better at photography. That camera was actually a gift from my dad."

"Ah," he said. "Go on," he said.

"What do you want to know?" she asked.

He gripped her hand, softly. "Whatever helps me get to know you."

Her chest did a flip and she inhaled. "Okay. Well, like I said I used to like drawing. When I was little I loved cartoons. I loved Disney movies. I still do." Don't blush. "People teased me about it but...I guess I just always loved colors. I've always loved fall, when the leaves change. I've always loved paintings. Any great blend of colors just...make me happy, I guess. But I was never able to draw or paint."

Barker was watching her so stiffly. His eyes were locked in her direction, hungering for whatever she said next. "So, when I was in about third grade my parents took me on a trip to Maine. All the scenery there was just so gorgeous." Despite herself, she forgot about Barker, forgot about his torment, about not wanting to give him too much, and just let herself be taken back. "No," she said to herself. "There's more to it than that. It wasn't just pretty it was…" She thought about the way the most violent, animated waters she'd ever seen crashed against the largest rocks she'd ever seen, and sprayed the cold air. She thought about the way the sunset turned the sky so many different shades and painted the water pink. "There was something…life changing. No, no. Something, deep and meaningful and…"

"Transforming," he finished for her. Melanie looked into Barker's eyes, for a moment, purely connected. He didn't look like Barker. He looked like a regular, kindly man wearing the monster's face.

"Yeah," she said, then remembered her mother's word. "Mom would have said 'Enlightening.'"

"That's a good word," he said. "Though I have some issues with the people who popularized the word. Anyway, continue."

"Well, I saw some great things and some great photographs in gift shops, and it just kind of hit me. I got into photography after that. Took pictures all the time with my phone. Looked up things on Google. Started watching movies I never thought I'd be into like The Godfather, because people told me the cinematography was legendary."

He was nodding his head. "Yes, you see amazing things in certain films. Great allegories to real life as well." He scoffed. "So is that what you were doing, that night? Trying to capture something transforming?"

"Mostly I was just excited. It was my first real piece of equipment. I wanted to take pictures all night. A couple of the ones I took I wanted to print out. It just made me so happy. It's funny. It was just a test. But the first time I took one that I liked I got chills. I wanted to keep it forever, show it to everyone." And it occurred to her for the first time that she missed her camera.

"What was it?" he asked.

"Just the stars. They were in a cool shape." She was starting to stream into embarrassing territory, and starting to remember who Barker was.

"What shape?" he demanded.

Melanie made "umm" sounds as she struggled to find the words.

"You love it so much but you can't remember?" he said, not aggressively.

"No, it's just dumb."

"Dumb? Come on now. Tell me." As always he'd backed her into a corner, but this time it was in a playful manner.

"Promise not to laugh?" she said.

"Sure," he said.

"I thought they looked like angel wings," she said. The revelation made her feel like she was about to get made fun of, but he just looked taken aback.

"Why would I laugh at that?" he asked.

"I don't know. Little silly, I guess?"

He straightened up from his leaning position and looked at the cabinets. "I used to think about angels."

"You did?"

"Mhm. Still do sometimes." He grunted. "Angel wings in the sky, huh? That's interesting." His eyes found her again. "You see, darling, I love photography as well. I would go out late at night, look up at the sky, the moon. The lights on the buildings. Go down to the beach. Film the ocean waves at night…Had a long list of pictures. A whole library."

"Can I see?" she asked.

He laughed. "Oh they're long gone. Unfortunately."

"Oh," she said.

"You know, Melanie," his voice was serious and stern again. "If I hadn't gone out to take pictures on a particular night…I wouldn't be who I am right now."

"What do you mean?"

"I mean I got myself into some trouble. Trouble finds you here if you're not careful."

"Men with guns?" she asked.

He nodded, frowning intensely. "I was just taking pictures, just like you, when they saw me."

"Who's they?" she asked.

"Agents of the Sect Crime Family." He was in another world. His hands were moving in odd ways, as if he was starting to grab onto something, but it was only thin air. "I was trying to capture the moon. Get a nice lasting shot of the moon. It was something I'd yet to learn."

"I don't know how to do that either," she said, meekly. Melanie felt like if she disturbed him in this state he would attack her, so she kept her voice low and her words few and far between. Barker started walking over to one of the stools.

"I witnessed a murder that night. Five men working for the Sect family attempted to kidnap a lady who'd walked by. But when she fought back they killed her. Shot her through the skull." Melanie flinched at the description, and added a new item to her list of prayers.

"What happened next?" she asked.

Barker was pulling the stool over to sit next to her. It screeched against the floor. "I took a picture," he said, and laughed. "I was so stupid. Sixteen years old, just like you. Thought I could take the picture with me to my friend on the force." He curled his lips. "Never thought he'd sell me out though."

"You had a friend on the force?" she asked, finding that hard to believe.

"Yes." He sat down next to her, slowly, stiffly. "His name was Stanley."

"I see," Melanie said. "I'm sorry. That it happened to you."

"I'm not," he said, and Melanie's heart jolted. She'd stepped too far. She didn't want to unlock all of his secrets. He might not even like that. He might decide she learned too much. And punish her. To protect his secrets. Melanie needed to just keep her mouth shut.

And yet, if she intended to escape, she needed to know her adversary.

"They hurt you, didn't they?" she asked. "The Crime family." Barker nodded, eyebrows up, eyes dazed. "Is that why you do what you do?" she asked. "To protect yourself?"

He shook his head, calm and relaxed. "No, child. I do it because I like it. Love it."

Her blood went cold and she stirred where she sat. Barker folded one leg over the other, and across the room the living room light flickered once.

"Are you going to do those things to me?" she asked. "Ever?" Barker folded his arms and gave her a sideways glance.

"I'm insulted," he said.

She shook her head. "I'm sorry. I didn't mean to, I—"

"Relax."

Melanie took a deep breath. "It's just...I have to ask. Understand. I'm just so scared. All of the time. Every day. Every minute." Her arms were hugged around herself now, as if bound. Barker stirred where he sat, arms still folded. He seemed to be deep in thought.

"Is there anyway I can help you with that?"

She wanted to suggest not tying her up anymore, but it wasn't time for that yet. He'd say no. No, she needed something else.

"I guess...Tell me more about yourself?" she asked. "I'd be less scared if I knew you better." Barker unfolded his legs and leaned his back against the counter, holding up his head with his left hand.

"You might take that back, but sure. I've wanted to tell you about myself...When I was six, my father took me out one night. Dad was a tall and, um, solemn man. He never frowned or smiled, just did something in between, like a thinker statue. That's all I remember about him. That and his name. Old Daniel Barker. He was my caretaker. Mom was useless, too crazy to function. She's still alive, you know."

"Oh," she said, amazed at the thought of Barker's living mother. What would she have to say about the way Barker kept his guests?

Barker scratched his head, and his eyes drifted to the blade over on the arm of the chair. "Anyway, one night he took me for some ice cream and on the way home can you guess what happened?"

"What?" she asked.

"We ran into a mugger." His eyes trailed. "The son of a bitch beat my dad bloody, spattered it all over me. Then he ran and I wandered home."

Melanie felt like she'd discovered the secret to the universe. If she'd been covered in blood at the age of six, how would she have turned out?

Barker went on, "I was fine. For years I was fine. A small trauma. All that changed was that I didn't mind blood. At all. Friends would gag and recoil at the sight of a mangled corpse but if I saw one...eh." He waved his hand. "It was all the same to me."

"Were you sad? Did you miss him?" Melanie asked.

"The mugger or my dad?" She went to answer and he said, "I'm kidding. Yeah, I guess for a time, quite a bit. At first I screamed and cried and howled to God on high that he stole my daddy away from me. Didn't last very long."

He stood up and paced the room. "Around high school I started raising myself, while Mom drank herself into slumbers. I was fine. Little socially awkward, but can you blame me? I had one dead parent, one absent parent, and an interest in blood." He stopped at the window and looked outside. "Drawing was how I took my mind off whatever. Whatever was holding me back. People didn't like what I drew of course. Eventually I started taking pictures...I was good at it."

She tried to picture Barker as a boy. She took the jet-black hair and cut off half of it, did away with the facial hair, the muscles. Made him skinnier and shorter in her mind, and much less pale. But the smile was the same. On the image of a small child, the smile looked even worse. Stretched.

Barker turned around and looked right at her. He continued to stand. "One night I went out and I saw what I just described to you. The mobsters and the lady. Yeah, got myself into some trouble. After that it was an ongoing fight for survival, and along the way I was introduced to a million amazing things about the world, things I didn't know existed.

People I never knew were real or plausible until they touched my life." He sat back down. "Oh, I have adventured."

"I'm sorry," she made herself say. To some degree she meant it. It sounded like a horrible life. But he looked bewildered.

"Why are you sorry?"

Was there nothing she could say correctly? "It sounds like you've been through a lot."

He gasped, like he was mortified. "Oh, no, Melanie. You don't understand." He reached over and rested his warm hand on her shoulder. "These were some of the best things that ever happened to me. They sent me on a path to where I am today, and I couldn't be happier."

Unbelievable. "Right, of course," she said, smiling. "Is that when you met Aethon Armata?"

His eyebrows went up and he leaned back. "You pronounced the name perfectly. Been eyeing the cover of my book?"

She nodded.

He smiled sinisterly. "Boy is that a tale. My self discovery."

"When you got stronger? Faster?" Melanie asked. Barker nodded and she pressed further. "Who was he?"

Barker nodded scratched his head. "Where to even begin?" He held up a few fingers to puppeteer a person walking. "Aethon was a pioneer. I met him in the Meridian."

"What is that?" she asked.

"After a few incidents in New Heim, I left home and started traveling. I went to Montana. This was back in roughly, 2012. You were just a baby. Back then, Montana had an exceptionally high crime rate."

"It did?" she asked. Melanie had never heard of Montana having a high crime rate. She didn't really know anything about Montana other than there were mountains and trees. It was never in the news. But Barker nodded adamantly.

"It's been much quieter for the past ten years. There's a reason for that, but that's a whole other story. When I ventured to Montana, it was still in the process of becoming," he paused. "The Meridian."

"Okay," she mumbled, still confused.

"It's an intersection. A place off the maps for people like me."

"People who have your…gifts?"

He stood up and poised himself as if giving a puppet show. "Some say we're aliens. Some say we're monsters." He gestured dramatically. "Superhuman. Unnatural." He put his hands down. "And some say we have genetic disorders."

"Like a virus?" she asked.

He stretched his index finger toward her. "Let's run with that theory for a moment. Yes, a virus would be close, but a virus can attack anyone. Picture instead a mutation, specific to certain individuals. A chosen few. A selective entity that begins as an obstruction, upon experiencing a trauma. Then later becoming an enhancement, upon further exploration. Upon self discovery."

"I…think I get it," she said. She began to picture Barker as a mutant. It helped her anchor an understanding of how his body worked and why he existed as he did. What she wanted to know was why scientists hadn't discovered it yet. And she still didn't know who Aethon

Armata was, but she didn't want to prod too much. That might test Barker's patience. Might be seen as rude. Might be strike three.

Barker went on, "The trauma is referred to as an awakening. And mine happened right here in New Heim. But to learn more about it, I had to venture to a place where people like me existed. A place I could be myself without the interference of the law. A place where outlaws ruled in secret, and the rest of the country were none the wiser." He came toward her again, but this time he had that book in his hand. "Aethon Armata was our leader and the visionary behind what was a truly short lived utopia. Sad, really. It had so much potential." His voice perked up. "But I'm on my own anyway. Doesn't affect me." He gently placed the book in front of her, and pressed his hand against the island, the other hot on her shoulder. "If you're interested to learn more, I would love for you to read this. Sometime. It's something very close to my heart."

Melanie pushed aside The Godfather and studied Awaken and Feast. The cover was white, and there was very cheap, basic art on the front cover, as if animated by a novice. It depicted four trees with several clouds of green to portray leaves. Across a speckled sky above, the titled was printed neatly in red. Melanie ran her finger down the spine. It was strong and upon looking closer, she realized that the book was truly well kept, no pages tearing out of the spine, no damage of any kind. She was afraid to touch it, but he had offered.

"I would love to read it," she said, placing her hands gently on top and smiling up at him. Barker smiled back, and brushed her chin with his thumb.

"Thank you," he said. "For listening."

"Of course," she said. "Anytime." Then she added, "I'm here for you."

He was staring down at her, like he was so very pleased. Like he'd known all along it would come to this. "Thank you," he said. Something changed in his face. "Melanie, I, they…"

"Yes?"

He shook his head. "Never mind. Come on. Time for bed."

Melanie took a deep breath and braced herself for the sting of the rope.

On some level, it was true. Barker had saved her life, and she owed him something in return. Despite however this started, there were simple ways she could repay that debt. She could repay him for protecting her, for feeding her, for keeping her alive all throughout this experience. Regardless of her feelings, her mother had taught her to repay kindnesses done to her. However, Melanie would not stop hating him. She would not give him everything. She would not relent until he released her. As long as he held her prisoner, she would repay that debt as well.

***

Barker lied on his bed once more, while Melanie rested upstairs. He thought about the conversation they'd had today. She'd opened up so much. He had her. It was going to work. He so hoped she would crack open the book. Oh, the things she would find. The ways she would begin to understand. The depth to which she might interpret what had occurred inside him. For the first time, someone would understand.

Barker dug the back of his head into the pillow, remembering, remembering it all. He'd almost let it slip. He'd almost showed her his weak side. A side he'd done away with. And yet, lately, his mind was more full of Stan than he was accustomed to.

Chapter 27

A Sick Feeling

After Stan and Andrea went to sleep, Justin laid on the couch staring up at the ceiling. He was alone with the darkness and memories of blood and a scream. By 6:00 A.M. he'd managed to sleep. Andrea roused him at 8:00 A.M.

"Wake up, sleepy head," she mused. Justin untangled himself from the ridiculous position he was, and sat up with a deep yawn.

"It's been awhile," he said.

"I know," she said, stroking her blonde hair. "About a year now?" she asked.

"Half a year," he said.

"Half?" She rolled her eyes up toward the ceiling and curled her lips. "Last time was?"

"The concert," he said.

Justin watched her eyes light up like a bulb. "Oh, that's right!"

He scoffed. "I mean, I enjoyed myself."

She tapped him on the shoulder. "Stop. I've had a lot on my mind."

After the moment of distraction, Justin's mind flashed to the night before, and a sick feeling fell on his chest.

"You okay?" she asked.

He shrugged. "Yeah, I'll be fine."

"Hungry?" she asked.

"I guess," he said.

"Great. I've got bagels." Then she was scurrying about the kitchen. Justin stretched and yawned, working out all kinds of knots. Then he was staring at the floor. He could tell Andrea was staring at him as she cut the bagels. There was silence between them, him lost in the shock of the previous night, and her, not knowing what the hell to do. The word for this was awkward.

And in all awkward silences, Justin had learned people try to break the tension. "Where's Stan?" he asked her.

"He's upstairs on the phone," she said.

"Important call?" he asked.

She nodded. "Yep. He's talking to the chief." She put the bagels in the toaster with a loud click.

Justin nodded. "Ah, I see."

Andrea ran her hands through her hair and yawned. "Yeah. Don't worry, everything will be fine."

"I know," he said.

"If there's anything you need from me, you know I'm here," she said.

"I know. Thanks Anne," he said.

She came around the island and sat down on the stool.

"Was there blood?" she asked.

Their eyes locked. Andrea was searching him for something, some sign of a problem she knew all the words and remedies for. A problem he'd had all his life, that she'd learned eight years ago when they met.

"There was blood," he said. "Quite a bit actually. They shot her through the skull."

Andrea grimaced. "Horrible. Horrible way to go," she said.

Justin leaned back. "Actually…I think that's an easier way to go. Just a pop and then you don't feel anything."

Andrea flashed him an old look from their childhood. "You know I hate when you do that," she said. "Someone died."

"I know," he snapped. "I was there."

Silence.

"Sorry," she said. "That must have been horrifying…I just. Well, you know."

"I know," he said. "You hope I don't get too desensitized. Stop caring. Just because bodies don't frighten me doesn't mean I don't get that someone lost her life. That's why I took the picture."

Andrea nodded. "That was really brave…Stan will get them behind bars."

"Stan the man," he said.

"Oh, God," she said, rolling her eyes. "Don't start."

Both of them laughed.

Justin was sixteen, and Andrea eighteen. At the age of ten, Justin was nothing but a victim for bullies, and that taught him to keep his distance from the rest of the kids, except for the one. The one who noticed, the one who understood. The one who heard his bizarre tale from years ago and didn't recoil from him. Instead she wanted to help him, stick by him. And although they didn't have much in common, if he wanted to show her a picture, or a comic strip, she always listened with a smile. Andrea was more family to him than his own mother, who spent all of her time tripping out on drugs.

Although their contact had lessened over the past few years, Justin and Andrea never threw out their friendship. She treated him like a family member, which was convenient now that she was seeing a twenty-eight year old cop, tough as nails and loyal to his loved ones.

In contrast to Justin and Andrea, Justin and Stan had more little things in common, movies, books, comics, and general interests, but there was much less love lost between them. Justin wondered in the beginning if Stan secretly hated him, but Andrea assured him that Stan was very fond of her childhood best friend. Justin later realized that Stan was simply a tough shell to crack, shielded. He was a warrior who'd committed himself to public service in a very dangerous place.

The bagels popped up, and Andrea looked at Justin with a wide smile. "Breakfast!" she said.

He chuckled. "What would I do without you?"

She was already buttering the bagel. "What kind of jam do you like?"

"Strawberry," he said. Then he added with a smirk, "Nice and red."

She slapped the dull edge of the knife on the counter. "Would you stop?"

He laughed. "Kidding." As Justin started to eat, Stan appeared at the bottom of the steps. He was in full uniform, his brown hair neatly combed over, face covered with intentional scruff.

"Oh ,look, a circus," he said.

"Thanks, honey," Andrea said. "I suppose now you'll be wanting some breakfast."

"No, thanks," he said. "I'm out the door in five."

"I could have a bagel ready for you in five."

"I'll pass. Thanks, honey." He walked over to the sofa. "How'd you sleep?"

"Alright," Justin said.

"That sounds like bullshit." Stan didn't sit down next to him. Really he knelt down, like a soldier, somewhat confrontational. "Here's the deal. You need to stay in this house until further notice. Understand?"

"That's nice of you, Stan, but I think I can lay low on my own."

"That wasn't a request," Stan said. "You're staying here." He looked over his shoulder, at Andrea. "Hun, do you think you could stop by his place after work and get some of his clothes."

"Sure," she said.

Justin looked between them both. "What's the situation?" he asked Stan.

"The situation is that those men work for Matthew Sect."

Justin's chest sank. Matthew Sect was about twenty-five years old, ruthless and powerful. He was the first son of Maxwell Sect, the most powerful crime lord in the city. Maxwell had territory that spanned about half of the city, a smaller portion belonging to Allen Marx, an up and comer. The city was divided between these two families, with the police struggling to achieve absolute control. There were rumors that one of the two families had the Mayor in their pocket, but no one knew which one. Matthew was in charge of several hit men in his father's employ. Justin had gotten himself seen by these men, and now he wasn't very hungry.

"Matt Sect, huh...That's great," he said.

"Yep. You're in some serious shit, son. But if you do what I say I'm confident I can get you out of this."

"I don't want to put you two at risk," Justin said. "I could just leave."

"What did I just say?" Stan snapped.

"I'm just saying, is there a better way?"

"No. This is the way. You'll be safe here. Do not go outside. You're welcome to our food, drink, TV, all of that. But stay away from the windows. Just leave it to me, alright. I'll let you know more tonight."

"Stan," Andrea said. "We can't just leave him here by himself."

"We go about our normal days," Stan said. "You know this. I go to work. You go to work. Nothing has changed here."

"That doesn't mean he should be by himself. Not after what he went through last night. Someone should stay here with him." She kept herself composed, standing still despite her aggression.

Stan pressed his fingers to his forehead. "Call your sister."

Andrea's eyes went up. "Good idea." She looked at Justin. "You remember Lorena, right?"

"Yeah I remember," Justin said.

Lorena was Andrea's older sister. Justin had visited Andrea's house more than once as a child. Lorena was an oddly named, oddly put together child, two years older than Andrea and much less social. She had a lot of odd pets and loved to draw, with the contents of her sketchbook an absolute mystery to all, even Andrea. Both girls hated their parents, and both had moved out now, Lorena starting a successful business in the city, and Andrea attending higher education with the help of Stan. Justin had not spoken to Lorena half as much as Andrea, but he had spoken to her enough times to be comfortable. Once, years ago, they had discussed blood.

"Haven't seen her in awhile," he said.

"She'll keep you company," Stan said. "Alright. I'm out."

Justin was looking at his knees when a large hand closed on his shoulder. Stan was looking at him intently. "It'll be alright kid. Got me?"

"Yeah, I got you. Thanks, Stan."

Stan put on his cap, kissed Andrea, and he was out the door. About fifteen minutes later, Andrea was done cleaning the kitchen and went upstairs to get ready for work. Justin was taking Stan up on the offer and pouring himself some wine when Andrea came down dressed in a red shirt and khakis.

"That has to be the worst job I've ever heard of," he said.

She blushed. "Yeah, but maybe one day I'll own a fancy restaurant," she said.

"You could always kill the owner. I think that's a good way to acquire a restaurant," he said, finger to his chin.

"Yeah, in cartoons," Andrea said. "Are you sure you're okay?"

"I'm fine."

"Alright. Well, I gotta go."

Andrea walked over and kissed him on the cheek, then turned and walked out the door. A gust of wind made her long blonde hair flow. Justin sat down on the couch and replayed the kiss in his mind. It was on the cheek, and he'd never wanted her sexually. But having a friend, someone who understood, in all the times that counted, even if they didn't talk very often; Justin decided very young that this was an irreplaceable treasure.

Later, Justin was using the bathroom as the sun continued to drop. He was waiting for Stan and Andrea to come home. It was 6:00 P.M.

Where were they? Both of them had worked eight hour shifts at this point. After washing his hands, he walked out into the living room to pick up his cell phone.

That was when he noticed something was amiss. If asked, he wouldn't have been able to explain it. Did he hear a noise? Did he see a flash of something out the window? He wasn't sure, but he felt like something was different than before. He had the lights out, still waiting for Stan to get home. Justin acted like he wasn't there. He was a shadow, a shadow with a knife in his hand. He'd left the steak knife on the counter this morning, and he picked it up now. Someone was turning the door handle, trying to get in. It was either Stan having trouble with the lock, Andrea having trouble with the lock, or Justin was about to be in serious shit.

The handle turned again, and he heard voices. Multiple voices. More than two. Either Stan and Andrea brought friends or…

They were here. They'd all have guns. What was one knife going to do. He needed to run. To make for the back door. He left the room. He passed the stairs. He got to the back door and opened it, quietly. A fist greeted him and he crashed to the floor, wind knocked out of him. A foot crashed down on his chest and he gasped for air. The front door flew open and they flooded the house. More hands grabbed him and started to drag him outside.

In the next few moments Justin Barker was looking at the moon, while numerous people pulled him in different directions. Two men were holding his arms, and another was dragging him by the collar.

"You trying anything, punk, and you're dead."

Justin struggled and freed one of his arms. He flung his elbow backwards and smashed into something hard. A few minutes later something cold and metal smashed into the back of his head and he staggered.

As they dragged him toward a car, one of the hit men opening the door, Justin looked up one last time at the moon. It was glowing, with a little white ring birthing light that seemed to cascade down. What a damn good picture, he thought, and knew that this little private fascination would be his final personal quandary, before the last gunshot.

Chapter 28

Ink and Water

T he next morning they dined on French Toast and blueberries, and Melanie made her next advance.

"Do you have a pencil and paper?"

He wiped his mouth with the napkin. "Maybe. Why?"

It was dangerous to lie to Barker, but today there was only one thing she wanted, one thing screaming her name. She didn't want to share it with him. It was something sacred, just for her. So she lied.

"After our talk last night, I would love to get back into sketching." She couldn't force herself to blush, but she acted like she wanted to.

Barker smiled at her, this time in the manner of a proud mentor. The way he nodded his head made him look like he was going to clap. "I'm happy to hear that," he said. "You certainly can. I'd love to see your work."

"It's just…" She stopped, provoking his curiosity.

"Yes?" he said.

"It's something I'd love to do in my room. In private. I know when I'm up there I have my hands tied but I wouldn't try to poke through the rope or anything. I promise. And you keep the door locked anyway."

He put up his hand. "That's enough, dear. Relax."

"Okay," she said.

"Tell ya what. I'll hang out in my room for awhile. And you draw. Deal?" he asked.

It was less than ideal, but maybe she could work with it, if she was discreet enough. "Okay. Thank you."

After Barker cleaned up the table, he brought her a notebook of white paper and a pencil. Melanie started to sketch something out, maybe a wing, like she'd described. Then after a few moments, after Barker was in his room, she put that sheet aside, and started on the letter.

What was best to say? Mom, Dad, I'm okay but I'm tied up every night and nearly got killed a couple of times. Oh, and he stripped me nude and chained me up. I got my head smashed by a cop and tear-gassed. Melanie held back a laugh, but as she started to find her words, a heavy weight fell on her.

Mom and Dad,

        I miss you so much. So, so much. I think about you everyday. I can't actually believe this is happening. I keep expecting to wake up. But I never do. And I'm so worried about you both. I hope you're okay. I'm sorry, so sorry. It was me he wanted. I wish he'd just taken me off the school bus and never touched either of you. I wish this would just end. I wish it would end. I hope you're not still looking for me. I hope you're not torturing yourselves. I guess, I just have to fend for myself now. And I really hope you both are too. Just, I guess, if you insist on looking for me, maybe try Washington. He brought me to Washington of all places. The cops here suck, Dad. I got out once and they sent me back. And this entire city was decimated by a mob family. It's horrible. The most horrible place I've ever been to. I miss Maine. Thank you both so much for bringing me to Maine. I loved it. And I love you.

Hugs and kisses,
Melanie.

Her nose was hot now, and she lost vision for a moment, water squeezing through. Melanie folded up the letter as small as possible and shoved it in her pocket, and tore up the half finished drawing of the wing. She went over to the trash can an tossed her failed draft inside. Then, for argument sake, she started sketching something else. But she couldn't stop herself from crying. And of all times for Barker to stroll in, he picked right then.

"What's wrong?" he asked. She didn't look at him, she just continued trying to sketch. "Answer me," he said.

Melanie sniffed. "I just hated the first copy. I'm so rusty. I wish I was good at this." She continued doodling on the paper, tracing what looked like the edge of a feather. Barker was walking up next to her, despite his stupid little offer.

"Most things just take practice, you know," he said. Melanie nodded her head, and another tear rolled down her cheek, cold. "Stop that," she heard him say, and cupped her eyes with her palm.

They were coming out hard now, hot and moist. "I can't."

"Please," he said calmly. "I don't...Come on, you have such a nice smile." His hands were on her shoulders, pressing hard, but then soft.

Melanie dropped the pencil and let her head sink down to the table, and Barker's hands continued to caress her.

When she'd finished crying, she asked Barker for a shower. She couldn't be near him. She had to get away. That meant two options. Returning to her room, to her leash and her muzzle, or retreating into her watery sanctuary. So here she was, the door locked from the inside. Barker never came in here. This was the one room in the house in which she had power. So it was in one of these drawers that she hid the letter. Underneath the tampons was probably a good spot. Even if he did come in she knew he'd never touch those.

Melanie had known about kidnapping all her life, but it was just an abstract concept. If she had to learn the hard way, she would have preferred to be a weekend long trial. Two days of torment, and then she could return to her normal life with some perspective. She felt like she'd been told at numerous points that when you really get into trouble, it doesn't work like that. There were things in life that would not offer a second chance, nor mercy. This proved it. It just went on and on. In moments where she felt like she needed to come up for air, Barker kept her submerged.

As she sank to the floor, her knee brushed something soft. It was the scarf she'd worn in her mouth the previous night. She grabbed it with two hands and pulled, trying to rip it in half. Or maybe she could bite through it. A silent protest on a device for silencing. But there was a reason she'd never bitten through a gag before, why she had to suffer them. As hard as she pulled she couldn't rip it. She was weak.

Melanie turned on the water, turning it up to a scalding temperature. When she stepped it felt like her skin was melting off, but only for a second. After that, it became easier, and took her mind off things. The steam allowed her to breathe, the pressure of the raining liquid allowed her to let her thoughts grow more narrow, and then allowed her mind to wander.

One time, in her past life, Melanie had cried for hours about a boy she knew. She never had much luck in school. A few were cute, and looking at other girls. A few were into her, but she wasn't attracted to them. She'd probably set unrealistic expectations, the way she thought about boys alone in bed at night. Once she'd had a boyfriend, and it only last a few months. Being as shy and timid as she always was, she never thought herself capable of emasculating a male. But somehow, she did just that. She might have suggested he turn down his music or make a small, very small, adjustment in some habit of his. Boys didn't like that. Really they were insufferable. That was when she'd learned about boys with low self-esteem. For a year she went on a passionate "boy's suck" rampage. Then she'd met Brandon Marters. Thinking now about his smooth skin and curly brown hair gave her a tingle between her legs, the first in a long time. Nothing had ever happened with Brandon; she'd been too damn shy. But she thought about him often, in her most private moments. And she was thinking about him now, regardless of Barker. This, like the letter, like the shower, was just for her.

Until the next day, when Barker entered her sanctuary.

The first thing Melanie did that morning, soon as Barker undid the gag, was ask for a shower. Once inside, she turned the knob and listened to the water sing. She looked at herself in the mirror. The mark on her head was so small she often forgot it was there, and she held her wrists up to her chin. Those marks were also faded. The scars might last forever, but who was complaining? Melanie slipped out of her clothes and into the raining waters.

Her thoughts from yesterday lingered on. Her train wreck of a first boyfriend was named Paul. She'd tried to voice her opinions, back when she constantly had freedom of speech, and one day when he felt too damn humiliated to work with her on a problem, he'd sent her home in tears. Her dad hadn't been happy, but he'd been less concerned with her feelings and more with whether or not she and the boy had sex. She remembered being angry with her father for questioning her, for being overbearing. Now she just remembered it as him having cared. Cared enough to fight for her when Barker came knocking. She wished she had appreciated her father then. She wished she hadn't been worried about his opinion of her, about the judgmental tone in his voice, about the fact that he treated her like a little girl. She wished she'd just thanked him, instead of saying I hate you.

When it came back to her, no amount of massaging water could soothe her. Tension built up in her chest. Her muscles tightened. Self loathing boiled her blood. One time Ronnie Kessler had called her name about ten times over in class and she'd snapped at him to shut up, and never apologized. She hated herself for that too. And she hated herself for trying to kill Barker so recklessly and so early on, because right now, if she had a strike to throw away, she could probably pull it off. She felt like she could destroy anything in front of her right now, and all that was there was a wall.

She smashed her hand against the wall.

It felt good.

She did it again. The blow echoed around the room, and possibly downstairs. She groaned. Roared. She let it all out.

Melanie took a few steps back and moved forward for the fierecest strike of all. That was when she slipped. Her legs buckled against the side of the tub and she took down the shower curtain. Everything spun upwards and she smashed against the ground, everything shaking and buzzing. Her head hit the ground almost as hard as her shoulder did, and she felt like something had wrenched free, sending pain like a giant needle through her right arm and right side of her torso. Then she laid there for a moment, waiting for things to stop swaying. All she heard was a hollow, echoic sound of flowing water.

Melanie honestly felt like she was about to pass out. She might have screamed, but couldn't remember finding the energy. There was one thing from this moment she did remember coherently. The moment when Barker forced the door open, took one look at her and grimaced. He disappeared and in a half second, he was back with a towel.

He gently slid his arms under her, wrapped her carefully. He didn't take advantage, he didn't touch her inappropriately, and he was careful with her shoulder. Somehow, Barker's steamy fingers were light as feathers.

The next day she stayed in bed, the rope tied around her left ankle instead of her hands. Her arm was stretched out on a series of pillows and she was advised to lie flat on her back. Barker had been coming and going, bringing medication to dull the pain.

It was nighttime, and he stepped into the room.

"Happy Halloween," he said, with an ironic tone. "Having fun?" He was teasing, but he was being gentle about it, far more gentle than she thought him capable. He sat down on the sofa, probably to avoid moving the mattress, sparking any pain. "Well, you won't be drawing for a little while."

"Sorry," she mumbled. Her injury had earned her a vacation from the scarves, but it was still hard to talk.

Barker got up and stood over her, pill bottle dangling in his hand. "Time for a dose," he said. Melanie started to lean up, but he put up his hand. She obeyed. "First, I want you to tell me something."

"Okay," she said.

"Why did you really want that pencil and paper?" The yellow brown eyes narrowed. "Do not lie to me."

Melanie swallowed and let out a deep breath, a few small tears forming. She'd do anything for those pills right now. "I wrote a letter to my parents."

Barker blinked. "Why?"

"I just wanted to put my thoughts on paper," her voice cracked but she'd gotten out all the words.

"And where have you hidden it?" he asked softly.

Through her tears, she said "The bathroom."

Barker nodded his head, and then he gave her the pills.

Later, when the pain was dull, Melanie just laid in bed, listless and helpless. Barker was sitting at the edge of the bed this time.

"You miss your family," he said. "That much I know."

Melanie didn't answer. It didn't sound like a question.

"That was a silly thing to do, that letter," he said.

"I'm sorry," she said.

He turned to her. "You don't have to be sorry. You can be smart instead." His voice softened, like a parent or a lover. "Melanie, dear. Tell me, wouldn't you rather see them again one day? In person?"

At first she didn't understand the meaning, but as she replayed the question again, she realized it sounded like an offer. "What?" she said.

"Would you like me to let you go home one day? And, you know, visit." He looked around the room, as if he were embarrassed. "Yeah, visit."

"I don't understand," she said.

He held up the long rope. "Wouldn't you rather, instead of this, one day just live in this house on your own terms. One day go outside when you want to. As long as you always come back? Wouldn't you love to travel wherever you want? Travel with me and let me show you amazing, adventurous things? As long as you remain with me and loyal to me? Wouldn't you love to be able to go home and visit your family? As long as you come back home?"

In the midst of his questioning, she actually sat up a bit. It was like a ray of sunshine. "You'd do that? You'd really do that?"

When Barker looked at her then, his eyes were fixed with passion. "Oh, Melanie. If you stop fighting me, if you're good to me, respectful of me, loyal to me, there's so much I'd be willing to give you."

Melanie watered up again, amazed at the suggestion. She'd thought she was in trouble. She'd thought that judgment was coming. But he was offering her a way out. No, he was offering a gift. In that moment, everything he'd just described became the things she wanted the most, and all she could do was timidly nod her head. Barker leaned down and touched his lips to her temple. It was truly soothing.

Chapter 29

Damages

E d Ryan's beard twitched beneath his grimacing face. He didn't look angry, per say, more taxed and ticked. Like it was all too much of a burden on him. "Tom. I know you've been to see Allen Marx."

Well, that was a great way for Tom Macklin to start his morning. "I don't–I beg your pardon, sir?"

Ryan smiled an ugly and rough looking smile. "Yes. Amazing isn't it? I'm New Heim's first psychic investigator."

Tom breathed once before answering. They say when you're stressed open with a joke. "Well, to be fair, sir, you were an investigator. Now you give orders to investigators."

Ryan chuckled. "Funny." He tapped his fingers on the desk, all at once, like a wolf scratching at the wood. Then he turned and adjusted himself in his chair. "Tom, let me tell you about a funny thing I heard. If you'll permit me, mobsters ran around our city with guns the other night. At 8:03 P.M., S.W.A.T. engaged the assassins on Main Street. I called in all of our units. Everyone reported in, save for you."

Tom started to feel like he was in a cage with a lion. And it was just waking up.

The Chief went on, with his hands raised. "Now, if I were psychic, this would be a lot easier. But since I can only speculate…" Slowly, Tom could see the rage developing in his boss's expression. "I certainly hope you haven't been double dealing with Allen Marx. I mean, sure. He's dead. Soon to be buried. But there's still, say, Orson Marx. I really hope you're not stupid enough to be double-dealing with them. Without telling me."

"I have no idea what you're talking about sir and if you would permit me, I already explained what happened. Three stragglers from their little militia attacked me. I was fighting for my life."

Ryan brushed his own chin with his index finger. "Do you like living, Tom?"

Tom considered what was behind the question. "Is that a threat?"

The Chief's reaction surprised him. "No. But I like the way you're thinking." He lifted his head and snapped his fingers. "Ugh. Fuck it. I'm no good at making jokes. Tom, I know what you did. And here's how I know."

"Sir, I—"

"Shut up. If you were to go behind my back and talk to the Marx Family, or anyone affiliated with them, why would you do it? Are you that broke? Are you plotting my death? Are you into the mob lord's wife? No. None of that sounds like Tom Macklin. No." The Chief leaned forward and drilled him with his eyes. "You went to carry out a plan involving Barker. A plan I wouldn't allow you to pursue." He took a deep breath. "So, you were involved in what just happened. The hit men. The deaths spread across the city. You had a part."

"I did not." But the Chief never heard him.

"You went to see Allen Marx to discuss killing Barker. They tried to kill him. It didn't work. So he manipulated us and the mob into the same place, and leveled the playing field. And Barker is, surprise surprise, still alive." The Chief inhaled deeply, and Tom saw his mouth half open. "The trick is though, someone warned Barker. He knew the mob was coming. I believe that someone was you."

Tom didn't hold back. "That is absolute shit." He leaned forward. "If I went to Barker, I'd be dead. How stupid do you think I am? Moreover, if I tried to kill him, I wouldn't involve you or anyone else. I'm not..." I'm not you. "I'm not Orson Marx. I don't drop bombs over a grudge."

The Chief never sat back. But he breathed more softly. "Don't lie to me, Tom. When we sent the Grier girl back to Barker I looked you right in the eye and I admitted to it. Like a man."

Tom gritted his teeth. Sold a sixteen-year-old kid into slavery. Like a man.

"I am not lying. I never went to see Marx or Barker."

The Chief looked unimpressed. "But you don't deny a part in the firefights."

"I had nothing to do with any of it. I responded to dispatch. That is all."

The Chief folded his arms. "Let me tell you something about me. I have a son, and, yes, he comes first, before any girl or criminal Barker wants to slaughter...but he's not the only one. Some of you, here at the station, most of you, are like children to me. The sons I never wanted."

"Thanks very much."

"But whether you want them or not, you always care, even if you'd like to kill them yourself sometimes." He leaned forward sharply. "Barker will kill you the way he killed Stan. You understand? What you're trying to do is stupid and mindless. So drop it. I will take your badge."

Tom lost his caution. "For what? You've no proof of any wrong doing."

The Chief's face slowly opened into a wide look of astonishment. "Careful, Tom."

"I've done none of the things you accuse me of, and even if I did, you have no proof. May I go?"

The Chief shot smoke out his nostrils. "You're being stupid, boy."

"May I go?"

"Dismissed," he declared.

Tom got himself as far away from his despicable boss as he could. Had he really just said Tom was like the son he never wanted? Truly? A son who could just get fucked six days out of seven? It reminded Tom very much of his real father.

One of the analysts stopped him. He was a short, stout man with red hair. He handed Tom a blank folder.

"What's this?" Tom asked.

"The thing we talked about." And then he scurried away.

Tom quickly walked out of the station, cradling the file like a child. A child he didn't really want, but needed. The report from a certain home invasion.

***

Melanie's shoulder was still in massive pain, her right arm in a sling. She must have cracked it, or worse. And her head was numb. But Barker said he didn't think she had a concussion.

Barker had told her to "be good," and lassoed a rope around her ankle again. But this time, after repeated begging and pleading, Barker had tied her foot to the living room sofa instead of upstairs in the dark stuffy room. Now he was gone, and any minute now, someone should be showing up to "watch her." Apparently she was three years old again. Well, fuck it. Maybe she could take advantage. Have everything done for her.

The rope was not incredibly long, and she couldn't make it out of the living room, into the kitchen, or even the bathroom, which sucked, because she was getting really hungry.

When she heard footsteps coming towards the door, she immediately assumed it was Barker. Then she realized how much lighter these steps were. And they didn't follow his rhythm. Barker walked with a bit of a stumble. Boom. Boom. Boom, boom. Beat. Boom. These steps came fast, following a straight pattern, and the knock on the door was light.

"Hello?" mused the voice of a girl. And then the door was opening. Melanie watched as Kris entered, long hair flowing behind her thin shoulder, still exposed by a sleeveless vest.

"How's it going?" she asked, shutting the door behind her. Melanie took a quick glimpse out the door before it clamped shut. The sun was shining behind clouds, giving the sky a somber gloom. It looked like a typical day in November.

"Alright," Melanie said. "I guess."

Kris gestured toward the sling. "Heard you took a fall."

"Yeah? Where'd you hear that?" Melanie asked.

Kris smiled. "You okay?"

"Think so," Melanie asked, half smiling back.

"Great." Kris's eyes drifted down to the rope around Melanie's ankle, but she didn't say anything. "Hungry?"

"Actually, yes," Melanie said. "If you wouldn't mind."

"What I do," Kris said, and headed toward the kitchen. "Babysitting. That's me." Kris opened the fridge, still muttering as Melanie sat on the sofa. "Watch the kid. Watch Melanie. Watch all the hostages. And what's this taking me away from? Oh, yeah, watching an entire fucking gang. Go me."

Melanie chuckled inaudibly. "Shame he doesn't pay you."

Kris set mayonnaise and cheese on the counter, followed by white bread. "Yeah well, he pays me in food. I suppose."

"How are things, you know, over there?" Melanie asked.

"Not good," Kris said. "This kid is so hard to control," she whined.

"Kid?" Melanie asked.

Kris went stiff for a moment. "Oh, right, fuck." She scratched her head. "Sorry but I'm not saying anything else. If you find out, you'll find out from him."

"Okay," Melanie said. "I mean its not like I would say anything to him."

Kris pointed a butter knife at her. "Quit talking like that. It's dangerous." Kris kept rummaging as Melanie tried to steady herself on the couch. Her shoulder jolted with pain and she gritted her teeth.

"Has everyone...everyone been okay since all the hit man stuff?"

Kris laughed. "Hit man stuff, yeah, we're fine. We're used to danger. How about you?"

"I've been better," she said.

Kris took a long gulp. "You should start drinking. You'll feel better."

Melanie let herself laugh. "If I get drunk enough I won't feel much at all."

Kris snapped her fingers. "Exactly."

They both laughed, and Melanie was happy she was here. She liked Kris. And Adam, and all those kids. She wished she could see more of them than Barker.

"How is everyone? Adam? The kids?"

"Everyone's great," Kris said. "Adam asked about you a couple times."

"Everyone's fed?" Melanie asked.

"Yes," Kris said. "Barker's been sending us a lot of cash. I've been able to feed everyone every night."

"That's great," Melanie said, happy for the little ones. And the boys too.

Kris was throwing around ingredients like a sloppy juggler. Melanie assumed she was making a cheese, lettuce and mayo sandwich. "Yeah. I still eat the least. But I'm fine with that," Kris said.

Melanie occupied herself by smoothing out wrinkles on the cushions with her free hand. Eventually Kris brought over a plate with a sandwich cut clean down the middle.

"Thanks," Melanie said, taking it and placing it on her lap.

"No problem, Princess." Kris looked around. "Looks like there's not much to do around here."

"I read a lot."

"I remember you saying." Kris sat down in Barker's chair, holding up the plate with her left hand. "Read anything new lately?"

"Not really. Mostly just been falling in the shower."

Kris laughed. "Well, books can get boring after awhile. No TV or anything. I'd like a TV. It's been years."

Melanie thought about Barker's suggestion to take her out on Thanksgiving. "I'd love some fresh air. Every once in awhile."

Kris took a bite of her sandwich, hesitating between bites. "You know, hun. I'd love to take you outdoors. Really, I would. But I'm not taking any liberties in his own house. Sorry."

"It's okay," Melanie said. "I'm not asking you to. I'm just saying. I'm fucked."

Kris set the plate on the windowsill. "No, you're not. You're alive." Her tone was gentle, but her words clearly annunciated. "That's more than others can say. Neither of us are fucked, not yet." But even as she said it, a shadow fell over Kris's eyes. She looked like she'd gone somewhere else, same as Barker tended to do. She brought herself back much more quickly, snorting. "Not yet."

"I know," Melanie said. "Thanks." She didn't know if she agreed. Melanie tried to replay the situation and see the bright side of things. She had not been raped. She had not been cut or hit more than once or twice. She had been nearly killed, but escaped every time. There were so many others she knew Barker had killed. So Melanie tried to comfort herself.

Once she did, she remembered a chill when she realized something was wrong in her house, a spasm of pain and fear that followed her for weeks, as her arms and legs were held down relentlessly, as every time she wanted to scream or cry, something was crammed into her mouth. She thought about how desperately she wanted just one thing, that God or some higher power had given her the right to. And how she was denied it. How every moment of her life was one cycle of apprehension, on edge to protect her life, for never committing a single crime. All the while, her eyes were on the rope around her ankle.

"It's agony," was all she said, and it was little more than a dull murmur. Yet, it seemed to affect Kris.

"I know," she said, leaning down, folding her hands, staring at the floor. "I know." Melanie's eyes drifted to Kris, and now the older girl was looking at her like she was puzzled about something. She made a "hmm" sound. "Can you keep a secret?" she asked.

"Of course," Melanie said.

Kris sat back in the chair. "Sometimes, I think about sending the kids away."

"Away, where?" Melanie asked.

"Anywhere but here," Kris said. "Barker would want to keep me, the boys, some spies. But I wonder if I could send the little ones off, discreetly. I think about it all the time."

"I didn't know that," Melanie said. "I can understand why, though."

Kris nodded. "This is agony."

It was dark when Barker returned, and Kris scurried out the door with a friendly, casual wave to Melanie. When the door was shut Barker stepped forth, arms loaded. He had one plastic bag. Gone for hours and back with one bag? Where had he gone? That bag did look pretty heavy. But he also had something long and dark over his shoulder, and she noticed there was a small hooked piece of metal coming out the top.

"This should help," he muttered. He pulled out several pill containers. And then he revealed the rest of the bag's contents, more books.

Perks of Being a Wallflower. Othello. Ender's Game. Bel Canto. The Shining. Dr. Sleep

Then he approached her with the long black structure. Melanie was slightly afraid, but when he unzipped it, she was enthralled. It was something she'd jump up and down if her mother had bought for her. It was blue, with gray fur on the inside, building out along the sides beside the zipper. She noticed it was just the right size for her.

"Like it?" he asked.

"I…"

She did like it. Very much. It was beautiful. Expensive looking.

"Try it on," he said, handing it to her. "I mean, you know, as best you can."

With her arm in the sling, Barker put the coat around her himself, and she slid her left arm through the sleeve. The other side he just hung over her. It felt soft and cool at first, before the warmth of the fur set in.

Barker said, "It is a…" He cocked an eyebrow and looked up. "Fleece…Faux…Fur, yeah, Fleece Faux Fur Winter Coat."

She fitted it around herself, adjusting it slightly, one hand holding it at the top, like a dress.

Barker continued, "That ought to keep ya warm, kiddo."

It was almost winter.

She stared down her own torso, admiring her gift. She had absolutely no idea what to think or feel. But she knew what to say. "I love it. Thank you."

"You're welcome," he said with a satisfied smile, and grabbed her head. He brushed her hair with a red hand.

Melanie recoiled uncontrollably, and he looked alarmed.

"I'm sorry!" she said. "I'm sorry, I didn't mean to. It's just…"

The blood was dry. But it hadn't been there when he left. He looked down as he curled his hand into a fist and made a face like he was in trouble.

"Oh…this." He brushed his thumb hard over his hand, as if that would scrape it off. "Sorry, didn't mean to frighten you…stopped to see an accountant on the way home."

"What happened?"

"Well, he was extremely rude." He shrugged and rolled his eyes. "Next thing I knew, I'd punched the guy out." And he laughed. And Melanie laughed too. Laughing was an experiment. What did he think of that? If she laughed with him, would he strike her? Was it a trap? No. He put his hand on her shoulder, and seemed ecstatic that she found the same amusement in life that he did.

Chapter 30

Trembling

One week passed.

Melanie spent her time eating, reading, and daydreaming about colors, pictures, and song lyrics. Barker came and went throughout the week. He was vague about the little missions he would go on. He kept mentioning a couple of names, one she knew well, from his story about Ghost Town. Orson Marx. The name she was less familiar with was Albert Ferris, but that seemed to be what his business was about. She didn't know if he was going out to talk with them, drink with them, or threaten them. He didn't tell her much about that. But he kept asking her about herself. Little questions about camerawork, some she didn't know the answers to. A few times, she feared he might even punish her for giving the wrong answer, but he never did. He asked and listened, like she was the most interesting person in the world. Then he would go off, into his own head, strolling around the house.

Melanie didn't have that luxury. Aside from meals, Barker still kept her foot lassoed to either the bed or the sofa. Before the accident, he had always gagged her as well. After the fall, it seemed like he was more interested in nurturing her than punishing her.

All of this came to a head a week later, when the sling finally came off. Her shoulder still hurt and it was hell to try and move it in a circle, but for all intents and purposes she was better, and now it was time to go back to the old routine: leash, gag, bell.

On November 7th, Barker tied her wrists together, and even her fingers, to keep her from picking at the ropes. As she awaited the scarf, she thought it was strange that Barker was suddenly taking more precautions. But then he kissed her on the head, and left the room. No gag.

He'd suddenly, without explanation, given her a small gift. Was it a message?

Now it was November 8th. She was still foggy on his frequent trips outside, though he never came back covered in blood. He said that mostly he was just observing. What, she had no idea. But tonight Barker said he wanted to stay with her.

"I'm sorry," he said as they sat in the living room. Melanie's wrists were lassoed to the sofa, but she could still hold a book. This time, it was a copy of Othello.

"Sorry for what?" Melanie asked.

"For neglecting you," he said. "This past week was important. Do you know much about war?"

"Can't say that I do," Melanie said. She had always hated when history classes arrived at wars. She found them to be the most boring subjects imaginable, and nothing was ever pleasant. World War II had been the only one remotely interesting to her, but that came with the most horrific stories.

"War is politics, then mobilization, bloodshed, and whoever kills the most people earns a surrender from the enemy. And that's it. Right?"

"Right?" she asked.

"Wrong," Barker said. "There's a kind of depression that follows a war. Economic, geographic, hell, even spiritual. A misery that lingers and an adjustment period as all those who were swept into the chaos watch the world go back to peace time without them."

"Makes sense," Melanie said.

"That happens even in small wars," he said. "So these past few weeks I've been keeping my eye on the enemy. Namely, old Orson Marx and Albert Ferris. They've been good, I have to say. They seem to know their places."

"Good," Melanie said. "So we won't have anymore trouble?"

He shook his head. "Not yet," he said. "I think I gave them a good enough scare. Are you cold?" he said.

"I think I'm okay right now. Thanks." She smiled at him.

He smiled back. "Okay. You let me know, though. Got it?"

"Got it." She turned her eyes back to the book, and Barker leaned back in the chair.

As she read, she found herself less focused on Shakespeare's lines, and more focused on what came next. Barker was a serial killer, but he didn't want to kill her. Serial killers typically had victims, but he'd been busy with the mob since they returned. Always looking over his shoulder. If things were quieting down, would he start killing again? Would she have to watch?

She turned a page. "What, um, happens now?" she asked.

"'Cuse me?" he said.

"You've been really busy since we came here. If things are safer now, what will you do next?"

He smiled, leaning forward slowly, dramatically. "Make fish tacos."

Her mind went blank. "What?" she said, hardly controlling her testy tone of voice.

"Want some?" he asked, as he got up and headed toward the kitchen.

"Sure," she said, fighting back laughter. At least he had a sense of humor once in awhile.

Barker opened the cabinets and drawers, grabbing taco shells and utensils. He wasn't cooking from scratch, God no, but he was at least putting the tacos together himself, even if it was pre-cooked fish. He opened the fridge and started taking out spices.

"What would you like on yours?" he asked.

She scratched an itch on her nose, keeping hold of the book with the other hand, and for a moment she smelled the paper. "Um, just some lettuce and tomato chunks. Please."

Barker stopped rummaging so suddenly it chilled her. When she looked at him he was completely different. Quiet, stiff, stern. Only a small change, but with his face it made all the difference. He looked like a killer again and she had no idea what she did wrong.

"What?" Her heartbeat was racing, and tears were coming rapidly. "What did I do?"

His finger went up to his lips, and she realized he wasn't angry at her. He heard something. So she stayed quiet.

After awhile, Melanie noticed it too. Something was moving outside. There were footsteps coming toward the door. Barker stood in the kitchen; Melanie sat on the couch. Together they awaited a knock on the door. When it came it was incredibly gentle. If they had been talking, she wouldn't have even noticed. Barker slowly glided toward the door and gripped the knob. Before he opened it he gave her a gentle but warning look, and she nodded back.

He opened the door and 'Kris was standing on the doorstep. Barker looked just as surprised as Melanie, and she didn't think that boded well.

"What are you doing here?" Barker asked sharply. "Did I miss your text?"

Kris shook her head. "No. I'm sorry." Tonight she was dressed in her usual sleeveless black top and dark jeans. She was wearing shiny gray boots, and her hair was draped practically over her face. Melanie looked closer, and saw dried blood on her.

"What happened?" Melanie asked across Barker, putting the book down with her bound hands. "Are you alright?" Barker looked back at Melanie almost inquisitively, and then back at Kris.

"Well?" he asked her.

"Can I come in?" She looked up at Barker with tears in her eyes. "Please."

Barker looked apprehensive. He was breaking records holding this distrusting frown. Usually he'd have broken a smile by now. But he stepped back anyway and ushered her in. He gently shut the door behind her. Kris kept her hands at her sides, and Melanie noticed that she was armed, a gun through her belt. She was shaking too. She must have just been in a fight.

"What happened?" Melanie asked again. "You're shaking." Kris still didn't answer, and Barker snorted.

"Don't make me ask again," he said, and the sound in his voice made Melanie want to scream at Kris to obey him.

"We were attacked," she finally said.

"Who's we?" Barker asked.

"All of us. All of us at once. Me, Dom, Adam, the kids." Her voice was shaking.

"By whom?" Barker asked.

"Ferris," she growled. "It was Ferris." Barker's eyes went wider than Melanie had ever seen, and his face had transformed into a glare.

"Go on," he said.

"He's gone," Kris said. "Took the kid. The hostage. We thought he was alone but he had assassins. They came out of nowhere. They fired. And…" Tears fell to the floor. "They're all dead." Her lips curled. "All of them." She covered her eyes with one hand, trembling, but staying on her feet.

Melanie's blood went cold. All of them? Dom, Adam, the girls, the other boys. The little ones. They were dead? She tried to picture the little faces, and Adam's kind interest in her, but the thought of any of them made her stop breathing. She tried to say something to Kris, but no words came out. Barker was taking steps back, aghast.

"He came to you?" Barker asked. "You should have texted me immediately. I'd have been over in three minutes."

Kris nodded, still crying. "I know. I'm sorry." Barker took a deep breath.

"And you shouldn't have come to my house without calling. You know the rules." Melanie wanted to punch him. Kris was clearly traumatized. Melanie had never seen her breaking down. She needed help, not scolding. Surely, if he could be kind to Melanie, even in small favors, he had to have a shred of soul left in him. It had to come out in moments like these, with the people who were loyal to him. It had to.

Barker turned around and looked at the kitchen counter for what felt like a long time, leaving Kris to cry. "Well I was just making dinner. I suppose you could rest here tonight until we figure this out. No one in their right mind will attack me here again so soon. Not after last time."

As he spoke, Kris stopped trembling, and Melanie began to. While Barker was looking at the counter she quietly drew her gun, and raised it. Melanie wanted to shout no, but instead she curled up, covering her face. Barker spun around and swatted Kris's hand.

Bang.

The shout rang in her ears, but the bullet had flown out the window, adding to the marks already made. Barker had Kris's arm in grasp and her throat in his other hand. Her feet had left the ground, dangling.

"Why you little bitch," Barker hissed. He was choking Kris so hard her tongue was hanging out. Melanie's chest was in pain from the panic alone. It was over in the next few moments. Kris's gun hit the floor as she went limp. Barker had either killed her or knocked her out. Barker had tackled her before, pinned her to wall and squeezed her throat with the strength of an elephant. She hadn't died or passed out. He must have gone easy on her.

He let Kris fall to the ground roughly, and stood over her with a sneer. He gripped his own ears, mouth agape and eyes shut. He looked like he was in a lot of pain, and once or twice he even staggered. He drew himself up quickly though. This man had survived being shot and stabbed. Whatever was hurting him now was just a flee bite, she was sure. His eyes drifted to Melanie.

"Are you alright?" he asked, his volume indicating that he couldn't hear very well.

She shook her head, but didn't say anything. Barker danced around Kris, who looked, surprisingly, relaxed where she slept.

"This little bitch," he was muttering. "Well, got to hand it to her. Bold. Ah." He groaned and grumbled. Then he raced out of the room and came back with one of his large knives. Melanie's wits betrayed her.

"No! Don't, please!"

"Shut up," Barker said. "You think I'll allow something like this?"

Melanie jumped to her feet, almost tripping over the rope, and stood opposite Barker. "Please! Don't hurt her! She didn't mean it!"

Barker cocked is eyebrows. "Oh, she meant it. You don't fire a gun if you don't mean it. Trust me." Barker's anger came with a condescending tone and face. Now he was talking to her like she didn't know anything about anything. But then his usual strange faces returned, mixtures of confusion, curiosity, dullness. "I guess I'll take you upstairs first," he said. "You don't need to see."

Melanie dropped to her knees. "Please. I'm begging you. Don't kill her. How would you feel if everyone you loved was killed? She's not herself! Please! Please!" Tears were pouring out and her nose was hot. Barker stepped back again, shoulders stiff, eyes wide.

"You care about her?" Barker asked. "That much?"

"It's her life!" Melanie said. "Don't you understand? Please!" She felt her own voice breaking into sobs. She wasn't just thinking about Kris. She'd pleaded for her own life before, and she was thinking of her parents. "Please."

Barker stared at her for a moment, still aghast. And then the knife slowly fell to his side, arm limp.

"Wow," was all he said.

Melanie stared up at him through the tears, and he stared down. Neither of them said anything, and Kris continued to sleep. Barker's first movement was slow, as he crept over to the island and set the knife down. His next movement was sharp and fast. He tore the lasso off the foot of the couch and yanked her to her feet. Then he was forcing her upstairs. She almost tripped once or twice and he didn't seem to notice. Then they were in the bedroom. Barker tied her hands to the foot of the bed as usual, the rope shorter now that he had torn it. She would have to kneel on the ground.

Then he was digging in her closet.

"What are you doing?" she pleaded. "Talk to me."

He drew a scarf and in an eye blink he knotted it and pulled it through her teeth. It pinched her tongue and almost choked her. Barker knelt down and pointed his finger in her face.

"Do not talk back to me. Understand?" Melanie almost stopped breathing again, and felt very sick. She cried and trembled, but managed to nod her head. Barker sighed, letting out some tension. Then he looked like he was starting to feel bad, like he'd lost control. He sighed again. And again, more than she ever thought he would.

"I won't kill her," he said. "I'll let her explain herself." He stood up. "We'll sort it all out in the morning. Get some sleep."

He turned and shut the door behind him, darkening her world once more.

Chapter 31

New Plan

Barker needed fresh air and he needed information. So he tied Kris up (much more uncomfortably than Melanie) and left the house. The air was brisk and the moon was bright. Perfect night for a slaughter. Too bad he hadn't been the one doing the slaughtering.

On the way to the gymnasium, Barker went into his phone and checked his special bank account. It was deactivated. Ferris was indeed gone. He must have done it just before he attacked. He wanted to kill both Ferris and Kris. Every time a gun went off so close to his ears he felt like he was struck by lightning, and he all he wanted was to slaughter everyone nearby who had a part in the noise. Kris needed a strict punishment...but what would Melanie say to that? Bah. So much work.

Barker assumed that the slaughter had occurred in the gymnasium. If not, then he would check the house he knew they crouched in. When he arrived at the gymnasium he immediately knew her story was true. There was just something hanging over the scenery, something most people might not perceive. Everything was just a touch more silent than usual. And far off, inside the building, he could faintly smell blood and the scent of dead flesh.

When he entered the large, dark room, he saw shapes littered throughout and dark puddles everywhere. He could see quite well in the dark, and was immediately able to do a head count of boys and girls. Six girls. Seven boys. There were more people in the gang than that, and there were the little ones. Where were the little ones?

Barker stepped over the bloody puddles and the carcasses, his footsteps loud and echoic in the mausoleum. He went toward the back door, trying to find the point of entry. He brandished his knife, in case any of them were still around. What he found in the locker room was the most recognizable and largest of the bodies. Dominic was lying on his side, several bullet holes in him. He was curled up, as if he had been protecting something or someone. Barker looked at his dead face in the pale light. His eyes were shut and his mouth hanging open, drool marring the floor next to him. The corpse reeked of shit, and Barker stepped away. Shame, Dom had been a nice strapping young man. A good mate for Kris, he always thought. But unfortunately, he and many of the rest were just more little nuts and bolts that constructed Ghost Town.

Barker stepped outside. It was beautiful, if just a little bit sad. More spirits surrounded the cursed slums now, and Barker was in need of new little spies. Ferris had stolen money and resources from him, and for a moment his chest tightened with hate.

"Well, you'd better hope I never find you," he whispered into the night.

The first time a mobster had taken something away from Justin Barker, it was Matthew Sect. And what he'd taken was precious, at the time. They had abducted Justin from Stan's house, and he was waiting for death in the back seat of a car. The car was small, fitting four people, two in back and two in front. The remaining two hit men did not get into the car. They ran off elsewhere and were likely following from somewhere far behind, in case anything went wrong. A tall blonde man with bright blue eyes and a long chin pointed his gun at Justin. The whispering man. He looked like he was chewing something.

The driver had a hat, dark coat, and what looked like a brown beard. The rest of him was shrouded. In the passenger seat was what looked like a thin man with a short crew cut. He was wearing a coat but no hat. He turned around and smiled at Justin with steely eyes. When he smiled, the skin on his cheeks bulged, showing some excess fat.

"You know who I am, son?" he said.

Justin was more focused on the gun being pointed at him from the side, but he shook his head.

"I'm Matt Sect," said the man in the passenger seat.

Justin looked away from the gun and studied the face of the devil. So this was the guy who wanted him dead.

"Pleasure," Justin said, voice quivering. Sect sniggered.

"Sorry for the rough pick up. I know my boys are aggressive." His eyes danced around the car for a moment. "How old are you, kid?"

"Sixteen," Justin lied, hoping that would earn him some sympathy.

Sect nodded his head. "You don't look sixteen. But whatever. Myself, I'm twenty-six. Handsome for an old man, ain't I?"

"Whatever you say," Justin said.

Sect laughed and pointed at the gunman. "I saw you glance at him earlier. This is Joe. Joe's one of my best guys. Has been since birth. That's right, he may not look like it but Joe is about twenty years older than us. He's been my bodyguard since I was a little guy."

"That must have been convenient," Justin said. He glanced at the gunman, who was glaring at him. "What's your problem?"

"You smashed me in the face, you little shit," Joe said in a deep voice.

"Now, now, Joe. Relax." Sect looked back at Justin. "See we have a little problem here. Joe's upset with you. According to him, you two met last night."

Justin looked at Joe, who was bearing his teeth. "Is that right?" Justin asked.

"Is it true?" Sect looked at him now with pondering, imposing eyes. "Were you on the boardwalk last night? Did you happen to see old Joe doing something, let's say, really fucking stupid?"

"No, sir, I was out for a walk in the city. Nowhere near the water," Justin said.

"Where were you going?" Sect asked.

"ShipDeck Bar and Grill," Justin said.

Sect motioned to Joe with his eyes. The gun was lowered for a moment, and Justin's head was bashed against the window, sending agonizing pains through his skull and neck.

"That's it. No more bullshit, alright?" Sect said with an unconvincing smile. "Joe here, whom I trust with my life, tells me a guy matching your description was on the boardwalk, witnessing something no one wants to talk about. If you did see it, it was likely a harrowing and miserable thing to behold. Did anything like that happen to you last night? It's okay. You can talk to me."

"I thought you said no more bullshit," Justin said through a bleeding lip, and Sect's smile vanished.

"Don't get smart with me, boy. Tell me what you saw and maybe we can still work something out. Talk back again, and you're dead."

"I still say we kill him," Joe said.

"I heard you the first time," Sect spit back. Then to Justin, "Talk."

Justin stared into Sect's face as the driver took them through a series of tight turns. They were cutting through the city and going somewhere near the coast. His eyes darted between the gunman and the rich man. He settled on Sect, and wondered what words would save him. He needed to buy time before he came up with them.

"How did you find me?" he asked. The gun jabbed into his stomach, and he struggled for air.

"What did I say?" Sect asked.

Justin inhaled deeply. "I was out for a walk last night. On the boardwalk. I enjoy the moon at night. Was just getting some air. I didn't see anything. I did hear a gunshot somewhere not too far, but this is New Heim."

Sect nodded. "Why does Joe say he saw you?"

"I don't know," Justin said. "I don't know what this is about?"

"Well, maybe where we're headed it'll start coming back to you."

Sect brought Justin to a very small beach somewhere at the Northern edge of New Heim, tucked away from the longer beach that stretched the coast of the city. The driver tore through the dunes and parked the car on top of a hill. When they dragged Justin out of the car they zip tied his hands behind his back, and marched him forward, gun nozzle digging into his back. They brought him down to the sand, miles away from anyone's houses. All he could see was the moonlight and the darkness beneath it.

Joe forced Justin to his knees and Sect stood over him. Now standing up, Justin noticed that Sect was of average height, with a slender figure and strong professional posture.

"You know where we are, Justin?" he asked, hands on his hips, looking around the area.

"Enlighten me," Justin growled.

"We're at Bronze Beach. Ugly name isn't it? Although I do love alliteration." He took his hands off his hips and patted them together. "I'm getting bored asking the same question over and over again, so I might just kill you now. But first, before I do, I want to at least let you confess. You know, for dignity's sake."

"You can't do this," Justin said. His heart was beating faster. The suspense was staring to rob him of his nerves.

Sect went on, "I'll just talk a bit about what happened. One of my ex girlfriends was strutting around the boardwalk the other night, ignoring all of my phone calls. So I sent my boys to pick her up. She fought back, things got a little violent, and my dear friend Joe did something very ill advised. That is, he shot her in the skull." He got closer to Justin, leaning down. "Now, although I am pretty pissed about that, do I want my childhood bodyguard, one of my most loyal friends, to go to jail for life? The answer is no."

"Then maybe you shouldn't go around killing people," Justin said. Sect punched him in the face so hard it felt like his face was smashed flat. He spit out some blood. Sect leaned close, face to face.

"Did you see it?" he asked again.

"Yes," Justin said. And then it hit him. Something that would save his life. "I have it on tape."

At first, Matt Sect was shocked, scared shitless, then his face turned to anger and he rounded on Joe.

"Is it true?" he asked. "Did he have a camera?"

Joe looked flabbergasted. "I…I thought it was a gun."

Sect smacked his hand against his temple. "You idiot." He turned back to Justin. A gust of wind nearly knocked them both over. "Where is it?" he asked.

"I gave it to a friend."

"Where. Is. It?" Sect asked again.

"If you kill me, my friend will make sure it shows up on the local news," he said with confidence. If he was dead, he was going to die like Sect said. With Dignity.

Sect took out a gun and pulled back the head. "Next loud gust of wind is your last. Where, is, the photo?"

"I'm going to need some assurances."

Sect pistol-whipped Justin sending more blood gushing out of his nose and gums. Justin could only imagine what he would look like in the mirror, and how much Sect was still going to do to him.

Sect moved toward Justin to hoist him up, but before he could reach him, flashes of blue and red swept the beach.

Three cars roared onto the scene and from them emerged close to a dozen cops.

"N.H.P.D.! Drop your weapons!"

From Justin's point of view, the cops were only silhouettes, but he'd never been so happy to see them. The hit men were pointing their guns at the cops. Matt was pointing his too.

Justin was on his knees now. The cops howled again, "Lay your weapons on the ground!"

Sect lowered his, but didn't drop it. "Do you know who I am officer?"

"Yeah, Matt. We know who you are. Drop your weapon, put your hands on your head, and walk towards us slowly. Tell your men to do the same."

"My father—"

"We don't give a fuck about your father. For the last time, drop the weapon."

Joe fired his gun at the speaker, and the cop hit the ground.

In the next moment, Matt sprang over Justin and the other hit man ran as well. Gunshots sailed over Justin, the sound pounding his eardrums in. The hit men were returning fire, and some of the cops were taken out from the back. The others Sect had brought for back up had joined the fight. Everything was a barrage of gunfire and smoke.

In a quiet moment, Justin jumped to his feet. He needed to move towards the ocean, away from the bullets, away from Sect, if he was still alive. With his hands tied, he ran toward the water. More gunshots sounded as the fight continued. As Justin ran, they grew more distant. And then there was a closer sound, like an explosion.

A bullet tore through Justin's shoulder, drilling through nerve and bone.

Justin staggered and tumbled into the water. Salt and liquid washed up into his sinuses and down his throat as the waves took him. His body was numb aside from the sickening drilling feeling in his shoulder, and his hands were still tied behind him.

He couldn't think straight. Either he'd die from the shot or from the water. He was upside down, rolling around in agony. The wound throbbed and seared, as blood continued to pour into the water. At one point he even tasted it.

Is this what happened to you, Dad? Is this how it felt?

He played with the restraints on his wrists, but it wasn't enough. He was just lying there, being swept up, face buried in wet sand. His head was getting fuzzy. It was getting harder and harder to stay awake. This was it. There was nothing he could do.

No. He had to live. He needed to get back. He couldn't die here. He couldn't give up. He wasn't weak. He needed to live. He could still live. He needed to live. He had to get up.

He strained against the zip ties, but they were so tightly done they probably dented the skin. Blood continued to pour, and he only felt more and more weak. No. Not weak. Not now. Never again. Not ever. He had to live. He had to get out of the water. He needed his hands. He needed to use his hands before he lost too much blood. Before he swallowed too much water.

He clenched his fist, and summoned every bit of strength he had. And in the next few seconds, the plastic circle around his wrists snapped in half. His arms flew apart, causing more pain to his shoulder, but he'd regained control. He dug his hands into the wet sand and pushed himself up out of the water. He coughed and hacked, blowing out his nose. He grabbed his shoulder, balancing on one arm as the waves smashed into him. Like an animal, he scurried on all fours toward the shore, kicking water backwards. With loud splashes he made his way out, fighting the pain all the while.

And finally he was standing on the sand, on two feet, with dignity.

He got a look at the carnage for a minute. All of the hit men were in cuffs, including Sect. Two cops were lying on the ground, and the rest looked furious. One of them was approaching him, and that was when the fatigue set in. He let himself fall, tasting a mouthful of sand, and then he was falling asleep under the cascading moonlight.

When he awoke, his head was pressed into a soft pillow. He wasn't in any pain, but he really couldn't move much. After his thoughts came together he realized he was in a hospital. Everything was murky white.

Andrea was there. Sitting next to him. As he woke up, he saw her dull, dejected expression come to life.

"How are you feeling?" she asked.

"Uh," he said. "What the fuck happened now?"

She started petting his head. "It's okay, Justin. It's all over. Matt Sect was arrested. The whole city is talking about it."

All over? Not if the mob was blaming him. Justin tried to get up, but she stopped him.

"Don't," she said. "Rest. Stan will be here soon."

"They broke into your house," he said to her. "They took me from your living room."

There were tears in her eyes. "I know." And then she burst into tears. Her cries came out in huge sobs, like a dog whimpering. She buried her face.

That was the end of that conversation. As the minutes rolled by a doctor came in the room to ask him a million questions, about what he remembered, then Lorena made an appearance.

"Hey," she said to him. Then she rubbed her sister's back. "You okay?" she asked Justin.

He nodded. And Lorena nodded back. She stroked her sister's hair and shushed her, looking like she was in an awkward, unfamiliar position. Their parents were outside, sounding livid. Their angry yells filled up the hallway, and some of the security guards were coming over. As Lorena escorted her sister out of the room, Andrea squeezed Justin's hand one more time, and for some reason, her face was wracked with guilt.

"It's not your fault," he whispered.

A few more people came in and out of the room, including a few cops, who brought flowers.

And finally, Stan.

He was still in uniform, and looked guarded, like he'd just been in a fight, and he didn't want to be talking.

"How you holding up?" he asked Justin. Justin shrugged. The sedatives were really kicking in now, and he couldn't move much. "This is a good place. They'll take care of ya."

Justin dug his head into the pillow, looking up at the ceiling, letting the drugs take him. He listened as Stan spoke.

"You're probably wondering right now what the fuck happened. Am I right?" He scratched his own eyebrows.

Justin half-nodded.

Stan took a deep breath. "I'm sorry, kid. But I don't want to lie to you. You deserve better than that."

Justin looked over at him and whispered, "Lie about what?"

Stan composed himself. "The police are working round the clock to bring in the entire Sect family. The two biggest targets are Maxwell, and his first son, Matt. The rest are easier targets. And they've been working on ways to get them...but you managed to nail a picture of Joe Royce taking a girl's life. That was big." He stood up, pacing the room, rubbing his face with his hands. He looked anxious about something. "When I told the station what you told me, and showed the evidence, they knew that the mob would come after you. They knew that if Joe was in danger of being seen, that Matt would come personally. They knew if they could catch him kidnapping you, they would have a reason to arrest them."

He stopped, and stared at Justin for a moment. And Justin stared back.

"So," Stan said. "Under orders...I disclosed your location to the authorities, and they dropped a hint to the mob." He came back and sat down. "I'm sorry, kid. I was acting under orders. By following them, catching them in the act, the police have brought down one of the biggest players in all of this. He's in deep. He'll never see the light of day again."

There was more silence. More stillness.

Stan broke it. "I didn't expect you to get shot. I'm sorry...really, I am."

The only thing that stopped Justin from jumping up and strangling Stan to death was the sedative.

***

Tom sat in his armchair (he was only comfortable reading this file at home) He had the outside lights on, and not many on in the house. He didn't want to advertise to everyone that he was home and what room he was in. He scratched his head to try and figure out what had happened back at the house. Something about that dark, empty house chilled him in the worst way. In New Heim, it felt much more safe to know where everyone was at all times. To know that Ferris was at home, that Orson was at home, and that Barker was in Ghost Town. When they were on the move, it was dangerous to take even one step. He sat down in the dark and put his feet up in the recliner chair. And there he dialed Debra Grier's phone number.

As the phone rang, Tom wondered how he would tell this woman that he'd found her daughter? Debra Grier would probably drive straight for New Heim, alert the police force, get ratted out and killed by Barker. Perhaps he could deter her. Tell her that he'd found a lead, and if she had to get involved, he would meet with her privately, to explain how best to go about the situation. The best way to go about the situation was not to tell her at all. Not until Tom had rescued Melanie. The phone had rung throughout his entire contemplation, close to eight times now.

Someone knocked on the door, and Tom turned off the phone, erased the number.

John Beckett was not in the habit of visiting Tom without calling. An unexpected guest meant Albert or Orson. Word around the street was that Orson was in a wheelchair since his scuffle with Barker. He probably wouldn't go to the effort of wheeling up to Tom's house. That left Albert Ferris. Or an assassin.

Tom loaded his gun and looked through the hole. No one was there.

What was it some kind of prank? That didn't typically happen on this block. Still he turned every lock on his door and kept the gun loaded, in case it were anyone meaning to do him harm. When he sat down, there was another knock. Tom looked through the hole again. No one was there.

He pulled the door open and aimed his gun.

"I don't know what you're playing at, but I want you off my property," he yelled at nothing, tracing the yard with the gun barrel. "Got it?"

There was something like a sudden gust of wind, something moving so fast he couldn't see until the man was already on his doorstep.

"Put that down," Barker said in a low voice.

"You," Tom said, his nerves ice cold.

"Can I come in, Tom?" asked Barker. He kept his hands in the pockets of his long black coat, yellow eyes bright in the dark.

"What do you want?" Tom asked.

"Very rude of you. I'm not even armed," Barker scoffed, scraping his foot against the cement. Unarmed, was he? If Tom took the shot, now, sucked it up and did the time in jail, he could save so many lives.

There was another snap against the wind, and something knocked Tom aside, smashing him against the doorframe. Barker was in his house now, and Tom on the porch.

"Would you like to join me inside?" Barker asked, hand extended.

Armed or not, Tom didn't have a chance against Barker. He kept the gun loaded, for comfort, but he wouldn't be using it. He stepped back into his own house and shut the door behind him. Now he was alone in his living room with Justin Barker. The tall, broad shouldered, black coated ingrate strolled around in a small circle, inspecting the room.

"Nice little place you got here," he said. "I might visit more often."

"That would be lovely," Tom said.

Barker stopped, hands on hips, and his eyes, accompanied by a cheeky little grin, drilled into Tom's. "Hand it over."

Though he wanted to resist, Tom relented and extended the gun toward Barker. Barker took it and gracefully unloaded it. Then he sat down on Tom's sofa, stretching his legs out. Tom stood with his hands folded. He wondered how many girls Barker had penetrated over the years. Barker tapped his fingers on the armrest.

"I didn't know you lived in this neighborhood. Right on the shoreline. How is it during the day? Nice, I bet."

"Very," Tom said. "Not trying to be rude but, could I ask what brings you here?" At this, Barker rested his head back.

"What's the best way to put this?" He snorted. "You're going to be my new accountant."

"What?" Tom asked, horrified.

Barker snorted. "Yep. Albert Ferris is gone."

"What?" Tom said, more aggressively. "What do you mean, gone?" Barker clapped his hands together.

"I mean, poof! Gone. Vanished. AWOL. Left a nice little mess before he went. Do I need to paint you a picture?" Barker said.

Ferris had skipped town, and left Tom to deal with Barker on his own. Tom's gut wrenched and he resisted the urge to kick over a chair. That old bastard had played him for a fool. Barker, too, apparently.

"I don't believe it," Tom growled.

"Yeah," Barker said, nodding his head. "Yeah. Anyway, he shut off my funds. So I need them replaced."

"I don't make much," Tom said.

"I'm sure you make enough," Barker said. "What's your annual?"

He had to answer. "Sixty-eight grand," Tom said.

"Perfect!" Barker said. "I'll take 15%."

Tom began by glaring at him, but quickly tried to reserve his gestures politely, at least until he heard back from Dennis Crawford. No one had ever beaten him down for money before, but Barker wasn't one to be argued with.

"I have bills to pay," Tom pleaded. "Can't you just get it from Orson? He's considerably richer."

Barker put up his hands. "Listen, Tom. You can just go ahead and quit your panicking, alright? Yes, I can also get money from Orson. I just came from there actually. You ever seen a 280 pound giant in a wheelchair, Tom? It's actually hilarious."

Tom was just a grand joke to Barker, but for now he needed to play ball.

"Alright, fine. 15%. Got it."

Barker stood up. "Don't look so put out, kid. I'm doing this because with Ferris gone, I not only need money, I need a new little team inside the walls of New Heim. I'd like to get to know you better." He stopped and cocked his head at Tom, staring straight at his face, or was it his throat? "Yeah, get to know you. And if you're ever in a jam, you just call me up and I'll help you out." He put up his hands again, as if offering peace. "Sound good?"

"Sounds good." Protect and serve, Tom. Whatever way necessary. Tom couldn't help anyone if he got himself killed tonight.

Barker cracked his neck, like he'd just been to the gym. "I've got to say, you're the least stubborn cop I've come across." He brushed his hair with his hand. "Cops. One half self righteous. The other half crooked. What do you do with them? In my opinion, you kill them. I've certainly had fun cutting down the cop problem around the nation. Been at it a long time."

Tom had known each and every time Barker was mocking him, and right now his insides were stiff with fury.

Tom stood firm. "Well, you're a good salesman. I may not agree with your nightly activities but as a show of good faith, I'm happy to help you with anything you need."

For a moment they stood in silence, and Barker's eyes drifted to the ground. Then he adjusted himself to be more comfortable, and spoke in a very low, gentle tone. "Good man. And, as a show of good faith, is there…anything I could do for you?"

He hadn't expected Barker to counter bribe him. This was a perfect time. It might cause him some pain, but he had to go for it.

"Yes or no?" Barker urged.

"There is one thing," Tom said, and Barker eyed him anxiously, smiling. "You have to understand, I have no conflict with you, but I feel very deeply for the people you've killed."

"Understandable," Barker said.

"I understand there's someone you currently have in your custody."

Barker's look changed to a deep frown, and Tom knew he'd stumbled into high water. He would need to tread carefully.

"All I'm saying is that I'm concerned about that living girl. I can't support a man I know is torturing another human being. I'd like to see that she is okay. That's all."

"You want to see if she is okay," Barker said. "You want to see my friend, Melanie?"

Barker literally had nothing to hide. He had no fear of the law. Unbelievable. If Ed Ryan would just grow a set, even if Barker still killed them all in the end, he wouldn't speak so recklessly.

"I just want to know that that girl is okay," Tom said. "I was Brolin's partner."

Barker nodded his head. "Ah, I see. That's how you know her."

"Yes. And it's been keeping me up at night. If you would just let me see her alive and well kept, I won't ask anymore questions."

He just wanted to get inside. See Melanie. Hint to her that it was okay. That he was coming for her. To hold on.

Barker kept nodding his head, contemplative. And then he smiled wide. "Alright, Tom…sure. Why don't you come over for dinner sometime soon?"

This just got better and better. "That would be very generous. Thank you."

And Barker burst into such high laughter that Tom actually flinched and flew into a defensive position. Barker gripped his own stomach, like he'd told or heard the world's greatest joke.

"You're so fucking fake," Barker said, pointing his index finger. "Stan never tried to hide his contempt for me. He knew he'd be as bad at it as you are!" He forced himself to stop laughing, gasping and snorting. Then his yellow eyes were narrowed and his tone more stern. "In fact, the night he nearly had me killed, he confessed to it immediately. And you know what, Tom?" His eyes rolled up to the ceiling. "Ignorance is bliss."

"I'll keep that in mind," Tom said. I'll fucking kill you for what you did to him. You understand? I'll have your fucking head. "I just want to know that the girl is alright."

Barker stepped forward. "Shake on it?"

Tom looked at the hand, wondering how many people it had fondled, violated, and killed, but like before, he relented. When their hands conjoined, Tom realized that Barker's skin was hot, like a steam vent. Just what the hell was this man?

After the handshake, Barker slowly let himself out of the house. Tom shut the door behind him and triple locked it. Then he began pacing all around his apartment, scratching his head, intentionally causing himself pain to relieve the tension.

Ferris had won this round. He'd gone back on their deal, abandoned Tom and thrown him to the wolf of Ghost Town. But as Tom rested his hands on the file Barker miraculously hadn't noticed, his thoughts were of Debra Grier, and the child buried in Barker's lair.

Chapter 32

Offer

Barker was very tired now. Kris had spoiled his dinner, and Tom had consumed the rest of his evening. He supposed he would sleep now. In the winter, when it darkened early, he tended to get his standard four hours in late at night. In the summer, he would typically stay indoors at day and prowl the night.

He officially needed some fun. He had to find himself a victim. And there was a perfect choice tied up in his room right now. But Melanie. She had cried, wept, pleaded for Kris's life. There was no sense denying it. Barker was jealous. He wanted Melanie to feel that way about him. He just needed more time, time for Melanie to adjust to him, and look the other way when he decided to appease his urges and cravings. He needed to punish Kris for what she did. It had to be done.

If he killed Kris, Melanie would never forgive him. He had to keep her alive. But he also wanted to appease Melanie. Bring her to his side. Give her something to make her smile.

Does she still need to be restrained?

Melanie had one strike left, and if she broke it, he would keep his promise. That in itself was a restraint. Would Melanie keep her word? Will you keep your word?

It all started to come together in his mind. He would go the neutral route. He would punish Kris and appease Melanie, and everything fall in his favor. And, he would get out the incredible urge he'd had since he saw all of those bodies, since he saw Tom Macklin trembling in front of him, the memory of Stan's confession bouncing around within his skull.

He had left Kris chained up on the bed, he had no idea if she'd woken up yet. Probably not. It had only been an hour or two. The thought of her lying there all wrapped up, scared, confused, dazed. It was already making him hard. And it wasn't even a choice anymore. It was something he needed to do.

First, make things right. Melanie, first.

Barker quietly glided into the house, and straight to the cabinets. He needed to get this just right. So he took the pills and folded them in a napkin. Then he filled a glass with water.

Barker unlocked his room and there she was, just as he'd left her. She tried not to stir, but did not succeed. He saw her move her foot in a sharp left pointed pattern. She was awake.

"I'm back," he said. "Look at me."

Kris rolled over, moonlight bathing her body blue. The chains were rapped around her shoulders, mid torso, wrists, and lower legs. He'd stuffed a rag into her mouth and secured it by wrapping duct tape. He'd made sure to press the tape against her long hair. She would not forget what was about to happen.

"Sleep well?" he asked. She only grunted at him. He reached down and helped her sit up. He slowly reached for her face, gripping it firm when she recoiled. Then he began to yank the tape out of her hair, slowly as possible. She grimaced and gasped, but eventually he'd gotten all of it off, then she spit out the rag.

"Keep your voice down," he warned.

Kris was pressing her chin against her own chest, eyes shut.

"So," he said. "Here we are." Now that he was here, looking at her, he knew he would not be able to resist. It wasn't even a choice at this point. It was a need. An act of nature. "I'm very sorry about your friends. What Ferris did was…horrible. But what you did was unacceptable. You could have killed me, or worse, Melanie."

Kris didn't answer.

"You'll have to be punished for this," he said.

Kris looked up at him, eyes bloodshot. "Kill me then." As he'd instructed, she kept her voice low.

Barker smiled. "Do you really want to die?" She didn't answer, only stared with red eyes. "I have a way out, Kris. An escape. All you need to do is follow my orders."

"No," Kris said. "No. I'd rather die."

"You don't have a choice," he told her. "One of two things will happen. Tomorrow I'll let you leave this house. Completely free." He snickered at his own word choice. "Not free to leave the city of course. But free to do what you want with your time. But only if you promise not to say a word to Melanie…about what happens next."

Kris was going red in the face, and Barker loved it. He wanted to take her now, but he had to be patient. Make things right with Melanie first.

"If you do tell Melanie about this…Well, I'll cut your throat. The end."

"Fuck you," she whispered. It was so feeble. She had no fight left in her.

"The choice is yours. You can take it and live. Or take it and die." He shoved the rag back into her mouth, loving the sounds of her protest. "I'll await your decision."

Barker locked her in and went back to the kitchen. He took out Benadryl, and poured a cup of water, then he was on his way upstairs.

He needed to see his friend. A strange sense he hadn't felt in years was hanging in the back of his mind. For some reason, he hated making her cry. It felt somehow…wrong.

He creaked the door open. He found her leaning against the bed. He hadn't left any space for her to lie down. Poor thing. He should not have treated her that way. Things were going to change soon, but half of that would be up to her.

Barker sat down next to her. She was awake, staring at him, lips puffy around the gag. He reached over and pulled it out, and she took a deep breath.

"How are you?" he asked.

She yawned. "Okay, I guess." Her voice was tiny, like when he had first brought her here.

"I'm…sorry for the drama tonight," he said. "I didn't anticipate it."

"It's not your fault," Melanie said. "Thank you."

"For what?" he asked.

"Not killing her. Thank you." It looked like she was about to cry again.

"Don't cry, Melanie. We can get past this. You understand?"

"How?" she asked.

"First tell me why you care so much about Kris. And don't lie to me. Don't say it was just because you didn't want her to die. I met with a man tonight who said something similar, and I know the difference between that and actually caring for someone. Now tell me why." He kept his voice gentle, but she seemed surprised by how many words he'd let out. After a loud sniff, she spoke.

"She was kind to me. Very kind. I just don't want her hurt. And I feel so terrible, about what happened. Do you know how much she loved those kids?"

"I do," he said. He really did. Kris was attached to them, the way Barker had gotten attached to Melanie. But she still had no right to do what she did. And if Melanie hoped to survive, she would need to learn that things in the Meridian, even all the way out here in Washington, things were different than what she was used to.

"I didn't want her to hurt you either," Melanie said, surprising him. "I wanted to warn you. I was just so…"

"It's okay," he said. "I understand…Do you like me, Melanie?"

"I'm grateful to you. Really, I am. You've protected me. You protected me tonight."

"I asked if you like me." Melanie froze, and he knew she wanted to say no. The child trembled, chin moving up and down, searching for just the right words. He wanted none of that. "Give me your honest answer. No matter what you say, it will not be the third strike."

Melanie looked both frightened and confused, conflicted. She stared at the carpet, like he'd backed her against a wall. All of these things Barker had seen many times through many victims, but this time, he wasn't playing a game.

"I mean," she started. "I don't really know you that well yet. I like you when we do talk."

"That was half-assed," Barker said. "The answer is no. You don't like me. I've made decisions for you. For your life. How could you like me, without learning to?" She looked flabbergasted, and he went on. "So, why don't we call tonight a little hiccup in an otherwise promising relationship. What say you that tomorrow, we start to make amends?"

She nodded her head rapidly. "Yes. Yes, please. I want that too."

Barker nodded back, and started to feel more comfortable talking to her. "Good, sweetie, good." He placed his hand on both of hers. "So. How 'bout this?"

She waited patiently, and he considered very carefully how the next few days needed to play out.

"Starting tomorrow morning, I no longer tie you up. You are still not permitted to leave this house, under any circumstances. But while inside, you have free reign?" He realized he'd forgotten something. "Oh. Except for my room. Don't come in."

Melanie's eyes widened. She looked humbled, flattered, excited. "I don't know what to say." She inched forward. "I promise, I'll be good. I promise."

He pulled both her hands open. "Shake on it?"

She nodded, and their hands enclosed on one another. Barker traced his finger over the ropes binding her. Then he decided to let her sleep in bed tonight. He undid the rope from the foot of the bed, and secured what was left of the string in another knot around her wrists.

"Then it's a deal," he said.

A tear fell from her eye. "Thank you," she said. "Thank you."

She squeezed Barker's hand with both of hers, tears dripping, mouth in a wide smile, the scarf still around her neck. And Barker liked it. He felt an odd sensation of satisfaction, being gentle towards her.

What the hell is happening to me? But it wasn't bad. It was something new. Just another thing he could take, another way he could prove everyone who knew him wrong. Anyone who thought he couldn't take power, slaughter hundreds, and make friends all at once, were wrong. They didn't know how capable and unique he was.

Barker pulled Melanie to her feet and sat her down on the bed. Then he presented the pills and the water.

"Here," he said. "This will help you sleep tonight. No nightmares."

Melanie took the pills without hesitation and popped them in. Then she took the water and drank deep. Barker undid the knot on the gag and pulled it from around her neck, then Melanie fell back onto the pillows. Barker backed away from her.

"Good night, Melanie."

Barker hadn't loved anyone since Lorena Phelps. Andrea's sister. And that had ended oh-so poorly. He was much happier making temporary friends. One night stands that ended in all of the things he loved. Power, dominance, sexual pleasure, blood, weaponry. Screaming. Tears. He had it all. But now he was taking something that he thought was desired only by his past self. He never thought in his new life he would desire a friend. A real friend. But he would have her, no matter how he had to compromise. It was worth it, and he was, as always, in complete control.

When Barker re-entered his bedroom, he was so aroused he could barley contain himself anymore. There she was, sitting there on the floor in a slightly different position. He'd done the chains perfectly. He could tell she tried to escape, but not much had changed. Excitement had his heart racing now, and he scratched a few itches born of sweat. For some reason, he thought of Lorena in this moment. And then the last time he'd had Kris. Would it be the same? Or was each experience unique, even with his first repeated victim?

"Ready?" Barker asked her.

One last tear fell from the gagged girl's eye, but she refused to whimper. Barker began the game. It had been so long he'd almost forgotten how much fun it was. How it felt like having a flopping fish in a net, a rabbit in a trap. How he felt more aroused and excited than any time a passing thought strolled through his mind. It was one thing to dream of prey, another to have it in front of you, dressed to perfection.

Barker took hold of Kris's neck with one hand and unbuckled his belt with the other. Then he pulled her close.

Chapter 33

Lorena

I t was 10:00 A.M. Andrea and Stan had left only hours ago, and they were expected by before dark. Justin had spent the duration of that morning monitoring the local news channels. He desperately wished that the mobsters had left the body at the boardwalk, that there was a big story circulating, that they had way bigger problems than one insignificant little photographer, who might have seen something. He wished.

There were three deaths in the news that morning. And none of them had anything to do with what he saw. Someone shot a man coming off the subway, someone else got hit by a car, and another was shot during a robbery. The beauty of New Heim was its shameless history with violence, and Justin had witnessed it first hand at the age of six, when his father was gunned down by a mugger. There was nothing on the news about the shooting last night. Knowing this city, if anyone heard the shots, they probably weren't coming forward. Fear of the crime families was more powerful than any moral conviction. Justin laid his head back on the couch, staring at the ceiling. He wanted this over. Dealt with, before it got any worse. Why did he have to go out that night? It was a dumb idea for a picture anyway.

There was a noise.

At first he thought he imagined it in his paranoia, but it was too loud to be imagined. It sounded like something slammed against the floor, toward the back of the house, behind the stairs. Justin got up and scaling the room for a weapon to use against whoever was in the house. In the next moment there was another loud bang—the back door shutting. Justin ran to the kitchen drawer and pulled out a huge steak knife. He was ready. He didn't mind blood. He'd seen it before. If he had to stab someone, he would.

Footsteps approached the kitchen, and Justin raised the knife.

A brown haired woman with huge diamond gauges in her ears and purple lipstick walked into the room. She wore mostly dark colors, silky shirt and pants that looked comfortable to move around in. Barker let the knife fall toward his waste awkwardly.

"Barker?" she said, green eyes wide and focused on the knife.

"Yeah…Glad you remember me." He looked down at the knife. "This is um…well, things have been a little um…" He set it down on the counter. "How've you been?"

She nodded slowly, crossing her arms, still looking cautious. "Fine. Better than you."

Lorena was twenty-one now. The lipstick and shadow on her eyelids, even here in the middle of a living room with no one else around, proved she still had her gothic interests, and she still had those bright green eyes like emeralds. Her hair was braided, and darker than last time he saw her. He'd only seen her in glimpses anyway.

"Why'd you come in the back?" he asked, still startled.

She cracked her back as she walked toward the counter. "Stan was adamant about me not driving my car here. Said he wanted it to look like no one was home. Told me not only to walk but go in through the back. The damn gate is bolt locked or some shit. I had to jump the fence!" she said. "Christ. I get two calls, one from Sis telling me to come watch you because you saw a murder or something, and then another from Stan making sure I'm clear on instructions and that I don't bring my car." She made a mocking gesture. "Sure, guys, I'll just walk fifteen blocks and hop your fence if you promise to leave the back door unlocked. God, my back. This is my punishment for being lazy."

Justin was laughing now. He didn't remember Lorena being this bitter and outspoken. He remembered her being quiet and shy.

"I'm glad you're amused, kid," she said. "So what happened? What did you see exactly?"

"I saw—"

"Quiet. Talk in whispers. In case, you know, anyone's stalking us." She looked over to check that all the blinds were drawn. "Nice and gloomy in here," she said low.

"I was just saying that I saw the mob shoot a girl in the skull."

"Like the whole mob at once? Or a particular member?" Lorena asked.

"Two men in coats. Sorry, I guess I'm still a little flustered," he spat back.

"Hey. I'm just kidding," she said. "Guess I'm baby sitting."

"I don't need a baby sitter," he said. "I just need company."

"Mhm," she said with a bent lip. "So I guess we'll watch some TV," she said. And she poured herself a drink. "So you don't know who they were?"

"Stan figured it out. They worked for Matthew Sect." He looked at her as intently as he could.

Lorena's eyes went wide. "Oh…shit. That's not good."

"No, it's not."

She poured herself another shot. "Don't worry, you'll be fine. Stan is the best cop in the city. Or so I'm told. You came to the right guy."

"I know," he said. Deep down, he hoped that she was right, and wished for some confidence.

"So," she said. "What do you say, kid? Can you handle a drink?"

For the next hour, Justin and Lorena sat in the living room, flipping channels with the blinds drawn. They didn't speak much, or have any lights on. Occasionally they flipped over some fun shows, like the X-Files.

"So," Lorena said. "Let's pretend this whole shooting business didn't happen. How have you been?"

"I can't complain. You know, trying to get my own apartment."

"You graduated right?" she said.

"Yep. Last June," he said.

"Nice. College?" she asked.

"Can't afford it," he said.

She widened her mouth, grimacing to show her teeth. "Sorry. So what have you been up to? Work?"

"I got some money as a graduation present from one of my uncles. He lives on the East Coast. Andrew, I think it was," he said.

"So what have you been doing?" she asked.

"I'm getting to that, geez. I've been studying photography."

"Oh, cool. You gonna be like a professional photographer?"

"Maybe," he said. He'd heard a story once about an up and coming photographer who was campaign photographer to the last president of the United States. Wouldn't that be amazing, to be someone important, faded into the background yes, but still more important to the thousand others in the same room?

"That's cool," Lorena was saying. "I still enjoy drawing."

"You have a business up and running, right?"

She nodded. "Mhm. Yeah, we've sold a good number of paintings so far. I pop out as many as I can. Don't sleep much anymore."

"What do you like to draw?"

"Lots of dark stuff," she said. "Anything black, blue, or red."

"Great colors," he said. A thought occurred to him. "Do you remember when we used to talk in your sister's house?"

"You mean my house? Yeah." Lorena was laying down now, head propped up by her right arm.

"There was this one time. We started to talk about things like that. Gothic, dark things. Andrea came in the room and asked what we were talking about. You said homework."

"I remember," she said.

"But one time, when we were alone, we finished our conversation."

"You mean when you told me about your dad?" she said.

"So you remember?" he asked.

She nodded. "It's not the kind of thing you forget. Some eleven year olds talk about T.V. and others about sports." She sat up and finished her drink. "You were talking about how your dad was murdered. How the blood sprayed in your face. Made you hemophobic for a few years until you conquered it."

Justin was flattered that she remembered their conversation, and all of these details about him, so vividly. Most of the time he spoke people forgot what he said a minute later.

"Hemophobic isn't a word," he said. "Hemophobia is one way of saying blood phobia, which I had a bad case of after dad died. I went through all the treatments, until I was completely desensitized to blood. Then I told one or two kids at school that and that's when my freak reputation started."

"Well, you should have known better than to share that with your bullies," she said, very matter of fact.

He laughed. "Yes, I should have. I think that experience taught me not to talk to kids at school. I wasn't sore about it or anything. I was fine on my own and I guess I just learned not to falter from that," he said.

"Amen," she said. "I've always been a loner. Andrea can't stand that. But I love her anyway."

"Andrea is wonderful," he said. All he wanted right now was to talk to Lorena more. He had to force out the words though, propel the discussion himself. "It was weird, having the blood phobia, and going through the treatment. I always felt weak. It sucks."

"Yes, it does." She rested her head on the pillow. "You don't look weak though. You look pretty damn impressive actually."

"Impressive?"

"Yep. You saw a murder last night and you haven't broken down yet. I'm impressed."

"Thanks," he said. "Seriously, though, I never want to feel that way again."

"Well, no shit Sherlock. None of us like it. But all of us are. Weak." she said.

"You think so?"

"Of course. All of us are grains of sand." She fluttered her fingers.

"Isn't that an atheist belief?"

"Oh, let's not get into that shit. I'm just saying. We're all part of a group of billions on one planet. We live under one hundred years and if something rams into us really hard, that's it. Lights out." She wiped her mouth with her hand. "We're all weak whether we like it or not. The best we can do is give it our A-game." She looked over, seeming a touch tipsy. "Right, buddy?"

"Right," he said, with a laugh. "Would you like another drink?"

"Oh, hell yes."

"I'll get it for you."

Justin got up and went to pour more for her. As he did he looked over at her lounging on the couch, and silently thanked Stan for choosing Lorena for a companion. "Thank you," he said to her.

"For what?"

"For understanding me," he said. "It just…means a lot, you know?"

She raised a peace sign. "Don't mention it." She didn't look at him.

He laughed, and brought her a drink. "Cheers," he said, and sat back down.

For the next several hours they just sat and flipped channels. Occasionally they discussed Lorena's artwork, and he learned that she now had an interest in sketching faces. She claimed to have a perfect sketch of the Disney character, Maleficent, noting the beauty of the dark jagged gown the character wore, and the sharp edges of the face. Justin learned a few things about Lorena until she received a phone call.

"Well, Sis should be home soon. I guess I'll be on my way."

The sun was starting to go down. "Do you need someone to go with you? You said its fifteen blocks."

She waved a finger at him. "Oh, no. You're not going anywhere mister. Stan's orders."

He felt a pang of frustration. "I can take care of myself. A walk around the block should be—"

She put her hand up. "Just do what Stan says. Okay? That's your best bet."

"Fine," he said. "Are you sure you're alright. Your sis could probably give you a ride back."

"Are you flirting with me?" she said, eye brows crooked.

"No," he said. "Why the hell would you…Don't flatter yourself."

She laughed and jokingly punched him. "I'm fine."

"You've been drinking."

"Hours ago. I'm good. Chill, bro," she said.

"You know, you really should pick a style to speak in. Just one," he said.

"Thanks, I'll be sure to do that." She strutted toward the back door. When she was past the stairs she stopped. "It was nice hanging with you."

"You too," he said, wondering what he was going to do with himself now.

She walked back to him. "Hey. It'll be alright."

He pulled away, embarrassed. "I know. Thanks."

She stared for a minute, then nodded. "Cool."

She turned and walked toward the back door again, this time slower. But she didn't stop.

Justin heard the sounds of the door opening and closing again, and this time they left him feeling bored. He wondered if Lorena would be able to figure out the fence mechanism from the inside. He spent a long time thinking about Lorena.

Chapter 34

Numbers

Melanie awoke to a knock at her door. Barker had guessed exactly when she would wake up, and here he was, extending his hands. He didn't say anything to her, and he didn't give his usual exaggerated grin. No, he reached forward, half smiling, half interrogating her with his eyes.

Gently, he untied the rope around her wrists. They slid off, and she took a moment to stare at her marked up, free hands. She looked back up at Barker, and he gestured for her to step out into the hallway. Melanie rarely left the room without an escort. Barker stood in her bedroom as she walked out into the small, dank dusty hall upstairs and into the bathroom. She glanced at him as she started to close the door of her sanctuary, and he gave her a sarcastic grin.

"Careful in there," he said.

Melanie nodded and shut the door.

In the shower, she thought about a time Ronnie Kessler had been crying in class. Someone had called him a long list of names and said that he should just commit suicide. Melanie couldn't remember if she'd said anything to comfort him. She remembered a time that Emily had been staring at the lunch table, obviously disturbed, but Melanie hadn't even thought to ask until they were walking out to next period. Melanie turned off the faucet, and started thinking about something besides herself or faces from her past. She started thinking about Kris.

When Melanie left the bathroom, she couldn't see Barker. Her bedroom door was open. There were no clothes left out for her. She'd have to get them herself. The rope, which had normally been dangling on the floor, was gone. And the scarves in her closet could be just that from now on. Melanie dressed herself in the most comfortable clothes she could find, to remind herself she was staying inside today. Maybe at some point, Barker would give her that as well. Until then, she wasn't going to push her luck.

To eat, she would have to go downstairs, on her own. But first she explored the upstairs a little bit more. She'd spent so little time just standing in the hallway. The floor of the upstairs was shaped on an acute angle. The top of the stairs led to two bedrooms, one of which was hers. On the way across the hall there was her sanctuary on the right. And at the end there were two large doors, leading to the master bedroom. When Melanie peaked inside, there was no walking space. Desks, chairs, torn up couches, bookcases, whatever kind of person Matt Sect was, but he certainly was a pack rat. Greedy. Gluttonous. Melanie shut the door. Nothing in that room interested her. Instead she walked back across the hallway and into the room neighboring hers. It was green. Green carpeted with a light brownish color on the walls, complimenting the carpet. It was empty, not lived in for years, and in the closet there were shredded papers funneling out on the floor. She almost picked them up, but she kept staring at the carpet. She liked this room better. Much better. Would Barker allow her to change rooms? Would that be a dangerous question?

No, only her reaction would be dangerous. If he was really starting to give her freedoms, then she was free to ask any question she wanted.

Melanie walked downstairs herself. Barker's door was shut, as usual, and he was at the stove making eggs.

"Good bath?" he asked her.

"Yeah," Melanie said. "Thank you...Is Kris still here?"

"No. Kris went home," he said.

"Home? Is she alright?"

He kept his eyes on the food he was preparing. "She's fine. She told me the whole story, and I let her go. I won't be asking her to do much for me anymore, and I'll give her some extra cash. Should be compensation enough."

Melanie contemplated what she was hearing, how much of it was true. Don't pry. Don't overstep. "Will she be able to make it on her own?"

"Well, I can't keep paying her for not working for me, can I?" He turned to her and showed her his teeth, like he was on some toothpaste commercial. "Sit," he said. "Almost done."

Melanie obeyed, folding her legs where she sat. "I guess, we won't see her again?"

"Oh, you cute little thing. Kris won't be leaving town anytime soon. At some point, I'll let you visit her." He brought her over a dish. "Sound good?"

Melanie nodded. "Sure. Thank you." She took a whiff of the peppered eggs in front of her. "Mmm, this smells great."

He sat down in front of her. "Yes it does."

Barker put a forkful into his mouth, and Melanie did the same. As he chewed his eyes flickered, like a thought occurred to him. "I found something in my trunk."

"Oh?" she said, taking a bite.

He got up for a moment and went over to the counter. Melanie braced herself for whatever disgusting joke he was about to pull on her, imagining only torture devices coming out of his trunk. And yet, he walked back over with a book.

"1984, by George Orwell," he said, presenting it to her. It was a small paperback, beat up from travel, but all of the pages in tact.

"Thank you," she said, taking it. "What's it about?" He sat back down and stuck his fork in a bite of egg, while she carefully placed the book to the side of the table.

"The impressionable," he said. "Dangers of Government control. All that good stuff. Every now and then it reminds me why I prefer this lifestyle."

"What lifestyle is that?" she asked.

"You don't know?" he chuckled.

"I mean, I know but...how would you put it in words?"

He gave her a searching gaze before answering. "A do what I want, when I want. I exercise my God given right to my own body and mind."

But only you. "Do you believe all people have that right?" she asked. To her shock he nodded his head, and she wanted to smack him, and present the marks on her skin.

"We all do, Melanie," he said. "But sometimes, people get eaten. It's natural."

"Natural?" she asked. Natural that she would be scooped up or killed, because she was weaker than him. "So you see everything, all of this, like a jungle? Strongest survives?"

He nodded. "And how do you see it?"

"Oh, I don't know," she said, wanting to grunt. In addition to being probed, she was being probed at breakfast. "I suppose, I see everything as a puzzle."

"A puzzle," Barker said, perplexed. "Interesting."

She nodded and took a bite of her breakfast. "Yeah."

"And can this puzzle be completed?" he asked her.

"Sure," she said. "Wouldn't be a very good puzzle if it couldn't."

"And what happens when you complete it?" He awaited her answer with apparent focus, and she felt pressure to answer correctly.

"You die," she said.

A wide smile appeared on his face, and he leaned back, making "hmm" sounds.

"Good answer," he whispered. "But you, school girl, need to learn just how much fun the jungle can be."

Later, Melanie was sitting on the floor in the green room, reading 1984. There was a quote in the book that stood out to her, noting that only numbers could defeat a tyrannical government. That's what Melanie wished she had. Numbers. With only her own feeble body as a weapon, she remained helpless against him.

The door opened and there he was, peering in, confused.

"What are you doing in here?" he asked.

"Reading," she said, closing the book on her thumb. "Did I do something wrong?"

"No," he said. "Just curious what you're doing in here."

"I like it in here," she said. "I like the colors."

"Ah, I see," he said. "Well, sorry to tell you this but, I'm going to need to lock you in your room."

What? What had she done? Had she broken a rule? She was supposed to have free reign of the house today. Then she realized, he said lock up, not tie up.

"You're going out," she said.

"Afraid so," he said. "I'm actually getting you a present, so, up up now."

She obeyed and walked into the dark blood colored cage, sitting herself down on the bed. She noticed that on the dresser there was an apple, some pretzels, a few tasty cake cupcakes and a glass of water.

"Thanks for the snacks," she said.

"I won't be long," he said. "Go easy on the water. I'll be back in say, an hour."

When he closed the door the lock was loud and echoic. Melanie looked around the room, from the dresser to the sofa in the open closet space, and to her own feet on the bed. There were still bars on the window, a lock on the door, but without the rope it felt less like a cage and more like a room. Maybe there was some work she could do on it to make it less glum. Any project would help her pass the time.

An hour and a half later, Melanie was looking at a hair straightener. It looked expensive and new, and she couldn't figure out if he'd stolen it or purchased it.

"Like it?" he asked.

"Love it," she said with a smile. "Thank you."

Barker's hot lips touched the top of her head.

Melanie ended up reading the entire novel that day and night, and then she went to sleep. The next day, when she awoke, she decided she needed to pay him back for every gift. So she got herself dressed and went downstairs in search of him. It was odd, searching for Barker within this house, where she had spent so much time waiting for him to come and collect her. She found him in the back, near the small door through which she'd escaped. He was doing laundry.

"Good morning," he said. "Sleep well?"

She nodded. "I really appreciate the gift you got me yesterday," she said. He put his hand up as if to say "Don't mention it," and Melanie pressed further. "Can I do something for you tonight?"

"Like what?" he said.

"I could cook for you again," she said. "Anything you want...that I know how to make."

He laughed out loud at that. She thought it would be more terrifying than it was. Really he sounded like a boastful uncle, getting too much amusement out of anything the kids did. "Sure," he said to her. "Actually, we could cook together a couple nights from now. On Thursday."

"Is something happening?" she asked.

He finished folding his shirt and narrowed his eyes, very more Barker-like. "Yes, dear. I'm going to need you to do a couple different things for me on that night." He took a breath, as if to say life was wonderful. "We are having a guest."

Chapter 35

Once You've Lost Your Way

What was proper to wear to Ghost Town? And why was he even going? Why was he strolling into Barker's domain, into his house, into his clutches?

Damn you, Albert. You got me into this mess.

Tom never should have trusted the mob. He should have tried bringing it to the Chief. The Chief might have ratted him out immediately, to save his son. He should have gone to the Meridian itself to find Crawford in person. He should have been more patient. He still had not received a reply yet. So now it was only Orson Marx as his ally, whom he hadn't even seen since the Manor incident. Appealing to the police would get him thrown in jail for conspiracy to commit murder and money laundering. So he was on his own with Barker.

Tom chose a black hoodie and dark jeans, something that made him just another dark illusion, until he came face to face with the gatekeeper. But as Tom opened the door and got into his car, turned the key in the ignition and pulled away from his apartment, he felt more and more lost. One thing he used to do when he was lost was call his mother, but he wouldn't so much as mention her existence in front of Barker. As far as Barker knew, his father had killed his mother in a drunken fit and gone to prison.

Driving through the city, Tom arrived at Main Street, right next to the restaurant where he and Melanie Grier had first met, driving along the road where the battle between S.W.A.T. and the Marx Assassins had taken place, only a block away from the Manor. On this street there were a series of allies that were a direct path to Ghost Town. If Tom wanted he could park the car somewhere on Main Street and walk discreetly into the dead district. Somehow, he thought that discretion would not be wise. Barker expected him, so Tom would announce his arrival.

Tom took the long route. He drove through Main Street, to the outskirts of the city, where there were several winding roads. These roads used to be busier when going all the way left meant driving into New Heim's South Eastern business district, but now that district was a shell, this winding road was barren. Tom followed the road and the noises of the city grew more and more distant, as he cruised into the blackened streets of Ghost Town.

This route to Barker's house was much more direct. He passed the old Power Plant on the right (and actually caught a glimpse of the short, rotund man running the place) and followed the road into a winding street with a line of houses. It used to be a rather nice suburban block, but now it was just a dead path to Copper Avenue. Tom arrived at Copper and made quick right. In two minutes, he pulled up to the house where Matt Sect used to abuse drugs with his companions of low birth. Or so the stories went.

As he parked the car, he felt this idea was madder than it ever had been. But he turned off the gas, and out he went.

The house was still covered in graffiti, same as it always had been, only now he'd see the inside. He knocked on the door. He could smell dinner from the doorstep. Smelled like steaks. The door opened and Barker appeared. He was wearing a white t-shirt and sweat pants. He seemed to have gotten comfortable. Barker ushered him in and he awkwardly stepped through the door. The inside of the house plain, walls barren and carpets poorly kept. The kitchen was simple, with an island and a small table. The steaks were on the stove top, and there was another pot cooking vegetables. Hopefully, he wasn't getting drugged or poisoned. Barker hadn't poured him anything to drink yet. Good. He would watch closely when he did, unless he was offered to help himself.

"Thank you," Tom said. "For inviting me into your home."

"Have a seat," Barker said, returning to the pots. "I'm just about done." He stuck his nose dangerously close to the pot of cooking vegetables. "Melanie did this up herself. She's got a lot to learn but I think she might have some cooking genius."

"She's alright?" Tom asked, looking around.

"Just missed her," Barker said. "She's in the bathroom."

"Ah," Tom said. He rested his elbow on the table. So far, he wasn't dead.

Barker banged a utensil on the side of the pot. "So, Tom. How are you feeling about our little arrangement? Anything I should be concerned about?"

"No, sir," Tom said. "Anything you need, I can provide."

There were footsteps on the stairs, and Tom turned. She was standing right in front of him, dressed in a black T-shirt and dark shorts. Her hair looked wet, like she'd just been washing, and aside from a scrape here and there, she seemed alright. Her face was blank, but she forced a smile.

"Hello," he said to her.

"Hello," she said back.

"Do you remember me?" Tom asked.

"Yes," she said. "You're Brolin's partner."

"Was," Tom said, and he heard Barker chuckle behind him. "I'm sorry. For what Brolin did. I had no part in it."

Melanie stepped forward. "I figured you didn't...You were kind."

"Kind," Barker said. "Hard to believe any friend of Stanley William Jackson would be kind."

Tom wanted to round on Barker and tear him to pieces, but he simply turned and said, "We don't always mimic our friends."

"True," Barker said. "Melanie, dear. Could you please set the table?"

And like magic, Melanie scurried past Tom, into the kitchen, following Barker's every command. Tom had expected to find her tied up or with some sort of leash around her but Barker had managed to contain her, and Tom was left wondering only one thing. Was she subservient to Barker, or was she just surviving? If Tom could get her alone, what would she say?

"Drink for you, sir?" Barker asked Tom. Melanie laid plates down on the table as Tom regarded Barker where he sat.

"Yes. Just some water would be nice."

Barker scoffed. "Oh, come on, Tom. We're both men who've been through war at this point. Why not share a real drink?"

"What do you have?" Tom asked.

Scratching his head, Barker walked over to the cabinet above the refrigerator. "Jack?"

"Perfect," Tom said. The stiffness in his own voice astonished him. This wasn't the first time he'd sat in the lion's den, after all. At Marx Manor he'd known to dress well, be respectful, not insulting, and get straight to the point. Make the offer quickly so that they would have reason to keep him alive. Here, he didn't know what to do. He didn't know how to prep for an unpredictable killer.

Barker took out Jack Daniels and poured two shots. Tom watched closely, but unless the entire bottle was drugged, nothing about Barker's actions seemed amiss. Barker brought the two glasses over as Melanie set the food down on the table. Tom took the shot glass.

"What shall we drink to?" Barker asked. Tom didn't answer, and Barker turned his head to the stove. "Melanie? What shall Tom and I drink to?" Melanie stopped moving and Tom saw her hands fidgeting as she looked at them both.

"Um, friendship?" She shrugged, and Barker looked back at Tom.

"To loyalty," Barker said, and as Tom raised his glass he added, "Something our mutual friend got a little bit backwards."

"To loyalty, then," Tom said, hiding the bitterness in his voice. How many cracks towards Stan would Tom have to endure before dinner was over? Melanie hadn't reacted, and held the pot in her hand with two oven mitts. Barker drank, and so did Tom, feeling the heavy liquor pour down his esophagus. When he gasped, he saw Melanie setting the pans down on the table. Steam and spices filled Tom's nostrils, and though the adrenaline stifled his appetite, he could imagine giving in. Barker picked up a fork, and Tom watched his hand carefully.

"Dig in," Barker said. Melanie brought over a fork for Tom. As she extended to him he caught her eyes for just a moment and searched them. As he took the knife from her, he spotted a half wink from her. Tom took it as an indication he was not about to be poisoned. So he dug in.

Melanie sat down next to Barker, and kept her eyes on her plate. She set about cutting up her steak, focused but relaxed. Tom did the same, his eyes jumping between them both, and tasted the juicy meat. Barker ate with his eyes fixed on Tom, and that caused Tom's taste for the food to come and go. Fortunately, he also glanced at Melanie here and there.

"Delicious, Melanie," Barker said. Tom watched her look up at him and smile.

"Thanks," she said.

"It is good," Tom said. "Wonderful." Melanie smiled at him, and returned her eyes to her plate.

When the trio were finished tearing through the meat and vegetables on their plates, knives scraping loud against the porcelain, Barker stood up and retrieved the bottle of Jack Daniels.

"I'm feeling like another one," he said, pouring a shot. "You?"

"Sure," Tom said, and Barker poured him another.

"How 'bout you?" Barker asked Melanie with a sideways glance. The girl looked flustered, unprepared.

"I mean, I'm underage," she said. Barker just raised his eyebrows at her, and Melanie shrugged. "I'd love one."

The three of them held up glasses.

"To good faith," said Barker, and they drank. Tom watched Melanie's face convulse at the taste, but she still smiled. And now Barker's eyes drilled into Tom's. "Is there something you wanted to say to my friend, Tom?"

It had to be a trap. Whatever Tom said would offend Barker, and he'd be killed for it. He'd waltzed right into the beast's cave, entertained him a bit, and now this was it.

"I just wanted to let you both know that I was concerned about your lives," he said. "We all heard about what was going on with the Marx Family, saw the assassins in the streets. I'm not stupid. I knew it was the two of you who came under fire."

"That's so nice of you, Tom. But you said you especially wanted to speak to Melanie. You know, to satisfy your concerns."

Tom looked directly at Melanie. "Seeing her now, how well cared for she is, has put my mind at ease." He looked back at Barker. "Thank you."

Barker poured himself another shot. "You're quite welcome," Barker said. "Now get out."

On his way to the door, Tom looked back at them both one last time. Barker whispered something in Melanie's ear, and she giggled. Tom's stomach turned, and with one last forced smile, he gracefully stepped through the doorway, shutting it behind him.

The next day, Tom trudged the boardwalk. He could see the ocean from his back porch, and often he would jog and stay fit on these wooden boards. When he wasn't working or trying to keep out of sight, he loved a good walk by the water. It cleared his mind. There was no reason to keep out of sight. Barker knew where to find him, and he could attack like a lightning bolt. Worse, the girl. She seemed completely adjusted. Tom kept wondering how much of it was fake, how much an act, and how much Barker was really getting into the girl's head. When Tom went to rescue her, who would she side with?

God damn it all.

The cold wind blew through Tom's face, chilling his torso. He welcomed it. That letter was never getting an answer. There was little hope left for Melanie Grier if Tom couldn't hire a proper gun, let alone in time to halt Barker's brainwashing. He was tired. Tired of ghost stories and carcasses in the streets. Fleshy sacks bearing stone carvings of dead faces, wracked with agony. Innocent children like Melanie, devastated parents like the Griers, and good men like Stanley. They needed justice. Killing Barker was worth Tom's own life. Even if the rapist had enough left in him to strike back and bite out Tom's throat, it would still be worth it. It was becoming a suicide mission.

As the thought dawned on Tom, the phone was already to his ear. He hardly remembered dialing. An articulate, carefully annunciated voice answered. "Hello? St. Vincent's."

"Hello," Tom said. "I'd like to speak to Elaine Macklin?"

"Name?"

"Thomas Macklin. Family." He heard some rummaging on the other end and assumed it was paperwork.

"One moment please," the voice said.

The moment was long, and Tom stopped walking, resting his arms on the railing, looking out at the water. When the line came back to life, an old, quivering voice answered.

"Hello?" she said.

"Hello, Mum. It's Thomas."

"Oh!" she said. "Hello, sweetheart. How are you?"

What a perfect question. He was absolutely miserable, and starting to think his current endeavor would cost him his life.

"I've been well, mother. Just getting through each day, as always."

"Oh, I'm sure," she said. "You've grown into a great man. I'm so proud of you." When she said those words her voice quivered less, and she even spoke louder. It was the one thing she assertively believed in, that her son had become a great man. So why didn't he feel like a great man, or even a man? It was interesting to have an oblivious family, far removed from this madness. Of course, now that Barker knew him, was obliviousness still a shield? Or was it a handicap?

"How are you?" he asked her.

"I'm okay…You know, spending most of my time with Diana. The weather is bad up here." Quivering aside, the sound of her voice always comforted him.

"Weather, huh?"

"Yeah. You know, I saw your father the other day." And away the comfort went.

"What?" Tom asked. "Why? How?"

"Well, he came to visit."

Tom's chest sank, and he clenched his fist. The distant waves hit the shoreline hard. "What did he want?" Tom asked. "Please, don't leave anything out."

"He wanted to talk. He said that he missed me, and you. And that he wanted to take me out for dinner sometime soon."

"Right…what does he want?"

"I don't know."

"You're supposed to call me when he tries to contact you, Mother. Next time, please put him on the phone with me. Would you do that, mother?"

"I don't think he means any harm. I think…I think he just wants to make amends."

"Yes, but regardless. I need to know. Promise me." There was a long pause on the other end.

"Okay, son. I promise." She sounded like she might start to cry.

"I'm just trying to keep you safe, Mum."

"I know," she mumbled. "I raised you right."

I was thinking about coming to visit you soon. But he stopped himself saying it. Just in case.

"Is everything alright at work?"

"Yes. Everything's fine at work."

"I heard stories." Her tone didn't change. It sounded as casual as if she were reading a letter. There was still a bit of a stern woman left in her, before the time where his father would beat and bully her.

"What stories?"

"People said there were shootings in the city. They said that the, the S.W.A.T. team was out."

"Yeah, that happened. But I'm fine. All of the culprits were apprehended."

"Oh, thank goodness. Were you there?"

"I was."

"Oh, Tom." Now her voice changed. "Can't you have picked a safer job?"

A year ago Tom would have told her this is what he wanted to do. He didn't want to sit at home and study math, literature, or philosophy. He didn't want a cushy job or a fun job. He wanted to do some good for the world. To save other people from the fate she had suffered. Being beaten by your own husband until your mind just shatters and you start self harming. Tom wanted to be the man who answered domestic dispute calls, who removed people like Allen Marx from power, who made parents and children feel safe going outdoors at night.

Interestingly enough, being the one who once made those calls for help, to save his mother, Tom's greatest foe had been drug abuse. It consumed his father and turned him vile, and Tom had no greater love than cuffing a violent drug addict. What was this now? Justin Barker. No drugs. Cruelty for cruelty's sake.

"I know it's not a safe job mother, but it's a good job. It's a good cause."

"Well..." said the quivering voice. "Just remember you're my boy. And I'll always love you."

"I know, Mum. I love you. I'll see you soon." He wished he hadn't said it.

"I would love that," she said. "Goodbye. I love you, son."

Tom called the front desk and warned them to contact him the next time Joseph Macklin attempted to contact his mother. Then he was alone on the boardwalk, watching the waves, chilling in the cold air.

***

It was six hours after dinner with Barker's guest. Melanie had brushed her teeth and gotten ready for bed. She started reading a book, expecting Barker to come talk to her. Was he still stumbling around down there, enjoying his liquor? That had been one of the most disgusting experiences of her life, to date. She wondered if it was okay to just go to sleep.

The cop, Tom Macklin. He seemed like a caring, kind man. He'd been so flustered and paranoid at dinner. She couldn't blame him. The entire time she'd wished she could say something comforting to him, but that hadn't been in the script. Her door slid open, with a low dark hum. Barker glided in like he was on ice.

"Hello, darling," he said.

"Hey," she said.

"Going to bed?" he asked.

"Yeah," she said. "Soon."

He sat down next to her. His eyes, eyebrows, and mouth could form such sharp images on occasion, making him look fierce and intense. But sometimes, his features softened, and his eyes looked so confused, like he was trying to take in a bunch.

"You did well tonight," he said. "I'm proud of you."

She just smiled back.

"What did you think of Tom?" he asked.

"Well, um, he seems okay. So he's working with you?"

"Yes. He's my new accountant."

"Ah. Okay." She figured it was good to know how Barker got his money. "Well he seems nice."

"Weird, huh?" He folded his arms and laughed. "I don't usually attract the nice."

"Yeah." She pulled hair out from over her eye. "I mean, I guess, this line of work doesn't...I don't think he'd murder anyone. Least not any kids."

"No. I don't think so either."

"Is she okay?" Melanie asked.

"She's fine," Barker said. He sounded very cruel. Like Kris wasn't even a person. But then his arm was around her, the special exception of Ghost Town. "I'm very proud of you. Our first couple days of this new arrangement have been perfect. You've been good."

"I try to be," she said.

He poked her nose with his finger. "I'm going to give you a treat tomorrow."

"Oh?"

He nodded. "Do you like the beach?"

That was one of Melanie's favorite things to do, something she thought she'd never see again. "I love the beach. I love the water."

"If you promise not to run, I'm going to take you there tomorrow. No ropes. No chains. Just good faith."

She nodded her head. "I'd love that. I'll be good."

He smiled at her. "I know."

Chapter 36

The Sun

Melanie took her shower, dressed herself, combed her hair, and looked at herself in the mirror. She held up her wrists beside her face, as if posing for a photo shoot. The marks on her wrists from the many days of ropes were faded, the mark on her head from Brolin's attack a little scab at best. The cut on her arm from when she tried to kill Barker was faded as well, though more noticeable than the others. Aside from these relics, Melanie had no damages to showcase her suffering. And perhaps that suffering was ending now. Barker was giving her a gift today. She liked gifts. If more gifts came, maybe life wouldn't be so bad. Maybe she could acquire the greatest gift of all.

It was always cold, so she wore her extravagant new coat and put a scarf around her neck. Then she went downstairs in search of Barker. He was standing in the doorway, holding a length of rope. At first, Melanie's heart stopped. She'd walked straight into some cruel trap he'd set for her. They weren't going to the beach, she was going back upstairs. And yet, as the incredibly long seconds rolled by, he did not come toward her.

"What are you doing?" she asked. He pulled something out of his pocket, holding the dangling rope as if it were a snake that would bite him if it got too close.

"Entertaining myself." He clicked the lighter and a small flame appeared. Then he was holding it to the bottom of the rope. Melanie folded her arms as she watched the spectacle. Barker stared with eyes more focused than even when he looked upon her. Rather than simply staring, his eyes were wrenched wide and the flame danced within them. Even his mouth was hanging open a half inch.

It took no time at all for the flame to ignite, nor very long for the flame to crawl upward on the line. But the burning was slow. It took a few moments for her to smell it, and a few seconds later a small black stream floated upward. Barker stepped out of the doorway and into the front lawn. The bottom of the rope was now completely aflame, and Melanie stepped closer. What amazed her was Barker's concentration. He seemed out of tune with the world around him, but it wasn't coming and going. He was fixed elsewhere. So fire got his attention. That was worth remembering. Still, as the minutes rolled by, Melanie started to feel uncomfortable.

"Um, do you want me to wait upstairs?" she asked. He heard her. His eyes didn't leave the flame, but his head drifted slightly in her direction.

"No, we can go," he said. He drew a knife from his pocket and sliced off the bottom of the rope. Then he stomped the flame out with his black boot. When he pulled his foot away, he proceeded to stare at the packed burnt mess. Melanie wished she could read minds, because right now she wanted to know if he was contemplating fire the element or fire the weapon, and what that meant for her.

Next he turned to her and smiled, "Ready?" he said. But Melanie continued standing in the doorway, staring at him, arms hugged around her. He motioned her forward with his hands, but still she hesitated. "What?" he asked.

"It's okay?" she asked him. "Not against the rules?" At this Barker titled his head and came slightly unhinged.

"Aw, you wonderful little thing. No, today I give you permission. Come now. It's lovely day."

Melanie looked at the doorframe for an extra moment. This had been her barrier for so long. Passing through it almost made her want to inspect it for traps. But that was ridiculous. He wasn't setting traps for her. He already had, and now that she was in it, he was kind. That's all he wanted, was for her to live here. She didn't get it, and she still hated it, but she could play the game.

Melanie stepped outside. The sunlight burned her eyes at first, but when her vision cleared, she saw a new perspective of Ghost Town. The front yard was about one hundred and forty feet long, and maybe twenty feet less in width. It was much larger than her yard back home, but the accompanying house was smaller than the Grier household. Across the street were the backs of several houses, seeming at an angle. There must have been a winding road straight-ahead, spanning beyond Barker's property. It matched up with what she saw the first night she escaped. Over the houses, the sky was murky blue with thin clouds splotched everywhere. She turned to behold her prison from the outside. The first thing she saw were four ugly words spray-painted across. Besides this, it was bland: brown siding, blue roof, nothing worth noting.

"Who wrote all that?" she asked him as he walked up beside her, hands tapping his sides.

"Different gangs to different people." He pointed at two of the words. "Those were written to Matt Sect as a memorial. And the rest were written to me."

"Ah," she said. "But I thought you only just moved in here." He nodded.

"I've spent time here before we moved in. Once, while Matthew was still in prison, I came here and murdered five of his women." He chuckled loudly, and Melanie breathed in at the thought of what they must have gone through. Barker seemed to sense the drop in mood. "But enough of that boring stuff. Let's go."

Melanie turned from the house. The color was awful, the graffiti deplorable. The grass around the house was dead. Her father would have called it a shit piece of real estate. They walked the cement patio cut through the dead grass, and Melanie entertained ideas of gardening for him. If he had any interest in a garden, she would be doing him a service, outdoors for hours. Hell, maybe she could make one spot in Ghost Town seem alive. They stepped into the street where the mob almost killed them both, where she would go left to New Heim or right to more of Ghost Town. When they got into the car, he turned the key and the engine roared.

"You know how to drive?" he asked.

She shook her head. "I had a couple lessons but I'm terrible at it."

"Aw," he said. "Driving is a necessity unless you can run at unnatural speeds. We could run to the beach if you want," he said.

"Whatever works best," she said. "Whatever you would like to do."

He slapped his forehead. "I'm joking," he said. "I didn't think you'd want your lungs smashed in for shits and giggles." And he proceeded to giggle, and she forced herself to laugh.

"Sorry," she said. "I'm slow sometimes."

He patted her on the shoulder, and spun the car around. They were headed to New Heim.

The skyscrapers were not lit up during the day, but Melanie recognized Main Street. It was not any less mobbed, and horns still honked loud. When they passed the ShipDeck, she searched the windows for the waiter, Carl Banning. Barker drove by too quickly for her to see. He drove straight through five red lights, then made one left turn and one right turn, following a new road for ten more minutes.

"You come here all the time," she observed. Barker was tapping his fingers against the steering wheel, eyes concealed by sunglasses. And when Melanie looked closer, she saw a small white object in his right ear.

"I grew up here too," he said. "Good old New Heim…Yeah, good old New Heim." Even with shades on, Melanie could tell when he was spacing out. Barker actually tended to move in place wherever he was sitting, even if it were just a few inches, back and forth. When he trailed, most of him went stiff. Melanie wondered if it were worth capturing one of those moments in a picture. It was like a sculpture.

They were driving on the outskirts of the city. It was much less busy on the road, and to her right were fifty story high black buildings, like some great long fortress.

"You must know everything about this place," she said, folding her hands on her lap and stretching her legs.

"I do." He drove with one hand on the wheel, other hand jittering on the armrest now. "When the mob attacked, I took the fight here." He pointed towards the large black fortress. "This was one of the spots. There's a nice alley complex in there. Killed four of them before they turned and ran."

"I'm glad it ended well," she said, not wanting to hear the rest.

They traveled five more blocks, then made another left, and another right. Now they were driving on a road with dunes to their left, and as they came to the end of the road, Melanie saw a boardwalk in the distance, lined with apartment buildings. Melanie couldn't believe how vast and wide open this part of the city was. She could see the sky, and the splotchy clouds were vanishing. The rays were shining through. Everything was bright blue. Barker parked the car right next in front of rising dunes with little green blades of grass.

"Ready for this?" he asked.

"Yes," she said.

The car doors opened, letting in the brisk air, but when she stepped out the sun rays warmed her skin. Barker took a small black bag out of the backseat, and then took her hand in his.

"Stay close now," he said. Thankfully, he walked fast. She could hardly contain herself, and she reminded herself not to get too excited, not to break any rules. Together they walked onto the boardwalk. It was fall season, so there were maybe three or four couples strolling the wooden boards, next to the apartments. Melanie was tempted for a moment to look at these strangers and scream for help. She would be dead, but he would be implicated.

No. She needed to be patient and appease him. In time, this whole nightmare could end without violence. As they stepped down onto the sand the wind started to get heavier. They approached the open landscape and she could hear ocean waves smashing against the shoreline.

The wind was ice cold on the beach, but Melanie didn't care. What she was seeing in front of her made her want to cry. Water. Vast, blue seas and skies, stretching on until it just looked like two large paintings colliding with one another. That was what she'd thought the first time she'd ever seen the ocean. And there was even a golden haze on a small section of the water. Everything she loved to look at was right here in front of her, and Barker was standing to her right.

"Want to get closer?" he asked her. She nodded, like a little child, and he said "Go on."

She looked up at him. "Go on?"

"I trust you," he said. "Go on. Go closer to the water."

She turned and look at it again. "It's beautiful," she said, so entranced. She obeyed Barker, and moved forward.

The splashing was loud in her ears now, and she began to suffer a memory.

Ready little lady?

Yes. Yes. Yes!

Alright, that's what I like to hear!

Her father had her on top of his shoulders that day. The sun beat against her black sunglasses, and the crystal blue water glowed. That day had been warm, the wind a relief from the heat. Her mother had been sitting on the beach towel, and her father ran around in the sand so much she'd started to feel dizzy. After that, all three of them had tested the cold water. It was one of her favorite memories.

Today the wind blue harder and the air grew colder. Melanie walked closer and closer to the water. As she did a spike of cold struck her so savagely that snot ran down her nose. She wiped it and pulled her scarf up over her mouth, immediately realizing the irony. I'm either tied up or bundled up. If I were home and it was summer, then I'd really be free.

She kept her hands in her pockets, tight against her sides, eyeing the water. She looked back at Barker. He was standing about fifteen feet behind her, staring back at one of the apartments. She thought he was just gazing at first but then she realized he was staring at a particular apartment. Melanie didn't know what he found so interesting about it, but she realized with a small pang of dread that she was stuck between Barker and the ocean. As beautiful as it felt and looked, it was just another cage. Although, if Melanie wanted, she could vanish into the water. No, Barker would pull her back out. He turned his eyes back to her and yelled over the wind.

"You know the closer you get the colder it'll be!"

She put up her thumb and turned her face back to the sand.

Waves smashed the sand. Waves funneled in the air and shattered into thousands of pieces. And although it was just another wall, it also granted Melanie the same sanctity of the shower. Barker stood far behind her, allowing her to live out the experience on her own, without interruption. Where there was water, Melanie was free.

Was it a glimpse he was offering her? Did he plan, somewhere down the road, for her to be his free companion? She would do it. At this point, if she had to maintain some deal with him in exchange for freedom, she would. But as she turned from the water, glancing back one last time, it occurred to her. What she truly wanted was a pair of wings.

The wind raged on, plugging her eardrums. Her favorite songs played to the fast rhythm of the waves, and she felt the warmth on her face.

"Nice day, isn't it?" said Barker.

She turned to see him right next to her, her heart skipping. She hadn't heard him coming. Then again, he might have only taken one step.

"This is so nice," she said. "I don't know how to thank you for this." He smiled at her.

"How about a picture," he said. He was already digging into the small bag, and she realized it was a camera bag. Out of the bag came a beautiful little device. It was made by Nikon, and attached lens seemed to stretch to at least 55 millimeters. It was perfect for a photograph.

"Give me your prettiest smile," he said. She obeyed, and as a wave splashed behind her, Barker snapped the photo. She couldn't hear the click, but she predicted what kind of count he did before he hit the button. He was looking at the monitor now. "Gorgeous. We could frame this. Come look."

She went over and looked down at a small square image of herself, all dressed in black, scarf over her chin, waves rising in the distance above her head. The light was dull, but the sand and the water behind her gave a nice 3-Dimensional portrait.

"Can I take one of you?" she asked.

"Certainly." He handed her the camera.

She ran her fingers over the buttons, adjusted the camera lens, much more expensive than anything she'd been able to get her hands on. It was like giving up training wheels. Barker stood in front of the waves and pulled his hood down for a moment. He smiled differently this time, almost obnoxiously, as she framed him.

She liked to take her time when she took a shot, so for a moment she was just zeroing in on Justin Barker, getting a good long look at her apparent destiny. Finally, she counted to 3-One thousand, and snapped the picture.

She hadn't captured a crashing wave, but she'd gotten what looked like a still canvas of water behind him. Our pictures should be reversed, she thought. Or maybe not. He's probably a lot more relaxed than I am. I'm the one who's crashing.

After reviewing the photo, Barker insisted on a selfie, of all things. You didn't take a selfie with a Nikon camera, you did it with a phone. Regardless, he held it up one handed and snapped the picture. When she looked at it, the two of them were standing, smiling, slightly at an angle, but well framed with colors and dimensions all perfectly balanced. He snapped a picture in five seconds, one handed, and it was perfect. Now she was jealous.

"Hold this," he said, handing her the device. "I'm going to go have some fun. Stay right there, now."

"Okay," she said. In the next few moments, she was happy no one else was on the beach with them, or even on the boardwalk at this point. He poised himself in the sand, and then he lunged forward, kicking up a huge amount. He was gone. Completely gone. And a moment later he was back.

So fast, she thought. *How is he so fast?*

Chapter 37

Tell Me

T hree days passed, and something changed.

Melanie realized it one night while they were eating dinner. As she twisted her fork with spaghetti, she realized that Barker was ignoring her. He obsessed about her, stared into her very soul, started conversations designed just so he could learn all kinds of things about her. And now, he seemed uninterested. In Melanie's experience, there was a difference between someone being busy and disinterested. Barker wasn't just spacing out. His mind was focused on something else. Melanie came second.

Melanie wiped sauce off her mouth and took the plunge. "Barker?"

He looked over his shoulder. "Yes?"

"What are you thinking about?" He stared for a moment, and she knew what was coming. He was thinking about killing.

"Actually I was thinking about fire," he said. His eyes were trailing, his face lingering in some wayward direction, as usual.

"I noticed you seemed infatuated with it the other day," she said. He nodded, leaning back in the armchair.

"I've been wondering," he said. "Wondering."

"Wondering what?" she asked. But he shook his head.

"Forget it…not important. Is there something on your mind?" His tone was pleasant, and he wiped his nose. The weather was getting colder.

"Well, I was wondering something," she said.

"Yes?" He flashed her a relaxed smile.

"Why do you go by your last name?" she asked.

His eyes didn't trail, but he stopped smiling. He looked downward, reaching up to scratch an itch on his head. "I just do," he said.

"So, you don't want me to call you Justin?"

"No," he said. "I'd rather you not. It's an old, forgotten name. Understand?"

She nodded. "Yes. Of course."

He stared ahead for a minute, and then he went and picked up a magazine, like he needed to occupy himself. "Is there anything else you want to know?"

She wiped her hands and drank some of the water in her glass before turning away from her dish. "We talked a little bit about your…powers." The sound of him laughing out loud was like an explosion, and she went to defend herself. Then he stifled his laugh and put up his hands apologetically.

"Sorry," he said. "Been awhile since someone took that approach. Go on."

"You said it's like an awakening. Something that changes inside you. What happened first? Were you strong first? Fast first? How did it all unfold?" she asked, thinking that was as clear as necessary. He motioned with two of his fingers.

"Come on over here, darling. On the couch. You can bring your food if you want."

She got up, leaving what was left of the pasta, and sat down on the sofa. She felt herself sinking for a moment and giggled.

"The strength came first," he said. "After my dearest friends betrayed me, I crushed a piece of solid metal with one hand. I tested out my power by overturning a car. There was, um, no one inside it. But that was what came first. The strength. And then, as I ran, I started to realize I could move faster."

"It didn't just all happen at once?" she asked.

"No, dear. I developed a capacity for it like a thunderclap. But the proportions of it, I had to train overtime. That's how it is for all of us."

"Who?" she asked. "That part confuses me a little."

"I used to be what they call a Meridian Killer," he said, emotionless. He put up a finger. "When you discover these abilities, you might think that you're on your own. Science hasn't really covered it. The public doesn't have anything concrete. Just ghost stories. But years ago, in Montana, when you were a baby, there was a man there with the condition. He gathered together people with the condition and formed a small underground society. A society I became a part of when I traveled there."

"And his name was Aethon Armata?" she asked, carefully pronouncing the name. For a moment, Barker looked annoyed.

"Yes, dear. I'm guessing you haven't really looked at the book I gave you." His tone was testy and aggressive, like a teacher's. Melanie put her head down.

"No," she said. "I've been meaning to."

"That's alright, dear. But all of the answers you seek are within those pages." He folded his arms. "I'd love to discuss it with you one day soon. There's much for you to learn."

"Okay," she said. "Sorry. I'll make sure I get to it next."

"Aethon wasn't the best writer but you'll find it a fast read. Straight to the point. That helped me a lot. I was able to read it in one night. He told me the first time we met that I had to adapt over night, else I wouldn't make it through the second day."

"Things were bad in Montana," Melanie said. "In the Meridian?"

"Everyday a fight for survival. And I loved it."

"How could you love it? It sounds terrifying."

He sat up. "Think about this place. You have myself, the king of beasts. And then you have the crime families, rivals, and the police, a feeble attempt at maintaining order. Then you have civilians. Typically, the civilians run and scream, the mobsters plot and scheme, and the police keep out of it. Ultimately, I do what I want. I have my own little playground."

She nodded. She knew all too well.

He went on, "In the Meridian, I would have to fight harder for territory. There would be one hundred Barker's running around at night, and all of us would be engaging in the Circle of Knives."

"What's a circle of knives?" Melanie asked.

"A game. The closest comparison would be what happened between the mobsters and I back in October. One lone subject, surrounded by predators. In the Meridian you had to prove your worth. And if you couldn't, it was over rather quickly. If you could, you got see just how much fun this kind of life could be." He closed his eyes and smiled. "The adrenaline, the rush. Going out into the big scary night that you feared so much as a child, and realizing that you aren't contained by it. That you control it. That you can fly up into the night and discover worlds of knowledge and experience. That you can live outside the normal established ring of society. That life isn't just the rules someone else sets for you."

There was silence then. Melanie had no response, and Barker shot her a look. A look that said he was reading her mind.

Then he said, "It was characteristic of a Meridian Killer, to take a prisoner."

"Oh?" she whispered, curling up.

"If a Meridian Killer decided he wanted something, he simply took it. And he introduced a young, pretty girl, or boy, to a new life. A life where they began in chains. And slowly, piece by piece, they would remove pieces."

"Pieces of the restraints?" Melanie asked.

"Hopefully," Barker said. "Some of them were assholes about it. But the bottom line is, sometimes a prisoner could do the same thing. Even without powers, a prisoner could persevere. Prove her worth."

"Ah," Melanie said. That was as far as she went.

"The moral of the story is, sometimes pain propels us forward in life. Makes us better," he said. "It certainly did me."

"Do you really believe that?" She hadn't meant for it to sound so aggressive, and for a moment she expected the knife. What she was trying to say was that pain left scars. Pain changed you into something arbitrary and you had no right to argue. She was wondering if he truly liked what he'd become or if he had simply given up. She hadn't meant it to sound judgmental, even if that was how she really felt.

"I believe it," he said. "And so should you." He got up and came toward her. Then he was standing in front of her. "You've been wonderful, Melanie. You've kept it together. Passed multiple tests. You fumbled a bit in the beginning, but lately you've proven to me that you're strong."

Melanie put down her head, staring at the floor. Having him this close, gloating over the chains he'd put her in, made her short of breath.

Barker went on, "And you've been honest. I haven't had to tie you up for the past week now, and you haven't acted out. Not even once. Not even outdoors. I'm very impressed."

"Thank you."

"Stop thanking me."

"Okay." She looked up at him and waited patiently for whatever he did next.

"Sooner or later, I'm going to let you start leaving the house on your own. There will be no more strikes. No more last chances. Just one promise between the two of us."

What he was offering her was irresistible. Whatever the condition, she would accept it. "What promise?" she asked.

"That at the end of every day, you will always come home," he said. "You will never run away from me."

"That's all?" Melanie asked. It wasn't what she wanted for her life, to spend the rest of it with Barker, but she had expected death all of this time. Torture and rape whenever he was done entertaining himself with her. What he was saying now gave her more hope than she'd had for months. "Just…remain loyal to you?"

"Yes," he whispered.

"And you'll let me come and go?"

"You won't be a prisoner, Melanie. You will live here. With me. Forever."

Forever. Barker, forever. Part of her couldn't breathe, or contemplate all of this going on forever. And yet, she was being offered a long life. The chance to become an adult. The chance to live for years, and eventually find a way to escape. But wait.

"You mean, like, if I want to go out for, like, a hotdog."

"You could go wherever you like. As long as you come home. As long as you tell me where you are going and how long you will be there. Respect me as your guardian. Treat me with the same respect I offer you now." There were tears in Barker's eyes. They weren't dripping, but she spotted the glassy layer. "I'll give you everything you could ever want, Melanie. You need only promise to be mine, forever."

Silence hung between the two of them, until Barker broke it.

"Someday, I might even let you see your family again."

Melanie jumped up to his level and he took a step back. "You would let me see them? You would let me go home?"

"If you come back to me, yes," he said. "That won't happen for quite some time but—"

"You'd let me visit them? Even for just an hour? Two hours? A day?" she pleaded. "You'd let me see my friends. Let them know that I'm okay. That it's all okay?"

"Not anytime soon, Melanie. Understand, that's something we would have to work towards. You'll always have to follow my exact instructions. But I'm not unreasonable."

He was offering her a life. A real life. She could leave the house when she wanted air. When she wanted food. She could have more people in her life than just him. The only condition was that she continued to live with him. To keep him in her life. Even after everything, if she could just be free. If she could just have this, she didn't care if Barker stayed in her life forever.

"I would love that," she whispered. "I'd do anything for it. Anything. I'd do anything for you," she said.

He smiled and petted her hair. "Time, Melanie. I'm not giving you any of this tomorrow," he said sternly.

She nodded through tears. "Right, right. I understand. I can wait."

He smiled. "I think we're off to a good start."

Melanie couldn't stop herself. She lunged forward and hugged him, buried her face in his hot chest, let the tears pour out. "Thank you," she whispered.

Barker's voice was proud and content. "You don't have to thank me."

Chapter 38

Tambourine

S omeone was knocking on Tom's door.
    It was loud, like someone large with large hands. Something told Tom that if it were Barker, it would be very light, almost inaudible knocks. So it couldn't be him. Not that aggressive. This knocker meant business.

Tom never put his gun away at home. Not anymore.

He pulled the door open, stopping at the chain lock to peek through, and saw a face he'd never before beheld.

Through the crack of the door, it looked like a pale man with no facial hair and a very pointy nose, not much hair on his head at all. Thirty, forty years old?

"Who are you?" Tom asked.

The man spoke in a North Jersey accent. "Are you Tom Macklin?"

"Who wants to know?"

"Me," the man said.

"And who are you?"

"Not giving you my name until you give me yours. I'm here about a certain...letter?"

Tom's heart pounded faster, and he felt more awake than moments ago. "Yes, I'm Tom Macklin. And I just want to say upfront that I am in full support of Mr. Crawford's organization."

"I don't believe that for a minute, kid. But don't worry, I'm not here to kill ya... gonna let me in or we just gonna keep staring at each other's pretty faces?"

Tom unlocked the door and let it fall open, bringing the man into full view. Almost bald, very pale with a round head and pointy nose. Broad shoulders and from what Tom could see, well defined muscles. He was dressed business casually and he had a bag over his shoulders. His face was like a mixture of Albert Ferris and Allen Marx, stuck between glaring and smirking. He seemed very laid back, at peace with whatever happened next, or wherever he ended up pointing his gun. He was closer in appearance to Barker than any of the mobsters. How about in genetics?

The man's footsteps were heavy on Tom's floor, and he dropped the bag like he was planning on moving in. "Nice place, I guess."

Tom stood on guard at the door, gun still in hand. "Thanks. It's a rental."

He turned, right hand on the back of his balding head. "Really? I thought you grew up in this tiny little apartment." He pointed toward the back room. "Mom and Dad would have stayed there and you, uh, I don't know where. Anyway, put down the gun. I don't like guns, especially not in my face. And regardless of my good intentions, if you provoke me, I will kill you. Clear?"

Tom lowered the gun. "I'd like to keep my gun...You can understand my need for caution."

The man didn't say a word, only put up his index finger and reached down to his waist with his other hand. He drew a large hunting knife and eyed it as he approached Tom. Tom raised his gun, but the man flipped the knife over.

"Trade? Hold onto this if it makes you feel safe. No guns."

Tom took the knife before he dropped the gun, and being double armed convinced him he would offend the killer if he didn't obey. He placed the gun down. The man swiped his hands through the air like a cloud of smoke and he had the gun.

"Nice. Cops get nice ones." He unloaded the bullets and threw the empty gun onto the couch before he sat down. "Okay, thanks for cooperating with me there." He pointed his hands inward toward his chest. "I'm Rodney Tambourine. Nice to meet ya...I'm sure you have questions for me and I have plenty for you. So we'll be here awhile. Got anything to drink?"

"Fresh out."

"Of everything? Beer? Liquor?"

"Fresh out."

"What kind of cop are you? Anyway, I can drink water, and if ya got a bag of chips or something that'd be great. Been driving for hours, what with you living at the farthest fucking Western edge of America. Seriously, what's Barker doing all the way out here? Anyway, if you don't have any, no big."

Tom went to the kitchen and poured the man a glass of water, and then one for himself, realizing the heat of the situation. He didn't have a bag of chips, but he found a small bag of pretzels.

He walked back into the room and tossed the bag into the man's hands. "Nice," Rodney muttered, tearing the bag open.

Tom put the water down beside the couch and sat down in his armchair. He'd be courteous if his life depended on it but he wouldn't be made to stand in his own house.

The man chomped on the pretzels, loud as a tire rolling over gravel. "So, you have a Barker problem."

"Yes. A rather large one."

"With him it always is...or so I'm told."

"Are you like him? A Meridian Killer?"

The man looked taken aback. "Well, that takes care of my first question." He dug into the pretzel bag again and folded his leg. "So you know the technical terms. What else?"

"I know that Mr. Crawford runs an organization of people with your special abilities. I know it's a mercenary organization operating out of I think, Montana, or at least used to be if it hasn't moved. And I know a few little details about the history. That you all started from outside Montana, little things."

The killer put his hand up. "Answer me one question."

"Okay."

The killer leaned forward, pretzel bag held in both hands like a glass. His face looked like a professor who was very invested in the class's trivia game. "Who is Aethon Armata?"

"I have no idea. Never heard the name before."

The killer nodded his head. "Alright. We can move on from that." He took out one pretzel and popped it in, eyes locked on Tom. "You found out about Crawford because of Stanley Jackson."

"Yes."

"Okay...well, he wrote a letter and was rejected. But you knew that. You wrote that in your letter."

"That's right."

The killer shook his head. "So you do realize you might walk away from this a bit disappointed."

"I don't think Stan ever won himself a house call. That makes me feel a little bit better about it."

"House call is just because Crawford doesn't like that he's gotten two letters now. He wants to put this to bed. He doesn't like people talking about him and what he does if he doesn't know who they are."

"Well...help me with the Barker problem and I'll shut up about it for the rest of my life. I just need support is all. The police force is completely whipped, as much as it pains me to admit it. I was forced to turn to the crime families of New Heim for support. But Barker's killed all of them."

"I understand. You're trying to off Barker, but you can't. And now he's cleaning the field and there's just nothing anyone can do but pray he trips and falls the wrong way. Or just gets a little too hungry one night and stuffs his air hole. You don't have to explain that. I get it."

"I'm glad."

"There's a lot of us, Mr. Macklin, and not all of us work for Crawford. Those of us who do sometimes have to go handle the ones who act out of line, or to quote Mr. Crawford himself, like savages. The technical term is Renegade."

"So you've done this kind of thing before?"

"Once or twice. But most renegades I've hunted are a lot weaker than I am. This is Barker. He's got a reputation...so I haven't said yes yet."

"Can I ask a basic question?"

"Go ahead."

"Hypothetically...can you do it?"

"Kill him? I think I can. You just have to know your prey, which Crawford's complimented me for. But the fact remains, we don't have much incentive."

"No, you do."

"Explain that to me."

"Barker lives his life isolated from most of society, and from an observer's standpoint, every now and then he gets lonely, and decides to, let's say, throw a party. The first time he threw a party in this city, several girls turned up dead. The next time he threw a party, cops started showing up dead. And then mobsters. In more recent years, he had a maniacal episode and killed the most powerful Crime family that's ever functioned on the West Coast. And this last time, he killed the second most."

"You lost me awhile ago, Macklin. Wrap it up."

"The point is, Barker is cleaning this city. He won't stop until everyone's dead. When there's nothing left here for him he'll just move on. He's a fundamental virus, and I think

Mr. Crawford should understand that kind of thing should be dealt with. Before it spreads to his territory."

"We like to throw parties too. We even have names for some of them. And I'm sure you know about his occasional trips all over America."

"Yes. I do."

"Coincidentally, he never stops in Montana. Why do you think that is? We're not worried."

Tom realized something in the midst of the back and forth. "You haven't mentioned price yet."

"No, I haven't…Crawford is paying for this one himself."

"What?"

"If I do it, he's not charging you. Crawford's had a long standing issue with Barker and he's currently weighing his options."

"What options?"

"None of your business, kid." He stood up. "Let's wrap this up…I've been asked to assess the situation, and it looks like it sucks. Dead girls, dead cops, dead hookers no doubt, you don't have to go into any further detail. With all the shit I've seen over the years, that pretty much sums it up. But I'm being asked to kill arguably the most dangerous fighter alive with no backup. It'll make me a hero forever or just get me killed. So…you're on. Convince me."

How would he convince him? What hadn't he said already?

"Barker is a problem. He's one of you, and in full control of this city. Even the Government keeps their hands off him…I don't think Mr. Crawford wants a rival like that. And…and you will be a hero. You'll be the most dangerous fighter alive. And I'd like to think everyone you work with, and everyone who opposes you, will know that fact."

The killer nodded his head, up and down. Then he picked up the bag. "I'll show myself out." He walked up to Tom and held out his hand. Tom gave him the knife and then the killer walked right past him.

"That's…that's it? You didn't say anything. You didn't answer me."

"You'll get my answer when you read about it in the paper, or don't."

And then he was gone, vanishing outside. Tom lingered in the doorway, wishing he could be more persuasive. Then he shut the door and locked it tight, putting a chair in front.

Chapter 39

Open Wounds

Melanie stuck her finger through the hole in the glass. A sniper's bullet, something she thought she'd only ever see in a movie. The hole in the window was probably the same size as the one in Barker's side. She stepped away from the window and went back to reading A Clockwork Orange. All the while, Melanie wondered if the author ever experienced bullets flying through his window. Melanie could probably write a good book.

Barker's bedroom door opened, and Melanie was tempted to glance inside. A clear violation of their agreement, but Melanie often wondered what went on in there. What she would see. The first time it had been too dark to see anything but him. What exactly was Melanie living with, besides a terrifyingly confusing man who was somehow starting to make sense to her?

"Hi," she said.

"Hello, there," he said. He scurried over to the refrigerator and took out a bottle of Yuengling.

"What's up?" she asked. It was a weird thing to ask your kidnapper, but not your guardian.

"Not much," he said. It was little more than a whisper. "Yeah, not much." His eyes trailed, and he didn't look happy, and she dropped her enthusiasm.

"What happened?" she asked. "Are you okay?"

"Of course," he said robotically.

"Okay."

He walked over to the counter and took a glass from the cupboard. He stood still for a moment before he filled it. From where she sat in the living room, Melanie could hear his gulping and exhaling as if it were right next to her ears. Barker seemed like he was just in a bad mood. She wasn't used to that, and she hoped it didn't mean things would change for the worse.

"Do you want to talk?" she asked.

"No," he said.

"Okay," she answered. A thought came to her. Maybe he was just flashing back. She knew he'd had some rough experiences. And though he played them off as beneficial, there had to be some part of him that was still in pain.

"I won't pry, but, I'm here if you ever need me," she said.

"You're a sweet thing," he said. He pressed his hands against the island, without looking at her. "Do you believe in souls, Melanie?"

She stood in place, unsure of how to answer. Melanie had been raised Catholic, but only to a point. Her parents weren't overly fond of church practices, and she'd been led to believe it was not a necessity. And that gave her an odd relationship with all things spiritual. Her life had been mostly based on practical, scientific reasoning, and yet, now that the abnormal had knocked down her door, was there a larger explanation for things she didn't understand?

"I was never a church person," she said. I guess, I just stopped thinking about it. they make you feel so guilty when you're not a church person. It's like, if you believe in souls you have to believe in God," she finished. Her blood ran cold when he appeared inches away from her. She'd never get used to that.

"Pure, unadulterated, bullshit," he said dramatically, straightening up. "Religion is cult work. And Christianity has nothing to do with my question. I asked if you believe in souls."

"I don't know." She contemplated his point. A soul did not require religion to exist. They were separate things. "I guess, the idea of a soul is too big for me to wrap my mind around."

"Nonsense," he said. "You're smarter than that."

"I guess I'd need to see it," she said, and laughed. "If that makes any sense." To her relief, he chuckled too. "Do you believe in souls?" she asked, already knowing the answer.

"I do," he said. Melanie sat down in the armchair as he continued, pacing. "There are other forces at work in this world, Melanie. I can promise you that." He opened and closed the magazine as he spoke. "And I believe the soul can mutate. Just like the body." She didn't answer that, and rocked back and forth where she sat. Barker asked her, "What do you believe in, Melanie? Use your imagination." But she already had her answer.

"I believe in kindness."

"Kindness?" He stared at her like he was stumped.

"Mhm." She nodded. "I think love is the most powerful thing any of us ever feel. I think it…governs our souls."

He stepped back and brushed his chin with his thumb. "That's true. I'll give you that."

He folded his fingers and rested his mouth on his knuckles, and his yellow eyes widened again, staring at the wall. She wished she knew what to say to him when he blanked out. She never knew what he'd say when he came back, or what kind of Barker she'd be facing. But now, she thought she saw something. She'd seen more of that in the past few days. He seemed less relaxed. More tense. Unhappy. But she didn't want to ask if he was alright, yet again, and get no answer. It made her feel stupid.

"I'm tired," he said. "I think I'm going to read a bit more and go to bed."

"Okay…I think I'll clean up and go upstairs."

He nodded. And she got up and walked to the table.

"Melanie."

She turned and looked at him. He was still looking down before his eyes finally found her. "It's not love. It's fear."

"Fear," she repeated.

He smiled. "Good night, darling."

The next day Melanie awoke to a new set of clothes on her couch. She hadn't even heard him come in. It was a tight black shirt and leggings, and short ankle shoes. There was a note that said, "Wear these ☺."

The clothes were clenching tight against her skin, but not uncomfortable. Melanie walked downstairs and was instantly chilled. The front door was wide open, and Barker was standing in the front yard. He motioned for her to come outside.

"Time for your lesson," he said.

"Lesson?" she asked, and he nodded.

"Remember when I said you need to learn how to defend yourself?"

"Oh, right." At first Melanie felt a weight on her shoulders. Sitting around reading all day every day didn't exactly put you in the mood to work out in the cold. Then again, maybe that would take her mind off things. But what kind of teacher was Barker? Melanie pictured herself getting cut and stabbed as lessons.

"Let's go," he said, and she obeyed.

Melanie stood opposite Barker. He was dressed in a black sleeveless shirt and shorts. His waist was holstered, knife sheathed at his side. It was so cold outside, but she knew his hot skin repelled the icy sensations just fine.

"What have you learned so far?" he asked her.

"I learned basic self defense when I was little," she said, shivering.

"Such as?" he said. His eyes seemed just as fixated as usual, but he was standing more straight and looked like he was getting ready for a party.

"Basically using the attackers own strength against them?" she said. "Couple little tricks."

"Funny, I'd have never known," he said. Anger welled in her gut. She didn't need to be teased about any of their violent encounters. But Barker pressed forward. "Go on. Use what you know on me."

He walked up beside her and counted to three. Then he reached toward her. Melanie grabbed his hand, and started to twist her hand in place, to readjust her grip. But Barker countered. He flipped his hand over, covering hers, and squeezed. The pain shot up her arm and she squealed. Then he let her go. "That was quick," he said. She gripped her arm and rubbed it fast, both for pain and cold. Then she looked up at him and grunted.

"That's all I know," she said. She'd been lazy as a child. Her father hadn't had much luck. Once she learned a basic technique, she assumed she was ready for anything, because nothing would ever happen. What a stupid little child. Barker paced around her.

"Here's what we are going to do today," he said. "It'll be safe and relatively painless. I promise," he softly sang.

"Relatively?" she asked, half laughing, half scolding.

"There's no training without a little bit of pain," he said. Melanie jumped up, terrified of whatever exaggerated test she was going to receive.

"No, I'm sorry. I can't. I'm sorry." As she begged he stared at her, perplexed. "I'm not cut out for this. I can't fight."

"Sure, you can," he said. "It's easy. I'm not asking you to learn Krav Maga."

"What the hell is that?" she asked, and he scoffed.

"A bit of nonsense is what it is. I can fight just fine without it." He advanced towards her and drew the knife, flipping it around. "Take this."

Melanie took Barker's knife in her hand. It was much heavier than a kitchen knife. It was eight inches long and weighed about an ounce. The blade was shiny white, as if it hadn't ever been used. The handle was dark and smelled like rubber. Barker was stepping back.

"Use that," he said. "Don't hurt yourself."

"What do you want me to do?" she asked, anxiety rapidly pumping her heart.

"You're going to try to kill me," he said. "You won't succeed, of course. However, the more you try, the more you'll learn."

"Barker, I don't know," she said.

"Remember our promise?" he asked.

She did. She had to obey. If Melanie resisted him, their deal would be off. He'd give her everything: fresh air, entertainment, the opportunity to actually live her life, and maybe even a family visit one day. But she wouldn't get any of it if she resisted him.

"Sorry," she said. "I'll try. I don't think I'll be any good."

He put up his hand, as if motioning for her to come forward. "I have more faith in you than that."

Melanie gripped the knife tight, extending it forward. For the duration of this lesson, Barker was her prey. If an accident happened, that would also free her.

Melanie lunged forward, and Barker vanished like smoke. He appeared at the other end of the yard, and she ran toward him again. For awhile, he jumped around the yard in eight different spots, forming an octagon. Melanie yelled at him to stop mocking her, and when she lunged again, he remained rooted to the spot. She stabbed forward, but he caught her wrist, same as that night in his room. This time he squeezed her wrist half as savagely, and instead of pinning her to wall, he lightly shoved her backwards. Melanie stood and heaved on the spot while Barker played with the knife he had taken from her.

"Not what you're used to, I know," he said. He walked over and placed it back in her hands, but this time she was holding it upside down. "That's how you hold a knife in combat, silly." He then demonstrated for her how much more likely you were to cut someone if you swung with the blade facing your elbow. When they were done he said, "If I'm going to let you walk away from this house, I'm going to make sure you're safe." For a moment, a vision of her father drifted into Barker's place.

Melanie still read books every day, and she still was not allowed to leave the house without Barker's permission. It was still only a promise. An offer for the future. But every day there was a new fighting instruction. Every day Melanie learned something new. Elbow strikes, palm heels, knee strikes. As the session went on she was less and less turned off. Barker proved to be far more gentle than she'd anticipated, as he often did. Melanie had come to learn the extent of his strength and speed, and during these sessions he hardly used any of it. Aside from a bump and bruise here and there, she came out unscathed, and with new knowledge. And shockingly, these lessons provided her with daily challenges. Something to ponder over night, expect in the morning. It drove other, more horrible thoughts out of her mind. It also gave her something to be proud of. If and when she completed a challenge, Barker smiled at her with pride, and it was the first time anyone had given her that since she was taken.

One day, Melanie realized that she might be getting as tough as Kris. And that was when time momentarily stopped. That was when Melanie remembered. Someone else was nearby, suffering.

"Have you heard from Kris?" she asked Barker one day.

"Not since she left," he said.

"Do you think she's back at the gymnasium?" she asked. Barker took another bite of his chicken drumstick, as if he wanted to change the subject.

"Probably."

Melanie wanted to ask if they could go see her, but she didn't know how far she wanted to push her luck. Maybe she could just go see her when Barker started letting her outdoors. Barker gnawed on that drumstick like a hyena feasting on a pig.

He was quiet for a moment before saying, "I'll take you." Melanie almost spit out her food.

"You will?" she asked.

He nodded. "After dinner."

The moon was pale over Ghost Town, and many doors blew open in the wind. Like the first time she took the trip, thunder was crackling overhead. Melanie remembered walking along the corridors of the school, rain banging against the outsides, like the inside of a giant instrument.

At a certain point, Melanie came across nothing but broken roads, until she had discovered Desolation Drive. That had been where she discovered the broken bridge and where Barker had brought her during the mob attack. Barker bypassed the broken roads by taking a few elaborate turns, then they were cruising through Desolation Drive.

"How long are we staying?" she asked.

"Long enough to check up on her," he said.

Barker rolled the wheels over a large amount of gravel before he finally parked in front of the school. Melanie got out and took a whiff of the cold air. It had been a couple of weeks. Melanie wondered if the bodies were still in there.

"Go on in," Barker said.

"You're not coming?" she asked.

"I'm coming. I'll flank you," he said.

"I don't under—"

"I'm here to keep you safe, Melanie, dear. I'll give you two ladies as much privacy as I can." He motioned for her to walk forward, and Melanie approached the dark corridors.

They looked the same as they once had, only Melanie expected to trip over bodies. But there were none. And it wasn't raining. The hallways were far more unsettling without the noise outside. Barker was walking about ten feet behind her, just watching. It reminded her so much of when she first tried to escape, and saw him strolling toward her in the distance.

When Melanie stepped into the gymnasium, she immediately saw one large blood stain on the floor by the back door, where some moonlight shined down. But there were no bodies. Kris must have gotten rid of them, given them burials. Still, the room was slathered with the presence of death. In the large gaping hole at the top of the room, Melanie heard the wind howling. As Melanie looked across the empty room where all of those people once spent their time, she thought of Adam. Kris had named him among the dead. He'd been kind to her. Interested in her, even. He seemed harmless. A nice boy just trying to survive. And the mobsters killed him. They probably didn't even hesitate. That nice boy was just dead now. He was never given a chance. As Melanie crossed the room, Barker stood behind her, peering in from the hallway.

Melanie walked toward the locker room.

Kris was there, lying on the ground with her hair hiding her face and a gun in her hands, head digging into her right arm. There was a bottle near her, looked very large, and she looked very under the influence.

"Kris?" she said quietly. When Kris didn't stir, Melanie was struck with worry. She stepped closer to the mangled, motionless, mess. "Kris!"

The girl came back to life, gasping. Her head darted all around and she pointed the gun, eyes settling on Melanie. Melanie put her hands up as Kris got to her feet.

"What do you want?" she growled. It sounded like she'd lost her voice.

"I just wanted to see you," Melanie said. "To see if you were alright." At this, Kris lowered the gun, setting it down on the bench.

"Peachy. Out." She pointed her finger.

"I'm sorry to barge in—"

"Out!"

"I just wanted—"

Kris lunged at her and tackled her to the ground. She wasn't nearly as strong as Barker but strong enough to stifle Melanie's breathing. The only breath Melanie got out was stuffed up with the scent of Kris's alcohol plastered breath. Melanie pushed up against her. She was going to defend herself, and she wasn't going to call for help this time. With a free hand, Melanie dug her fingers into Kris's arm. Kris screamed as Melanie raked her, Kris lunged upward and momentarily released Melanie. As Kris prepared to come down on her, Melanie jabbed her palm upward, striking Kris in the chin.

Then Barker had his arm around Kris's throat.

"Calm down," he said quietly. To Melanie's shock, Kris was immediately quelled. Melanie got to her feet and it brought she and Kris face to face. It was only for a second, but Melanie saw it. Kris's eyes were tearing, and her jaw quivered. It was the same look her mother had given her that day.

"Did you hit my friend?" Barker asked her, tightening his grip.

"She's drunk," Melanie said. "I'm okay." Barker looked at her over Kris's terrified shoulder, and grinned.

"Nice reflexes," he said, and winked at her. He dropped Kris and she fell to the ground, sobbing. She scooted forward and hid her head underneath the bench. Melanie wanted to kneel down and put her hand on her shoulder, though she feared she might lose it in the process.

"Come," Barker said. "We're done here."

On their way out, Melanie asked him, "Is there anything we can do for her?"

"Yeah. Give her time and space, and keep our doors open to her...That was nice of you though, coming down here."

She didn't want to give up just yet. There had to be a way to get through to Kris. But there was a gun in there. "Sure." Melanie looked around the empty gymnasium one last time. "You don't think...you don't think she got rid of them all herself?"

Barker scoffed. "That'll make you crazy."

Chapter 40

The Burrow

A s the days rolled on, Melanie continued to hone her skills. She was still no match for Barker, but after twenty days, she was starting to feel like she could at least hold her own in a fight. But she would need to keep practicing. It was strange to be focusing so much on something she never had an interest in. But a memory from her previous life came a couple of weeks later. It was Thanksgiving.

"Where are we going?" Melanie asked Barker. They were standing in the living room, about to head to the car.

"To a very nice restaurant," he said. "It's called 'The Burrow.'" From the sound of it, it wasn't in fact a nice restaurant.

"What kind of stuff do they have?"

"All kinds of stuff. American, Mexican, even a little Chinese."

"Cool," she said. "I can't wait." She gave him the most genuine smile she could manage. But things weren't half as stressful lately. Melanie was still a prisoner, but he was training her, arming her. Treating her with respect. Giving her something to make her feel less helpless. She realized now that the helplessness was where the anxiety truly stemmed from.

Melanie was dressed in a pink shirt and black jeans, covered by her Fleece Faux Coat. She'd combed her hair very neatly to hide the mess she'd made of herself in the training. And Barker had cleaned up as well. He'd shaved the stubble that was just growing back. Melanie hadn't ever seen him this nice looking. He'd combed his hair to the side and moisturized his skin. For clothing he wore a blue button down underneath a dark coat, thinner and cleaner looking than his usual trench coat. When she'd inquired about the occasion for such a change, he joked that every now and then the beard gets too itchy.

When they arrived at The Burrow, Melanie was looking at a small door in a large building, with two other shops on either side. This place wasn't very big. When she passed through the doors it was like looking down a dark alley, with neat and polished wooden walls. At the end of the alley a brick floor and an open door to a bright yellow room. It had to be the kitchen. Next to the door was a right turn that likely led to the dining hall. Barker approached the hostess and raised two fingers. The girl drew two menus and walked ahead of them. It was strange to see a girl around her age look upon herself and Barker and be undaunted and unaware. She was a game player like him now. The thought of being on a date with him was repulsive, but it wasn't like that. It was more like a brother, sister kind of thing. Or just two friends. Yes, two friends.

The dining room appeared on their right, and had all of twenty tables. This place sure didn't look like much. The hostess set the menus down and the duo sat.

"The waitress will be with you shortly."

"Thank you," said Barker with a wide smile Melanie knew was fake.

Melanie opened the menu, and read through and abundant number of food choices. She looked around at the restaurant, dim and dank as the house she lived in.

"You like these kinds of places, huh?"

"What?" he said.

"I just mean it reminds me a little bit of the kitchen at home."

He cocked his head for a moment and said, "Yes. I suppose it does."

And then he went back to reading the menu. Melanie could get the entire restaurant's attention right now. She could scream and call him out and all of them would jump to her defense. Or would they? The police wouldn't help her. If these people tried, he'd kill them. Everywhere was a prison.

"I was thinking, I'm a little worried about something," she said.

"What's that?" he asked, eyes on the menu.

She looked at his distracted, clean face for a minute and said, "Well…suppose one day, if this all works out, you let me visit home."

"Yes?" he said, like he didn't know what she was getting at.

"I think my parents might have trouble understanding."

"Yes, probably." He turned a page. He looked like he was reading a book rather than a menu. Melanie liked to read menus quickly, and she probably sat stiff when she did.

"So…how would it work?" she asked.

"You have to be patient," he said gently, still not looking at her. "In time, we will make it work."

"Okay." She went back to the menu, and her eyes sailed over a blur of words before settling on "Steak Burrito." Something died for that, Emily said to her once. Her friend was vegetarian, and had even convinced Melanie to try it out for all of one week. She'd felt sick and ravenous for meat by the end of the week.

Emily was like Kris. Emily had been in pain when Melanie met her. Something about her home life was clearly abusive, and Melanie couldn't figure out if it was her mother or her father. She did notice that one day Emily came to school with bruises. Only once. But Melanie had reached out to her then. She didn't like the thought of other people in pain. And it was strange to think back on the past two months, being tied to that bed, gagged, stripped and cut. Melanie didn't know how to respond to herself as the victim. She hadn't known how to respond to Emily, beyond 'are you alright" and she sure as hell didn't know what to say to Kris.

A waitress walked up to them. She had brown curls and tan skin. Her name tag read "Ashley."

"Hi guys, welcome to The Burrow. Can I start you off with something to drink?" She was bubbly with a loud, high-pitched voice. It sounded like she wanted to be their best friend, not just bring them food. Barker looked up at her and smiled.

"Ashley, pretty name," he said.

"Thank you," she said enthusiastically. "I don't usually get compliments."

"You don't? Unacceptable," he said. Melanie could hear the complete difference in his voice. He wasn't at all himself. What was he playing at?

The waitress was laughing, hand on her collarbone. "Oh, no, it's okay. Can I start you guys off with something to drink?"

"Fire away, Melanie."

"Melanie," said the waitress. "That is a gorgeous name! Way better than mine."

Melanie smiled, her teeth pressed together. "Thank you, that's really sweet."

"Tell her what you want," Barker said.

"Can I just have a water with lemon?" Melanie asked.

"Sure!" the waitress said and turned back to Barker. "And you, sir?"

"Water without, please. My sweet tooth leaves something to be desired." When he smiled his teeth were bright.

"Two waters coming up," she said, and scurried away. There weren't many people left in the dining room, but there were enough to fill the room with noise.

"I haven't seen you eat anything sweet," Melanie said.

"Nope." He cracked his neck and folded his hands. "Bigger fan of meat."

"Ah. So what meat are you getting tonight?"

"Actually tonight I might just get some soup. Or maybe," he said, sliding his finger along the menu, and stopping it hard on one spot. "Oh, maybe a bread bowl."

When the waitress returned, they ordered their food and she scribbled it all on a newspaper. Looking closer, Melanie noticed besides the curly brown locks her eyes were a pretty shade of green. What Melanie noticed the most about her was her carefree smile, like there was nothing wrong with the world. That there wasn't a serial killer at her table. He can change. He almost died for you. It came to her like a slap in the face, and for a moment Melanie was numb and thoughtless. It took both the waitress and Barker to get her attention.

"What?" she said, eyes darting.

Barker's eyebrow was up. "It's your turn to order, silly."

"Oh. Can I have a Steak Burrito please?" The waitress wrote at the same place a moth flapped its wings.

"Will that be all," she asked them both, hugging the clipboard to her chest.

"Actually, may I have a glass of this?" Barker asked, showing the waitress an item on the menu.

"Coming right up!" she said. Then she was gone again.

"What did you order?" Melanie asked.

"Wine," Barker said, in a pleasurable tone like he was already tasting it. "You like?"

"Tried it once...Liked it better than beer."

"Certainly sweeter," he said with a wink. "Anyway, tell me more about Fargo."

"What do you mean?"

"If you visited, who would you be visiting besides your family? Did you have any friends?"

"Um...well, I had one friend. Emily."

"Just one?"

"Pretty much." She scratched her own scalp, remembering an incident she was turned away by a group of well dressed, overly done up girls. "I wasn't popular."

"Neither was I," he said. "You have to love yourself." He took a sip of water and pointed with his left index finger. "Of course it's a bonus to be loved by the right people."

"You know there was a boy I was mean to a couple of times."

"Really?" he asked.

"Yeah," she said. "His name is Ronnie. He had a lot of problems. He was hyper, loud, really over emotional, always paranoid and crying. I was nice to him here and there and he kind of latched on to me sometimes. And I don't know, sometimes I think I was a little bit mean. I didn't mean to be."

"Melanie," he said, dropping his tone. "When I was your age, I had bullets going through me. What I had to do to survive was start being mean. You understand?"

"I do," she said. But she still wanted to see Ronnie again one day. Apologize to him. Check in with Emily. Maybe even visit a few teachers. A memory flushed through her of saying the wrong thing to one of the popular girls and being labeled a whore. "I still think those girls were mean," she said. Barker laughed at that.

"And what kind of person is Emily?" he asked.

"She's funny. Really witty. Always talking, always complaining about her mom." She remembered the bruises. And the last thing Emily said to her before she met Barker. "I think she gets abused."

"Abused?" he said.

"Yeah, I think they hit her."

"How long have you known that?" He sipped his water.

"Not long. I was thinking about it the other night. Little hints she gave me."

"Ah." He looked down, then up. "Were you good to her?"

"I tried to be." I try to be.

"No doubt," he said with a smile. "I'm sure that meant something."

"I hope so."

The waitress returned with their food.

"Here you go! One Steak Burrito." She put a sizzling plate down in front of Melanie. Then she gave Barker his bread bowl. "And shrimp bisque bread bowl."

"Thank you, Ashley," he said.

"No problem! Can I freshen up your waters?"

"Yes, please," Melanie said.

"Sure, Ashley. Sounds good," Barker said. Was it possible for his smiles to get even wider? Like, fall off his face. That'd be interesting.

"Alright. I'll bring you guys a pitcher too. You guys enjoy."

As she walked away, Melanie sniffed her food and the smell was mouth watering. She immediately tasted it, and the moist meat, cheese, and several spices made it the best Burrito she'd ever had. The restaurant didn't look like much but the food was excellent. Barker hadn't touched his yet. He was staring over Melanie's shoulder, at the waitresses.

"This is really good," Melanie said to him.

He picked up a spoon and tore at the top of the bread. "I know," he said. He looked over her shoulder again. "I love this place."

***

"What's so urgent about this sir?" Tom asked the Chief.

"Don't sit," said Ed Ryan. "This won't take long."

"Okay," Tom said. He tapped his feet as he stood in the dark office of Ed Ryan. The Chief was reading a file, elbows pressed against his large wooden desk. His voice was robotic and had a feint bit of disgust.

"The New Heim Police Department recently began an investigation into Allen Marx, before his untimely death. The contact was Albert Ferris."

"News to me," Tom said.

"Let me finish," the Chief said. He returned his eyes to the paper. "The intention was to obtain information from Albert Ferris, to implicate him in the attempted murder of one Justin Barker. Allen Marx, along with over fifty men under him and several relatives, would have been charged with conspiracy to commit murder, pending Ferris's testimony. The officer assigned to the case was Gene Brolin. However, no sooner was the case given to him than he was killed by Justin Barker, the would be victim of the Marx family."

"That's bullshit," Tom spat, and the Chief glared.

"Let me finish," he said again, grunting. As he read on, he bared his teeth. "In a corresponding occurrence, Officer Tom Macklin was scene conversing with Albert Ferris in the streets of New Heim. Macklin was warned by Chief Ed Ryan not to engage with the Marx Family, and disobeyed. A report from the contact places Tom Macklin at the Marx Family Manor, the night of the attack." He finished by locking his eyes with Tom's.

"What is this?" Tom demanded.

The Chief slapped the papers down on the desk and folded his hands. "My justification for your paid suspension."

"How dare you," Tom said.

"I suppose now that the jig's up you're just abandoning caution, eh Tom?"

"Everything you just said was a lie," Tom said. "I won't let you do this to me." But at this, the Chief merely leaned back in his chair.

"Who do you think the Mayor will listen to? Me or you? Drop it. Take it like a man."

Tom's chest twisted and he clenched his fist. "You're suspending me for no reason."

"For not listening," the Chief said rather gently. Tom lost control, flailing his hands.

"How did you even know I went to see Ferris?"

"Hah!" the Chief gasped. "Barker has spies. Maxwell Sect had spies. Allen Marx had spies." He leaned forward. "Who do you think I am? You think I don't play ball with these people? You don't think I have my own network?" He slammed his fist down on the desk. "Barker seems to think so, but he's wrong. This isn't just his city. The Mayor and I may let him do whatever he wants, for the sake of our families, but this is not his city. It's mine!" Tom was at a loss for words for a moment. There was no shame, no remorse, and apparently no longer discretion within these walls.

"You had me followed," Tom said. "You violated my rights."

The Chief wave his hand dismissively. "Let's not, Tom. Hand over your gun. Get out. Keep your nose out of all this nonsense. Believe it or not, what I do, I do to protect you and all the rest from meeting Brolin's fate. We keep the peace in New Heim, we uphold the law, we do not go after Barker. He could kill us all no matter how many guns we have, and I take care of you, the rest, and all of our citizens."

"Letting them die is a piss poor way of protecting them," Tom snarled. "You suck."

The Chief glared and grinned his teeth so hard Tom thought they might break to pieces. "Get out, boy. Learn some wisdom."

As Tom went to hand Ed Ryan his weapon, a cold chill went down his neck. "You have to let me keep the gun."

"No," he said.

"You don't understand," Tom said. "Barker knows about me."

The Chief gasped. "What?"

"You want to punish me for disobeying you, fine. But don't leave me defenseless." It was more of a command than a plea. For a half second Tom was pleased with himself.

"God damn it, Tom," the Chief hissed. "I was trying to help you. Now you've gone and gotten yourself mixed up with this…God damn it, boy!"

"Do I get to keep the gun?" Tom said.

The Chief slammed the desk so hard the sound blasted Tom's ears. The man was on his feet now, looking like he could jump over the table and strangle Tom, but such a savage blow never came. The Chief stared at him, heaving, unable to process the situation.

"Keep the gun," Ryan said. "And keep your head down," he said. "You'll get no protection from me. I won't risk the lives of our men for your stupidity."

"Thank you, sir," Tom said. "Truly, thank you," he hissed in turn. Tom then turned his back to the Chief and left the room, concealing the weapon. He didn't say a word to anyone on the way out, walked right past John Beckett, who tried to stop him.

The whole way to his car he only thought of Melanie, and the disgusting report he'd read about the day she was taken. And the way she was wandering around the house, like a little friend to Barker. He wondered what kind of lies he'd told her, was still telling her. How she'd feel when she found out the truth about what he did to her family.

Chapter 41

A Spell at Night

B arker looked around the room at the tools he'd assembled. Four racks of chains. Three boxes of clamps. Four or five ball gags. Ten rolls of duct tape. A large amount of nylon rope. And of course, plenty of handcuffs.

He'd taken it easy on Kris. Feeling her, inside and out, had quelled his cravings that night. This time, he was going to have fun. He was going to be inventive, artistic even. And he wouldn't let this one live. Once he'd left a girl alive after he was done using all of his fun toys on her. He'd wanted to have another go at her, and see how the police responded to her testimony. But he'd gone all out, and when he left her, she killed herself. Strangled herself against the rope around her neck. He'd decided then that if he ever used the tools he kept it would be all or nothing. Tonight he wanted to use them. He had the girl in mind. He walked out into the living room, shutting the bedroom door firmly behind him as always. Melanie was reading on the couch, finally reading, Awaken and Feast.

Barker hadn't needed to ask her, and he felt a deep wave. A comfort. A pride in her. But it wasn't time to give her attention. He needed to release. And then he could focus on Melanie. What to do with her in the meantime?

"Melanie," said Barker.

"Yeah?" she said, putting down her book. "It's really good," she said. "Interesting."

"I'd love to hear about it sometime, but right now we have to talk about something serious," he said.

"Okay," she said, and carefully put it aside.

Good. He nodded. "There is something going on. I'm concerned about our friends. The leftovers from the crime family. The police officer."

"Macklin?" she asked. "Is he planning something?"

"I think so. I need to go and look into the matter."

"Alright," she said. "Want me to stay here then?"

"No," he said. "I want you to go to Kris."

"Okay," she said, seeming suspicious. So he stabbed onward.

"I want to try out our suggested arrangement. I want to let you go outside. Without me." Her eyebrows went up, and she got to her feet.

"You do?" she asked. He nodded back at her.

"You've been wonderful these past few weeks. Not one problem. And you've been doing well in our lessons. I think you could sufficiently defend yourself. So I want to try out this little idea. I'm going to let you go out on your own, and you must promise to come back by the end of the night. Say, no later than two in the morning?" That was all the time he needed.

"I mean, yes. Of course I would," she said, stumbling through her words. Barker walked over and patted her on the shoulder.

"I know you will. But just in case anything goes amiss, I want Kris with you. For protection."

"Are you sure, that's a good idea?" she asked.

Just nod your head, Melanie. "Yes, dear. She'll behave herself tonight." Everyone will. "I'll make sure of it."

***

This surprise test caught her off guard, but she was ready. Ready to prove to Barker that she could be trusted. If he offered her freedom tomorrow, then she would take it. Sooner than expected? The odds were turning in her favor, and she wouldn't dare cross Barker. In her mind, she pictured herself running toward her family, as Barker dropped her off outside the gym.

"You okay?" Barker asked. There was real concern on his face, as always.

"Yeah." She pointed over her shoulder. "I guess I just go in?"

"That's right," he said. "Oh, and before you go." He dug in the glove compartment and pulled out a long knife. "If there's a problem, I trust Kris will call me. But if she acts up, you can use this to defend yourself."

"Okay," she said, gripping the knife tightly.

"I'll see you a little later. Okay, cutie?"

"Yes, sir," she said.

He smiled and turned the wheel. The brown mustang slowly turned around and cruised away. Melanie was alone now, and faced with the giant gymnasium. Back she went to the sight of the massacre, the spot where her friend lived. When Melanie walked through the doors, her footsteps were loud on the hollow ground. This time Kris was sitting on one of the bleachers, smoking a cigarette.

"Hello," Melanie called to her.

"Hey," Kris said, blowing smoke. She was high off the ground on the fourth bleacher up. Melanie eyed a spot right next to Kris.

"Mind if I sit?" she asked.

"Go nuts," Kris said.

Melanie walked up the bleachers and sat down next to her friend. For a moment she just looked at her, wondering if she'd get punched as soon as she spoke. But Kris seemed more together tonight. She wasn't trembling or crying, not darting her head in multiple directions. Just chilling out and smoking.

"How are you?" Melanie asked.

"Are you really asking me how I am?" Kris snapped back.

"As in, are you hungry? Need food?" Melanie asked. Kris sucked on the stick and blew more smoke.

"I could eat," she said.

"Where would you like to go?" Melanie said.

"Nowhere," Kris said.

"Okay."

It looked like Kris wasn't going to cooperate, but how far could Melanie pry. As much as she did not want to sit in this cold dark room in silence, that might be exactly what she needed to do, until Kris was ready. Emily had sometimes needed Melanie just to be there. She was always confused by that. She felt like she wasn't helping at all, and if someone didn't want her to talk or give advice, then what did they want? But Melanie was starting to understand that. Fearing for her life for so long, the last thing Melanie needed or wanted was advice. She wanted someone who was not Justin Barker to be there with her. Although lately, he wasn't quite as bad as he used to be.

"I'm happy to sit here with you," Melanie said, cursing herself for being so awkward. "I hate what happened here. I hate what happened to you. And all of them…If I can help you, I just need you to tell me how."

Kris didn't answer, and Melanie stretched her legs.

"That's all," she said.

Melanie learned in the next twenty minutes that Kris was incredibly stubborn. They just sat there, and Melanie's stomach growled here and there. Melanie made a game of counting all of the shadows in the room, and trying to decide who had died where. She hated thinking about it, but she wasn't really thinking about them or what they went through. She was just painting the choreography in her mind. And in the midst of this, Melanie realized that it wasn't stubbornness that kept Kris from speaking. This girl had to keep her mouth shut, for a long time. She couldn't let any emotions slip, for the sake of the little ones.

"I feel terrible," she said to the darkness. "I've had it easier. I hate how horrific it's been for you." As she finished muttering to herself and counting shadows, Kris stood up.

"I know an awesome bar. Want to go?" Kris sounded more firm, like Melanie was used to. More resolved.

"Okay," Melanie said. "I mean, I'm underage."

"So am I," Kris said. "It's New Heim. No one cares. And this place has great burgers."

"Sounds great," Melanie said. Kris stood up and came down the bleachers with four loud steps, cracking her back at the bottom.

Melanie followed Kris out of the room, stepping over giant snowflakes of moonlight. Through the locker room and out in the field, Kris walked towards a small truck. She hit the keys and the car beeped alive. Melanie got in the passenger side as Kris slammed her door shut.

"Welcome to my humble abode," Kris said. Melanie just stared. "That's what Dom would always say. He talked about this truck like it was our real home."

"Did you guys move around a lot?" Melanie asked, buckling her seatbelt.

Kris turned the key. "We drove around a lot. We knew where we slept but sometimes, in the beginning, Dom and I used to go on long rides. We'd pick up food, load up the truck, drive around Ghost Town, reminisce about the ones we lost. Good times."

"That's really amazing, Kris."

"What's amazing?" she said.

"The way you took care of everyone. Really. I can't even imagine the courage you had, have."

"I'll bet they all feel differently, wherever they are."

"That's not true. They must have known how much you loved them all."

"Actually, they forgot on a nightly basis," Kris said.

"Well, that was on them," she said, and Kris flashed her a dark look. "I'm sorry, I don't want to insult them but…fuck it. You were a hero to them. You deserve a pat on the back, at least."

"I'm not," Kris said, dully. "I'm just a girl."

"A girl can be a hero," Melanie said. "Even if she's lost and scared. Especially when she's scared."

"That's some nice rhetoric dear, but when did you become so vocal?" she asked. "Moreover, when did you get tougher?"

"Barker's been training me," she said. "In case some lunatic tackles me."

"Yeah, sorry about that," Kris said, with a gentle laugh. "Being alone in the dark for a long time…Makes you a little spastic."

"Tell me about it," Melanie said.

After talking back and forth for awhile, once they were well into the city, Melanie was delighted to hear Kris start talking unprovoked. Speaking whatever was on her mind.

"Fuck this neighborhood," she said, passing by The Burrow. "We're right by Nester's. That's where a lot of the kids came from. They beat, starve, and sexually abuse the kids there, and no one has arrested them yet. Dom actually killed one of the workers there. He said he might as well take advantage of Ghost Town. The cops don't follow you there."

"I'm glad he did," she said.

"The place we're going to is called Joe's. Clever, right? Me and the girls used to love this place. It's dank, and disgusting and noisy, but no one ever bothers you. No one gets killed there, shockingly. And it feels normal being there. Ghost Town gets quiet."

"I know," she said. "You said they have good food?"

"They have shitty salads, pastas, and their specials are the worst. But by some miracle they can pull off a burger."

"Great," she said. "Yum."

Kris looked over at her and tapped her on the shoulder. "Thanks, Melanie."

"Of course," she said. Melanie smiled with pride as they reached their destination.

***

I like this place, Barker thought as he sat down alone in The Burrow. He saw Ashley right away. Whatever abominable hours they had this girl working meshed perfectly with Barker's plans. Yes.

Restaurants were a difficult game. If a man walked into a restaurant and walked away with a new waitress every night, and each one of those waitresses were never seen again, people would remember the man's face. There was an art to it all. If you drove from town to town, state to state, then you could stop wherever you wanted, unrestricted, unbothered, as long as you got out of dodge. Staying in one city for more than a month? It was about where and when you showed your face, and how effectively you changed that face. Tonight, the grungy, messy, Justin Barker had combed his hair and shaved his beard, dressing in all blue. He'd called himself Daniel. That was his go to alias, but he never put it in writing.

And sometimes he went by Justin, or even Barker, just to see if terror exploded in their eyes before he knocked them out.

He loved terrified expressions, and he wondered what Ashley's would be.

"How are you doing over here?" Ashley asked him.

"I'm doing well, yourself?"

"I'm good! Can I get you a refill?"

"If you could," he said.

She giggled. "Coming right up."

"You're just a sweetheart aren't you?"

She blushed. "You're not so bad yourself."

Any minute now. "Really? I should start coming more often, then."

"Well we'd love to have you," she said.

"I could even hang around till your shift is done tonight."

She looked taken aback for a moment, but then pleased. "I'd like that," she said. "It's not much longer till I'm cut."

He just smiled and nodded. *I can't wait.*

***

Kris parked the car.

"Here we go. Buccaneers." The sign was large and lit red. Inside was dark, as Kris said, with small lantern lights in every window and bright white light coming from the kitchen area, but no overhead lighting. Melanie pictured trying to get a good camera shot of this place. It would be a train wreck. The socializing seemed to be a free for all. The music was loud and the people at the bar counter even louder. They raised glasses, cheered for their football teams, cursed out people who supported the other team. There was no host or hostess. Kris tugged Melanie on the shoulder and led her over to a wooden booth. After what felt like an eternity, a waitress came over and offered them drinks. Kris ordered a beer and got one without having to show I.D., and Melanie asked for a burger and a water. Then the woman was gone.

"Not quite as nice as The Burrow," Kris mused.

"Yeah. It was nice," Melanie said, looking around at the rambunctious crowd. There was a football game going on, but she couldn't hear or see the names of the teams.

"I'm glad he's treating you better," Kris said. "Anymore bondage?"

"No. Thank God. He trusts me now." Melanie spotted a jealous glint in Kris's eyes.

"Good. Keep it that way."

Melanie nodded. "He said he's meeting one of them tonight. The mobsters."

"Who?"

"He didn't say." Kris inhaled, and brushed her long hair out of her eyes. She seemed to be scratching her forehead.

"Did he say what for?" she asked Melanie.

"I don't know," Melanie said. "He just said he was dealing with things." At this, Kris gasped, and folded her face into a deep frown.

"Oh, Melanie."

"What?" she asked, gritting her own teeth.

"That was bullshit."

"What do you mean?"

"He sent you to me 'cause he doesn't want you to see something."

"See what?"

"What do you think?" she hissed, and silence fell between them.

Melanie wanted to believe Barker. He'd told her he was going out to deal with their enemies, and that was exactly where he was. Still, what proof did she have that he wouldn't lie? He didn't lie to her about anything the past few weeks. He said he'd be kinder, and he was. He said he'd give her more freedom, and he did. He said he'd spare Kris's life, and here she was. But throughout all of it, Melanie gave him what he wanted. That didn't mean he wouldn't ever lie. A pit grew in Melanie's stomach, and her appetite vanished.

Kris remained firm and aggressive when she said, "Never forget what he is, Melanie."

***

Barker was home again. He'd uncombed his hair, redressed in his usual look, and dressed up the waitress to his liking. He decided that a ball gag complimented Ashley's face. The strap rested beneath her lovely curls. For the rest of her, chains. Not very creative. Maybe as the night went on, he could make some adjustments. He hoped Melanie was off somewhere having a good time, because he was planning on going slow.

Ashley was awake, reacting the same way they tended to. Trying so hard to scream, tears streaming and bed shaking as she tried to escape. Barker left momentarily as she screamed. Poured himself a heavy drink. Enjoyed the music.

Then Ashley released one incredibly loud scream. They could probably hear it all the way in the alleys bordering Ghost Town. He loved those screams best. She did just the way he was used to. Close to a wail. It sent chills through his body and made him hard. It was like receiving something you'd craved an entire year. Hell, even about to go out for a night of fun at the movies.

He walked back into the room, cup in hand. His shirt was off. She was spread eagle, the way he left her, and writhing so hard he thought she might kill herself the way the one did. He still couldn't remember that one's name. Megan? Maria? He shrugged.

"So, my dear," he said. "Is there a special way you like it?"

She sobbed, water flying out her nose. Then, with a soft whimper, she dug her head back into the pillow. He liked to give them pillows. It looked cute, and gave him something to rest his head on while blood poured out their throats. While he held them close.

As she continued to cry he walked along the side of the bed, crossing to the front. His chests were open, and inside them were toys and tools. He picked up a long, sharp toy. As he inspected it, something loosened in his mind. The waitress screamed at the sight of the object. It echoed, bounced off the hollow walls of his skull.

She'll never forgive you.

He swiped the device downwards. To hell with Melanie. This was his night.

You'll ruin everything. She'll hate you. You'll have to put her down.

Barker dropped the toy and picked up a tool, a long serrated knife, feeling more aggressive now than aroused. Her eyes widened like two big stones as he came closer. She started thrashing.

Stop it. This will spoil the whole damn thing.

But I want her. I want this.

Barker always got what he wanted. No one could take that away from him.

You'll have her tonight. You could have Melanie forever. It was Barker's turn to widen his eyes, and he stepped back from the bed, stomach tightening. No, no, no, no.

He couldn't back out now. Not because of Melanie. This had nothing to do with her. She wasn't supposed to have power over him. She wasn't meant to be an obstacle. She was supposed to be his friend. He was supposed to have a friend now. He was supposed to prove Lorena wrong.

No, Melanie would understand. He'd make her understand. The waitress looked at him and cried, the tears so thick and eyes so squinted that he could hardly see her face anymore.

"Don't hide your face," he said quietly. He smiled at her. His customary smile. It was the perfect shield. Shield? What are you so afraid of?

He threw the weapon down and turned from the bed. He rubbed his forehead with three fingers.

Accept the consequences.

He rubbed and rubbed until his iron fingers could have poked holes in his skull. And then he raised his head to look at the wall, and the photograph he had of Melanie, tied to the bed, gagged, sleeping.

Guess she was right.

"No!" He beat a hole in the wall, and the picture shook in its frame. The waitress was screaming again.

"Please shut up," he muttered, far too low to be heard.

You can't make her love you. You can't even make her like you. And all of the things you crave will just bring you more pain. She was right. You'll just run yourself right into the ground.

He strained his own neck.

"Fuck." His blood was cold with anger. And in his chest there was nausea. Yes, this he remembered. It had been a long time, but he remembered this humiliating mortification. The kind that made you sick. That raging, burning, conniving dead bitch, was laughing somewhere. He could hear it.

Fuck you.

He turned back to the waitress. She was weak now, struggling as feebly as a butterfly in a web. Barker moved towards her with the same grace as the spider, never faltering. He leaned over her.

"Do you know who I am? Do you know my real name?" She trembled, looking somewhat ugly now. But eventually she nodded.

"Then you know the stories. The crime families. The victims. The spontaneity of the incidents? Yes?" She nodded again, crying loud. He slapped her. "Listen…you know that if you ever utter a word, I will find you again. You know that right?"

She nodded.

"So when you go home, are you going to tell people about me?"

She shook her head. It only took him a half second to cross the room and back. He held the knife to her throat.

"Promise me, now."

She nodded and mumbled and cried out. Then he untied her and threw a jacket on top of her.

"Get out."

As she ran out the door her screams carried across the darkness, and inside Barker had gone numb, his thoughts as black a void as Ghost Town itself.

***

As Kris drove down Melanie home, the road in front of them was lit only by high beams.

"Was it always this dark?" Melanie asked.

"Well there used to be people living here," she said.

"I know that!" she said. "I meant after the airstrike. Has it always been like this? Since you've been living here."

"Yep," Kris said.

Her mind flashed to the power station. She'd do anything to distract herself from what Kris had implied. From what Barker was doing. "Do you know the guy at the power station?" she asked.

"Charlie?" Kris asked. "Yeah, I know him. I went to him for food and he chased us away."

"Oh, yeah, I remember. Sorry."

Kris went on, "I said we were both working for Barker and that we should have each other's backs. He said that he served Barker, not his rats. I wanted to kill him but I thought I'd be in deep shit if I went over Barker's head. And Charlie said he'd shoot one of the kids if I repeated that. So—

"Kris!" Melanie howled, when she saw the girl in the street. The high beams lit her up head to toe and Kris slammed on the breaks. The car stopped and the girl pounded her hands flat on the hood. After the smallest moment of eye contact with the stranger, the girl slipped around the car and kept running. She was screaming.

"What the hell was that?!" Melanie asked.

Kris was gritting her teeth. "Damn. We need to get you home."

"Do you know her?"

"No, idiot. Use your head!"

"No, no. Oh God." Melanie felt immediately sick. But where was Barker? Wouldn't he be chasing after her? She didn't see him. Kris drove faster now, in a straight line towards the house.

Oh, God, no. He wasn't. He couldn't. She wasn't going to see it. It couldn't be happening. Please.

"I'm going to throw up," she said.

"Hold it together. I'm going to get you home safe." Kris broke all speed limits. She must have figured if Barker was in the road, he'd dodge a car going 120 mph. He'd just jump up to a roof top.

Before long, Melanie was home.

Nothing seemed amiss, aside from the front door hanging open. She left the car, and Kris was right behind her. She marched up the sidewalk, across the dead grass. When she and Barker first met, everything had seemed fine at her house too, save for the extra cars in the drive way. It was only after she got close that she saw the door was creaked open. This time, the door wide open, she looked into the house and saw Barker's bedroom door wide open, but she still couldn't see inside. When she'd looked into her house, she'd found her father, half dead.

Tonight she saw Barker, the living room. On the floor.

She wasn't used to this. Wind whistled through the open door as she took a few steps closer to her protector. He was sitting with his knees close to his chin, a knife in his hands, staring at the wall.

"Barker. What happened?" She didn't reach him. He heard her, but his eyes never moved.

"You're home."

"I am. What happened?" She dropped to her knees. He gripped the knife with two hands, arms resting on his knees, as if she meant to hurt him.

"Nothing," he said. His voice was as emotionless as a cold man, but quiet as a sickly old man. "I was remembering things."

"What?"

"I was..." He put his head back. "I was...thinking about a church...and knives...fire."

"What?" She scooted closer, every bit as cautious as the night she tried to kill him. But right now he didn't look like Barker. At all. Her father had the same look when Barker was torturing him. It was like they'd merged together.

"I...didn't do it," Barker said.

"Didn't do what?"

"Did you see her?" he asked. "Did you see her running?"

"Did you hurt her?" she asked.

"No," he said, mouth hanging open for a moment. "Promise."

"Then what happened?" she asked. "What's wrong?" And with a sudden tremor, she saw that his eyes were tearing. Barker's eyes were tearing up. He looked terrified, like some larger beast was staring her down. Her father had been fearless until Barker came knocking, and now it was Barker's turn. Whatever it was, whatever happened, it had him shrunken. Quivering. Crying. Just like she had at his hands. So why didn't it give her any pleasure? Melanie heard Kris step into the room behind her, as a tear trickled down Barker's face. Melanie's heart broke, and slowly she reached out to him, toward his incredibly warm hands. She placed hers on his, above the knife. And at her touch, he lowered his hands, letting his legs uncurl, so that he was sitting flat on the ground.

"Are you alright?" She couldn't stop herself. When Barker looked at her, his eyes remained wide with terror. It made her feel like the captor.

"I'm... sorry, Melanie."

Kris grunted, and Melanie turned. Kris's hand was on her gun. Melanie jumped to her feet. The two girls stood eye to eye, just in time for Kris to point the gun at Barker. He hadn't even seemed to notice, and Melanie stood between them. Kris jerked her head, motioning for her to get out of the way, and widened her eyes when Melanie remained rooted. Melanie didn't say a word. The only word she would have been able to come up with was "no." Both of their eyes were locked, and Kris's face was now wracked with horror. Melanie had stepped in it now. This was the perfect opportunity to kill Barker, and Kris would go right through her. They were both about to die.

No, Melanie could help her. She could kill him now. And be free.

And imprisoned with guilt for the rest of her life.

Kris let out a deep sigh, and lowered the gun. "I'm here for you," she said.

Kris slowly turned and left the house. Melanie walked forth and shut the door behind her. Then she turned to Barker. He looked dazed, like he was falling asleep. Slowly, he covered his own face, and Melanie went to him and put her hand on his shoulder. His whimper was almost inaudible, but it rang loud in her ears.

Chapter 42

Bang

In Melanie's old life, two months could go by and she'd feel like nothing happened. She wouldn't look back on a large chapter in her life until she was looking back on the entire school year. After Barker had taken her, she'd woken up in a new world. And now every day was a new experience. Three months felt like three years.

Barker had tied her down. Gagged her. Beaten her. Bullied her. Stripped her. Endangered her life. Cut her. Nearly killed her. Then he'd saved her life. Slowly, tried to make amends. And last night he cried in her arms. Melanie had no idea what to make of any of it. She only knew she hoped that the girl he'd nearly raped was alright. That he wouldn't go after her again.

And even more so, Melanie wondered if Barker had permanently changed. If she would be released.

And she was worried about him.

He's a serial killer, Melanie. He took you away, violated your rights, and he nearly killed me. Her father's voice was loud in her ears, and yet the man she saw last night didn't look like the same man. It looked like a younger man, a sane man, who woke up in a monster's body. Was it possible? Was there hope?

Barker didn't talk about that night. He only said one thing.

"Don't leave the house."

For two days, she tried to talk to him, and he never responded. In his own head he prowled around the house, made her meals, drank nothing but water. And Melanie read her books. No fighting lessons. No conversations about souls. Just silence.

Soon it was December 2nd. She would never forget December 2nd.

Barker sat alone in his armchair, eating a turkey sandwich. Melanie was eating a ham sandwich, sitting on the couch. This had become her spot. Barker's was the chair. Barker chomped on his sandwich like all was right in the world. But the smile. His habitual smile. It was gone. And he only did it when she addressed him. It was forced.

"Barker," she said.

"Yes?" he said, not unpleasantly.

"Can I ask you something?"

"If it's about the other night, don't waste your breath."

"I know, but—" He groaned, and she gathered herself for a moment. Careful. "Barker, I—I'm worried about you. I've never seen you like that."

"And you never will again," he said, softly. "So please, let's just leave it." He smiled. She put her plate down beside her and pressed forth.

"Can I just ask one question? Just one and I'll never bring it up again. I promise."

"Okay," he said.

"You said something about a church?" She could put together the bit about the girl herself, but the things he muttered. She wanted to know more. He breathed heavily and his face ticked.

"That's... private."

"Didn't you want to share things like that with me?" she asked, feeling especially brave. He looked at her with something that resembled fear, and she pushed harder. "Isn't that why you brought me here?"

This time he dropped his own plate. He still didn't look or sound like Barker. She'd never seen this. He was pacing rapidly, excited or terrified. His face was always in a frown. His body didn't even look quite as imposing. Not unless he drew himself up the way he did.

"Melanie," he whispered.

"I'm happy to talk to you," she said calmly. "I want to. I want to know that you're alright."

He leaned forward, pressing against his own knees. "Melanie." His head was pointed down, and she curved her own to search for tears. They didn't upset or disturb her now. It empowered her.

"I just..." She picked her words carefully. "I want to be your friend. Your equal. I want to be able to help you. To understand you."

He grimaced. "Don't be scared, Melanie."

"But...if you could...let me see my family...You know I wouldn't walk out on you. Remember, Emily? Remember when I told you about Emily?"

"Yeah, I remember Emily."

"When I saw her bruises, I was so scared. Scared for her. I wanted to help. I couldn't sleep unless I'd at least said something to her. I don't want anyone I know to be in pain. That's why I stood up for Kris."

"I know, Melanie. I know how you are."

"If you let me go...I wouldn't abandon you. I can't stand what I saw last night."

"I've thought about it," he said. "I have."

Melanie said nothing. She held her breath.

He turned sharply. "But I don't want—" Bang.

It flew by so close to her face that little bits of something whipped painfully against her temple. But just like last time, glass shattered, and the bullet missed her. But Barker hit the ground. The house shook. Blood had burst from his shoulder and spattered along the couch, all over her. The bullet had slammed into the wall next to her head, and she temporarily lost control of her bladder. Barker was on the ground, covered in blood. Melanie sat numb and sick for a moment, afraid to move for fear of another bullet. But another bullet never came. Only Barker's moans and groans. He was in agonizing pain. She could hear it. Even when he'd taken a bullet for her he'd never cried out like this.

"Ugh...Melanie," he grumbled.

She dropped to her knees beside him. "Are you okay?"

"Are you alright?" he asked.

She held down some bile, and nodded. "Yep."

He nodded. "Stay down, behind the chair."

She did as he said.

"Now, wait him out, whoever he is."

They waited, and no other bullets ever came.

"Is it the mob?" she asked.

"I don't know." He grunted. "Orson, perhaps. Or someone new. Who knows?" He sounded more curious than scared, like the idea was a game. He sounded like Barker.

When no more bullets came, he said, "Stay low, keep staying low."

"Okay."

He pointed in the kitchen. "Over in the bottom drawer is the first aid kit. Bring it too me. And a pair of tweezers."

She crawled into the kitchen and did as she was bid. She had to reach up to get the tweezers, right in front of the window by the counter. She tried to do it quickly, but her hand faltered in the drawer. She could be shot if she stayed in front of the window any longer. There was a burst of wind next to her; Barker was beside her, hand in a drawer, and then he hurled a kitchen knife through the window and the shattering glass squealed all over the room.

He stood hunched, nursing his shoulder, but still fearsome. Melanie never asked how far the knife flew. Or if it hit wherever he'd aimed. She brought him the things he asked, and he crawled to sit at the front door. His shirt was torn near the shoulder and the wound was enflamed with blood trickling out. It was disgusting. He snapped his fingers and she handed him the tweezers. Then he was pointing them toward the hole. A wicked and crazed smile was on his face now. "Good lord, this stings." And the tweezers were in.

Melanie turned away and vomited all over the floor.

"You'll have to clean that up," he said. "I'm gonna need to rest a bit."

Melanie didn't look, but he yelled loud and then dropped something onto the floor. She assumed it was the bullet.

"Melanie," he said.

She forced herself to look. The wound was covered by his wet red hand. "Sow me up," he said.

"What?!"

"I need you to sow me up. Get on with it. Please," he said.

"Barker, you need a doctor. I'm not, I'm not qualified for this."

"Just do it. Please." Some of his scared voice was back, and he closed his eyes.

Melanie was in danger of throwing up again, but she took out black thread and followed Barker's instructions.

"Don't hate me if I vomit on you."

He chuckled.

Sticking his flesh the first time made a noise that nearly brought it all up. But she held it down. As she threaded it through, it got a little bit easier.

Barker continued to groan and wheeze. "Damn," he muttered.

"Are you okay?" She continued threading.

"I think so," he said.

It was scary thing to hear. "Is there something I can do?" she asked.

"You're doing it. Thank you, Melanie."

She might have been saving his life right now, and that made her feel something. Some twinge of satisfaction. It was in that moment Melanie realized that at this point, she truly cared about him.

***

Barker had forgotten himself, and the one behind this was going to suffer.

Chapter 43

Doubt

A nother week passed. It was December 9th.

For the entire week, Melanie and Barker had barely spoken. Barker sat in his armchair, listening quietly for any disturbance. Melanie moved very quietly and didn't say a word. She made herself food quietly, and spent all other time in her room. She ate granola bars and apples when she read on the bed. And like he said, she stayed away from the window, all the way in the corner of the room.

All of it smashed together in her mind and she felt the need for Advil. The last time he'd been injured he'd tied her down, just in case. He didn't want to be vulnerable against her. But now he trusted her. And she hadn't seized any opportunity. She couldn't take it. Seeing him on the ground suffering. She couldn't.

"Melanie," a voice called from a distant place. It was the beckoning that gave her chills. She didn't want to answer, but when she realized it was Barker, she felt safe enough to answer.

"Yeah?" she called.

"Come down," she heard him say.

She got off the bed and slowly came downstairs, checking the window before she finished the descent. Barker was in the armchair. He wore thick clothes to hide his bandage, and he refused a sling. "Come here."

She obeyed.

"Sit down."

She obeyed.

Just keep obeying said her father.

Barker looked at her with a tired but confident expression. "Thank you, for last week."

"How is it?" she asked. In response he put his hand near the wound.

"A lot better. I can move around easier."

"Good." She smiled at him.

"It means a lot to me, that you would help me like that. Thank you."

"You're welcome," she said. "What are we going to do?"

"I'll tell you what we're going to do. We're all going to have a nice day out. Kris is taking you to the beach." He sounded so matter of fact, and she crossed her arms, not obnoxiously.

"What about you?" she asked.

For a moment he looked exasperated, eyes wide. "I'm going to handle our little problem."

"Are you sure? What if you have to fight? Shouldn't you heal first?" He returned with a smile, bearing his perfect teeth.

"I'll be fine. Thank you though...You know I love you, right?"

"I know." And what she said next was true, if appropriately exaggerated. "I love you, as well."

He chuckled. "Thanks for that."

There was the sound of an engine outside.

"That'd be Kris. Let's go."

***

Tom read the file over and over. Melanie had just come home from school one day, and found her family in a crisis. Reportedly, Barker had violated them, left them in ruins, with their daughter in the backseat of his car. It was horrible. He hadn't heard a damn thing back from that killer he'd hired. He didn't even know if he was paying him or paying Barker or if he would be killed by the end of the day. Technically he wasn't even on the force. It was all falling to pieces, and there was a family that would never receive justice.

"Please," he muttered. "Something needs to go right."

***

Barker stepped out of the car, leaving Melanie with Kris.

"Go on," he told them. "Off to the beach." Kris shut the door and Melanie stared after Barker as the car pulled away. He blew her a kiss. Then he was alone in front of Orson Marx's house. Instead of knocking, he sent a text message.

Get out here.

Barker stood for a moment and admired the scenery. The air was cold and dank. There weren't many noises, not cars, not people, not birds. The sky was gray.

The door opened and the tall man appeared. He walked on two crutches.

"Orson," Barker said. "How're your legs."

"See for yourself," Orson said from the porch. "What do you want?"

"You know about what happened with Ferris?"

"Yes, you already questioned me about that," Orson said, folding his large arms.

"Good...how bout last week?" Barker asked. Orson's eyes told him nothing.

"What was last week?"

"Someone shot me and ran off."

"How bout that?" Orson said, and Barker now saw a glint of satisfaction in his eyes.

Barker began taking slow, long steps.

"What do you know, Orson?"

"Nothing," said the giant, skin and hair moistening with a rapidly beating heart. "Nothing. Pardon me for not being too upset after what you did to my legs."

"You'll lose more than your legs this time. No more bullshit. Where is he? Who is he? Tell me, Orson."

"I don't know," he said, slowly, drawing out each word. "I don't make plans anymore. I didn't know anything about Ferris's plans and I wash my hands of Macklin's."

"Macklin's?"

Orson raised his eyebrows. "Yeah. The kid obviously wants to kill you. Didn't you notice?"

"I did notice...Tell me more."

"I have nothing else to tell," the mobster said. "I don't know anything."

"You know something."

"I know things, just not the things you want. I know that he's a sniveling little prick, and that he thinks he's Dudley fucking Doo-Right. I know that he's stupid. And I know that he loved your old buddy, Stan."

"This assassin was good. What kind of friends does little Tom Macklin have?" Barker was convinced Orson was lying. The punk of a cop may have wanted him dead but he couldn't have such powerful mob friends. He just didn't seem the type.

But something changed in Orson's expression. He looked like he'd just realized something, and that he wanted to keep it to himself. Then he grimaced, like he was sucking it up.

"Actually," Orson said in a lower tone. "There is one thing."

"Tell me," Barker said. And say the right words.

"When Macklin and I last crossed paths, all he kept talking about was this plan of his. This big plan. He said it was fool proof, and that you'd be dead. We tossed his ass out the door."

"And what was this perfect plan?"

"Ravings of a mind as disturbed as yours. That's what it was. He kept saying there were more people like you. Hundreds. That we could find a killer just like you."

Barker's chest tightened again, and he felt stiff as stone. Crawford.

Orson was still talking. Barker put his hand up. "Say no more, Orson…Say no more."

Barker turned his back on Orson Marx and walked forward. He wasn't going anywhere in particular, just forward. Processing everything. Betrayal. Twice betrayed with one bullet. Barker felt like the game board was just turned upside down. Every plan he'd made for his future had just gone up in smoke, replaced by the wrongs he was now going to right.

***

It was a gray afternoon at the beach. This time with Kris. Melanie was sitting in the cold sand. The waves crashed, this time more slowly, sailing toward the shore, only to wreck at the end of the path. The air was brisk, and the wind frigid.

"So somebody fired a shot through the window," Kris said, trying to understand.

"Yeah." It had almost struck her. "I'm very lucky."

"Damn right you are," Kris said, wiping her nose.

"Do you know what he's doing right now?"

"Probably killing someone." Kris shrugged, a solemn look on her face. "No one likes being shot."

"I guess not," Melanie said, digging her foot into the sand. She didn't mind getting sand in her socks at all anymore. She'd learned greater discomforts. And now she needed to be brave. Face Kris and justify what she had done.

"Speaking of killing," Melanie started. "Have you heard anything? About that girl?"

"No," Kris curtly replied.

"Oh…" Melanie turned her attention to the water, wits all gone.

"You know he raped her, right?" Kris spat.

The naked girl in the coat flashed through her mind. And Barker's tears. "No. I don't think he did."

"Whatever," Kris said, groaning and cracking her neck. "Whatever gets you through the night."

Melanie turned to face her. "Listen. I'm sorry that I...got in your way. But...I don't think he did it. You, you don't understand."

Kris shook her head. "I understand just fine."

"No, you don't. I...I think." I think he changed. I don't think he was Barker that night. "Look, just trust me. He didn't do it. I know he didn't. I couldn't let you kill him. Not then. Not like that."

Kris turned away. Hard as a rock.

"Kris." Melanie tugged on her arm. "Kris, he didn't rape that girl."

Something struck Melanie's head and her world spun, waves splashing in the distance. She hit the ground hard and got a mouth fool of sand. Her eyes were wet and her skin hot. She sat up and spit out the sand before it reached her throat. Then she looked up at Kris. For a minute, she was afraid Kris would hit her again, but her friend just brandished her fist, rubbing her knuckles.

When they met, Kris's face was stone. Stern. Cool headed. Today, her glare was wracked with pain. Her jaw trembled, and she looked like at any second she could break down.

"He raped me."

And Melanie was struck again. This time by words. It had to be a lie. This could not have happened. Barker couldn't have raped her friend. Strapped her down, covered her mouth. Watched her cry. Attacked. Not her friend. Not Kris. Melanie hugged her knees and looked away from her. Tears came easy then. She cried so hard that she trembled.

"Twice," Kris said. "Twice, he raped me." Melanie heard her coming toward her. "So don't tell me what he is."

Kris struck Melanie and she went straight down, choking on sand. Images were sailing through her mind. Her mother. Her father. The waitress. Kris. All of the kids. Even the dead mobsters.

Barker's face was always the same, because anytime he stared at her his face would change. From happy to grim to sinister, to tearful. He played a wonderful manipulation game with her, but she belonged to him now. And he was her only way out. And he was her friend now. But...she was meant to sit and watch him torment everyone else.

"I'm sorry." Her voice broke. "I'm sorry." Kris reached for her hand, and something snapped inside Melanie. She knocked Kris's hand away and jumped to her feet, building some distance.

"Where are you going?" Kris called. "Get back here!"

Melanie started to run, and she knew Kris was running behind her. Melanie left the beach, the wind bashing against her face. She hadn't run in so long, not since the attack. She'd sat and played the game, when all she wanted was to run. And now she was running, and she was faster than Kris. Barker had taught her to be fast. Melanie raced onto the boardwalk, straight into a man with a slushie. It spilt all over her and chilled her through to the bone.

"Oh God! I'm so sorry!" the man yelled. He started trying to apologize, but she hardly noticed him. She was trying to think how she would escape. She noticed Kris bounding towards the boardwalk and speedily walked along the wooden boards, past multiple people.

Poor Kris. I can't believe it. I don't want to believe it. God, I should have let her kill him. I'm such a bitch.

"Melanie," said a familiar voice.

She turned and standing next to her was a tall and skinny man in a long white jacket, not that much older than her and Kris. He was just as handsome as he was the last time she'd seen him, his light brown whiskers more personified today.

"You," she said.

Macklin nodded, looking over his shoulder. "What are you doing out here on your own? Is he here?"

"No," she said. "She is." She pointed over Macklin's shoulder, at Kris. Kris finally caught up with them but stopped at the sight of Macklin.

"Who are you?" she asked.

"Who are you?" Macklin asked her. "Work for Barker?"

"None of your business," Kris spat. She walked past the cop and gripped Melanie's wrist. "You ever do that again, I'll fucking kill you." She gave her a fierce yank. "You hear me?"

Melanie tried to pull away, but suddenly Macklin had his hands around their connected wrists.

"Stop," he said. He was looking at Kris. "I work for Barker too," he said.

"Yeah?" Kris said. "What do you do?"

"What Albert Ferris used to do," he said. "Ever hear of him?"

Kris broke her hand away and Melanie held her breath. Macklin had said the wrong words. For a moment, that look was back on Kris's face.

"Oh," Kris said. "You're the new Ferris. Wonderful. Let's see how many innocent children you can kill."

Melanie watched Macklin grimace as he stood between them both.

"I'm not him," he said. "Can I just have one moment with Melanie? I don't think Barker would mind."

"Your funeral," Kris spat at him. Then at Melanie, "I'm watching you." Kris stomped away, giving them about twenty feet of space. Melanie faced Macklin.

"No offense, but I'd like to be alone," she said. But Macklin gripped her shoulders.

"Melanie. Where is he right now?"

"I don't know," she said. "Running an errand."

"What kind of errand?" he asked.

"Leave me alone!" she screamed. People were looking, noticing, whispering. Barker wouldn't like this. Macklin didn't like it either.

"I'm just trying to help you, Melanie. I've been trying to help you." Melanie searched his eyes. He wasn't lying. This might have been the most genuine person she met yet in New Heim.

"You want to help me?" she asked. "Why?"

"Why?" he asked, incredulous. "Why not? I won't let him do this to you." He glanced at Kris. "Who is she? Is she a prisoner too?"

"Stop asking so many questions," Melanie urged. "He'll...he'll kill you. Just leave us alone. We'll be fine."

She tried to walk way but Macklin still gripped her shoulder tightly.

"You are not fine," he said. "I know what he's done to you. When I came to the house I thought he might have brainwashed you but now I can see it's just fear." He put his hand up, as if to stop her from leaving. "Listen, Melanie. We can get out of this. I can get you out of here and back to your mum. But I need your help."

"I can't help you," she said. "Barker could be here any minute. Just leave me alone."

She pulled out of Macklin's grasp and walked back to Kris. Melanie's beach day hadn't lasted very long. She was stuck between the both of them. Kris was probably going to pummel her when they were alone, but for now she stood beside her, opposite the cop.

"What are you doing here anyway?" Melanie called over. "Weird coincidence."

He pointed over their shoulders, at one of the apartments. "I live here."

Melanie remembered the first day at the beach, when Barker had been glancing at the apartments. From the beach, to the police station, to the eerie streets of Ghost Town, it was all one giant web.

Melanie looked over at Kris, who had her arms folded. Melanie didn't know what to say to her, how to help her, or how to make up for poking those wounds. Before she could, Kris raced over to Macklin.

"Take her advice," Kris told him.

"I know the both of you are scared. But you'll die if you don't let me help you."

"Fuck you," Kris said. "Got it?" She pointed back at Melanie. "She's fine. He likes her. Loves her. She gets a pass. Just let her have it."

"Let me—"

"I've survived a long time without you," Kris said. "And so has she. What have you done? Where were you, you fucking pig? Where were you and the rest of them when my family was killed? Where were you when all of those girls were dead in the streets? Where were you when that piece of shit, Ferris, killed everyone I loved? When my best friend jumped on top of me and took ten bullets? We don't need you. Now fuck off, before you get us all killed."

Kris stormed back to Melanie and slowed down next to her.

"Want to walk near the water?" she asked, voice still scratchy. Melanie sniffed, the cold air unhinging her sinuses.

"Sure." Melanie glanced once more at Macklin. He looked flustered, shocked, like she'd really done a number on him. Melanie wanted to thank him for caring, but instead she turned her back and followed Kris back to the beach.

As they walked near the water, Kris stared at the waves, her hair blowing in the wind.

"I'm sorry, Kris," Melanie said, more coherently than before. "I don't know what else to say."

"Don't say anything," Kris said. "I've lived with it a long time now... Fuck that cop. He doesn't know what it's like. None of them know what it's like in Ghost Town. They sit with their families, hoping Barker never comes knocking." Kris stopped moving and Melanie with her. "They don't know what it's like, to be wandering around that place at night. Where everything is dead. Where all you can see are shadows. And then one of the shadows moves. And then someone has their arms around you, choking you, stuffing something in your mouth, holding your arms. They don't know."

Every single word struck Melanie's heart, and her eyes seared with agony. In place of her sobs, the waves crashed next to them.

"I'm so sorry," she said again. "I want you to know."

"I know, Melanie. Thank you."

The waves kept crashing.

The drive home was bitter. Neither of the girls spoke, with one exception.

"Why do you care so much about me? Why does that cop?" Melanie asked.

"Because you're the only one of us who has a fighting chance, Melanie," Kris said.

When they arrived back at 125 Copper Avenue, Barker wasn't back yet. So the girls sat and waited in silence. Melanie composed herself and went to find one of her books. This time she picked up The Perks of Being a Wallflower.

She tried to lose herself in a book, but it was too much. It was all too much. She couldn't live here anymore. She couldn't live with Barker anymore. The man who tied her down and took a bullet for her. Fear and guilt. That was her life now.

Both girls were sitting in Melanie's room. Away from the windows. Kris was sitting cross-legged on the ground, right on the spot where Melanie's leash used to hang.

It would be fine. She used to be trussed like a dog. Now she lived here. She could keep working her way up. To freedom. If that didn't work, maybe she could just kill herself.

"Is it true?" Melanie asked Kris. "Did Dom die protecting you?"

"Yes," Kris said. "Most of them tried to fight, some of them went down right away, some of them tried to save the kids, and Dom protected me."

Melanie didn't say anything. Both sat silently.

"Do you know what that's like?" Kris asked. "Someone dying to keep you alive?"

Melanie thought about her father. She thought about his face, his whimpers, the way he bled, and how she had no idea if he was okay, only Barker's word.

"No," she said. "I don't...but I know guilt."

Chapter 44

Come Out

T om was thinking about Melanie, the girl, and Stanley. In a way, the girl was right. Tom was failing them all. She told him he didn't understand. It wasn't the first time he'd been told that. It wasn't the first time Tom, with all his good intentions, was told he didn't understand, that there was nothing he could do, that he was only human, that he was failing.

Stan had even told him once, and for some reason, Tom was swept with very real guilt. He'd done nothing for these girls. Done nothing for anyone.

"We don't know, Tom," said Stan. They were walking side by side on the boardwalk. The moonlight was pale. Same was drinking a soda, and finishing the last of his French fries. Stan would sometimes go on the boardwalk by himself, to walk and ponder everything he'd experienced. At some point, Tom started joining him. Because he knew the man's soul was broken. He knew that if he could get him talking, maybe he could help him. Stan had taken him under his wing. It was the least he could do in return.

"We read the stories. We see the bodies, but we don't know," he said to Tom.

"I know," Tom said. Stan laughed.

"No you don't," Stan said.

"No, I mean, I understand, what you mean," Tom stuttered.

"You don't know," Stan wheezed, smiling through gritted teeth. "You don't know what my wife experienced. You know Andrea died. You don't know how she died."

"I'm sorry, Stan," Tom said. "Is there anything I can do for you?"

Stan leaned against the railing, looking up at the moonlight, while Tom watched him closely.

"You do enough, kid," he said. "But when you get to my age you'll realize. Enough is never enough."

Barker was in Tom's dreams now. And in those dreams, Tom put a bullet through his skull, his brains spattered across Stan's grave. It felt terrible to know the mission was so futile. To feel like he abandoned Stan to an unanswered crime. But then hadn't Stan abandoned him? Tom begged him over and over not to go after Barker. The same way the Chief warned him, the same way Albert Ferris warned him. But Stan hadn't listened. And now he was dead. What did Tom Macklin owe a dead man?

He needed to get out of New Heim. He needed to find his mother and make sure she was somewhere safe. And father, yes father too. He'd have to make sure they were both safe. Could he still get Melanie and that other girl out?

God. What a mess.

Tom stood in silence, contemplating getting a drink. He was far too tense to function right now. So he stood in silence. And that was when he heard the footsteps. Coming toward his door. They were light, hollow. When the knocks started on his front door, they were almost rhythmic. He took lights steps forward, fearing who might be on the other side. He already had the gun in his hand. Tom might always hate his boss, but at least the fool had let him keep his gun. But it didn't make him any less terrified when a monstrous force hit the door. It sounded like wood breaking, and he felt like the whole building shook. Tom took multiple steps back into the kitchen, pointing the gun. There was another smash against the door. It almost came out of its hinges and dust was flying.

Tom fired the gun. Abominable sounds rang out throughout his small apartment. He put four holes in the door, and the attacks stopped.

Silence.

He kept his hands on the gun. Then he heard footsteps coming up the porch again. Tom made for the back door as the front door was thrown into the house, smashing down on the ground and kicking up a huge wave of dust. Before he slipped out the back door, Tom glimpsed the silhouette of the man he most despised. Tom was in his backyard now, hugging the side of the apartment walls. There was a small space between his building and the next, where he could slip through and get to the front. He heard footsteps upstairs in the house and thought about shooting up through the floorboards. But if he missed he'd just give himself away.

He heard the heavy footsteps going through his apartment, to the back door, and now they were outside. As Tom slipped through the space between the houses, he saw the back of Justin Barker on the deck, black hair and black coat heavily lit by the light atop the door. He came down the stairs.

Tom crawled to the front yard, quiet as a caterpillar.

From the backyard he heard a voice say, "Tom."

Tom continued to crawl, past the destroyed doorway, along the grass. Barker was standing in the backyard, checking for any evidence of his hiding place.

If Tom stepped on a twig, that would be it.

"Tom," the voice said again. "Come out."

Tom was almost to the curb now, beneath a streetlight that had burned out two and a half months ago. Darkness was his only friend. That and this loaded gun. It was pointed right at the small crawl space. There was only one way out, and that was where Tom aimed. Barker's footsteps were coming through the alley now.

"Understand something, Tom. You are going to die...It's just a matter of...how." Tom heard a chuckle.

Tom backed away along the alley, away from the house, in the dark. His feet didn't make a sound. His gun stayed fixed on the same spot. There was a sudden movement, and Tom fired. The bullet struck brick. Something was flying at him in the dark, and he barely sidestepped the soaring knife. It hit the concrete blocks behind him with a loud chime.

"Tom," the voice said, much closer.

Barked looked him in the eyes. Tom fired the gun, and Barker knocked it out of his hands with a strike like a boulder. Tom had no weapon now and he lashed out with his fist. Barker caught him and threw him to the ground. The concrete cracked one of Tom's teeth and scraped his gums and chin. Barker rolled him onto his back and held him down tight.

"I have to hand it to you, Tom. Hiring a Meridian Killer. I never even guessed."

"I'm your accountant!" he screamed. "Kill me and you have nothing!" he screamed. Barker faltered and Tom delivered a kick to Barker's head. He slipped out of Barker's grasp and rocketed to his feet. As he ran he noticed some people were coming out of their houses. But they wouldn't help him. If a cop was the victim, it was hopeless.

There was a gust of wind next to him and Barker was in front of him again. His face was the cruelest thing Tom had ever seen: completely relaxed, with a goofy smile. "How do you want to die Tom? Shall I bleed or bludgeon you?"

Tom backed away.

"Neither, you need me."

In seconds Tom was in his grasp again.

"Not quite," Barker hissed.

The strike came fast, bending Tom's arm like a pretzel. Then came the agonizing pain.

Chapter 45

No One Can Know

Melanie and Kris had decided to sit in the dark. If anyone were stalking the house, it would pay to make it look like no one was home. Kris had her gun cocked, in case of the worst. Melanie was holding a flashlight to the text of her book. Kris had joked that she should try it out, like camping. The words of this book didn't look any less sinister in the sinister dim light. She hated Awaken and Feast. Every single word, a justification for her abduction. Melanie was so grateful for her books. It was such a wonderful escape, but there was no escape.

They heard a car pull up. Kris pointed the gun forward, just in case.

"It's probably him," she said.

Melanie heard a door shut and another door open. Then she heard some noises that sounded like a struggle. And a scream. Kris jumped up while Melanie was stiff on the bed. Downstairs the door flew open and the screams came inside. Something hit the floor, and the door slammed shut. Kris immediately left the room with her gun cocked and Melanie searched for the courage to follow. She found it when she remembered that Barker was her friend, and it was safe for her to go downstairs.

This time she descended the stairs like a lightning bolt. When she reached the landing, she saw Kris was at the bottom, holding the gun out slightly but looking powerless. Tom Macklin was on the floor, clutching an arm that looked horribly injured. And Barker stood over him, coated in black and hair a mess, his white skin starting to grow back his scruff. He grinned like a wolf on the hunt.

"What's going on?" Melanie shouted. Barker pointed at Kris.

"You. Get out." He pointed at Melanie. "You."

"Barker, what happened? What's going on?" she pleaded.

"Upstairs," he said. "Do not make me tell you twice." He looked back down at Tom, smiling wide. "Welcome home, Tom."

Tom tried to push himself up with one arm. He was bright red and all of his veins were bulging. His arm was broken. Melanie nearly gagged at the sight of him, and she already wanted to jump between Barker and his latest victim. Barker kicked Tom and he yelled so loud it Melanie want to scream too. Kris was backing away, still pointing the gun. Barker was pushing him toward the bedroom now, and though Tom tried to struggle, Barker pushed him into the room and onto the bed. Then Barker rounded on Kris.

"I told you to get the fuck out!"

Tom jumped back up and tried to hit Barker with his good arm. Barker caught his wrist and twisted. Tom screamed again, and Barker wrestled him to the ground of the bedroom.

Kris glanced up at Melanie, and Melanie silently pleaded with her not to leave. But Kris ignored her, and bounded out the door.

"Barker please! Please talk to me."

Barker ignored her and started tearing off Tom's close. With his foot he kicked the door shut, and Melanie heard the rustling of chains. She ran forward and tried to open the door. It was locked. Tom screamed again, and Melanie stood, locked out.

***

Tom was on the bed, and Barker was thinking arousing thoughts. He already knew which tools he wanted to use. For now he settled for getting Tom's clothes off. It was a fierce struggle on the part of the punk cop, but nothing Barker couldn't handle. With a flaring wound in his shoulder still, Barker might have had a sensitive spot for Tom to hit. That was what Barker called an even playing field. He'd set things straight by handicapping Tom with a broken arm. Now he was as helpless as the rest.

Barker slid off Tom's pants, exposing his parts. After that he delivered a fierce punch to Tom's stomach. The blow could have killed him if he wanted it to, but this time it only paralyzed. And in that moment, Barker quickly set down the chains. He fastened Tom's arms and legs to the bed, spreading them all apart. He then stretched Tom's broken arm and the policeman howled in pain, stretching his jaw so wide Barker thought it might fall off. Perfect time to shove in the ball gag.

Tom was one of the most fun yet. Why hadn't Barker done this sooner? He couldn't believe how infrequent his killings had become. He missed it. It was because of Melanie. Things needed to change. She'd just have to understand. Would she though? Maybe he should talk to her, before he went to work on Tom. He didn't want to, but leaving someone alone like that, with this?

She'd never forgive him. He needed her to. He groaned and got up. "Don't go anywhere, Tom. I'll kill you soon."

***

Melanie had spent the last five minutes walking around in circles, wanting to scream. She was hot, and she knew she was going red. She'd done circuits in the living room. The door was wide open. Everything was ice cold. The door to Barker's room opened and he emerged. He was calm and collective, more like he always was with her.

"Melanie," he said.

"What the fuck?!" she screamed. "What's going on?"

"Shush," he said. "Please sit."

Melanie vibrated where she stood. "I can't sit! I can't!"

"I'll talk to you if you relax, like the good girl you are," he said.

She sat down, but her feet tapped the carpet every half second. Barker stood in the middle of the room. He rubbed his shoulder wound once. Only once.

"Macklin is the one who sent the shooter. So I'm punishing him." Melanie didn't say anything, and Barker added, "That's it. That's what's happening."

"Why would he do that?" Melanie asked. "I thought you two were partners."

"So did I. He's a manipulative little punk. And he's learning his place."

"Are you going to kill him?"

"Yes," he said with an eager grin. Melanie jumped back up.

"No. Please don't."

"None of that, Melanie," he said, putting up his hand. "Listen, you'll just have to accept…" He looked way, as if searching for words. He made dramatic hand gestures, pointing at her and to his heart. "In my life, it's sometimes necessary for me to do this. I'm sorry. I really am. But you'll have to live with it."

"Please." Right now she would have given anything for him to let Tom go. That scream was the most horrifying she'd heard yet. And she could still hear him moaning and whimpering in the room. "Please." Tears leaked down her eyes.

"Go upstairs and listen to some music. Or better yet, take a sleeping pill. You'll wake up tomorrow and everything will be fine."

A sleeping pill. Like whatever he put in her water, the night he raped Kris.

"No, I'm not moving from this spot!" Where they stood, he towered over her.

"If that's what you want." Then he turned his back on her and went back into the room.

***

Tom bit down on the gag, hard as he could. He hoped to snap it in half but it was no use. He was already drooling and his arm was in so much pain. Like being on fire. Or having a slab of concrete pressed over it. He was naked too, exposed. He banged his head against the pillow and coughed. He wrenched against the restraints with his good hand. Nothing. He kept trying.

I'll kill him. I'll kill him. I'll kill him. I'll kill him. I'll kill him.

Barker returned.

"Sorry, Tom. Where were we? Ah yes." He rolled his hands through the air. "I was trying to think about what tools I would use…"

He walked around the bed but then stopped, stared at free space, and looked at Tom again. "There's a big difference between toys and tools…yeah…big difference. A ball gag, that's a toy. Handcuffs? Toy. Hell, maybe even chains and clamps. But a tool." He raised a fist and beat it in midair. "A tool, Tom." He bent over. And when he stood up he was holding something. "A tool is something like this."

It was a wood saw.

***

Even though he was gagged, and Barker's door was shut, Tom's screams filled the house. They sounded choked. Poor thing. She was just going to stand here and listen to him die in misery, terror, and pain. Melanie rocked back and forth on the couch.

Tom screamed again. It sounded more like crying than screaming, and Melanie buried her face. But then there was a howl, and she could hear something like cutting. Through it all she heard Barker "shush" him.

Melanie got up and ran out of the house. Outside was an icebox to the point where she didn't think she could survive for very long out here, not without her coat. But it was safer out here. It was better out here.

"Melanie," Kris said from the car. She hadn't left yet, and she motioned with her hand. "Come on."

"No."

"Come on, Melanie. There's nothing you can do. You don't need to see this."

"No!" She shook her head. "No, no. No, no, no, no." And she ran back into the house. She couldn't leave him. She couldn't. They were supposed to be friends. Barker was too dismissive. He had to listen.

Tom was gasping and moaning through the door, and she kept hearing pops, like Barker was hitting him with something hard. A hammer?

"Barker?" she called. "Barker! Barker!"

The strikes stopped, but Tom didn't. He cried and whimpered as the door slowly opened. Barker poked his head out like a confused child, and she could tell his shirt was off now.

"Something wrong, dear?"

"Yes, something is wrong." She growled and paced the room. "Please stop this…Can't we talk about it first? This is all happening so fast. Can't we, you know, hear him out?"

Barker stood with his sweaty chest and black jeans, breathing heavily and looking perplexed.

"Hear him out?" He looked over his shoulder. "You care about him, Melanie?"

"No. I just don't want to see this. Please."

"Melanie." He put his head down and he stepped forward. He pressed his hand against the wall and sagged against it. Inquisitively, he said, "I've tried to protect you from this for a long time…but there are some things you'll just have to experience, living with me. This is one of them. So please, just relax, and let it happen. Or if you want, like I said, go back to sleep." He pointed his bloody hand at her. "But don't interrupt me again. Okay?" He finished with a smile.

Melanie was sobbing now. She didn't try to fight that anymore. It was a weapon to use against him, or just to let it all out. Hoping she would win him over. Hoping to feel his arms around her. But they never came. And she opened her eyes when she heard the bedroom door shut in her face.

***

Barker cracked his neck and took some deep breaths. He looked down at Macklin. He was still spread eagled on the bed, hands and ankles bound. His dick was about as soft as a deflated balloon, given all of the pain. If Barker really wanted to have some adventurous fun he could beat Tom off before he killed him. What would old Stan say to that? For now, he just picked up a nail. It was a thin, shiny, long piece of metal. Touching it to your skin felt like a little prick. Shoving it through would be agonizing. As for Tom…Barker had made three lacerations on the torso with the saw. One laceration up the arm. Two on the left leg. The one on the left arm was especially deep, and that was the arm Barker hadn't broken.

He took the pin and watched as it glistened in the light. And then he knelt on the mattress next to Tom. Gently placed the point within the open wound. He moved it along the wound and Tom thrashed and moaned. Then Barker twisted the metal, and Tom's howls returned.

Excellent.

The ball gag popped out of Tom's mouth and he shouted, "Melanie. Melanie! Oh God. Oh Jesus…. Oh Jesus." Barker had stopped for a moment, offended that Tom called for his friend.

"Melanie isn't going to help you, Tom. You can get over that right now." He reached for the gag to put it back in place.

Before he did Tom said, "Fuck you. Fuck you." Spit and blood flew from his mouth. "Fuck you all. Fuck Stan. Fuck Melanie. Fuck Andrea. Fuck Lorena."

Lorena.

Barker dropped the ball and grabbed Tom by the throat. He knew. How did he know? He knows.

"How do you know Lorena, Tom?" How does he know? He can't know. No one can know. Tom spat in his face, and Barker fought the urge to slit his throat. He pressed harder. "How did you know Lorena?"

"I didn't," Tom moaned.

"You must have, or you wouldn't mention her." He brought the long nail to Tom's throat. "How?"

"Stan told me everything," the boy said.

"Stan didn't know everything, you obnoxious little shit. What did he tell you exactly?"

"Go to Hell." Tom said.

"Answer me, Tom."

"Fuck you."

And Barker shoved the nail through Tom's eye.

***

Melanie, Tom had called. She stood in the living room, horrorstruck. I have to do something. I have to.

But there was nothing. She couldn't stop Barker. She couldn't do anything.

She poured herself a glass of water, and drank deep. Then she started to fill the glass with tears.

Mom...Please.

Every bit as helpless as the night she arrived in this house. I don't want to be here anymore, Mom. Please, help. Please...I want to go home. Please Mom. Dad. Someone please. But no one was coming. And Barker wouldn't keep his word. He'd keep her here forever. She'd been stupid.

Melanie was seized with rage and hurled the glass across the room, shattering it everywhere. She stood and watched the sparkling knives fly for a little while, so dazed that she hadn't noticed Barker creeping behind her. When she turned to look at him he had spots of Tom's blood on his body, and he was elsewhere. Not in this world.

The face was back. The other man's face. Mixed with the crazed eyes of Barker.

"Barker," she said, her voice gentle.

"Lorena," he said, a purely crazed expression on his face.

"What? Who's Lorena?"

"No one can know," he shook his head and eyed the carpet. "Please, Melanie. You can't tell anyone."

"Tell anyone what?" she asked, flailing her hands. "What?"

He was stiff, thinner, his arms tight against his sides, his chin sagging.

"They hurt me...No one can hurt me."

She could stop him. She could tame him. She grabbed his hands and caressed them. He reeked of sweat and blood, but she ignored it.

"Barker, please. It's okay. I'm here for you." He wasn't resisting. "What happened? Who hurt you?" He didn't answer. She grabbed his shirt and beat her hands against his stony torso. "Please. Just tell me!"

He pulled his hands away from her grasp and said, "I can do whatever I want, Melanie. That's my right."

"What about me? Why can't I?" She buried her face in his chest.

"You can."

"No, I can't. Right now I want all of this to stop." She looked up at him through tears. "That's what I want. And you won't let me have that."

"Yes I will...just give me time."

"Time? What do you mean?"

"I'll show you how to live like me." His voice was a low mutter. "It's easy...really...just gotta break a few eggs...no one can hurt you. No one can take anything away from you."

"Justin," she said.

She thought he'd chastise her. She thought he'd say I told you never to call me that. But instead he muttered, in a curious, innocent tone, "Yes?"

"Please, can't we just go somewhere safer? Can't we go talk? Can't we sit down and talk? You said you love talking to me."

His eyes trailed all over the room and then they settled on her. He smiled. "I made you a promise."

"Yes. You did." His smile faded. Bags nearly formed under his eyes, as his face dropped. "Oh, Melanie. I'm so sorry."

Tom wailed again.

"He's going to die," she said.

"Yes, he is."

"Please. Don't hurt him anymore. Hurt me if you need to. I can take it." At this, Barker looked down, incredulous.

"I will never hurt you, Melanie. I love you." He ran his hand through her hair, and she swatted it away.

"Stop! Stop doing this!"

He looked bewildered. "But Melanie...you don't understand."

His face changed again. Sadness turned to anger. Confusion turned to tension, eyebrows raised and mouth still curled. "You don't understand."

"What don't I understand?"

Barker's eyes jerked right, toward the window. "Did you hear that?"

"Hear what?!" she yelled.

Barker raised his knife as if for battle, and she stepped back. "Our new friend is back."

Chapter 46

Men of the Meridian

T om laid on the bed, one eye gone, limbs torn open, and the rest of him barely in tact. Barker was gone. Where, Tom didn't know. The pain had yet to numb, but he was dozing off though, unable to handle much more. It was hopeless.

He was dying.

Careful, Tom. Voices in his head spoke in unison. And they all said the same thing.

Careful, Tom.

I warned you, Tom.

You fucked up, Tom.

Tom. You're dying.

***

Barker stepped out into the darkness. A Meridian Killer was here. Tom Macklin had been more resourceful than he ever expected, and he likely had Stan to thank for that. It was a strange idea, to be mocked from a grave. But where and who was this particular killer? Someone he knew? Or someone who'd come in after he left? Barker flipped his blade upside down and readied for battle. He listened carefully, to the buzzing of insects, to the roaring of cars over in New Heim, to the wheels of Kris's truck, slowly backing away from the house.

And then.

"Got you."

The killer sprung from within the house next door, two knives flying in the moonlight. Barker dodged them both, and kept his own handy. The man was on the ground now, right in front of him. He was almost bald, and very muscular. He wore a black tank top and army pants. He held two knives while Barker was content with one. He didn't know this man.

"And who might you be?" Barker asked.

"Rodney," he said.

"Rodney... last name?" Barker asked. The man grinned.

"Beat it out of me," he said. Barker grinned back.

"That's what I'll do."

The two killers sprang for one another and when they clashed, Barker was met with a force stronger than any he'd felt in years. For a moment, it was frightening. The two were locked in a pressing match that tensed his muscles and made his injury flare up. But he worked through it and as always, he kept the smile.

Some day, when I'm dead, they'll say I never stopped grinning.

The men sprang apart, Rodney throwing Barker back over the fence and into the neighbor's yard. Painfully, Barker felt wood break under him.

This is fun.

The man leapt high into the air, about thirty-five feet. He had a gun. The bullets were loud and they cut into the grass. Barker flipped over and ran the other way, leaping into the streets of Ghost Town, through the yards of old neighbors, cutting all manner of corners. Rodney followed.

The two pivoted around houses and slipped through cracks for the next ten minutes before they met again. Rodney went for Barker's throat and their knives clanged together. Barker jumped back and Rodney disappeared, shaded in the dark. Barker leapt to the rooftop of a three-story house. There he searched the houses, seeing all there was to see but not what he wanted to see. There was nothing out in the darkness of Ghost Town. Come on now. Don't be a bore.

And then a black speck leapt onto a rooftop and more bullets came flying at him. Barker went to the ground as they continued to rain. With all his strength, he tossed his knife into the air, toward where Rodney was perched. He might never see his knife again, but something told him it made contact. Regardless, the bullets didn't stop. Barker slid into the darkness of another large house. The inside was dusty and dim. He slipped under an open window and hid himself.

More bullets rained outside. Then stopped. For the next thirty minutes, nothing happened. Nothing except for strange, unlikable sounds in the distance back home, and later one familiar looking truck racing by at 85 mph. He faltered when he realized what might have just happened, but then he heard footsteps coming down the street. Rodney was waddling, a knife wound in his gut. Barker had made contact. He could throw a knife fifty yards. He hadn't tried in quite a while. He was proud of himself. Rodney stumbled by the house, looking for Barker, and Barker dove from the window. It was rough, but he managed to get his arm around Rodney's neck. Now the two were rolling through the streets of Ghost Town, and Rodney dealt Barker several painful blows, more pain then he had felt in a very long time. And from the bare hands of another man, (or elbows). Oh to fight with a Meridian Killer. It had been far too long.

He didn't lose his grip. He pressed against Rodney's throat. "If you're going to kill a man," he said to Rodney. "Don't shoot him in the shoulder."

"I aimed for your head."

"You missed."

He managed to get Rodney on to his back, and to hold him down with one hand. It wouldn't last though. Barker needed to act quick.

He picked a knife off Rodney's belt. First he would question him about Crawford.

"I want to know what Craw—"

Rodney delivered a fierce knee to Barker's crotch, and that very nearly took him out. To end the threat, Barker shoved the knife into Rodney's heart, and twisted with all his strength.

When he yanked it out there was a fountain of blood.

Chapter 47

Let It All Out

Melanie experienced a moment of ecstasy. Barker was long gone, off fighting the shooter. He'd walked out into the darkness, peacefully, without bullets flying. And then a fight started. Now she was alone with the prisoner.

If she disobeyed Barker, disobeyed him like this, it would be the third strike. Was it worth it? Tom wasn't moaning and groaning anymore, and it let her keep her thoughts straight for a moment. And then she realized, silence could have meant death. Her heart raced and she raced into the room. The boundary broken, Melanie took a moment to glance around the room. There were chains and ropes everywhere, with disgusting weapons and sex toys lying on the floor. The bed was covered in blood and the stench was thick. Tom was cut up all over. His eye was destroyed, horrible blue and black marks all over his body, a broken arm looking like the skin of a torn string bean. Her friend had done this to him. And she'd just stood there and cried.

"I'm so sorry, Tom," she muttered. Tom gasped loud, like a cross between a cough and a scream, and Melanie's heart jumped, propelling her forward. If she could get him out of here then he might survive. Barker had run off. He'd left the car. She could use the car...

Melanie unfastened the chains, every moment making her feel condemned. For a moment she wanted to stop and refasten the chains. Take Barker's side. The safer side. But she couldn't. Tom needed help. It was too late to turn back. Melanie pulled the wet, disgusting ball from his mouth.

"Melanie," he wheezed in a destroyed and deformed voice no different than her father's. "Melanie."

"Shhhh, it's okay," she whispered, gently rubbing his cheeks. "It's okay. Hang in there," she whispered. He was undone now, but still naked. She found his pair of underwear and slid them back on him. At the very least he could have some dignity. She went back to his ear and started whispering again. "Come on. You need to stand up."

He had no strength left to stand, so Melanie had to pull him to his feet herself. His weight almost took her down but she stayed on her feet. He cried out once when she bumped into a few of his injuries. They were everywhere. He was destroyed. A bloody, disgusting mess of a body.

Barker. How. Why? Why?

She dragged Tom out of the bedroom, into the living room. Afraid she might drop him, she stopped for a moment.

"Are you okay?" she asked him. "Are you still with me?" she asked him. He did something resembling a nod, and she knew there was still time. She braced herself and dragged him outside.

The truck was still there. Kris jumped out.

"What the hell are you doing?"

"Take him. Take him please."

"Take him where?" Kris demanded.

"Anywhere. Far away. Please take him."

"Melanie you know I can—"

"Just do it!" Melanie yelled. "Take him and run. Both of you, run. Get him to a hospital."

"Jesus Christ, Melanie. If I do this, I'll have to leave the damn city."

"Then leave! Come on, Kris. Don't let him die!"

"He won't survive the trip," Kris said. Melanie was still holding him and Kris was taking deep breaths with a closed mouth. Melanie saw on Kris's face the same hesitation that she herself displayed, fueled by a desire to survive.

"He'll make it. Please, Kris. Please."

"Melanie," she said.

"Look, what do you have left here anyway!" she snapped. "Don't let Tom die too!" It came to her thoughtlessly, because somewhere inside she knew it would work. Kris opened and closed her mouth a few times, then grunted and reached out to help her carry Tom. As they pulled him to the car, both girls kept speaking.

"Where am I supposed to go?" Kris said.

"What's the closest place to here?" Melanie demanded.

"Long Beach."

"Then, there. And then keep moving."

They reached the car.

"Got damn it, Melanie," Kris said with clenched eyes.

"We can't let him die!" she shouted. She was so desperate for something to go right. For everyone in her path to just stay out of her way. She wouldn't let Tom die. Not unless her hands were bound.

It was difficult to get Tom in the car, and he even coughed up blood in Kris's face. When he was in, Kris grabbed hold of Melanie's sleeve and wiped her face with that. Then she got behind the wheel. Melanie stood outside the passenger window, looking at Tom. His head was pressed against the window, mouth agape as if the ball were still there.

"Hurry, please," Melanie said.

"I will when you get in, dumbass," Kris said loudly.

Was this it? Could she escape right here, right now?

"No."

Kris looked as if she'd been punched. "Melanie, get in the car."

"You go. Run. I'll keep him at bay."

"At ba—Melanie get in the car!"

"Someone has to stop him coming after you. He'll listen to me. If I go with you he'll chase us and kill us all."

"No!" Kris howled. So Melanie ran back into the house, to make it easy for her. A few moments later she heard another loud, furious howl, and the car wheels rolling against the gravel. There was a loud screech in the Kris's wake, and they were gone.

It was quiet now. Melanie heard nothing but gentle wind.

She turned and took a few steps through the doorway, peering out into the night. She'd saved them. They were escaping. Melanie rested her hand against the doorframe of her new home, as the stars lined up overhead. Now she waited for Barker to return.

Melanie didn't sit on the couch. She didn't wait in her room. She was bold tonight. She went into Barker's room again. She sat on Barker's bed. She'd looked around at all the toys, trying to make sense of it. And now that she could sit still, she saw something on the wall. It stared back at her like a wolf. Drooling, bearing its teeth. Forcing her to look away. It was a girl, tied to a bed, gagged, asleep. Red walls surrounded her, and in sleep she looked at peace. Unaware to the horror she was about to wake up in.

A different Barker took that photo. He didn't care about me then.

He'd get rid of it. He had to. She kept waiting for him to return. This suspense, the sick feeling in her stomach. She was in limbo. This room had saws, and knives, and needles and drills. White walls. She saw the bloody hammer lying on the floor. Blood was all over the bed, save for the spot she sat on. In other chests there were disgusting things. Ball gags. Penis shaped devices. It was any real person's nightmare. And she firmly resolved she no longer lived in the real world. She was in a large Pandora's box, a freakish nightmare that refused to subside.

There were footsteps outside. The went all around the house. And then they were near the front door.

"Melanie," said Barker, from the hallway. "Come out here."

Melanie stood up slowly. She was terrified, her chest tightening, but she obeyed.

She walked out of the room and turned right. With the door open behind him, Barker stood with a bloody knife in his hands. His right eye was twitching, his free fingers fidgeting. And his breath was not steady.

"Why are you in my room?" he said.

She didn't answer, and he started to walk toward her.

She stepped aside so that he could see what she did, so that her confession could be wordless. She backed away, toward the door. If she needed to run, it was open. But first she could try to reason with her friend. Her friend who was staring at the open door of his own bedroom, and had his hands down at his waist. Shaking his head, denting his own chin. Then he looked at her, and his face shocked her. He looked purely furious.

"What happened?" he said. Her nerves abandoned her.

"He got out." Barker studied her like reading a bad joke book.

"How?"

There was no point in denying it now. Honesty might soften the punishment. She didn't draw herself up. She didn't express confidence in her words. That might help her cause.

"I let him out."

His eyes rolled up and he turned away. If his mind was scattered, his voice was the exact opposite, sharp as the blade.

"You. Let. Him. Out."

"Yes," she whispered. He kept his face toward the back of the house, fingers still jittering. He wiped the blood off on the leg of his pants.

"Why?"

"I begged you. I begged and pleaded. I sobbed. And you wouldn't listen. Do you know how horrible that is? Do you know how frightened I am? Do you know how horrific it is to watch something like that? I felt like you were killing me."

He turned to face her.

"This is my fault, then?"

"Can we sit down and talk about this?"

"We'll talk right now. Why? What made you choose him over me?"

You kidnapped me. "He was screaming."

Barker scoffed. "So if I made sure the next one doesn't scream, we should be perfectly fine, yes?"

Run. Run, Melanie.

"Barker, please." He shut his eyes and the lines in his forehead appeared. He looked like he had a searing headache. She pressed on. "Justin, please. You're scaring me."

His eyes snapped open. "Justin?" he roared. And then he had her against the wall of the kitchen, his hands crushing her throat. "I am not Justin, you little bitch."

For a moment she just struggled to breathe. It wasn't until the moment lasted that she started to fight back. As always, his grip was inescapable.

"You betrayed me," he growled. She tried to shake her head.

"No," she coughed.

Barker gritted his teeth.

"God damn you. You got into my head!" His voice deepened and echoed across the room.

He let go of her and she dropped. This time she landed on her knees, upright. She coughed some more. "Barker, you're unbalanced," she whispered.

"No shit," he grunted back. "Thanks for that."

She had her hand on her throat. "I didn't choose to be here!" she growled.

He took a long breath in and stepped back. "No. No you didn't." He took a few more steps as Melanie tried to get to her feet. "And you father didn't choose to die."

She felt cold. Frozen.

"Wh...what?" Blood dripped off Barker's knife, spattering the carpet. Now he wore a look of defeat, as if she'd caught him in the lie herself. "What did you say?"

Barker rolled his eyes.

"You know, sometimes I get so carried away I screw myself over. I get that. I went to town on your dad before I put the knife in his back. Didn't you feel the blood when you hugged him?"

Wet blood on her father's back.

You're going to be okay. She said.

Oh, Melanie. He said.

Barker went on, "Tried to cover it up with a fake phone call to the hospital...Not my best work. I guess I just hoped in time you'd forgive me."

"You." She lost all other thought besides rage. "You."

He grinned. "Oh, and another clue. I told you the first time you ran away, if you did it again I would drive back to Fargo and kill your mother."

Melanie snapped. "You son of a bitch!" She jumped to her feet and struck him with an open palm, right in his shoulder wound. He gasped and recoiled. Then she tightened her fingers into a fist and took another strike. She landed a hit and Barker screamed. Still she roared, "You son of a bitch. You fucking bastard!"

She tried to strike him again but he came around with his elbow and she was flying across the room.

"Oh, Melanie," he whispered. She heard him patting his wound and grunting.

He was upon her and he yanked her upwards. Melanie had one free hand and she found the bullet wound. She smashed her thumb against it, pressing as hard as she could into the stitching. Barker screamed and bent downwards, trying to throw her off. She thrust upward with her head, smashing against his jaw. It did more damage to her than him, it seemed, as he grabbed her hair and ripped. He threw her to the side, slamming her down and shaking the house. Melanie jumped up again.

Barker was a liar. He'd killed her father. He'd pretended to be her friend. He'd brainwashed her, like Macklin said. He'd even cried in front of her. The bastard. He'd taken her by the throat and trapped her. God, she hated him so much. She tried to strike him again, with one of the moves he taught her, but Barker shook himself into reality, wiping his bloody wounds. He was upon her in seconds, restraining her arms, yanking her hair, bending her backwards. Her face and throat were exposed. Barker raised the knife.

"Oh, dear Melanie," he said, letting out a deep sigh.

Then the blade tore through her.

Chapter 48

Clarity

Though it was often cloudy in New Heim, at dawn the sun lit up the sky. The first bit was a little red streak. It stretched across the sky, pale orange rolled out above it. As the streak grew it got wider and thicker. It continued to bleed until it was a stream.

Barker sat on the front porch, flipping the knife over in his hands. The Meridian Killer's body was somewhere out in the streets. There weren't really burials in Ghost Town.

Everything was different now. He'd renounced Melanie.

Her betrayal stung. A lot. In fact it broke him. He finally woke up.

A house guest? A friend? And all over a camera obsession. What the fuck?

He never used to get attached. He never hesitated to kill. And he never let anyone dictate his decisions. Worst of all, somehow, she sent him back. Back fourteen years. To the fear, uncertainty, anger, and sorrow. All of the more poisonous things he'd long forsaken.

How could he have made such a mess of himself? Unbelievable. It was all Lorena's fault. She'd been the first to get inside his head, and Melanie just slipped in where the damage was already done.

Well, fuck them both.

It felt good to be back. Peaceful. Safe. Secure. He took a deep breath of the winter air. He'd matured. Yes, he could have whatever he wanted. Whenever he wanted. But all things were temporary. And he would have to enjoy them for as long as they endured. And make sure he himself endured the longest. For that was what he most treasured. Himself. Barker would live a long and happy life, happier than anyone else in the world, still lost in their self degradation. He'd live long and happy and enlightened to the bliss that was life. But not forever. Eventually, he would die too. And what really mattered was assuring his time was precious. For even the great Justin Barker, the most dangerous man on Earth, could never defeat the one supreme killer, that stalked every human born on Earth since the dawn of their species. He wasn't even interested in trying. But maybe, when that mysterious figure came, Barker would greet him as an equal. So what to do with Melanie? Kill her now? Draw it out? Have some fun with her? Some real fun. Chains, shackles, and broken doors. Breaking the sacred wall of Melanie Grier. Yes, that sounded fun. There was still more to do with her. And then he she would die. He straightened himself up and strolled back into the cage he built. When the red faded in the sky, the dark clouds emerged.

Chapter 49

Marked

Melanie went in and out of sleep. In her dreams she saw her father. Sometimes he was walking in from work and she was giving him a hug. Other times he was teaching her how to drive, yelling the entire time, but giving her a pat on the shoulder anyway. Other times he was hurt on the floor, crying, bleeding. Once she was sitting at dinner with him and Barker. Both men were laughing and cracking jokes in her direction. Either one of them might have commented that the circumstances between them were supposed to be uncomfortable.

Whenever Melanie came out of sleep, she recognized the red room, but she faded just as quickly. She always remembered the walls, the amount of light that came in from the window, the feel of the bed, the smell of the compacted air. Most of all, she remembered a tight feeling on her wrists. A tiny little bite, like something was pinching her. Melanie was never fully sleeping, never fully awake. Her head was a feather and she was ball of lint. Whatever was on her mind, her father, her mother, Barker, it didn't matter. Once when Melanie awoke more completely and she noticed it was hard to talk. Something was wrapped around her face. Another gag? No. It was soft, like gauze.

In some dreams, Melanie saw Tom Macklin. He and her father sat down together, discussing their work on the force. Both of them had been friends for a very long time, and they shared a few laughs. Melanie called to them but they didn't answer. No one ever answered. She sat in the corner of the room, unheard and unseen. While her family continued to laugh and talk she walked out of the room, into the bathroom. And in the mirror, she realized that she had tape on her mouth. No wonder they couldn't hear her.

Melanie was finally fully awake. This time she'd be able to get up. But the pain...It hit her as soon as her other senses. Something in her face, like she'd stuck her face in the oven. She tried to move but the pain made her lay still. Her hands were tied in front and gauze covered her face, leaving space open for her nostrils and eyes. She looked all around the red room, as she tried to pull her hands from the bedpost.

A monster was there, cloaked in black. It peered down at her, smiling with bright teeth. She yanked her hands up as far as they could go, then she let them fall again. She was in so much pain. It was enough to kill her.

"What," she said. It hurt to speak. She could only whisper, "God."

The monster cut the cords on her wrists and her arms fell apart. Then he slowly departed the room. It took a lot for Melanie to roll over, even more to get to her feet. But when she did her steps were steady, even if she was weak on her feet. It was hard to see with the bandages on. But she found her way to the bathroom. Once she'd called it her sanctuary. Now it just looked like a bathroom. She might be dead any minute. But right now she looked in the mirror at her mummified face. She remembered him grabbing her hair. She remembered the knife...The knife. Her flesh tearing.

It was like a drill had forced its way through her face, and twisted it until she was completely deformed and in ruins. With the amount of blood she lost she thought the drill wouldn't stop until she was dead. But she was on her feet. How was she on her feet? How had she not suffered a heart attack? How had she not died on the first night? How had she trusted and loved a monster? She'd traveled so far from her poor father and mother. Her only friends were Kris and Tom, and they were both gone. For all she knew, Tom was dead. If she could have one prayer answered now, it would be for Tom to live. At least she wouldn't be killed for nothing. All of this and more, everything that had passed through her mind the last three months, circulated within her along with dread for the people who'd tried to help her.

She started to unwrap the gauze, gently untethering his work as she stood within her sanctuary. The gauze loosened more and the sides of her hair puffed out. Melanie started to see her skin again. And then a glimpse of what he had done.

At first it just looked like a little red line between her eyes. As the gauze started to slip down toward the floor, Melanie watched it expand into a streak. Then a bundle of fabric rested at her feet, and Melanie saw his completed work. It was like she'd been cut in half and sown back together. Or even better, taped back together. A torn photograph. A happy memory, destroyed.

Melanie pressed her hands against the wall, staring at herself. Her mother used to comb her hair. Do her makeup and lipstick. Make her feel pretty. Encourage her to take on any challenge. Encourage her not to cry, not to despair. What would she say to her now? Would she even dare touch her deformed daughter? It didn't matter. Melanie was now convinced she would never see her mother again.

Melanie reached into the drawer and found that beneath the hairdryer he'd gifted her. The letter she had written to her parents was still there. She unfolded the paper and gazed upon her words, eyes settling on the first sentence. Then on the last. Again and again she read those words, wishing somehow that instead of ink and paper, it could be real. That they could all be together. Alive.

Downstairs, a horrid voice called her name, and Melanie shredded her words.

Chapter 50

The Onlookers

All the lights were white. Opening his one eye was painful. Abysmally painful. He really couldn't move at all. And he had no memory of what happened. How he got here. What the treatment was. Nothing.

When he could finally look around the room, he could only see a portion of it. And focusing his eye on the room took effort that exhausted him.

There was a nurse next to him. "Mr. Macklin," her voice was gentle and sweet like spring winds. "Mr. Macklin." He focused his eyes on her soft and happy smile. She was an older woman, brown haired and wrinkly in the face. Bright blue eyes. "Mr. Macklin, blink once if you can understand me."

He blinked. Why couldn't he talk?

"The pain medication we have you on makes it a little difficult to speak. That'll clear up in a few hours." She placed her hand on his. "You are very lucky to be alive, Mr. Macklin. I don't know what kind of beast would do such a thing, but you have angels watching over you."

He remembered something now. Being poked and prodded at, not just by Barker, but by doctors. He remembered a moment when the pain was so excruciating, and the fatigue so incapacitating, he was tempted to let himself pass away.

But something inside him spit in the face of that temptation, and he'd held his strength.

Barker had taken him effortlessly. Hell, even the mobsters had him on the ground easily. He wasn't a good fighter, but he wasn't easy to kill. He wouldn't give up without a fierce fight.

"We put a phone right next to your left hand, Tom. Please don't try to get up. Ring for us whenever you need anything. Physical therapy will start soon. Your father will be visiting and he's already paid for it."

That was an information overload. His father was coming? Paying for physical therapy? Coming to the rescue. How opportunistic. But how did he find out?

"The girl who brought you in is still here. She'll be in shortly."

The nurse left and Tom was alone in the white room. The pillow against his head was extremely comfortable. He felt like a king in a palace. Everything was so numb he was trying to remember where Barker had cut him.

He remembered it all too well. The broken arm. The shackles. The wood saw against his stomach, chest, left arm, legs. The needle in the open wound. The hammer smashing against his rib cage and his knees. The needle in his eye.

He was most aware of the missing eye and the broken arm. The arm would heal. The eye would take an amount of money he didn't have.

Someone sat down next to him. A young girl with dark hair and a tattoo over her right eye.

"Hey," she said. She put her chin in her hand. "How are you feeling?"

He really couldn't speak yet. Trying to was painful. He nodded his head.

Kris said, "You'll be alright."

After a moment, Tom realized she was staring at him with pity. "I told you not to get involved," she said. "Christ, Tom."

He turned his head away and he must have grimaced, because she put her hand on his. "You were stupid...but really brave. I'm sorry for what I said. You're no pig. You're a lot better than a pig."

He nodded his head, but he didn't believe her. He watched. Just like the Chief. For years, he stood by and did nothing, because he didn't know what to do. And when he finally tried, he was so in over his head he almost lost it from his shoulders. He didn't feel brave. Just stupid. And now deformed.

"I called your dad," Kris was saying. "His info was in your wallet." Kris leaned forward. "He sounded real concerned but...you know you can't go home right?"

He nodded. Good lord. My poor mother. I need to make sure she is safe.

Kris massaged his hand with hers. "I'll watch your back. If that helps. I have no where else to go." She stared at the wall for a moment, then looked back at him. "Thank you for trying, Tom."

Tom needed to speak at least once. There was one thing he needed to know. When he spoke it was the smallest whisper, just the slightest bit he could release. Three words. But Kris understood, and her face darkened.

"Melanie stayed. She said she would try to stop him coming after us...I went back after you were admitted. To see if I could sneak her out...there was no one there."

Tom's heart dropped.

Kris ran her hands through along her scalp. "The whole place was deserted. Barker's car was gone. I went up to the room he kept her in. That was cleared out. No clothes. None of her books. I went down to his room. That was empty too." She put her head down, groaning. "It's like they were never there."

Tom looked at the ceiling. All white. Washed out. Every little detail revealed by the sun. The exact opposite of Ghost Town. And Tom never wanted to see it again. Not Ghost Town. Not New Heim. Not the Chief or his badge.

I'm sorry, Stan. I'm sorry, Melanie. I'm so, so sorry.

That damn police report stuck to him like a leech. Debra Grier was sitting at home in Fargo, longing in sickness for news of her daughter, and Martin Grier was rotting in the ground. Melanie Grier might be suffering a death more agonizing than either of them.

If Tom had taken her from New Heim the night they met, instead of trusting that wretched community, she might be home safe right now. Every decision he made since that night had been stupid, half assed, and futile.

What were we thinking, Stan?

"Do you know where he's headed?" It was Kris who spoke back, not Stan. Tom looked at her, as she peered at him with a hungry, hopeful expression. He understood. Both of them agreed on one thing, one person they wanted to be saved. But even though Tom had a very fine idea where Justin Barker was headed, he doubted Melanie was still alive. As Tom

Macklin rested in a comfortable bed, his thoughts were wracked with grief for the one they left behind.

Acknowledgements

Looking back on my life, I realize that I have always had a terrific support group at my side, and the support that went into completing my first novel is no exception. For *Barker's Rules*, I cannot express enough gratitude to the following people.

First, a heartfelt thanks to Jennifer Hecker, my wonderful cousin and first project manager, who introduced me to Sevenhorns Publishing and made my dream of being published into a reality. Thanks again to the wonderful team at Sevenhorns Publishing, and to Tasha Grant, for creating my first published books. I will always cherish the work we did together.

I worked on this novel for a number of years with the committed editing and revising of an awesome workshop crew. A heartfelt thanks to Kimberly Koering, Nikki Rae Colligan, Marisa Sciarappa, Brielle Elise, and Sarah Baginsky. Thanks especially to Brielle Elise Bogdzio for reading it over twice! Without the support and creative thinking that each of you brought forward, this book would never have gone half the distance.

Shout out as well to Daniel Yukob, Stephen Reynolds, and Paige Conticchio for proofreading the book and giving me great advice. Thanks to the creative community at Stockton Student Television for keeping me sharp and active in the creative realm, and thanks to the Stockton Literature Faculty for their truly excellent teachings.

A million thank you's to three of the most supportive people in my life, my mother, Donna, my father, Albert, and my brother, David. Without their enduring support, I very well might not have known that I could become a writer. From movie theater trips, to comic book discussions, to Broadway visits, world traveling, and hours spent watching Dave play story-driven video games, this author's mind has been groomed since childhood.

A warm thank you to the amazing author, Nikki Rae, for designing the Meridian Trilogy's cover art! Thank you very much to Andrew Bast, my best friend, fellow writer, and partner at One True Promotion, for his extensive work in helping me develop and promote these books.

Finally, a warm thank you to two people in Heaven. Thank you, Grandma Dot, for rooting me on and telling me that you couldn't wait to "see my name in the Headlines." Thank you, Grandpa Jack, for supporting me from the start and reading some of my earliest work. I never knew a man could read so fast! Rest well.

Made in the USA
Middletown, DE
19 June 2021

41297592R00170